A Modern Legionary

John Patrick Le Poer

Methuen's Colonial Library

A MODERN LEGIONARY

UNIFORM WITH THIS VOLUME

A FRONTIERSMAN
By ROGER POCOCK

A
MODERN LEGIONARY

BY

JOHN PATRICK LE POER

METHUEN & CO.
36 ESSEX STREET W.C.
LONDON
1904
Colonial Library

A MODERN LEGIONARY

CHAPTER I

ON a January morning in the early eighties I found myself in Paris with less than a dozen francs in my purse, or rather my pockets, for I have always had a habit of distributing my money between waistcoat and trousers, so that if one pocket be picked the contents of the others may have a chance of remaining still in my possession.

How I arrived in Paris is easily explained. After two years and a half in a boarding-school I had become so tired of its monotonous routine and, indeed, of the idleness which prevailed there—for the masters never tried to teach, and, naturally, the boys never tried to learn—that I resolved, when the Christmas vacation came to an end, to leave my home in the south of Ireland and seek my fortune through the world. Accordingly, instead of going back to school, I set out for Dublin, whence I started for London by the first boat. In London I spent a day, and then came on to Paris, filled with vague hopes and vaguer misgivings as to my future. Thus it happened that I at the age of sixteen was walking the streets of Paris on the 6th of January 188—.

I considered anxiously what lay before me. I could not go home, even if pride did not forbid. True, I could write for money, having enough to maintain myself until it came, but that would be too great a humiliation. To dig I was not able, and to beg I

A

was ashamed, so I saw but one course open to me—to enlist. Having made up my mind, which I did the more easily as I had been brought up in a garrison town, and like most boys loved to follow the soldiers in their bright uniforms and to march along with head erect, keeping step to the music of the band, I at once set about carrying my resolve into effect. I was not long in beginning. As I walked along the streets I saw a soldier with a gold chevron on his arm, and, going across the road, I addressed him. I did not speak French very well, but had something more than the usual schoolboy knowledge of it, as I had read a good many French books and papers when I should have been at Greek or Mathematics in the study hall. Very soon, therefore, he learned my purpose, and a conversation ensued, somewhat as follows :—

"You are English; is it not so?"

"No; I am Irish, from the south of Ireland."

"Very well, my friend; but you must go to the Foreign Legion, and that will not be very pleasant, you may well believe. Always in Algeria, except when serving in Tonquin and other devil's colonies on the earth."

"I do not mind that; in the English army one has to go to India and South Africa, so what matter?"

"Ah! and you are doubtless without money, and one has to live."

"Let us go in here," said I, pointing to a wine shop. "We can talk better over a glass."

"Good comrade! good comrade! he cried, slapping me on the shoulder; "I see that you will be a soldier after my own heart. Have no fear," he continued; "I will tell you all, and you may rely on me as a loyal friend."

When we entered the shop my new-found friend asked me whether I should drink *eau-de-vie* or *vin ordinaire*, and, on my refusing the brandy, commended my discretion, saying that young soldiers should never touch brandy as it interfered with their chances of promotion, and, moreover, they did not usually have money enough to pay for it. Thereupon he called for *eau-de-vie* for himself and some wine, rather sour I thought it, for his young friend, and when we had clinked glasses and drunk, our conversation was resumed.

I shall not try to reproduce the dialogue, which would, indeed, be wearisome, as we sat and talked for full two hours, with many repetitions. During this time I drank little, and the sergeant, though he had his glass filled more than once, took no more than he could safely bear. One thing I must say of him, that although he painted the soldier's life in glowing colours yet he always kept me in mind of the fact that he spoke of the French army in general and his own regiment in particular. What he said had no reference to the Foreign Legion. That corps was not to be compared to his. There were in it men who had fled from justice; from Russia, though, indeed, the offences of these were in most cases political; from Germany, and yet many were Alsatians and Lorrainers who wished to become French citizens; from Austria, Belgium, Spain; from every country in the world. And, whatever their crimes had been, they were of a surety being punished, for their stations were on the borders of the great desert, where were sand and sun and tedium so great that an Arab raid was a pleasant relief.

"But there were French soldiers also there, were there not?"

"Oh yes; the zephyrs, the bad ones who could not be reclaimed to duty, to discipline, or even to decency, and who were sent to form what one might call convict battalions in places to which no one wished to send good soldiers—men who respected themselves and the flag."

"But the Foreign Legion could not be always in Algeria, on the borders of the desert?"

"Oh no; there were many of them in Tonquin on active service, and these, of course, were just as well or as ill-off as the regular French troops, but still they were rascals, though, he would confess, very good fighting men. There was a war in Tonquin against great bands of marauders who carried a variety of flags, by the colours of which they were known: I must have heard of the principal ones—the infamous Black Flags, who gave no quarter to the wounded and who mutilated the dead. These were helped by the regular Chinese soldiers, and had among them many Europeans, dogs that they were, who gave them advice and instruction, because these Europeans were Prussians or English who hated the great French Republic and viewed its expansion with dislike and distrust."

"But was there not a good chance of promotion in the Legion?"

"Oh yes; if one did one's duty and willingly obeyed orders and did not get into trouble. Oh yes; there was always justice for the good as well as for the bad. If one was not a corporal in five years there was little use in staying; one could take his discharge and go away."

That decided me. I was sixteen—in five years I should be twenty-one—better spend the time learning experience in the world than in the dull, dreary idleness to which I was accustomed, and which filled me with disgust. I said so to the sergeant. He looked me up and down, and said:

"How old?"

"Sixteen," I replied.

"You cannot enlist; the recruit must be at least eighteen."

I thought a moment. "I will be eighteen; they cannot see the registers of my parish."

"Very well, very well, my son; you are resolved. I will say no more to prevent you—I will help you—you shall be a soldier of the Republic to-morrow."

He kept his word. We spent the day together; he showed me his barrack, his room in it, where to dine and sleep, and leaving me at nine o'clock, with a parting injunction to meet him at eight in the morning at the barrack gate, went away saying:

"Poor devil! poor devil!"

On the following morning at ten minutes to eight I was at the gate. Indeed, I might easily have been there at six, but as the morning was cold and nothing could be gained by being out and about too soon I remained snugly between the sheets until seven. Punctually at eight the sergeant appeared, and we walked towards one another smiling. I asked him to join me at breakfast. He readily consented, and soon we were seated together in a small restaurant before a table at which we appeased the hunger induced by the sharp morning air with eggs, bread and butter, and coffee. Breakfast over, the sergeant asked, as he said, for the last time, if I were still resolved to join the Foreign Legion. I replied that I was, if I should be accepted.

"Very good; we have half-an-hour, let us walk about until it is time to meet the doctor."

While strolling through the streets he gave me much advice. I was to be respectful, alert, step smartly, and, above all, be observant.

"Watch the others," he said, "and you will very soon learn soldiers' manners."

I promised to do so, and reminded him that I had grown two years older in a single night. He smiled, and said encouragingly:

"Good child! good child!—alas! poor devil!"

I asked him what he meant by alluding to me as a poor devil, and again he abused the Foreign Legion with a vocabulary as insulting as it was extensive. I had never heard or read one-tenth of the words, but it was not hard to guess the meaning. I stopped him by laying my hand upon his arm, and said:

" You forget that I may be one of the Foreign Legion before noon."

" True, true ; but I do not apply the expressions to you, only to those who are already there." And he pointed with his finger towards the south.

" Very good ; but surely not to all ? What can you say against the political refugees from Russia ? "

" Ah ! they are different ; they——"

I stopped him again, and said :

" And what can you say against a political refugee from Ireland ? "

" Ah, ah ! I understand ; now I see clearly. Oh, my friend, why did you not tell me yesterday ? "

From that moment he believed me, a schoolboy of sixteen, to be a head centre of the Fenians, or at least a prominent member of some Irish league. This belief had consequences shortly afterwards, pleasant and unpleasant, but we live down our sorrows as, unfortunately, we live down our joys.

Well, soon it was time to " meet the doctor," so we went towards the barrack, and passing the gate approached a portion of the square where about twelve men in civil dress were already assembled. I was told that these also were would-be recruits, not all, however, for the Foreign Legion, as some were Frenchmen who volunteered at as early an age as possible instead of waiting to be called up. Not far off a small party of *sous-officiers* stood, criticising the recruits, and laughing sarcastically at an occasional witticism. These the sergeant joined, and I was at leisure to observe my companions. They were of all sorts and conditions. One, a tall man with white hands, at least I saw that the right one was white, but the left one was gloved, who wore a silk hat, frock coat, and excellently got-up linen, looked rather superciliously at us all. Another, in a workman's blouse and dirt-covered trousers and boots, had his hands in his pockets, and, curving his shoulders, looked intently at the ground. A third, about eighteen, in a schoolboy's cap and jacket, was humming the Marseillaise; he was a French lad who *would* be a soldier. There was a dark-browed man, a Spaniard as I learnt afterwards, tugging at his small moustache; a few others whom I have forgotten; and, lastly, standing somewhat apart from the crowd, three or four medium-sized, heavily-built men, with the look of the farm about them, and, indeed, the smell of it too, who proved to be Alsatians.

I was still engaged in observing the others when a door was thrown open, and we were all ordered into a large room on the ground floor of a building, over the entrance to which were painted some words which I now forget. Here we had to strip to shirt and trousers, but as there was a stove in the place, and the windows and doors were closed, that did not hurt too much. After a short delay the tall man was summoned, and left the room by a door opposite to that by which we had entered. Others were called afterwards, and I, as it happened, was the last. As I passed out the sergeant—I forgot to mention that he and the other *sous-officiers* had come in with us, and all had spoken encouragingly to me, having been told that I was a rebel against "perfide Albion"—the sergeant, I say, tapped me on the shoulder, and said:

"Have no fear, be quiet, respectful, attentive, good lad."

I thanked him with a nod and a smile and passed in. I now found myself in a smaller room, where an old soldier with a long grey moustache—I thought at once of the old guard—gruffly bade me take off my shirt and trousers. I did so, and felt a slight shiver— it was January—as I stood naked on the floor. I had scarcely finished shivering when the schoolboy came from the doctor's room looking as happy and proud as a king on his coronation day. It was quite evident that he had been accepted, and already his early dreams of military renown seemed on the point of realisation. Poor devil! as the sergeant said of me. I met him afterwards twice; the first time he was a prisoner under guard for some offence, the second time he was calling out huskily for water in the delirium before death.

As he went towards his clothing I entered the apartment he had just left. It was a large white-walled room, with a couple of chairs and tables, a desk and stool, and a weighing machine in a corner, as its chief furniture. A couple of soldiers were present, but evidently the chief personage in the room was a tall, thin man with a hooked nose and sharp grey eyes, whose moustache bristled out on each side. He was dressed in uniform, and wore some decorations, but I cannot recall more than that now. I doubt, indeed, if I ever fully grasped how he was dressed—his eyes attracted my attention so much.

A few questions were asked—my name, age, country, occupation, and others—which were answered by me at once and shortly. I did not forget the sergeant's advice. Then followed a most careful observation of my body. My height and weight were noted, as well as other things which I did not understand. I remember I had to breathe deeply, and then hold my breath as long as I could, to jump, to hop, and to go through every form of work of which the human body or any part of it is capable. My eyes were examined in various ways, and there was not a region of my person left unexplored by the stethoscope or by the bony fingers of my examiner. All the while he called out various words and sentences, just as a tailor calls out while he measures you for a suit of clothes, and a soldier at the desk took them down. The other soldier acted as his chief's assistant, covering my right eye with his hand while the left one was being tested, holding a stick for me to jump and hop over, putting on the weights while I was on the machine, and doing all these things at a nod or other sign from the doctor.

At last the examination was over. The doctor took

the sheet of blue paper on which the soldier at the desk had been writing, and, looking alternately at it and at me, seemed carefully considering. I stood erect, hands by my sides, looking steadily and respectfully at him. It was very quiet. After some time he said:

"How old are you?" (in English, with just a trace of an accent). I waited a moment, but that moment was enough.

"Eighteen, sir."

Had I answered on the spot he would have learned the truth. He paused a little, still keeping his eyes on me, and then, slightly lifting his eyelids, asked:

"Seventeen?"

"No, sir," I replied; "eighteen to-day."

"When and where were you born?"

"Seventh of January, sir, in the year ——, and at the town of ——, in the south of Ireland."

He still gazed at me in doubt, but I met his gaze steadily. Suddenly a door opened—not the one through which I had come—and a short, stout, bustling man, dressed in blue coat and red trousers, with a gold-laced cap on his head, came in and, glancing carelessly at me, shook hands warmly with the doctor. In the conversation which ensued it was apparent by their glances and gestures that I had more than my share of their attention. Finally they approached, and the short man asked me my age. I replied as before. Turning sharp round he said with a merry smile, which ended in a short, quick laugh:

"Oh, my friend, he is eighteen; he says so, and who knows better? Would you destroy the enthusiasm of a volunteer by doubting his word? My fine fellow"—this to me—"you will be eighteen before you leave us."

That settled it. I was accepted, sent away to dress, and, as I had said to the sergeant, before noon I was a sworn member of the Foreign Legion, sworn in for five years.

The swearing-in was not impressive. All I remember about it is that in a room with a very wide door an officer in a gold-laced cap sat at a table, repeated a form of words which I in turn repeated, holding up my right hand the while, and then I kissed a book tendered to me by a *sous-officier*. Some questions were asked, and I answered, telling the truth, as, indeed, I had told the truth all through, except about my age, and also except about the insinuation that I was a political refugee.

That night I slept in the barrack. About eighteen or twenty other recruits for the Foreign Legion occupied a large room with me. We were of all countries in Europe, but the Alsatians outnumbered the representatives of any other, and next to them came the Belgians and Lorrainers. A couple of Poles, a Russian, a Hungarian, a Croat, the Spaniard whom I have already mentioned, and myself completed the list. We looked at one another rather suspiciously at first, but after some time we became more sociable, and tried to explain, each in his own execrable French, how we had come to enlist, and it struck me that, if all were to be believed, my comrades were the most unfortunate and persecuted set of honest men that the sun had ever shone upon. I changed my opinion in the morning when I found that the last franc I had, nay the last sou, had been taken from my pockets during the night, but what was the use of complaining? It was a lesson I had to learn, therefore the sooner I learned it the better, and it was well that I learned it at no greater expense than a couple of francs. When we got a blue tunic, red trousers, and kepi, with boots and other things, I sold my civilian clothes to a Jew for one-tenth of their original cost, and that money did not leave my possession without my consent. I did not spend it all upon myself, but neither did I spend it indiscriminately, a jolly Belgian and the Russian had most of the benefit.

A little circumstance occurred which at first gave me great pleasure, though afterwards its effects were rather serious, at least in my opinion at the time. I had not been an hour in the room when the sergeant came and gave me some tobacco and a small bottle of wine. I insisted on his sharing the latter; as for the tobacco, that went in the night along with my money. I saw some very like it afterwards with one of the Poles. When going he shook hands warmly, bade me be of good courage, and was about turning away when someone, an Alsatian, I think, jostled against him. Immediately the flood-gates of his eloquence were opened, he cursed and swore, and that not alone at the cause of his anger but also at others who were near. No reply was made, and he went away, still cursing and fuming with anger. How this event affected me will be told in due course; suffice it to say that, young as I was, I saw that his evident partiality for me and his undoubted contempt for the others would likely bring unpleasant results before long.

In two days our numbers had increased to about thirty, and we were despatched to Algeria under the orders of a sergeant and two corporals. During the journey we learned a little more about discipline, but all that and the journey itself must wait for a new chapter.

CHAPTER II

LET me first describe the sergeant who was in chief command of our party. He was a small, active, sharp-tongued man, wearing a couple of medals and the Cross of the Legion of Honour on his breast, neat in his dress—I believe he would, if it were possible, polish his boots forty times a day—having a constant eye to us, such an eye as a collie has for the flock. When he gave an order, it was clear and abrupt; when he censured, you felt no doubt about his meaning, for tongue and tone and eye and gesture all united to convey contempt and abuse; if he gave ten minutes for a meal, we had to fill our stomachs in that time or go half hungry; and as for accepting a drink from one of us—for some had a little money—he would as soon have thought, he let us know, of accepting a glass of hell-fire from Satan. He was one of those men found in every army in the world—men who cannot live out of barracks, who feel comfortable only in uniform, who look upon civilians as beings to be pitied for not having the military sense, just as the ordinary man pities the blind, the deaf, or the dumb. Such men's minds receive few, and these transient, impressions from outside their own corps. To hear the regiment rated soundly on inspection day is a greater calamity than the cutting off of a squadron by Berbers or the ambushing of half a battalion by Black Flags; in fine, they are soldiers of the regiment rather than of the army.

We were divided into two squads, each under the immediate control of a corporal. My corporal was a jolly, good-humoured fellow, a bit malicious, a Parisian gamin in uniform. He told us terrible stories of the

Foreign Legion, and said that we should get through our purgatory if we only lived in it long enough. But in the end he defeated his own object, for, as some tales were obviously untrue, we had no difficulty in persuading ourselves that all were lies. The other corporal, a tall, lank man, seemed to me moody or, perhaps I should say, pensive. However, he had nothing to do with me, so I scarcely observed him.

With regard to the journey, I can only say that we marched from the barrack to a railway station, travelled by train to Marseilles, thence by transport to Oran, where we were handed over by the sergeant to a *sous-officier* of our own corps. Some incidents and scenes of the journey I must relate, as they show how my military education began. And first I must tell about the unpleasantness which I spoke of in the first chapter.

Of course, a woman was the exciting cause—the match to the gunpowder. Women can't help it; they are born with the desire of getting you to do something for them. The average woman merely gets her husband to support her; she would like to have every other woman in the parish there to see the weekly wages handed over, the wages which, if he were a bachelor, would represent so much fun and frolic and reckless gaiety. But there are women who would incite you to commit murder or to save a life with equal eagerness, just to feel that their influence over you was unbounded. However, this has little to do with the present case, which was merely a casual flirtation and its ending.

At a certain station, which had more than its due share of loungers, our train was stopped for some reason. We were allowed to get out during the delay, and the report quickly spread that a squad or two of recruits for the Foreign Legion had halted at the place. We were soon surrounded by a curious group, many of which passed by no means complimentary remarks upon our personal appearance and the crimes they supposed us to have committed in our own countries before we came, or rather escaped, to France.

In the crowd was a rather handsome woman of about thirty who pretended great fear of us, as if we were cannibals from the Congo. The sergeant, however, reassured her, told her that we were quite quiet under his control—pleasant for us to listen to, wasn't it?—and volunteered to give her all information about us. Well, he gave us information about ourselves too.

He described the Pole as a dirty Prussian who had robbed his employer and then made his escape to Paris. The Spaniard became a South American who had more murders on his soul than a professional bravo of the Middle Ages. The Russian was a Nihilist who had first attempted to blow up the Tsar and afterwards betrayed his accomplices, so that in the Foreign Legion, and there only, could he hope to escape at once justice and revenge. An Alsatian was described as a Hungarian brute: "these Hungarian dogs are so mean, sneaking, filthy, and cowardly"; while the poor Hungarian, who had heard all this, almost at once found himself pointed out as an Austrian, a slave of an emperor who was afraid of Germany. Unfortunately, as it turned out afterwards, I escaped his notice, and what I congratulated myself upon at the time I had reason afterwards to regret.

While the sergeant was thus trying to advance himself—the vain fool!—in the handsome woman's favour and was getting on to his own satisfaction, if not to ours, into the crowd struts a young corporal of chasseurs. As soon as she saw him the woman turned her back upon our sergeant, put her arm affectionately through the corporal's, and brought him, vacuously smiling, down to us to tell the sergeant's stories over again. She muddled them, but that was of course. We never minded anything she said; but weren't we delighted to see our *sous-officier* so excellently snubbed!

"And where, my dear Marie, did you learn all this?" queried the happy and smiling chasseur.

"Oh, pioupiou told me." And she pointed with the tip of her parasol at the man who a moment before had mentally added her to the list of his conquests. And pioupiou was angry; his cheeks got all white with just a spot of red in the centre, his eyes glared, he twisted his moustache savagely; he turned on us and ordered us back to the carriages. But that was not all: the crowd laughed, Marie laughed, the corporal—another fool—laughed. Some of us laughed, and we paid for all the laughter in the end.

Nothing was said while we were in the station, but as soon as the train was again on the move the sergeant began. The first to feel uncomfortable was the corporal of my squad. He was told that he did not enforce discipline, that he was too free with these rascals, these pigs, that he had no self-respect, that he was ill-bred, and much more to the same effect. We came in for worse abuse, the Hungarian and a Belgian being made special marks for the sergeant's anger because they had been the first to laugh when Marie called him "pioupiou." The abuse was kept up, with occasional intermissions, for over half-an-hour, and no one was sorry when our tormentor sought solace of a more soothing nature in his pipe. It is very hard for men to listen to angry words which they know they cannot resent, and, sooner than have no relief for their pent-up passion, they will vent it on one of themselves, as I found out before long.

We had stopped for ten minutes' interval at a station, and the three *sous-officiers* had gone to a small refreshment room after ordering us, on various pains and penalties, not to leave our seats. Scarcely were they on the platform when the Belgian, who had been most insulted, began to rail at me. I was astonished. My surprise increased when the others joined with him. I was asked why I should be spared while better men were being treated as dogs and worse than dogs. The visit of my friend, the kindly sergeant who brought me wine and tobacco, was raked up as an instance of favouritism, and the rather violent language which he had applied to others in the barrack room was also recalled. I felt indignant at the injustice but knew not how to reply. Indeed, there was but a small chance of doing so, as all were speaking loudly, and some even shaking their fists at me. At last the Belgian, who had started the affair, struck me lightly on the cheek. This was too much. I jumped at him, had him tightly by the throat with the left hand, and set to giving him the right hand straight from the shoulder as quickly and as strongly as I could. He was altogether taken aback, and, moreover, was almost stunned by my assault, for every blow drove the back of his head against the wood-work of the carriage. Before anyone could interfere I had given him his fill of fighting, and when I was torn off his mouth and nose were bleeding and the skin around both eyes was rapidly changing colour. Before the fight could be renewed the sub-officers returned, and we all sat silent and sullen in our places.

The sergeant at once grasped the situation.

"What, fighting like wolves with one another already! Very well, my fine fellows, it does not end here; to-day the fight and the arrest, to-morrow the inquiry and the punishment."

Thereupon he ordered the men on each side of us to consider themselves our warders. "If they escape, if they fight again, there will be a more severe punishment for you, whose prisoners they are."

"A beautiful way to begin soldiering," he continued, looking alternately at the Belgian and myself; "go on like this, and life will be most happy for you."

At the next station he ordered the Belgian to be transferred to the compartment in which the other squad, under the silent corporal, travelled. When he left, to give orders, I suppose, about the prisoner, the jolly corporal turned to me, and said:

"My worthy fellow, you have begun well; where did you learn to use your hands? No matter, the commandant will talk to you; he will settle all. But, my son, what was it about; did he insult you?"

"It was all the fault of the sergeant," I cried——

"Hold, hold!" interrupted the corporal; "take care, you are foolish to accuse your officer, and, besides, he was not present."

This gave me a hint.

"No; he was not here, and the corporals were not here either."

"Then it was my fault too?"

"Not yours so much as the sergeant's—you merely deserted your post—but he in addition to that abused the men so much before going away that their passion was aroused, and when men are angry they cannot help fighting."

"Yes, yes," said the corporal; "he did abuse people, there is no doubt that he was in bad humour, and would have abused his own brother at the time."

Little more was said, but the corporal was very thoughtful, and evidently was chewing a cud he did not like.

At the first opportunity, it was when we halted for a meal, the corporal took the sergeant aside, and a long conversation ensued. The upshot was that I was taken from my guards and brought by the corporal to where his comrade stood. The latter asked me to tell him the truth about the quarrel, and I spoke as he wished me to. I mentioned everything—the kindness of the first sergeant to me and his abuse of the others, his own harsh treatment of us from the beginning, his wrong and malicious descriptions to the woman—he winced when I mentioned her name—his fearful abuse of the men afterwards, and I took care to point out that I was the one who had been least hurt by his tongue, and I wound up by declaring that, if he and the corporals had not gone away, leaving us without any *sous-officier* in charge, the affair would not have taken place.

B

"I believe you have told me the truth," he said. And I knew well that he knew it, for all the time that I was speaking he kept his keen eyes fixed upon mine, and they seemed to read me through and through.

The Belgian and I were almost immediately relieved from arrest, but my opponent received strict orders to stay in the centre of the squad while marching, so that as little chance as possible might be given to the curious to note his bruises. He was furthermore told that for his own sake he had better tell anyone in authority who might chance to make inquiries that he had been suddenly, and when off his guard, assaulted by a drunken man at a wayside railway station. He afterwards did tell this tale when interrogated by an officer, and, as we others corroborated his statement, he escaped all punishment, and so did I. All the same, the sneers and whisperings of my companions during the remainder of the journey were at least as painful to me as his injuries were to the Belgian. In fact, I was more than boycotted by all, and the fact that none of my comrades would associate with me in even the slightest degree was gall and wormwood to the mind of a sensitive youth. How I wished that the first sergeant had not been so kind and the second so sparing of abuse to me. I was glad that in the depot for recruits I was altogether separated from the rest, and I may add now that, when I met some of them afterwards in the East, they seemed to have forgotten all the little annoyances of our first acquaintance.

I wish to say but little now about the rest of the way. The chief thing that remains in my memory is the scene aboard the transport that carried us from Marseilles to Oran. It was so striking that I fancy I shall never forget it.

There were troops of all arms aboard. I need not describe the party I was with, as I have said enough about it already, and of most of the others I can only recall that the various uniforms, the different numbers on the caps, all impressed me with the idea that I belonged to one of the great armies of the world. Having been, as I have already mentioned, brought up in a garrison town I at once noticed distinctions which another might pass over as trivial. I saw, for instance, that all the soldiers of the line did not belong to the same regiment in spite of the strong likeness the various corps showed to one another, and I knew that the same held true of the chasseurs and zouaves. I admired the way in which disorder was reduced to order ; the steady composure of those who had no work to do, which contrasted so much with the quick movement and tireless exertion of the men told off for fatigue ; the sharp eyes and short, clear orders of the sergeants ; and, above all, the calm, assured air of authority of the officer who superintended the embarkation.

While I was noting all this my glance fell on a party of men, about fifty in number, wearing the usual blue tunic and red trousers, who had no mark or number in their caps. Now the Frenchmen of the line had each the number of his regiment on the front of the kepi, and we of the Foreign Legion had grenades on ours. Moreover, these men were set apart from all the rest and were guarded by a dozen soldiers with fixed bayonets. The men seemed sullen and careless of their personal appearance, and when a Frenchman forgets his neatness you may be sure that he has already forgotten his self-respect. Curiosity made me apply for information to the corporal over my squad, and he told me that these were men who for their offences in regiments stationed in France were now being transferred to disciplinary battalions in Algeria, where they would forfeit, practically, all a soldier's privileges and be treated more like convicts than recruits. I at once remembered what the sergeant whose acquaintance I had first made had said about the zephyrs, the men that could not be reclaimed. I saw them often afterwards, and, though in most of the battalions they are not very bad and are treated fairly enough, in others which contain the incorrigible ones the officers and sub-officers have to go armed with revolvers, and the giving out of cartridges, when it can't be helped, is looked upon as the sure forerunner of a murder. Figure to yourself what a hated warder's life would be worth if the convicts in Dartmoor had rifles and bayonets and if the governor had occasionally to serve out packets of cartridges, it being well understood that all—governor, warders, and convicts—are supposed to be transferred to, let us say, Fashoda, where there is now and then a chance of a Baggara raid.

I don't know much about the voyage across the Mediterranean as I was almost, but not quite, sea-sick. It has always been so with me, the gentlest sea plays havoc with my stomach. We got into Oran at about six o'clock in the evening, and our party at once disembarked. We were met on the quay by a sergeant of the Foreign Legion, who showed us the way to a barrack, where we were formally handed over to his control. That night we stayed in the barrack, and I suffered a little annoyance from my comrades, from all of whom I was separated next day, when we were transferred to our depot at a place called Saida. I do not know whether this is to-day the depot for the Foreign Legion or not, as I heard men say that an intention existed on the part of the military authorities to place it farther south. Here I spent some time learning drill, discipline, and all the duties of a soldier, and this was the hardest period of my military life, for my knowledge of French had to be considerably increased before I could quite grasp the meaning of an order, and very often I was abused by a corporal for laziness when I had the best will in the world to do what I was told, if I could only understand it.

CHAPTER III

WHEN we arrived at the depot we were at once divided into small parties, each of which was sent to a company for drill. I was attached to No. 1 Company, and though four others of my comrades came to it with me they did not remain there long. Two of them were Belgians, one an Alsatian, and the fourth a Pole. All spoke French well, and it was very soon seen that they had learned something about drill already in other armies, and, therefore, they were sent almost at once to the battalions on service at the edge of the great desert. Thus it was that I found myself the only member of the detachment in No. 1, and of this I was very glad, for my last experience with them had not been of the most pleasant kind.

And now let me put on record the only complaint I have to make about my life at Saida. On account of my speaking English all agreed that I must be an Englishman, and the Englishman is well hated abroad. Consequently on the drill ground and in the barrack room I was continually addressed by the expressive sobriquet of "English pig." Now "cochon anglais" is not a nice nickname, and though I dared not resent it from the corporals and other sub-officers I made up my mind that from my equals in rank it was not to be endured. There was a big Alsatian in my squad who was most persistent in insulting me, though I had often tried to explain to him that I was neither a pig nor an Englishman. With him, therefore, I resolved to deal, confident that, if I could put a stop to his insolence, the rest would be quiet enough. I determined, as he was my superior in age, strength, weight, and length of arm,

21

that it would be only right to take him unawares and, if possible, finish the business before he could quite understand what I was about. For three or four days after settling this matter in my mind I got no opportunity such as I wished for. Seeing me take the nickname quietly, for I no longer even remonstrated with him, the Alsatian went further than before and raised my anger to boiling point. At last the chance came. As I entered the room one afternoon I noticed lying near the door a rather large billet of wood. The corporal was out, so were most of the men, and those who remained, five or six in number, were lazily lounging in various attitudes about the room. I put aside rifle, belt, and bayonet, for I had just come in from a punishment parade—that is, an extra parade ordered to men for some slight irregularity—and looked straight at the big brute, as if to challenge him.

"Ah, my fine fellow, how do English pigs like punishment parades in this weather?" he began.

"As well," I answered, picking up, carelessly as it were, the billet, "as Alsatian dogs like this." And I brought the heavy block down upon his head with all my strength. The cap, though utterly destroyed, saved his head, but still he was so stupefied by the sudden assault and by the force of the blow that I had time to strike him again and again. The others jumped up quickly and seized me, crying out that the Alsatian was dead. And, indeed, he looked as if he were dead, for his head was covered with blood, and one almost imagined that his brains would protrude through the wounds. However, after some time he came to himself again, and truly no one was better pleased than I, for as I cooled down I began to be fearful of consequences.

When the corporal heard about the affair he told the sergeant, the sergeant went to the captain, and the captain came down to investigate the matter for himself. I told him how I was continually annoyed, and when he asked me why I struck the other when off his guard, I pointed out that to do so gave me the only chance of revenge. He measured us both with his eyes and seemed to agree with me. Anyway, the Alsatian was sent to get his wounds dressed and I was ordered extra drills, extra fatigues, and to remain altogether in barracks for a fortnight.

Now I wondered how I got off so lightly. Well, in the Foreign Legion a fight between men of the same squad is not considered half so serious as one between men belonging to different squads, just as no one minds so much about a fight between brothers as about one between members of separate families. If a soldier of No. 1 squad beats a soldier of No. 2 all the men of No. 2 will look for revenge, and all the men of No. 1 will know that, and, therefore, at any moment thirty or more men may be, to use an expressive phrase, "into" one another with Nature's weapons and anything lying handy that will do a man damage. Sometimes when the quarrel is more serious than usual—as, for instance, when it is about women—bayonets may be used, but, indeed, the soldier very seldom has recourse to his accustomed weapons in a fight with comrades. But if a dispute arises between a battalion of zephyrs and another of the Foreign Legion there is but one way of restoring order—call out the cavalry and the guns.

As the Alsatian and I belonged to the same squad the captain contented himself with punishing me slightly and warning us both against a renewal of the quarrel. The story went around, and I don't believe I was called an English pig ever afterwards except by an Irishman or an Irish-American, who, of course, spoke only in jest.

Our company consisted of from 160 to 200 men. Sometimes it was strong for a week after the arrival of a number of recruits, then again it would go down as a squad or two departed for the regiment. My squad varied, I think, from ten to seventeen, and, taking us all round, we weren't very bad, as soldiers go. What language did we speak? French on the drill ground and on duty and in reply to superior officers; amongst ourselves a Lingua Franca, made up chiefly of French, especially the Argot, but with a plentiful admixture of German, Spanish, Italian, Portuguese, and other languages, including in some squads even Russian, Turkish, and Arabic. What I say now refers not merely to the depot but to the Foreign Legion in general: every battalion, every company, I might almost say every squad, had its own peculiarity of idiom; Sapristi and Parbleu gave place often to Caramba, Diavolo, and Mein Gott. In fact, before I was six months in the Legion I could swear fluently in every European language except English; the only English curse they taught me was Goddam.

The *sous-officiers* were pretty strict with us in the depot, but the punishments were not too severe. The favourite one was to keep you altogether in the barrack and compel you to sleep during the night in your ordinary uniform on a plank bed in the guard room. That was the worst of it, in the day no one minded the confinement to barracks—for what was the use in wandering about a dirty town if one had no money in his pocket, and our pay did not last long?—but in the night the plank bed was not an ideal resting-place. I did not get into much trouble, the row with the Alsatian was my chief offence, and what kept me right was the dread of sleeping in the guard room at night.

We drilled every day except Sunday, but there is no use in telling about that, as drill is the same all the world over. Our drill instructors were certainly eloquent—all had copious vocabularies—and the wealth of abuse and cursing that any of them could expend in an hour's work was, indeed, extraordinary. While I was unable to fully understand I felt angry; by the time I understood every word I was too philosophical to care. Moreover, I am sorry to have to say that I was rapidly acquiring a fairly extensive vocabulary of my own, and every time I heard a curse directed at myself I thought one for the benefit of the drill instructor's soul. It's a tradition in every army just as it is in every navy, fighting and mercantile, that nothing can be got out of men without bad language, and I do believe that there is a good deal of truth in the tradition. One would fancy that skippers and sergeants wish to familiarise their men with the names at least of the lower regions and their ruler, in the firm belief that the men will at some time make the acquaintance of both. That's as it may be; at anyrate we learned a good deal more than our drill from our instructors.

We had a remarkably fine band. It was chiefly composed of Germans, I think, and it does seem strange that ten years after the Franco-Prussian war the majority of a French regimental band should be composed of the sons of the men who crushed Napoleon the Third at Sedan. The band played very often in the square, and every evening that it turned out I felt no desire to leave the barrack. I don't understand music but I like it. In the square the women and children of the depot used to walk about listening, talking and laughing; the officers' wives at one side and the wives of the *sous-officiers* at another. As for us, we lounged about at a short distance and made remarks, not always in the best taste, about the women of both classes. A good deal of quiet, oh, very quiet, flirtation used to go on, and this gave rise amongst us to rather broad jests and hints. Of course, many people from the town came in also, and these we considered fair game as well. One very fat man, accompanied by a tall, extremely thin woman, evidently his wife—they seemed to have no children—came regularly at least three times a week to listen to the music. If he and his lady knew all the fun they provided for us and the jokes uttered at their expense, I fancy that the square would never see them again. What they did not know did not trouble them, and so they came as long as I remained in the depot and I daresay for long enough after I left it.

A very important consideration with a soldier, as with any other man, is his food. I think we got nearly enough—that is, the fellows who were used to it got enough—but the poor devils who were not used to slops and bread were badly off, especially those who, like myself, had schoolboy appetites. I have seen—this was in the battalion—veterans leaving part of their rations untouched and young soldiers, men under twenty-five, hungry the whole day long. Early in my soldiering I learned the blessed consolation of tobacco. Often when I was more hungry after a meal than before it, the soup and bread rather exciting my stomach than satisfying it, I have smoked till no sensation of emptiness remained. I don't know what a soldier in a Continental army would do without tobacco. Nearly all our scanty pay went to buy it, and, wretched stuff as it was, I have never enjoyed the best Havana as I used to enjoy the delicious smoke when all work and drill for the day were over and the pipe of comfort and blessed forgetfulness made paradise of a barrack room.

We were good enough to one another. If the Spaniard had no tobacco he could generally get some, unless it were too scarce indeed, and then he had to be satisfied with half-a-dozen puffs from every pipe in the room. I say the Spaniard advisedly, for he was always without money; he had such an unfortunate trick of getting into trouble and losing his pay. At the same time I too have had to do with the whiffs when I longed for a pipeful of my own, and when you wanted to feel the taste of the weed in your mouth it was very good to get even them. When tobacco was very scarce with all we had more than one device for getting a smoke; but there, these are only silly things, not that they seemed silly to us at the time.

While at our drill we were the most obedient fellows in the world, so were we too when doing the ordinary work of the soldier. But when the day's labour was done we were not to be ordered about at the will of any sergeant or corporal. Well they knew it too. Why, when a squad in No. 2 Company was bullied—out of hours, be it well understood—by their corporal a strange thing occurred. The corporal was found one afternoon—at least the corporal's body was found—in one of the latrines, and it was quite evident to the doctors that he had been suffocated. Suspicion fell at once upon the squad he commanded, but, and this was the strange thing, every one of them could prove that it was impossible for him to have hand, act or part, in the business, for some were on guard, and others were at drill, and others—rather peculiar, wasn't it?—had been directly under the eyes of the sergeant-major of the company. There was a sentry near the latrine, who, of course, had not left his post, and this man could tell within five minutes the time the corporal entered. He saw no others enter at or about the same time, but that was easily explained : a large hole had been broken through the back of one of the compartments, and half-a-dozen men could easily get through this in as many seconds, and, once in without being observed, the rest was easy. Nobody was ever even court-martialled for the murder, and, though many might be able to guess the names of the murderers, he would be a fool who did his guessing within earshot of even a corporal. One thing is certain, we had a fairly quiet time afterwards while I was in the depot, not that we weren't sworn at and abused just as much on parade—oh yes, we were—but when the quiet time came the *sous-officiers* had sense enough to leave us to ourselves. Well, it's all over now. The man who carried the business through died in Tonquin—he was a Russian—and he will turn up again in this narrative as ringleader of one of the most exciting incidents of my life.

I did not form any friendships in the depot. True, there were fellows in the squad whom I liked better than others, but I never showed preference even for them. One thing chiefly prevented me from making friends: I was beginning to learn something about the world and its ways, or perhaps I should say about human nature, for with us conventionality was dropped when the belt came off for the last time in the evening and we spoke very freely to one another. If you liked something in a comrade's words or acts you told him so; if you disliked anything you were equally outspoken. Did a thought enter your mind worthy of being communicated, in your opinion, to the rest it made no difference whether it were immoral, or blasphemous, or against the law, or contrary to discipline, out it came, and generally with a garnishment of oaths and obscene expressions. We very seldom spoke of what is good, except to laugh at and revile it. When we saw a woman evidently very fond of her husband we said: " Ah, she is throwing dust in his eyes ; she has more than one lover." If we noticed a husband very devoted to his wife, why, it was certain that the devotion was only an excuse for watchfulness. Everything good was looked on with suspicion ; everything bad was natural, right, and obviously true.

We were always looking forward to the future. When in the depot we yearned to be with the regiment; afterwards, when with the regiment in the south of Algeria, I found my comrades and myself thinking eagerly of the chances of going to the East. Life in Tonquin could not be so monotonous ; there was always fighting going on, and in any case you got the chance of looting on the sly after a battle or even a petty skirmish. This looking forward is, however, common to most men, but we had a special reason for it, inasmuch as we were never comfortable or content, our lives being made up for the most part of work and drill and punishment, with an occasional fight, which wonderfully enlivened the time for those who had not to pay for it.

When we had learned our drill pretty well the officers began to take more interest in us. Don't imagine that they were kind and nice to us, that they complimented us on our smartness and intelligence, or that they even dreamt of standing us a drink in the canteen. Oh no; they were somewhat worse than the sergeants, and if their language was not so coarse it was equally cutting and abusive. By this time, however, we were case-hardened, and, besides, we knew that at last we were leaving the depot for ever, and the excitement induced by the expected change was in itself a source of joy. We who were about to go went around smiling and in good humour with ourselves and all the world. The men who knew that their stay would last for some time longer consoled themselves with the thought that at last it too must come to an end. Simple philosophy, wasn't it? but wonderfully comforting.

We speculated about the battalions, about the stations, about the Arabs, about the Moors, about the war in Tonquin, about everything that we could think of as possibly affecting our after-life. I, mere school-boy that I was, was one of the most excited, and indulged in the most extravagant fancies and dreamt the most extraordinary dreams.

At last the glorious day came. We were aroused at three o'clock in the morning, had finished breakfast, and were on the parade-ground at a little after four in full marching order. There we were addressed in a farewell speech by the commandant, who called us " my children," as if he cared especially for each and all of us. I had almost to smile, but a smile at such a time would surely entail punishment.

The band played us out of the gate, and off we marched, about 200 strong, all in good health and spirits, for the little station where lay the battalion for which we were designed.

CHAPTER IV

WE went altogether by march route to our destination. Every day was like the preceding one, and a short description of any day will do for all. Reveille at four o'clock, then while some pulled down and folded up the tents others cooked the morning coffee, at five or a little after we were *en route*, at eight usually, but sometimes later, a halt was called for the morning soup; that over, we put our best foot foremost until about eleven or half-past. Now came the pleasantest and sleepiest part of the twenty-four hours. We ate a little, we smoked a little, we slept, or rather dozed, a little, until the bugles warned us at half-past three that another stretch of dry, dusty, throat-provoking road had to be accounted for. On again at four until six or seven or eight, with occasional rests of ten minutes each, and then there was nothing but cleaning up after the evening soup. When all was right and the sentries had been posted for the night you might talk and smoke if you liked, but as a rule you smoked first and fell asleep afterwards.

It was not strange that we, who had been cooped up in the depot so long, enjoyed this march. It seemed to us that we were soldiers at last, not mere recruits, and dust and thirst and other inconveniences were matters to be put up with and laughed at. On the road we often sang; at the end of the midday halt, while we helped one another with knapsack and belts, you might often hear songs of every country from the Urals to the Atlantic. Every man's spirits were high; the long-expected change had worked wonders, and the officers, nay, even the sergeants and the corporals, had little of abuse or swearing for us. True, our *sous-officiers* were not drill instructors; of all things in the world teaching is the most wearing on the temper, and perhaps that is why there was so great a difference between the sergeants in the depot and the sergeants on the march.

I think we did on an average about three miles an hour. It was good enough too, for there were the rifle and the knapsack to be carried, and the greatcoat and the blanket and the ammunition, and all the other impedimenta of the soldier. The straps of the knapsack galled me a bit, and I soon found out the difference between a march out from barracks for a few hours and a day-after-day tramp through the heat and the dust with the knowledge that you carried your bed and most of your board upon your person. The rest at the end of the hour, for we always halted for ten minutes after a fifty minutes' march, was a great help; and, again, I was a little too proud, or too vain if you like to call it so, to fall out of the ranks while my comrades were steadily marching on. After all, pride or vanity, call it what you will, never hurts a youngster, though it should make him slightly overwork himself in trying to keep up with those who are his seniors in age and his betters in endurance. All the same, when the day's march was over, it was delightful to pull off knapsack, boots and all, and to feel that there were before you eight or nine hours of complete freedom from toil.

One night, however, things were not quite so well with me. It was my turn for guard, and when we halted for the night I with others was turned out of the ranks at once. The first sentries were soon posted, and the remainder of us had a couple of hours in or near the guard tent to enjoy our evening meal. When that was over we all had a smoke, and at nine—we had halted at seven—the reliefs were wanted. I felt very lazy as I got up, took my rifle, and set out with the corporal of the guard to my post. There I remained until eleven, was relieved until one, and went again on sentinel duty until three. At four the usual routine began, and I remember that, after the wakeful night, the day's march seemed very long. When we halted at midday I fell asleep, and when the march was over I forgot to smoke, and, curling myself up in my greatcoat and blanket, became utterly oblivious of all that occurred until the reveille next morning awakened me to another day. I don't remember much of the country through which we passed. Most of the time my ears were more engaged than my eyes, for many a good story was told and many a happy jest passed as we tramped along in the dust and sun. Some fellows told us stories of life in their own countries, and if they did not adhere exactly to the truth, why, that only made the stories better. Others could not see a man or a woman —especially a woman—on either flank but straightway they criticised and joked, and very clever we used to fancy the criticisms and jokes were. Some again were good singers, and these were constantly shouted at to sing, especially the men who sang comic songs. I daresay some of these songs, if not all, were scarcely fit for a drawing-room, but as no ladies were present it did not seem to make much difference. Then we had a bugle march occasionally—say half-a-dozen times a day— and I for one found the bugles wonderfully inspiriting. While the bugles were playing none of us seemed to feel the road beneath our feet; we stopped talking, we almost gave up smoking, the step became more regular, and the ranks closed up. I suppose a musician would call a bugle march monotonous; well, it may be so, but how many men out of 200 are musicians? But we had more music than that. Some of the fellows had brought along musical instruments of small size— tin whistles, flageolets, and such things. Very well they played too. Many were fairly good whistlers, and so there was a variety of means to drive away dull care;

indeed, I think we were the jolliest and most careless set in the world. Even when the sun had been very hot and the road more than usually dusty we had always the thought that the end of the annoyance would come when we reached our battalion and that every day brought us nearer to the men who were to take the place of home and country, friends and relations, for five years. We fancied that they would be just like ourselves, and we liked one another too well not to be satisfied.

It was while on this march that I first saw how soldiers are punished when there is no prison near or when it is deemed best to give a short, sharp punishment to an offender. Of course, I refer to cases where the offence does not merit a court-martial. We had halted for the evening near a small village, and some fellows had gone to it, more, I suppose, out of curiosity than because they had any business there. I was not with them, and I never fully learned what occurred but I know there was a woman in the case. Whether she deserted the corporal for the private soldier, or refused to leave the private when his superior made advances to her I cannot tell, but some words passed between the men, and the corporal made a report to the sergeant, who passed it on to the captain. Very few questions were asked; the man was taken to a spot near the guard tent, where he would be directly under the eyes of a sentry, and there he was put, as we termed it, *en crapaudine*. This is how it was done. First his hands were pinioned behind his back, then his ankles were shackled tightly to each other, afterwards the fastenings of his wrists were bound closely to the ankle bonds, so that he was compelled to remain in a kneeling posture with his head and body drawn back. After some time pains began to be felt in the arms, across the abdomen, and at the knees and ankles. These pains increased rapidly, and at last became intolerable. Yet he dared not cry out, or at least no one would cry out until he

c

could not help it, for the sleeping men ought not to be disturbed, and at the first cry a gag was placed between the teeth. This poor devil did not get much punishment. I think he was *en crapaudine* for only an hour or so, but, take my word for it, if you place a man in that position for four, five, or six hours, he will be in no hurry to get himself into trouble again. There are other punishments too—the silo, for instance—but I shall not describe these now, as I shall have occasion further on to tell all about them when I am dealing with life in the regiment.

We did not always lie under canvas on the march. Sometimes we halted at a garrison town or at cantonments, and then some, if not all, of us were placed in huts for the night. We saw all kinds of soldiers there. We met zouaves, chasseurs, turcos, spahis, zephyrs, but with none had we much intercourse. This was due to several reasons. We came in hot and tired and with little desire for anything except food and rest, and besides we had to clean up clothes, boots, and arms for the parade and inspection in the early morning. Then the regular French troops, and even, I must admit, the native Algerian soldiers, looked with contempt upon us, and you may be sure that we of the Legion returned the contempt and the contemptuous words with interest. They never went very far in showing their feelings towards our fellows, for we had an ugly reputation ; more than once a company or two of Legionaries had made a desperate attack on a battalion even, and it was well known through Algeria that when the Legionaries began a fight there would be, as was often said, "blood upon shirts" before the fight was over. Therefore the others stood rather in awe of our men, and they did not quite like the idea of having anything to do with us, even though we were only recruits on the way to the battalion, for every soldier knows that the recruit is even more anxious to follow the regimental tradition than the veteran. The latter feels that he is part and parcel of the corps and that his reputation is not likely to suffer; the former is only too eager to show that he accepts, wholly and unreservedly, the ideas handed down to him, and, besides, he has not been altogether brought under discipline. Thus, though we saw men in many uniforms we got to know very little about them—indeed, all our information came from the corporals—and I may add here that the corporals impressed upon us that we were never to fight individually with Frenchmen or natives, but that, if a general quarrel took place, we were to remember our duty to the Legion and make it " warm weather " for our opponents. Afterwards on more than one occasion we followed that advice.

Once or twice a little unpleasantness arose amongst ourselves. It never went very far; the others, who were not desirous of seeing their comrades get into trouble, always put an end to the business before any real harm was done. I had nothing to do with any of these disputes save once, when, in the *rôle* of peacemaker, I sat with another fellow for more than half-an-hour on an Italian who was thirsting for the blood of a Portuguese. The Portuguese was receiving similar attentions from two others at the opposite side of the tent. It was funny how the thing came about. The Italian had got, somewhere or somehow—I suppose he stole it—a bottle of brandy, and, instead of sharing all round, gave half to his comrade the Portuguese and drank the other half himself. When they returned to the tent they were quarrelling, and evidently drunk. After some time they began to fight, and we left them alone, as they had been so mean about the liquor, until we saw the Italian reaching for his bayonet. Then the rest of us joined in, and the precious pair of rascals, who had forgotten their comrades when they were happy, got something which made them rise in the morning with more aches in the body than they had in the head. They apologised the next day and we forgave them. This was another lesson to me. I saw that when a man got anything outside his ordinary share of good things he was supposed to go share and share alike with the rest of his squad. Many a time afterwards I have seen men who had at one time been of good position at home, and whose relatives could and would send them money, openly show the amount received in tent or hut or barrack room, and we others went out to spend that money when the evening came with just as much belief in our right to do so as if the money had been sent to the squad and not to the man. Well, the rich ones did not lose in the end, for they got many a favour from their comrades which the average soldier would be a fool to expect.

The corporal of my squad on the march south was a rather good fellow. I am not quite sure whether he was a German or an Austrian by birth. He had seen a good deal of Algerian life, and was determined as soon as his term was up to get clear away for ever from Africa. This was not pleasant news. Here was a corporal, a man of over four years' service, whose whole and sole idea it was to leave the Legion and the country. It plainly proved that the life before us was not the most attractive in the world, and the thought often crossed my mind that perhaps I had been a fool to try soldiering in such a corps. With the happy-go-lucky recklessness of youth, however, I quickly got rid of these fancies, and I could console myself that five years would not be long passing, and at the very worst I should have learned more, situated as I was, than if I were to spend the term at school, and at such a school as the one I had been attending.

I got on fairly well with the others of my squad. I have never been inclined to affront people, and I can honestly say that I have never shirked my work, and these qualities, added to a natural cheerfulness of disposition which caused me to look at the bright side of things, helped me very much all through my stay in the Foreign Legion. Indeed, there was only one man who was disliked by all. He was a Pole, a German

Pole, I believe, and he had the most sarcastic tongue of all the men I've ever met. His sneering smile was almost as bad as his cutting tongue. While speaking politely he said little things that one could not very well resent, and that, therefore, hurt one the more. It's bad to be an idler, and worse to have a nasty way of openly abusing and insulting people, but the worst gift of God to a man is the gift of sarcasm. The sarcastic man never has a friend. There are, of course, always men who will fawn upon and flatter him, but that will be only through fear of his tongue—even they who most court him rejoice inwardly at his misfortunes. He can't be always lucky, he must take his bad fortune as it comes, and when it does come he cannot help knowing that all who know him are glad.

It was well, I think, for our friend the Pole that the journey did not last a week longer. Somebody or other would be sure to lose his temper, and if one blow were struck, twenty would surely follow, for we all hated him. He said something about a gorilla one day, looking hard all the while at the Italian already mentioned, and it was a wonder that there was no fight. There would have been, I feel sure, but that the bugles sounded the assemble for the last march of the day, and the Italian, who was no beauty, had a few hours of marching to get cool. The Pole was quiet enough for the next couple of days, and by that time we were within six hours' march of our destination.

Before describing the battalion to which I now belonged I must say a few words about the Foreign Legion in general, so that the peculiar characteristics of the corps may be understood. All that I shall mention in this chapter is that one sunny afternoon about four o'clock we marched into camp on the borders of the Sahara amid the cheers of our future comrades, and that within an hour our 200 men were divided amongst the four companies that constituted the 2nd Battalion of the First Regiment of the *Légion étrangère*.

CHAPTER V

FOR centuries the armies of France have had a certain proportion of foreign troops. Readers of Scott will remember the Scottish archers, and there is a regiment in the British army to-day which was at one time a Scottish corps in the service of the Most Christian Kings of France. Almost everyone has heard of the Irish Brigade, a force whose records fill many a bloody and glorious page of European history and whose prowess more than once turned the ebb-tide of defeat into the full flood of victory. It has been computed that almost 500,000 Irishmen died in the French service; and we may well imagine that half-a-million dashing soldiers did not yield up their lives for nothing.

In the time of the great Napoleon there were many foreign brigades in the grand army. Everybody has read of the famous Polish lancers who time and again shattered the chivalry of Prussia, Austria, and Muscovy in those combats of giants, when kingdoms were the prizes and marshalships and duchies mere consolations for the less lucky ones. These Poles were magnificent fools. Poniatowski and his riders clung to Napoleon, led the way in his advances, covered the rear in his retreats, and all the while the cynical emperor had little, if any, thought of restoring the ancient glories of Poland, and thus repaying the country for the valour and devotion of her sons. Other foreign cavalry he had as well, but they became more or less mixed with the native Frenchmen, and thus do not stand out so boldly to our mental vision as the Poles. Chief amongst the great emperor's foreign infantry brigades was the Irish one. Indeed, to this one alone of them an eagle was

38

entrusted, and it may do no harm to remark here that that eagle, much as it was coveted by certain enemies, was never lost, and was handed back to French custody when the Irish Brigade ceased to exist as an independent body after the final defeat at Waterloo. Most of the brigade, not caring for the monarchy after having so long and so faithfully served the empire, took advantage of the offer made to them of taking service under the British monarch, and were incorporated in various regiments of the British army. Indeed, in the late twenties and early thirties of the nineteenth century it was by no means uncommon to meet in Irish villages a war-worn veteran who had been in most of the great European battles—Jena, Austerlitz, Borodino, Waterloo —and had finished his soldiering under the burning suns of Hindostan.

In the Crimea, again, a foreign legion, somewhat like the legion formed by the British Government for the same campaign, was amongst the troops sent out by Napoleon the Third. I know very little about this corps, but I am quite sure that it got its full share, and more, of danger, hard work, and privations. Anyway the Crimean campaign, except for a few battles, was more a contest against nature than against the enemy.

In the Franco-Prussian war we next find mention of the Legionaries. At the battle of Orleans, when that city was captured by the Prussians, the Foreign Legion and the Pontifical Zouaves covered the French retreat. When we learn that out of 1500 of the former only 36 remained at the end of the day there will be little need to ask where were the Legionaries during the rest of the war. It must be remembered also, that the 1500 men who fought and fell outside Orleans were the remains of the Legionaries brought from Algeria, and that their comrades left behind were amongst the most distinguished of those who quelled the rebellion of the Kabyles in the year '71. It is only just to mention that the Pontifical Zouaves covered themselves with glory at this fight; they went into action along with the Legion on the 11th of October 1870, 370 strong, of whom only 17 survived the day.

The Foreign Legion, as I knew it, consisted, as I believe it still consists, of two regiments, each containing four battalions. As a battalion numbers 1000 men the total strength of the service soldiers may be put at 8000. In addition there are depot men, including band, drill instructors, and recruits; but I have said enough about the depot already, so I shall now confine myself altogether to the service soldiers.

Every battalion is divided into four companies, and thus a company contains, approximately, 250 officers, sub - officers, and soldiers. The officers are three—captain, lieutenant, and sub - lieutenant. Next comes the sergeant - major of the company, a sub - officer who keeps the accounts. There are two sergeants, one for each of the two sections into which the company is divided, and under them a number of corporals in command of squads, every squad being, be it understood, a distinct unit in the economy of the section to which it belongs. The men are divided into two classes, the first and the second, and from the first class are chosen the corporals as vacancies arise.

The uniform consists of kepi with a brass grenade in front, blue tunic with black belt, red trousers, or white, according to the season. With the red trousers go black gaiters, with the white ones white spats, somewhat like those worn by Highland soldiers in the British army. The knapsack, greatcoat, and other impedimenta are rather heavy, especially when 150 rounds of ball cartridge are included. I don't know the exact weight, but I remember that I used to feel an ugly drag on my shoulders at the end of a day's march. The pouch for ammunition at the side also pressed heavily against the body, and we often wished that those who had the arrangement of a man's equipment should wear it on the march, day in day out, if only for a month. There might be some common-sense displayed by them after that. But in all ages and nations a man's accoutrements—I use the word in the most general sense—have been decided on by tailors and good-for-nothing generals—oh, there are plenty of them in every army in the world—and, worst of all, by women, who twist and turn the said generals around their little fingers. Look at a private soldier of any army when standing at attention in full marching order; you are pleased with the sight; his head is erect, his straightened shoulders seem easily to support the heavy pack behind; the twin pouches look so beautifully symmetrical. Ask that soldier how he feels at the end of a thirty-mile march. If he isn't a liar, he will tell you that the rifle is rather heavy, but he doesn't mind that; that the pack galls a bit, but that's to be expected; and that the pouches weighted with ammunition have given him a dull, heavy pain in each side just above, he imagines, where the kidneys are, and if that pain could be avoided he would think little of all the rest. Many a time I have taken the packets of cartridges from the pouches before we had gone a quarter of a mile and stowed them away between the buttons of my tunic—there they had ribs and breast bone to rest against. Why don't the people whose business and interest it is to get the best out of the private soldier give the private soldier a chance? But they won't. Of all the humbugs on the face of God's earth the military officer of, say, twenty years' service is the worst.

The soldier of the second class wore no decoration on his sleeve, the soldier of the first class had a red chevron, the corporal wore two red chevrons, the sergeant a single gold one, and the sergeant-major two gold ones. It was a good thing to be a soldier of the first class, not because you wore a chevron or got extra pay, but because, when a charge was made against you

by sergeant or corporal, the officers would listen carefully to your defence, and you generally got what the
second-class man rarely got—a fair chance as well as a
patient hearing.

Squad etiquette was rather peculiar. You were
assigned to a squad, and on entering were made free,
as I may say, of the mess, and how you got on afterwards with your enforced comrades depended largely
on yourself. You might be very well liked, or thoroughly
disliked, but violent likes and dislikes were rather uncommon. As a rule, you had just a little trouble in
asserting your right to a fair share, and that always, of
what was going. If you had a dispute with another
your comrades looked on and listened; if you came to
blows they prevented the affair from going too far; and
unless the corporal was a brute he allowed his squad
to arrange their own affairs out of working hours in
their own way. But you dared not form friendships with
men outside the squad; if you did you were set upon
and punished in every way by your comrades, and your
friend was served in the same way by his. Let me give
an instance. A rather nice, quiet fellow, an Alsatian,
was in my squad at a place called Zenina when we
received a new draft of recruits from the depot. Amongst
these was another Alsatian, who came from the same
place as my comrade, and, as was natural, the two
became fast friends. Under the circumstances nothing
was said at first, and had either asked for a transfer to
his friend's squad all would have been well. After
some time, however, the comrades of both began to
object. Why, we asked one another, should Schmidt
openly abandon us and our genial company for a man
who should by right be good comrade with others?
Well, Schmidt was abused, and bore the abuse calmly;
he got only half a share at meals, and still did not go
further than a meek protest; he came back after seeing
his chum, and found all his kit flung outside the door of
the hut, his rifle fouled, his bayonet covered with salt

water, his straps dirty, and his buckles dull; still he bore with all. Next evening he went to visit his friend, and, while he was absent, we formed a soldiers' court-martial and tried him. One man represented the accuser, another took the part of Schmidt, but the result was quite evident from the first. He was found guilty of neglecting his duties as a comrade, and as he had openly abandoned his squad and thereby shown his contempt for it, at the same time exposing us to the derision of all the battalion, it was high time that the squad should adequately punish him and thus vindicate its character.

The chief difficulty was about the punishment. It was first proposed that we should put him *en crapaudine* for a night, seizing and binding him while all in the cantonments were asleep, and releasing him in the morning before the reveille. However, it was pointed out that the corporal would not be likely to permit that, and, if he did permit it, Schmidt might report the matter and get the corporal into trouble. Now the corporal was a good fellow. He swore at us and abused us and would allow not even a sullen muttering in reply, but he would not, if he could help it, of course, get a man into trouble with the sergeant or the captain or the commandant. Occasionally he would find a bottle of wine, half-a-bottle of brandy, or a score or two of cigarettes in his corner. He said nothing, and as soon as the bottle was empty he did not have anything more to do with it: it was removed without a word by some one of us and quietly, I may say unostentatiously, deposited where its presence need not be accounted for by any of our squad.

After a good deal of talking we finally settled on a plan. What it was will appear in a short time. That night we could not do as we had resolved, for the corporal came in at an early hour in the evening as drunk and as abusive as a man could be. He rolled against me, and cursed me for a dirty, drunken pig, who could not carry his liquor like a soldier. He stood tottering in his corner of the room, and gave out more bad language than he had ever done before. And we were not quiet. He got quite as much as he gave; we described for his benefit our conceptions of his father and his mother—his father was a dog and his mother the female of the same species—we attributed to himself all the bad qualities that we could think of; we even called him coward, and dared him to report us at once to the sergeant or the captain. He knew, and we knew, that if he did so his arrest would at once follow and that the chevrons on his arm would not be worth one of the brass buttons on his tunic. We overpowered him with abuse at length, and he fell asleep muttering curses and threats, which were altogether forgotten in the morning.

Next evening the chance came. The corporal had taken a hint that it would be just as well for him for his own sake to have some appointment that would keep him away until the last moment before roll call. I may admit that when he woke in the morning he looked, and I suppose felt, very ill, and even refused his morning coffee when it was first offered to him. I took the coffee then from the man who had offered it, and, while all the rest, as it had been arranged, turned their backs, poured into it nearly a quarter of a pint of brandy. He saw what I was doing and took the mixture from me. Smelling it carefully first, he swallowed a little; liking the taste, he swallowed some more; and in less than two minutes he handed back the empty vessel to me, with a wink and a nod of the head that told me how delightful had been the little surprise prepared for him.

As he was going out another man held out his hand with a couple of cigarettes. "Thanks, my comrade, how you are kind!" said the *sous-officier*.

When he came in for soup, I again poured some brandy from the bottle into a tin cup in such a way that the corporal saw but the rest did not, being discreetly engaged. He did not wait to have it carried to him, he came swiftly round, took the cup, and drained it at a gulp. Then somebody left six or eight cigarettes near the corporal's bedplace, and all walked out except the corporal and myself. I went to the door, looked out, came back to my own bunk, took out a bottle of wine nearly three-quarters full and the tin cup, walked over to the corporal, filled the cup to the brim, and dutifully offered it to my superior officer. He drank, and returned the empty cup to me. Filling it for myself, I finished the contents, and then asked him for a cigarette—just one. The corporal gave it me, and I began the conversation.

"Bad for us others if you lost the chevrons, corporal."

"Why? Why? what did I say last night?"

"Oh, nothing to speak about; but, corporal——"
Then I stopped and looked straight at him.

"Well, my comrade, what do you wish to say?"

Now he was afraid; he began to fear something hidden by the kindness.

"But, my corporal, could you not make an appointment now, so that after the evening soup you would be engaged until roll call—away from this place and in good company?"

"Oh yes, yes; that is easy."

"And your comrade might like to smoke and drink a little; if so, my corporal, after the evening soup, when we others leave the room, look behind your knapsack."

"Good comrade; but will anything happen?"

"Yes; a man will go to hospital for a week."

"To hospital?"

"Yes."

"Only to hospital?"

"My honour; only to hospital."

"And for a week?"

"Well, perhaps for ten days."

"But only to hospital?"

"Have I not pledged my honour?"

"Very good; I will see my good friend Jean this evening. But you, you will remember, only the hospital."

After the evening soup, as all were going out, he called me.

"It is settled, my comrade; only the hospital?"

"But yes," I answered.

"Not this?" said the corporal, fingering a bayonet.

I shook my head.

"Not this?" and he touched the butt of a rifle.

I answered as before.

"And only hospital; word of honour?"

"Word of honour," I replied.

"Be it so then; I am well content."

Then he looked behind his knapsack and found half-a-bottle of brandy, a bottle of wine, and six cigars. He turned, put out his hand to me, and said:

"You are my good comrade. Have no fear; if there should be trouble, it is you, it is you that I will save." I laughed and shook his hand; he gave me a cigar, and the next moment was sorry for his generosity.

Schmidt went off after the evening soup to see his chum.

"Very well, very well," we said to one another. Lots were quickly drawn—we had not a sou amongst us to toss with—and Nicholas the Russian, Guillaume the Belgian, Jean Jacques from Lorraine, and I were chosen as executioners of justice. The others lounged outside in different places, all anxious to let us know in good time of the arrival of the condemned. About an hour after soup we were warned that he was coming towards the hut. At once the blanket which was ready was laid on the ground directly inside the door, and each man stood at his corner waiting for the victim. The others outside gaily saluted him, and the fool did not suspect the unusual courtesy; he was humming an air to himself as he stepped through the doorway on to the blanket. In a second we had raised it at the corners; he stumbled and fell, in a limp heap, in the bottom. We jerked the blanket upward, and crash came his head against the roof of the hut. We let go at the word of command, given by the Russian; flop went his body against the floor. Again and again this was repeated, till our arms were tired, and the others who had crowded in and had been excited by the fun swore that he had not been punished sufficiently and that they would take our places. I was glad enough to surrender my corner to an Italian, for, indeed, my arms were weary, and my feelings—I was only a boy, you must remember —were shocked at the sight of the unresisting and almost insensible bit of humanity in the blanket.

After a short time the Russian said the game should stop, and we, the other appointed dispensers of punishment, backed him up. Some grumbled, but Nicholas, to give him his due, was not a man to be turned from his purpose, and his reputation was such that nobody was very anxious to fall out with him. So the blanket was dropped for the last time, pulled from under the Alsatian, replaced on his bed, and we all went out, leaving the wretched fellow groaning on the ground. After a short talk we came back, gave him a drink, put him to bed, and prepared to meet the corporal on his return.

The corporal came in a little before roll call.

"What's wrong?" he asked as he heard the moaning of the Alsatian. Nobody answered. The corporal went across to the injured man's cot and again inquired. The poor devil told him as well as he could, and the *sous-officier* at once ordered us all not to leave the hut until his return. He went out, and came back in a few minutes with the sergeant of the section. There is no need in telling all about the inquiry that followed; suffice it to say that the corporal was the only man sleeping in the room that night—the Alsatian was in hospital and we others under guard.

Of course, our conduct was approved of throughout the battalion. Regimental tradition is dearer than justice, and we were regarded as good soldiers and good comrades who had merely vindicated our honour. But the army tradition is : when a charge is made and proved, punish. Officers *may* sympathise, but they *must* punish. Therefore we of the squad, corporal and Alsatian excepted, were sentenced to do extra drill every day for a month and sleep in our clothes under guard every night. It was a hard punishment. The weather was hot, we had little change of underclothing, and when we lay down on the planks for the night with the shirts and drawers on that we had worn during the day our sleep was restless, fitful, and uneasy. It is a wonder we did not mutiny ; however, that would be going too far, so we counted the days and nights that intervened until we should be free soldiers again. The Alsatian was transferred from the hospital to another battalion, and I came across him again, and was glad to find that he bore no malice ; indeed, he admitted that we were justified in acting as we had done and that it was his own fault, as he had not asked for a transfer.

The incident I have related will give some idea of my life in the corps. I shall have soon to relate another story, which will show that jealousy might arise between companies as well as in a squad.

CHAPTER VI

ABOUT this time there were signs of a disturbance amongst the semi-savage tribes that hold the oases on the borders of the great desert. These are not, and I daresay never will be, brought completely under subjection. They are to the French in Algeria what the hill tribes of the Himalayas are to the British in Hindostan. They are by nature, proud, fierce, suspicious; by religion, contemptuous of Christian dogs; by habit, predatory. They are fairly well armed, indeed, they make their own weapons and ammunition. When they go on the warpath there is always more trouble than one would expect, considering their numbers; they are so elusive, so trained to forced marches, so dashing in attack and swift in retreat, that the Government has to allow at least three men for every Arab. If a general could corner them and get well home with the bayonet after the usual preliminaries of shell firing and musketry, or if the rascals would only come on and have done with it, a quarter of the number would suffice. But these pleasant things don't occur—I mean pleasant for the man with the modern rifle—at least, if they do, it is only when all the oases of the district have been seized, and then the Arabs may prefer to hazard all on a big fight, but as a rule they bow to destiny and surrender.

Well, one morning we noticed the commandant and other officers jubilant and smiling, and very soon the news got down to us through the *sous-officiers* that our battalion was for active service. How delighted we were! All punishments in the battalion were at once remitted; we had no more to suffer for the affair of the Alsatian; and the other squad, which had treated

Alsatian number two in a similar manner, was also included in the pardon.

We were not long getting ready for the march. The day after the good news came the battalion tramped out of cantonments nearly 1100 strong, every man in good condition, and with 150 cartridges in his pouches. A significant order was given on the parade ground, when we formed up for the last time in column of companies. We were told to break open each man a packet of cartridges and to load. We did so, and the commandant addressed us, and gave us fair warning that he could not permit *accidents*—he laid great stress on the word and repeated it more than once—he told us that if an *accident* did occur it would be bad for the man whose rifle should be found to be discharged; he quoted the Bible to us, saying something about "a life for a life and a tooth"—yes, I think it was a tooth —"for a tooth." The old soldiers understood, and we others learned the meaning before we came to the first halting-place.

The fact is, in every regiment, and nowhere more than in the Foreign Legion, there are unpopular officers and sub-officers, and there are feuds amongst the men, and what is easier than to loose off a rifle accidentally and, accidentally as it were, hit the man you dislike? In action the thing is done far more commonly than people suppose—and that is the safest time to do it; but after a fight, when all the men's rifles are foul, and when a cartridge can be flung away as soon as used, a bullet is sometimes sent through a tent on the off-chance of hitting the right man within. So the commandant was justified when he warned and threatened us about accidents.

We marched about twenty-five kilometres every day, and did it cheerfully. We did not mind the country through which we passed, for all our thoughts were turned to the work before us. The veterans were in good humour. What advice they gave! "When the

Arab charges you, mon enfant, or when you charge the Arab, which is better, thrust at his face the first time and at his body the second." "But why?" "Ah, my boy, give him the bayonet in the body and still he will strike ; give it to him in the head, and then you can finish with a second stroke. And, again, the glint of the bayonet will disturb his aim, and, even should you miss with the first thrust, you can always get your weapon back and send it home before he recovers—of course, that is if you are quick enough. Moreover, the Arab expects you to lunge at his body, and you must always, if you are a good soldier, disappoint your enemy. Then there is no protection for his face ; but a button or a piece of brass, even a secretly-worn cuirass, may turn your point and leave you at his mercy."

We eagerly drank in all this and similar hints from the men of experience. The old soldiers were delighted. We were all as happy as schoolboys out for a holiday ; we endured the heat and dust without muttering a complaint ; nay, even old quarrels were forgotten, and the man who would not look at his detested comrade a month before now helped him with his knapsack or offered some tobacco, with a friendly smile.

When the halt was called in the evening, the sentries were posted, the fires lit, the little tents put up, the messes cooked for the squads ; but very soon the air of bustle and activity gave place to an appearance of quiet ease. When the last meal of the day was over, and the rifles, bayonets, straps, clothes, and everything else had been cleaned, we lay about the camp in small parties, here two or three, there half-a-dozen, yonder a full squad. Again we listened to the *vieux soldats* ; we made them repeat their stories of war and pillage ; we eagerly questioned them about the chances of loot. Some of our fellows had fought in the Russo-Turkish war of '78 ; Nicholas, whom I have mentioned, was believed to have commanded a company of Russian guards at the siege of Plevna, and, though he never

said in so many words that he had even carried a rifle
and knapsack in that war, he told us stories of it that
could be told only by an onlooker, and it was easy to
see that he was a man of birth and education, and,
judging by the money with which his purse was often
filled—not for long though, as he was a prince to spend—
of wealth as well.   It was during this march that I
learned for the first time the privileges of a soldier as
the soldier conceives them—I mean his chances when
the fighting is over and the enemy's camp, village, or
town is in his hands.   Perhaps I had best say nothing
or, if anything at all, but little of them.   One thing I
may mention ; it is foolish for people to suppose that
fighting men of to-day are at all different from their
compeers of yore—the only change is that the rapine and
the pillage are not boasted of so openly—but there is
just as little of the spirit of Christianity in a so-called
civilised army as there used to be in a legion of Julius
Cæsar, perhaps even less.   Many people will regret
this, and yet you always find the goody-goodies and
even the women loudest in crying out for war to avenge
the wrongs, or fancied wrongs, of their country or to
acquire new territory and new trade.   I say this : if the
women of the world only once realised to the full what
war means to the women of the losers they would
throw all their weight into the scale of peace.   And
remember, armaments are such to-day that no nation
is absolutely safe from invasion ; social questions, the
relations between capital and labour, the currency,
slave labour amongst whites, even in the United States
—most happily situated of all countries—the eternal
feud between whites and blacks in the South—any of
these may at any moment cause a war worse than a
war of invasion, because more bitter, more relentless,
more capable of leaving a heritage of hate.   Who is
the more to be blamed : the rigid moralist at home who
admits that most wars are the devil's work but pro-
claims that the war which he favours and shouts for

is really blessed by God; or the soldier who, after dreary weeks or months of weary marching, with broken boots or no boots at all during the day, and chilling nights with only a tattered greatcoat or a ragged blanket to save him from the dew, with the memory upon him of hunger and thirst, of dust and fatigue, of constant knowledge that any moment may see him a corpse or a maimed weakling on the ground, forgets the Ten Commandments and even his natural humanity when the final charge has been successful and the chance has at last come for, in part at least, repaying himself, as soldiers have since war began repaid themselves, for toil and trouble and danger in the conquered town? Blame the man who does wrong if you will, but blame more the foolish people who, fancying that rapine and pillage can never stalk abroad in their own happy land, let loose the dogs of war upon their neighbours. The Carthaginian maids and matrons acclaimed their re-turning heroes; the day came when the Roman legion-aries taught those very maids and matrons the real meaning of war. How proud the Roman women were of their gallant warriors when the gorgeous triumph unfolded itself on the long road to the Capitol! With what different feelings did they look on war as the news came that Attila had forced his way into the rich plains of Lombardy; or, even before that, with what agonised apprehension did they not look forth from the walls at the red glare in the sky that told of the presence of Hannibal? We abuse Turks and Arabs, Filipinos and Chinese, the Baggara from the desert and the tribal mountaineers from the borders of Afghanistan because, forsooth, they do not make war as Christianity dictates. And what about the allied armies in China of late? They were Christians—by repute at least; but what were they in reality? Just a little worse than the Boxers, that is all. Do I blame them? No; I know the temptations; I know how quickly the soldiers of Chris-tian, so-called Christian, armies are taught to forget the

Ten Commandments. I am not surprised, nor do I feel called upon to censure. I shall leave the casting of stones to the people who are always strong to resist their passions, especially those passions which soldiers feel and yield to most readily—lust of others' property, which your virtuous stockbroker will never allow to enter into his bosom; lust of strong drink, which never affects the shouters for war in the streets; lust of—well, another lust which need not be spoken of here, as I have already hinted more than enough of it and its consequences. ¯

However, I've done with moralising. We young soldiers heard, and heard with an awakening of delight, of pleasurable anticipation, the things that might happen when the fighting for the day was done. And war does not seem all war. You've got to cook and eat, to forage and drink, to mount guard or sleep, just as if you were back in cantonments, and the daily routine soon grows upon a man—at anyrate it soon grew upon me.

At last we joined the general. We were the first of his reinforcements, and very soon, as others arrived, the defensive gave place to the offensive. I can't tell about the progress of the little campaign; all I know is our share of it, and for me that was quite enough. For a few weeks we were cornering the enemy, seizing a well here, a caravan of provisions there, and having slight brushes, in which a dozen or two men killed and wounded represented our losses. The Arabs, having been beaten back by the men originally attacked, did not seem to care to give the general a good stand-up fight now that his forces had been increased, and after some time we began to fancy that they were merely holding out for good terms and would at last surrender in the usual way. Not that we grew careless about our guards, pickets, and vedettes, discipline prevented that, and luckily, for when all the oases had been seized and garrisoned except one, the Arabs, in desperation I believe, determined to throw all upon the hazard of a battle. This was my first real experience of fighting, for I don't count it fighting to advance in skirmishing order and fire at constantly moving figures half-a-mile away. I judged their opinion of us by ours of them, and, indeed, we never even ducked the head, for we could not fear bullets at such a range.

Our cavalry had been pushed forward to locate the enemy and hold him if possible. My company and two companies of native infantry and three or four guns were sent in support, and the main body, coming along slowly and laboriously owing to difficulties of transport, moved in our rear, the flanks well protected by out-lying horse. One evening when we were about fifteen kilometres in front of the general—too far, of course, but some officers do so want to distinguish themselves when they get a separate command—the chasseurs d'Afrique and the spahis rode back upon us. They reported the enemy in a strong position at the last oasis left to them, about twelve kilometres away, and our commanding officer sent back the news at once, halting meanwhile for instructions. He acted somewhat wisely too in getting us to throw up a sort of fortification on a piece of rising ground. A circular trench was dug; the stuff taken out formed a weak rampart; a biscuit or two and a glass of brandy were served out to every man; and then we lay down on the hard ground without a tent or even a blanket for shelter or covering. The horse-men fell back on the main body; their work was done, and they would be worse than useless in a night attack.

Most of the night passed quietly, and I, who had done two hours sentry-go before midnight without seeing or hearing anything which could disquiet me, began to hope that the savage devils would wait to be attacked. About an hour before sunrise the corporal in charge of the outlying picket called me for another turn of duty. I arose from where I lay, took my rifle from the ground, and prepared to set out for my post, about eighty paces in front. I was to relieve Nicholas the Russian. As I took his place he whispered: " Look out, young one ; the dangerous hour !"

When the corporal and his party went away I gazed intently into the darkness towards the south. I knew by experience gained in many a night watch that very soon the sun would, as it always seemed to me, born and bred in a northern land, jump up on the horizon and send his welcome arrows of light across shrub and rock and sand. Once the light came the sudden rush in upon the camp would be impossible ; the modern rifle would stave off all attack ; spear and bayonet would clash together only when our leaders saw that the time had come when we should be on the rush and the enemy on the run.

As I gazed I fancied that there was a movement in my front. I could not at the time, nor can I now, though I am a man of wider experience to-day, swear that I actually saw anything, but that an impalpable, strange, indefinite change was coming over the blackness of the desert, I neither doubted nor misunderstood. Raising my rifle to my shoulder, quietly and cautiously as one does whose own body may be in a second the target for countless bullets, I aimed steadily at the blackest part of the blackness and fired. As I turned to run to the picket an awful shriek rang out, telling me that my bullet had found a billet, and then, while I ran shouting: " Aux armes, aux armes !" a hideous, savage cry ran in a great circle all about the camp. When I closed on the picket the corporal was giving his orders: " One volley, and run for the camp." The volley was fired, and we all ran madly back to the entrenchments, crying: " Aux armes, les ennemis !" not, indeed, to warn our comrades of their danger, but to let them know that we were the men of the outlying picket fleeing to camp and not the mad vanguard of the attack. We got inside the little rampart, helped over by willing arms, and at once the crash of musketry began. Our men had their bayonets fixed; for a double purpose this—for defence if the Arabs came home in the charge, to lower the muzzle if only shooting were necessary. Luckily our firing became so successful that the Arabs stopped to reply, and, you may take my word for it, when a charging man halts to fire he is already weakening for retreat.

Well, we kept the enemy at a safe distance till the blessed sun sprang up and turned the chances to our side. Yet still they hung around, and a dropping fire was maintained on both sides. They did not now surround the little camp; they had all collected in almost a semicircle on the southern side. While the desultory firing went on our commandant eagerly turned his gaze from time to time towards the north, and he was at last rewarded. He sent orders to give a ration of brandy to every man—the rascal! He had seen the glint of lance heads on the horizon, and he wanted to take a little of the pursuer's glory from the cavalrymen. Glory, glory! what follies are committed in thy name! The brandy was given out, the news went around that the horse were coming up at the gallop, the men looked with blood-lust in their eyes at the lying-down semi-circle to the south, the commandant flung off jacket, belt, scabbard, keeping only sabre and pistol, and with a wild cheer and cries of "Kill, kill!" we rushed from the camp straight at the enemy. They were not cowards. They gave us a wild, scattered fire, and then, flinging away their rifles and flintlocks, came daringly, with loud cries of "Allah!" to meet us. And in their charge they covered a greater distance than we did in ours, for they came along every man at racing speed, and their line grew more and more irregular, whereas we, disciplined and trained to move all as one man, easily fell into the regulation *pas gymnastique*, and so went forward a solid, steady, cheering line, officers leading, and clarions at our backs sounding the charge.

As we neared one another a great shout went up from

us. Nicholas the Russian, who was my front-rank man, dashed forward and stabbed a yelling demon rushing at him with uplifted spear. I ran into his place, and saw almost at once a dusky madman, with a short, scanty beard, coming straight at me with murder in his eyes. I remembered the advice given by the *vieux soldats*, and as he raised his sword I plunged my bayonet with all my force into his face. He half reeled, he almost fell, and as he recovered again I lunged and struck him fair and full on the breast bone. Again he reeled, yet still he tried to strike; I thrust a third time, and now at his bare neck; the spouting blood followed out the bayonet as I drew it forth and back to strike again. Before I had time to do so the Arab fell, a convulsive tremor passed over his body, the limbs contracted, the eyes opened wide to the sky, the jaw fell, and for the first time I saw my enemy lie stark and cold in death before me. I stood watching, with a curious feeling at my heart, the body that lay so strangely still upon the sand. I felt no desire that life should return to the corpse, nor did I feel at all inclined to drive my weapon home again; it seemed to me that my assailant and the dead were not one and the same, and the animosity which I had felt for the living foe was lost, nay, utterly extinguished, in wonder at the awful change my handiwork had produced. Remember, I was only a boy, and I had taken that which no man can restore. Many times since have I looked without a shudder, almost without a thought, on the face of my dead foeman, but on that morning in the desert my mind was shocked by the new experience.

Suddenly I heard a trumpet and a cry. I looked towards the right; the spahis were riding at top speed with levelled lances on the foe. Our men were scattered, fighting in squads and parties over the plain, driving the Arabs back. The press of battle had gone beyond me. In a moment the horsemen swept into the Arab ranks; the lances rose and fell with terrible significance as the mass rolled on. Our work was over; the cavalry so rushed and harried the fleeing enemy that the rebellion was practically at an end, for that time of course, before noon. When the main body came up the chiefs were in our camp, prepared to accept any terms offered by the general. These were hard enough. All arms to be surrendered, a heavy fine to be paid, their villages to be kept in our possession till all the petty fortifications should be dismantled. Yes; my company kept a village and an oasis, and I fancy that the next generation of Arabs was whiter than their forbears. But that is war; and the people—the goody-goodies and the stockbrokers and the foolish women—who believe that honour dwells in the heart of a soldier on active service will lament our wickedness and get ready for the next occasion when they can send off their own soldiers to war, glorious war!

CHAPTER VII

NOT long after the end of the little war my company and another were ordered on garrison duty to a place which we called, for what reason I know not, Three Fountains. I never saw three springs in the place; of course, there was an oasis but whether this, before being walled in, had really been divided into three separate wells I cannot say. Probably the name was a fanciful one given by a soldier and taken up by his comrades.

Alongside us lay about five or six hundred Turcos. They did not like us and we did not care overmuch for them, so you might imagine that here were pretty grounds and opportunity for a quarrel. Not so, indeed; they kept away from us, for they knew well what would happen should one of them dare to enter our lines. We gave them a wide berth, for the African is always—like the Asiatic and the American and the European—ripe for treachery to men of another race and colour. No; the races did not fight, but we of the higher breed, —how angels and devils must laugh when people speak of higher breeds!—had a very pretty fight amongst ourselves.

It came about in an unusual way, but for the invariable cause. There was a Portuguese in No. 4 Company who loved a girl—a Cooloolie girl who had followed him in all his marches and campaignings. A Cooloolie, I may explain, is the offspring of a Turkish father and an Arab or Christian mother, and as a rule when a Cooloolie woman gives herself to a man she does it in a thorough manner and without any reservation save one—the woman's right to change her mind. And this lassie did change her mind, and of her own accord made love to a Greek who belonged to my company, as handsome and well-formed a man as I have ever had the good fortune to see, and a downright good soldier. Certainly I should not care to see him too near my knapsack—brushes and such things have a strange knack of disappearing—but I know very well that he was a right man in a fight and a trump to spend his money when he had it. He did not have it often, and when he had you generally heard next morning that an officer's tent had been visited—yes, visited is a good word—by someone not invited.

Well, the Cooloolie girl flung over the Portuguese, with bad words and worse insinuations, and openly followed the Greek around, like a dog after its master. And Apollo, of course, who probably did not care a button about the woman, must go here and there, head up, with smiling face, cheery talk, and queer jests. He visited every corner of the camp: first the part where we, his own company lay; then, still followed by the woman, the Turcos, who showed their white teeth and grinned and muttered: by Jove, he was a handsome man, and she, though rather dusky and stout, looked a perfect beauty in such a place, remote from civilisation; last of all he came towards us through the company of his predecessor in the Cooloolie girl's favour. Flesh and blood, least of all the hot blood of a Peninsular, could not stand it; with a hoarse cry and an awful oath the Portuguese rushed at the Greek, but Apollo was quite prepared. Slipping aside he struck the poor devil full under the ear at the base of the skull and sent him headlong to the earth, senseless. Apollo, seeing that his opponent did not rise, calmly walked to his own quarters, the girl now hanging upon his arm and uttering all the endearing words she could think of, looking up the while into his face as one entranced. None of the men of No. 4 Company interfered. It was a common thing enough for two men to quarrel about a woman, and, though they must have felt sore that their comrade had been worsted, still that was no reason why outsiders should interfere. The matter would have been settled by the interested parties for themselves had it not been for the devilish desire of creating mischief that always possessed Nicholas the Russian. Indeed, Nicholas loved mischief like a woman.

Now Nicholas was a man who often had money and spent it like a gentleman, a soldier, and a rascal. He never got all that was sent to him, any more than the Crown gets all the revenues collected in its name: to greasy palms coins will always stick. If 1000 francs were his due—sent by friends, of course—he reckoned himself lucky to be able to spend half. This time he must have received a more than ordinary sum, for instead of following the custom of the Legion and showing us, his comrades, a little bit of paper, which the commandant would cash next day, so that we, his good comrades, the men who liked and loved him, might know exactly how much drink and other things to be had for money each might fairly reckon on, he said:

"Our comrade, Apollo I mean, has taken the girl; let us be good comrades to him; let us take the two cabarets to-morrow, and keep all the drink and all the tobacco and all the cigars for ourselves, and give the happy pair a right good wedding."

He pulled his moustache as he spoke, and then, turning his eyes round the squad, he showed devilment and fun enough in them to entice the ordinary good man to break not only the laws of God but to do a still more risky thing—to break the laws of his society.

The word was passed around quickly that the Russian would be a good friend to all the company, and not merely to his own section or his own squad. Everybody was happy; we forgot squad distinctions and shook hands with one another and handed freely round our tobacco, for was not to-morrow the glorious day when *eau-de-vie* and wine and cigars and tobacco were to be had by every one of us, even without the asking? Ah! the good Russian, the worthy comrade! Ah! the handsome Greek! Ah! the wise woman, who knows the company to select her lover from! Ah! you, good soldier, of another squad it is true; shall we not drink and smoke together to-morrow and curse the pigs of No. 4? How they will groan and curse and envy us to-morrow! Good-night, brave comrade; good-bye till I see you again to-morrow!

The morrow came, with its drills and fatigues and duties. Some of ours were for guard, others for camp picket; how they envied us who were free for all the fun of the evening! The last meal was over, the last duty for the day done, when Nicholas and Le Grand and I went out to negotiate with the two cabaret keepers of the place.

Let me say something here about Le Grand. He was the biggest man in the battalion, some fellows said in the Legion, but there were others who denied this; anyway he was a fine, strapping Dubliner, whose real name I do not care to give. He was in my company, but not in my squad, not even in my section, so he and I passed each other when we met with a friendly "English pig!" "Irish pig!" "Go to the devil!" "Yes, yes; have you any tobacco?" "Yes; here, do not forget me to-morrow." Another word and we separated.

But let me pay here my tribute to the comrade of whom I shall more than once have occasion to speak. He was brave—I learned that on the battlefield, I have it not by hearsay; he was generous—I learned that many a time when we were together in Tonquin; he was kind and honest—that is, honest for a soldier— to all he met with, and his only fault was hastiness of temper, which made him knock you down one moment and, with the corresponding virtue, pick you up the next. But he never struck a boy, he never struck a veteran whose limbs and features showed the effects of war, he would die of thirst sooner than take a drop of water from the hot-tongued youngster in the fight who had the desire to go forward and the weariness of the rifle and pack, and the moist heat of socks and the dull, heavy, deadly pain of pouches at the sides. I do not know where you are to-day, Le Grand; wherever you are take a little, a very little, tribute from one of your comrades. Great as was your frame, our liking and love for you were greater.

Well, we walked slowly, as befitted men bent on so important a mission, down to the collection of mud huts where the sutlers were. Nicholas, as the giver of the feast, had the centre, Le Grand was on his right, and I, the youngest and least of the three, supported the Russian on the left. We did not speak, but Nicholas now and then laughed, while a constant smile, cynical, sarcastic, and malicious, was on his lips. The Russian was evidently calculating on the fun he would have, for he, if no one else did, forecasted accurately the result. He was paying, and paying for a purpose; excitement was to him the breath of life; he had no fear of consequences; if he were punished he would take his punishment with that calm ease of manner which was the despair of all his superiors from the commandant down.

The first cabaret we visited was kept by a retired soldier—a man who had spent most of his life in Algeria, who had in fact, almost forgotten France. An ugly, old Kabyle woman, whom, I daresay, he had picked up a young girl in some forgotten desert raid, lived with him, cooked his meals, and helped to swindle us poor fellows out of the wretched pittance we were paid.

When we entered the host came forward, smiling, gloating I should say, on Nicholas. The fellow evidently knew about the money. The Russian came straight to the point.

"How much, *mon vieux*, for all in this hole?"

"What! all?"

"Well, you may leave out madame and the domestic furniture. How much, I ask you, for the hut, the drink, the tobacco, the glasses, the tables and forms, and all the rest of your property?"

"Well, well, I do not understand."

"Let us go to the Jew then," said Nicholas to Le Grand.

"Very well."

"What do you say, my friend?" This to me.

"A Jew can't swindle more than this old ruffian."

We turned to leave.

"No, no, no; I will sell all," cried the sutler.

"Very well," said Nicholas; "show me all you have, and quickly. I will make an offer; if you take it I will pay the money at once."

The sutler showed us what he had: so much brandy, the strongest in France, he said—so much wine; how beautiful, would we not take a glass?—so much tobacco, and so on; he praising and Nicholas critically valuing as the goods were shown. When everything had been shown Nicholas offered 500 francs for all.

"Oh no, not at all; that would ruin me."

"Very well; let us go to the Jew."

As we were passing out he ran out after Nicholas, and said:

"Six hundred."

"Five," said Nicholas.

The sutler shook his head.

"Give me five hundred and fifty and take all, in the name of the devil."

"For the last time, five hundred."

"Oh, you have a hard heart, very hard for so young and brave a soldier."

The temptation was too great; he would not let us go to the Jew, so he accepted. The money was paid, and Nicholas gave the old soldier and his wife ten minutes to get out their personal belongings, leaving me on guard to see that nothing else went out by mistake.

E

A similar scene, Le Grand afterwards told me, took place in the Jew's. At anyrate, in about a quarter of an hour Nicholas came back alone, having left our comrade to watch the other sutler's departure, and told me that he was going away to summon the rest.

"Fill a couple of glasses for ourselves first," he said; "I want to give the Jew time to get his things away."

The old soldier cocked his ears.

"You have bought the Jew's stuff too, my boy?"

"Yes," said Nicholas; "my company will drink, this evening. Get madame and your property to a safe distance, as there may be trouble."

The old man took the hint and hurried away; he was too experienced a soldier not to easily guess what would happen when a poor and thirsty company looked on at the carousal of a rich and happy one.

Well, down came the company, laughing, clapping one another on the back, jumping about, for all the world looking partly like schoolboys out for an unexpected and unhoped-for holiday, partly like a commando, as the Dutch say, from the lower regions. There was not room for all in the huts, but the barrels were quickly rolled out and broached with due care, for who would spill good liquor? There was no scrambling or pushing; in spite of the excitement every man waited good-humouredly for his turn, for was there not enough for all? Eight or ten of us selected by Nicholas were filling the glasses; a man came to me and asked for brandy, I gave him a glassful, he drank, passed on to a second and got a ration of wine, and then went off to the place where the tobacco was distributed, giving way to another. This went on continuously until all had received an allowance of brandy and another of wine and a third of tobacco, and then Nicholas, this time also accompanied by Le Grand and me, went for the *nouveaux mariés*, as he called them. We brought them down in triumph, Apollo smiling and bowing, the Cooloolie girl beaming with happiness, Nicholas as

solemn as a judge, Le Grand and I breaking our sides
with laughter.   Such cheering and such compliments!
Such a babel of tongues!   The soldiers were all shouting out, every man, or almost every man, in his own
tongue, and those words I caught and understood did
not certainly err on the score of modesty.   Nicholas
amidst renewed cheering handed an immense vessel of
wine to the lady; she drank some and passed it to
Apollo, who drained it to the bottom.

When the cries had somewhat subsided Nicholas
made a short speech.   He alluded in graceful terms
to the happy pair, and hoped that their children's
children would in the years to come follow the flag in
the old Legion, in the old regiment, in the old battalion,
above all, in the old company.   He praised the company;
he said we could fight any other company on the face
of the earth; as, he concluded by saying, our well-loved
comrade has taken, and will keep, the woman he wants
without asking any man's permission, so we have taken,
and will keep for ourselves, the liquor in the camp.

He spoke in a loud tone, so that certain men of the
other company might hear.   These were looking envi-
ously on at the orgy, and were quite near enough to
make out the general tenor of his remarks.   And
Nicholas meant them to hear his words.   He was no
fool, and he knew what his speech would provoke; he
was no coward, when the fight came, he stood up to
his work like a man; he was no liar, for at the investigation he told exactly what he had done, and kept
back only his purpose in doing it.

I may mention here that there were no *sous-officiers*
and no soldiers of the first class at the carousal.   We
were all men of the second class, who neither hoped
nor wished for promotion, therefore we were quite careless as to what might happen.

Very soon the fellows of No. 4 Company began to
come out of their quarters by twos and threes.   As we
saw them approaching we raised our voices, we shouted,

sang, danced, cried out toasts, and did everything in our power to make them at once angry and jealous. The Cooloolie was in the centre, seated in Apollo's lap, the Greek himself having improvised a sort of arm-chair out of the staves and ends of an empty barrel. Even then things might not have been too bad, but nothing can keep a woman quiet, especially when her tongue is loosened with wine. She called to the men of No. 4 to go and fetch the Portuguese, and we all laughed. She openly and without shame showered kisses and other endearments on her lover, and the laughter was redoubled. She called out to the poor, thirsty and tantalised devils outside the charmed circle that her old sweetheart was—well, let me leave her words to the imagination of those who have ever listened to an angry, reckless woman's tongue—and she ended by saying that the Portuguese was only a fair sample of his comrades. The men of No. 4 were now all around us, and those of us who, like myself, had partaken only sparingly of the wine began to scent a fight. There was no premeditation, I believe, on the part of the others; indeed, the only man who desired to make trouble from the beginning was Nicholas the Russian, and truly he got his wish gratified to the full. A few bad words passed between some of theirs and some of ours, a blow was struck and replied to; in a moment a wild rush towards the combatants was made by all. A general melee ensued, and in a second almost, as it seemed, a little spot of ground was covered with the struggling, twisting, writhing bodies of four hundred angry, swearing men.

As I was running down to where the press of fighting was, I came full tilt against a man of No. 4. He and I staggered and almost fell from the shock. Luckily I had a half-empty bottle in my hand, and though when he recovered himself he almost made me totter with a swinging blow on the chest, yet I sent him fairly down with an ugly stroke of the bottle across the head.

The next man I crossed tumbled me fairly over.

What followed immediately afterwards I do not know. The next thing I remember is that I was standing on a table, striking out on all sides with the leg of a chair. A sudden rush on the part of the men of No. 4 drove back our company, the table was overturned, and I found myself sprawling on the ground, trying as best I could to regain my feet. Our fellows rallied and pushed back the others, and a tacit armistice took place. Not for long, though. The others got together in a mass, we formed up in a circle round the barrels and the tobacco, and the fight recommenced. And the Cooloolie woman was the best combatant of all, for though she herself did not do more than claw a man or two, who broke away at once, not wishing to hurt a woman beloved by men of both companies, yet with her cries and execrations she lashed them and us into a fury of fighting which made all men perfect devils. I have seen worse fighting, but then we had weapons. This fight was really the most savage save one, which I shall speak of afterwards, for there was no care of hurting comrades, there was no hanging back in the rush, there was no yielding of even a foot in the defence, and all the while the white guards looked on in horror, and the Turcos crept back to their part of the encampment with deadly terror in their hearts.

Half-a-dozen times we stopped for a moment or two to take breath. Then one of ours would rush at a man of No. 4, or one of No. 4 would come with an oath against a man of ours, and in a second the fray would be re-commenced. The officers and the *sous-officiers*, the guard and the picket, tried to separate us. It was all in vain ; they might just as well have tried to pull apart two packs of wolves. Moreover, half of the soldiers brought down to quell the trouble belonged to ours, and half to No. 4, and the commanding officer was very much afraid that these might join in the fight, and they carried arms and ammunition. But, you will say, why not use the Turcos ? Ah, that would never do. The commanding officer might succeed in putting an end to the disturbance with their assistance, it is true, but the consequences which were sure to follow were too serious, for the Turcos would never afterwards be safe from an attack. All the legionaries, not merely the men of the companies in the camp, but all the legionaries throughout Algeria, would resent the interference of the native troops, and heaven only knows what scenes of bloodshed might arise in unexpected quarters, and from trivial causes. Had there been even half-a-company of Frenchmen in camp all would have been well, but the nearest French soldiers, a squadron or two of chasseurs, lay a few kilometres away. To them, however, a mounted messenger was sent, and when we were almost weary of fighting, and began to think it time to look after the wounded — the place looked like a battlefield where regular weapons had been employed — we heard the trumpets of the cavalry and saw not a hundred yards away the long line of horsemen thundering down with raised swords at the charge. Before the chasseurs we broke and fled, but they were on us too soon for safety, and many a man went down before the charge.

As I was running to a hut a sergeant of chasseurs overtook me. Instinctively I jumped aside and lifted my right arm to protect my head. It was no use; down came the flat of the heavy sabre on my shoulder, and almost at the same time the charger's forequarter struck me sideways on the breast. I fell, and wisely remained quiet and motionless on the ground until the charge had passed. I then got up and reached the hut, which I found almost packed with men of both companies, whose appetite for fighting had altogether disappeared. In a short time we were all prisoners. My company was marched to the north side of the camp and No. 4 to the south, and we lay out all the night; and nights are very cold in these warm countries—the more so by contrast with the heat of the day.

Now about the casualties. I cannot tell the exact number killed outright in the quarrel or charge, or of wounded who afterwards died, but it was certainly not less than a score. More than 100 were seriously injured, and there was not a man of all the fighters without several ugly marks on his body. The Greek, who had fought well until, as I heard, a blow of a stone brought him insensible to the ground, had his brains knocked out by a horse's hoof; the Portuguese, we learned, died in hospital of his hurts. As for the Cooloolie girl—well, what would you expect? She wept for a week, and then took to herself a new lover out of the many who sought her favour, for your famous or notorious woman does not long lack suitors.

How we made up the quarrel and escaped severe punishment — heaven knows we punished ourselves enough as it was—must be told in a new chapter.

CHAPTER VIII

NOBODY was surprised when, on the morning after the affray, a corporal of chasseurs and half-a-dozen men came to escort Nicholas, Le Grand, and me to the commandant's quarters in the camp. Nicholas had his head swathed in rags, and limped more than slightly with the left foot; Le Grand showed a beautiful pair of black eyes and confessed to a racking headache. Every part of my body felt its own particular pain, my right eye was closed up, and I had an ugly cut on the forehead, the scar of which still remains. When we arrived at the place of inquiry, we found every officer in the camp, our own officers and those of the chasseurs and Turcos, assembled around the commandant. For a few moments there was silence, while they eyed us and we looked steadily at the commandant. At last this officer spoke, slowly and in a quiet tone: "The affair of yesterday was serious, indeed serious." He fixed his gaze on Nicholas. "You, I hear, bought all the drink and tobacco from the sutlers. Did that lead to the quarrel?"

Nicholas saluted respectfully and asked permission to make a statement. When it was accorded he began to tell all the story, just, indeed, as it happened, or almost as it happened. In narrating the dispute between the rivals he placed all the blame upon the Greek, for he knew at the time that the Greek was dead and therefore could not be punished. He said nothing, however, about certain encouragement that Apollo had received before and during his vainglorious parade through the camp with his new love on his arm; nor did he mention certain sarcastic expressions concerning the Portuguese which he himself had uttered in the hearing of the Cooloolie girl; also, he seemed to forget that these very expressions were used most frequently and with most infuriating effect by her when she was sitting, almost lying indeed, in the Greek's arms just before the fight. No; he told the truth, but not all the truth, and he told everything in so open and candid a way that Le Grand and I were almost deceived. He let fall the nickname Apollo, as it were by accident, and then, turning respectfully to the captain of chasseurs, who could not be supposed to know the man, he explained: "We called him so, monsieur le capitaine, because he was so handsome." "Quite true, quite true," acquiesced the commandant; "he was a veritable Apollo." Afterwards we heard that the cavalry officers went to see the Greek as he lay stripped in the hut of the dead, and, although the face was disfigured out of all human semblance by the horse's hoof, yet the beautiful curves and splendid proportions of his body, marked even as it was by countless bruises, proved that the nickname was well deserved.

One good effect was produced by Nicholas' statement. Everything was so honest and straightforward, so natural and true-seeming, that anything he might afterwards say was likely to be believed. Moreover, though the officers had not seen the parade of the lovers through the camp, yet they had evidently heard of it; and, again, the *sous-officiers* could be brought to prove the truth of that part of the story.

When the Russian was asked about the buying of the sutlers' property for the use of only one company, he again begged leave to make a rather long statement, partly, he admitted, about himself, but chiefly about the customs of the corps. He said that without such a statement the business could not be clearly and thoroughly understood by the officers, especially by those officers who did not belong to the Legion. Again leave was granted to him to tell his story in his own

way, and the commandant was graciously pleased to
allow Le Grand and me to stand at ease; he even said
to Nicholas: "You need not stand altogether to attention, make gestures if you wish, speak freely, just as
if you were telling a story to your friends." Nicholas
bowed with a courtier's grace; he wore no kepi, being
a prisoner at the tribunal; the chasseurs looked at
one another in astonishment, wondering at the aristo-
cratic air that could not be concealed even under a
private soldier's tunic or by a bruised and battered
face. Ah! little they knew of the wrecked lives, the
lost souls, that came to us from every country in
Europe, that made the Foreign Legion, if I may say
so, a real cemetery of the living.

Nicholas explained that, when a man had money,
he was bound by all the rules of the corps to spend
it with the men of his squad; that, when the money
was more than usually plentiful, he was supposed to
entertain his section; that, in the rare cases when
thousands of francs—how the chasseurs opened their
eyes at this!—were in a man's possession, all the rules
of regimental etiquette obliged him to spend the money
royally and loyally with his comrades of the company.
Beyond the company one could not go. Were one as
rich as a Rothschild one could not do more than give
a few francs to a man of another company if he were
a fellow-countryman—all, or nearly all, had to be spent
with one's comrades of the company. Our officers
recognised the truth of this, they understood our un-
written laws, and again Nicholas added to his reputation
for veracity. But he said nothing at all about giving
a percentage to the sergeant-major, nor about the taxes
levied by the sergeant of the section and the corporal
of the squad. The sergeant-major, who was present,
looked relieved when this part of the Russian's statement came to an end—for were not two hundred francs
of the Russian's money in his pocket at the time?
Nicholas knew what to tell and what to keep back; there

would be no use in alluding to the money which he was practically compelled to give to his superior officers; it would only cause anger at the time and produce trouble and a heavier punishment for us afterwards.

Nicholas went on to state that he had received a large amount of money from a friend in Europe, and that he had at once resolved to pay for a good spree for his comrades. For a joke he called the affair a wedding *déjeuner* in honour of the Greek and the Cooloolie girl. He thought—at least he said he thought—that the other company would not mind; they knew the rules of the Legion as well as he; a little fun about the new connection ought to hurt nobody except the Portuguese. But, poor, misguided fellow that he was, he had never calculated the damage that might be done by a woman's tongue; he, simple, ignorant baby, thought that we should have a couple of hours of jollity and drinking and that then all would go quietly back to quarters. He had always held the men of No. 4 in great respect; he would, indeed, be the last in the world to insult them, or in the slightest degree to make little of the company. He admitted with sorrow—the hypocrite— that his action had been injudicious—it would have been all right only for the woman; he had paid for drink and tobacco, but not for insults to any man or men of No. 4; it was the woman who insulted people; he did not want to fight with anybody, least of all with the men of No. 4, but, when his company became engaged in an affray, he would have been indeed a bad comrade, nay, a coward, had he remained out of the fight. We wished for only the drink and the tobacco; we soldiers had no desire but to enjoy ourselves in peace and quietness in the evening after the hard work of a hot and dusty day; we had no malice, not even now did we harbour evil thoughts, towards our fellow-soldiers of No. 4; but what will you? who can stop a woman's tongue?—we could not even expostulate with her without insulting our good comrade Apollo; if she drove the others to attack us by her ugly words, were we, men not afraid of death, to tamely surrender? That, they all knew, was impossible. Without actually saying it he flung the whole blame for the fight on the woman's shoulders. I thought at first that this was not quite fair, but I soon saw that Nicholas was really doing his best to save us all. Everybody knew the wild way she spoke and acted before the first blow was struck, but Nicholas knew quite well that nobody would hold her accountable for her language, while everybody would admit that the men of No. 4 had reasonable grounds for attacking us, and, of course, we when attacked were quite justified in defending ourselves. This was what the Russian was aiming at all along: to put the blame on the Cooloolie girl, who in the first place could not be court-martialled for a soldiers' quarrel, and in the second would most undoubtedly be sympathised with for the loss of her lover. At the same time, a case of extenuating circumstances was made out for No. 4 Company, and we, the attacked party, who did not apparently seek to provoke an attack, would be adjudged guiltless of offence because we merely resisted. It was a splendid plan—it saved us—but we had, in addition to becoming reconciled with our comrades and getting some punishment, to volunteer for the war. That, however, will be told of in its own time and place.

When the Russian had finished his statement a few questions were asked of him, not in the nature of a cross-examination, but for the evident purpose of clearing up matters that were not quite understood by the hearers. He answered these with readiness and to the point, preserving always the bearing and language of an aristocrat, with the tone and temper of a simple soldier in presence of his superiors. When they had done with him the commandant questioned first Le Grand and then me, but we merely corroborated our comrade's story. Not that there was at the time any doubt in our minds that Nicholas had desired a fight and had paid for the gratification of his desire, but who can give evidence of what has passed in another's mind, and who would betray a generous comrade?

At last the commandant sent us away, and we returned under escort to the place where our company lay under guard, hungry, thirsty, without change of clothing, and every man aching all over, and cursing as the effects of the fight began to make themselves felt. The other men crowded around us to learn what had happened. Nicholas, in the centre of a ring of eager, interested listeners, told exactly, without change, addition or omission, in a loud voice so that all might hear, the tale of the inquiry. All were satisfied so far, many, indeed, gave up their preconceived beliefs, and thought that the Russian's account of the affray and what led up to it was "the truth, the whole truth, and nothing but the truth." We, Le Grand and I, confirmed the account, we made no secret of our belief that all would yet be well, we swore it was the woman who led our good friends of No. 4 to assault us, and surely no one could blame us for defending ourselves.

After some time Nicholas called Le Grand and me apart, and we held a consultation for nearly a quarter of an hour. The others marked us, they noted the earnest words and persuasive gestures of the Russian, they watched the eager, attentive looks of Le Grand and me. When we had settled the matter to our own satisfaction apparently Nicholas led the way to the centre of the little camp—prison I should call it, for the sentries looked inwards and not outwards. In a moment, as it seemed, every man that was able to drag himself forward was in a group around our little party. Nicholas waited until a hush fell upon the meeting, and then addressed them somewhat in the words that follow. I have no doubt about the essence of what he said, but I cannot hope to reproduce the eloquent language, the expressive features, the seductive tones, above all, the general air of the born orator that Nicholas assumed. From time to time he appealed to Le Grand or to me for confirmation of his words. There was, indeed, no necessity, the men were at his will before he had spoken for two minutes.

In brief, this was what he said :

"My comrades, we have had an ugly quarrel with our fellow-soldiers of No. 4, and we cannot, I think, blame them for attacking us, nor can they with justice blame us for defending ourselves. But there is no doubt about the real origin of the affair. The woman used to belong to one of theirs ; she chose, as she had a right to do—that everyone admits—to give up her lover in their company and to give herself to a man of ours. Well, we must acknowledge that she and the Greek were not discreet, and I will confess that, for my own part, I did not act with discretion either, but what could I do when I had money in my pocket but spend it with my companions of the encampment and the battlefield ? If there had been no jealousy about a woman, we should have had a peaceful, enjoyable evening ; if there had been no money in the company, the jealousy would have been settled by a fair fight between the rivals in the usual way that we all understand and appreciate, without four or five hundred men being drawn into the quarrel. We are under guard and are sure of punishment ; in all respects they are faring, and will fare, no better than we. Let us try, now that the Greek is dead and the Portuguese, as I hear, is dying, to become reconciled to our comrades of No. 4. Trust me, if we can settle the matter amongst ourselves, so that all may understand that we shall not renew the quarrel, the officers will be only too glad to have an excuse for passing over the affair as lightly as possible. What I recommend then is this : let a deputation of four be appointed from amongst us ; let us ask permission to visit the prison camp of No. 4 ; let us ask them to appoint four of their number to confer with us; believe me, we shall soon, for the sake of the men of both companies, come to a satisfactory arrangement, and we all shall be friends again, and, indeed, be better friends than ever before, because we have learned to respect one another."

The Russian's proposal was agreed to on the spot. Someone said that Nicholas ought to be chief of our embassy, but this he would not agree to. He would be a member, if they wished, but only with the same rights and the same responsibilities as the others. Le Grand, a Hungarian, and I were chosen as his partners in the delicate business, and some way or other we all seemed to be satisfied that our troubles would soon come to an end.

The first thing to be done was to get permission to go across, under escort be it well understood, to the prisoners of No. 4. This was obtained by the aid of our sergeant-major. He must have spoken very strongly to the commandant, for the latter came down to us in a great hurry, asked Nicholas point-blank whether we were serious in the attempt to settle the affair amicably, and if he thought we had any chance of succeeding. Things were bad enough, heaven knows, as they were, but it was rather risky to keep nearly 400 fighting men without their weapons and ammunition in the very centre of the scene of the recent operations. Had the Kabyles attacked the camp on the night after the quarrel, they would have slaughtered us, the unarmed ones, like sheep, and in all probability would have easily carried with a rush the little fortification that had been set up around the huts. Therefore the commandant was only too glad to get a chance to put us under arms again, if he could only believe that we would not use them against one another. The quarrel was an ugly thing, but that could be explained, and we should in any case receive punishment, but a disaster to his command would spell ruin for his chances of promotion. He was pleased, therefore, when Nicholas laid his hand upon his heart and promised upon his honour—yes, he said upon his honour—that we would do our best to settle matters, that we would in no way again raise the anger of the men of No. 4, and, finally, that he was himself prepared to apologise for his part in the affair.   This expression, I am sure, the command- ant took to refer to the buying up of all the drink and the tobacco; we, who knew better, remembered the irritating speech that the Russian had made after the *nouveaux mariés* had pledged each other.

Well, after a little hesitation he let us go across. We were escorted this time by the men of our own company—soldiers of the first class, who had taken no part in the fight, and soldiers of the second class who had been either on guard or on camp picket.   The escort was under the command of our sergeant-major, and I am sure that he was sent so that the commandant might get a trustworthy account of the negotiations. We could not object to any arrangement; we were very well satisfied to get the chance of making it up again with our fellow-soldiers, for, as I have already said, the nights are cold in Algeria, and we feared that news of the quarrel might have already spread amongst the Kabyles, and we knew that the exposed position in which we were placed left us completely at their mercy, should they make up their minds to attack.   Moreover, the soldier, even in a peaceful country, hates to be deprived of his weapons and his belts; how much more then did we, in a hostile land, dislike the deprivation of them!

When we arrived at the cordon of sentries around No. 4 Company we were halted, and Nicholas, stand- ing slightly in advance of us, his fellow-ambassadors, told them why we came and asked them to be so kind as to appoint four men of theirs to confer with us, so that the dispute might be settled and the com- panies be at peace with each other again.   He was

listened to with attention, and when he had finished
his message he said that we four should wait, with
the sergeant-major's kind permission, for half-an-hour
to give them time to deliberate and, if they should
agree to the proposal, to select their delegates.

Before the half-hour was over the men of No. 4 Company had made up their minds to accept the proposal,
and at once appointed four of theirs to arrange matters
with us. Two of the four were Alsatians, one a Lorrainer, and the fourth, and, indeed, the most important
—their Nicholas, as I may say—a bronzed, sharp-eyed
and sharp-witted Italian. As soon as these ambassadors
were nominated, our sergeant-major took the eight of
us away a short distance from the escort and told us
that we might speak freely, as he and the sergeant-major
of No. 4 would be the only listeners, and they would in
every way respect our confidence. The second sergeant-
major said the same thing: "Speak freely," he continued, "and, for the love of God, settle the affair for
ever. It is not pleasant to see so many brave soldiers
without arms in such a region; who knows when the
Kabyles will attack?" The hint was not lost upon us,
and I believe that the seven others felt, as I did, that
the sooner we were again good friends and under arms
the better.

Nicholas made the first speech, and said in almost
the same words what he had already told the commandant. He did this, I believe, purposely. Our sergeant-
major was very attentive, and Nicholas guessed, as all
did, that he would make a report to the officers, and it
would be just as well that the statement made then
at this meeting should be on all-fours with the statement made previously at the tribunal. But he went
further. He explained that he had made up his mind
to give a good evening to his company when money
came to him from Europe, and surely no one would
blame him for that. Then he went on to say that he
was truly sorry for the affray and for any language or

F

acts of his that might have brought it about. Had
he but remotely guessed what would be the result, he
would have burned the money sooner than let it be the
cause of strife between companies which had been so
lately fighting side by side against the enemy and
which had never before fallen out with each other. For
his own part, he hoped and prayed that the former good
relations might once more exist between us, and he
believed that they would, and that we should respect
one another more than ever on account of the gallantry
which No. 4 Company and his own had displayed in
that unfortunate struggle. Many other things he said
to the same effect, and when he had finished it was easy
to see that all, with the exception of the Italian, were
satisfied. Not that the Italian desired to prolong the
disagreement, but he saw—what his fellow-delegates
either did not see, or, for the sake of peace, pretended
not to see—that Nicholas had deliberately resolved,
when the money arrived, to get up a quarrel between
the companies through pure devilment and love of excitement. The Italian wanted to show clearly to all
that he at least understood and was determined to
publish his opinion, and it must be admitted that he
was quite within his rights in doing so, though it would
have been more discreet on his part to keep his thoughts,
for the moment any way, to himself. He developed his
plan of attack in a Socratic manner.   •

"Why," he questioned the Russian (I may mention
that all through he ignored the rest of us), "why did
you not spend the money with all?"

"Because I never go outside my company," replied
Nicholas.

"Very good; but why did you buy up all the drink
in the two cabarets? Why did you not leave some in
one of them for us?"

"Because I thought that all would be scarcely enough
for my own comrades, and one thinks only of his own."

"True," continued the Italian; "but then why did

you not give us notice ·that you were taking all for yourself and your companions?"

"Because I thought that such a notice would be an insult and would certainly provoke a quarrel, a thing which I was most anxious to avoid."

A low muttering of approval followed this, but Cecco only smiled like one unconvinced. I was looking at Nicholas at the time; truly he had the air and bearing of one who would suffer martyrdom rather than tell a lie. He puzzled me. For a moment I almost believed him innocent, he seemed so calm and steadfast, his manner was so open and ingenuous. Here, a stranger might remark, is an upright, God-fearing man, whose heart knows no guile, whose mind is lofty and self-respecting, whose bosom swells with love and friendship for his fellow-man. Cecco's comrades seemed almost to believe, but the Italian was too cunning, too experienced in the world—above all, too full of knowledge of his own rascality—to be convinced.

"Well, well, well," he said; "we were insulted, and you best of all know it. Shall we not have even an apology? There cannot," he went on, "be an excuse. No matter about the woman and her fickleness; no matter about the wine and the tobacco; what can be said of the ugly words spoken of us, the comrades of the Portuguese?"

"Ah," replied Nicholas in a tone of contrition and with an assumption of sorrow that would have deceived Vidocq himself, "that is what wounds me. I, alas! have been indiscreet. I confess that I was overjoyed when I saw around me my comrades happy and free from care, and that in a moment of excitement I said things which were altogether wrong and uncalled for. Let me beg your forgiveness for my offence, and, as an evidence of my regret and a proof of your forgiveness, let us spend, both companies together, the remainder of the money sent to me by a kind friend in my own country."

The admission that the Russian still had money, and enough too to provide fun and pleasure for both companies, was quite sufficient to settle the whole affair. Even Cecco was satisfied, as he remarked : "What was the use of abusing one another for a thing that could not be undone, when it was so much better to shake hands and clink glasses and be good friends as of old ?"

"What indeed ?" assented the Lorrainer. "What indeed ?" said we all.

We shook hands earnestly and gladly with one another, and each quartette departed to its own company. All were pleased to hear the report. The men of No. 4, indeed, cheered Nicholas as loudly as we did. The commandant was satisfied ; he knew well that the men were only too glad to become reconciled, but he took care when the rest of the Russian's money was spent that it was spent in the encampment and that half-a-squadron of chasseurs were standing by their saddled horses until the last man had gone quietly home to quarters. They were not wanted, indeed, but the cunning fox was taking no chances, as a serious renewal of the fight would, if not at once put down, be bad for his military reputation.

So we became friends again. But we suffered a little, and judged it best to volunteer for the war in Tonquin, for the soldier going on active service, especially as a volunteer, generally gets his punishments remitted, and is received back again into the favour of his superiors.

CHAPTER IX

OF course, the affair did not altogether end with the reconciliation of the companies. Punishment had to be awarded to both, and as ours was the more guilty one we received more than the men of No. 4. As so many were included it was obviously impossible to punish us in any of the ordinary ways, but we got extra drills, extra duties, unnecessary most of them, and in addition each of the companies had to furnish all the guards and pickets for the little camp on alternate days. This relieved the Turcos and those of our men who had not been in the fight, but it was very hard for us others to do double drill and double fatigue, let us say on Mondays, Wednesdays, and Fridays, and on Tuesdays, Thursdays, and Saturdays to be on sentry or on picket during the day and to sleep in our clothes, with only a greatcoat to cover us, during the night. And even then there was no chance of sleeping much, for when night fell one of the sections was on guard and outlying picket for two hours, and then the other relieved the first for the next two. Thus, if my section went on duty at eight o'clock in the evening after, be it well understood, doing our fair share of guard and camp-picket work from eight in the morning, we were relieved at ten for a little rest, went on again at midnight, and were relieved at two; took up the duty once more at four, and remained on until six, and then we had two hours to get our morning coffee and clean up our things to come off guard at eight. You might think that it was hardest on the officers, sergeants, and corporals; but no, only one officer and one-third of the *sous-officiers* mounted guard on any morning, so that all of these got five

nights in bed out of every six, whereas we, the troublesome ones, got only one night in every two.

We bore it well enough, however, though I must
admit that we used bad language occasionally, but, as
there were so many of us included in the punishment,
no one minded it so much as if he were the only de-
linquent. It helps a man wonderfully to bear hardship
and disgrace when he sees many others undergoing the
same misfortunes as himself, and this is the rule even
though he does not wish evil to his comrades in distress.
One man on a sinking raft will in all probability go
mad before it takes its final plunge beneath the waves;
a dozen men similarly situated will have less fear of
the great deep and the great unknown, because each
is, as it were, consoled by the knowledge that others
too must pass through the grim portals of death at the
same time and place and by the same means as he.
Thus it was that, though we grumbled and cursed one
minute, the next we laughed and rallied one another;
and we had, moreover, one great consolation — we
knew that the story would rapidly run through the
Legion, and that our good comrades, 8000 in number,
would laugh with fierce delight when they heard of the
encounter and its causes, and would admire and envy
the men who had the spirit and the devilment to provide
such a relief from *ennui* in the little camp on the border
of the desert. We eagerly figured to ourselves how
they would gloat over the story of the Cooloolie girl
and her lovers—the handsome Greek and the passionate
Portuguese; we knew how they would envy Nicholas
and his money; we felt quite certain that the story
would go down to succeeding legionaries with embel-
ishments, as was natural, and finally become one of the
best-loved traditions of the corps. It is still too early
to call it a tradition; but, take my word for it, the
fight between the two companies at Three Fountains is
talked of to-day in many a barrack-room, in many a
lonely village round an oasis in the Sahara, over many

a camp and watch fire, in many a canteen and cabaret, where the *vieux soldats* pull their grey moustaches and tell the eager-eyed recruits over the *eau-de-vie* and the *vin ordinaire* the wonderful story of what happened when a Cooloolie girl changed her lover and a Russian prince, in exile and disgrace, received thousands of francs from a friend, "most likely a woman, *mes enfants*," in Europe and spent it as a soldier should. Ay, even the officers are proud of the story to-day, and, when they go to France on leave, our little escapade is told in the family circle and to all the friends and relations who are continually asking for tales of *ces affreux légionnaires*.

I had almost forgotten another part of our punishment. While all the others turned out for parade without knapsacks, those of us who had been in the affray had to appear in heavy marching order, as English soldiers say—that is, with all our *buffleterie*, knapsack, and pouches on our persons. In fact, looking at us one would imagine that we were just about to start on a campaign. Another thing was that Nicholas, Le Grand, and I, as to all appearance the ringleaders in the affair, were not allowed to stir out of the camp or even to go much through it; a sergeant or a corporal would quickly order us back to our own quarters, if we were seen at any distance from them. Moreover, we three lost all our pay; but that made little difference, it was not much anyway, and our comrades gave us as much tobacco as we wanted and as much wine as we really cared about or they could spare.

While we were thus getting a foretaste of purgatory, into the camp one sultry afternoon rode the colonel of the regiment. That evening he spent in talking to the officers and examining some sergeants and corporals, who were believed to have most knowledge of the quarrel and of those engaged in it, especially the corporals who commanded the squads in which the Russian, Le Grand, and I were. Le Grand, I have already said, did not belong to our squad, not even to our section.

Next morning at six a company of Turcos relieved No. 4
Company, which had been on guard and outlying picket
all the night, and at seven, immediately after the morning coffee, the two companies of legionaries were formed
up in line first and inspected, and then in column of
sections, No. 1 section of mine being the front, and
No. 2 of No. 4 Company the rear, of the half-battalion.
While in this formation we were addressed by the
colonel of the regiment.   I cannot give a detailed
account here of what he said; all I remember is that
he abused, threatened and cursed us for nearly half-an-
hour.   We did not mind that, however, as we were
case-hardened enough already; but what we did mind
was the Parthian shaft he let fly as he turned to leave
the ground: "Remember, remember well, that all the
punishment has not been endured; when the commandant is satisfied I shall wish to be satisfied too."
To say truth, then, he frightened us.

When we were dismissed from parade, we indulged
in many gloomy speculations as to the extra punishment awaiting us.   We knew, or rather guessed, two
things at once—first, that the extra fatigues and guards
would soon be discontinued, for our officers were not
likely to make us disgusted with our duties, because we
should then become careless, and who could foretell
what danger might arise from the inattention of a sentry
or the unwilling response to orders on the part of an
advance-guard?   Secondly, we quite understood that
very soon we should turn our backs on Three Fountains,
where everything kept us from forgetting the dispute
and the fight, especially the little mound at the eastern
side of the camp, that marked the last resting-place of
the Greek and the Portuguese and our other comrades
who had fallen—an ugly reminder of an ugly fray.   As
soon, therefore, as other white troops could be sent to
our camp we should pack and march—the question was,
whither?   Now, there are many bad stations in the
south of Algeria.   There are places where one may often

not wash his face and hands for a week, so scarce is water there. To do the French Government justice, these places are usually held by native troops who do not mind thirst and dirt so much as Europeans, but it was well known that white men had on more than one occasion been sent to such stations and kept there until they almost despaired of ever becoming civilised again. Moreover, in these spots there is a great lack of other things besides water; there is no wine save that which comes to the officers; there is only the tobacco sold to one by the Government. Worst of all, a woman must be very much in love or very ugly before she will consent to follow a man thither. These are the suicide stations, if I may call them so—the stations where a shot rings out in the night and all rush to arms, fearing an attack of Touareks or Kabyles, but when dawn comes there is only a dead sentry making black the yellow sand at a post. When one man shoots himself an epidemic seems to set in; men hear every day in hut or tent or guard room the ill-omened report; soon they go about looking fearfully at one another, for no one knows but that he is looking into the eyes of a comrade who has made up his mind to die. The corporal counts his squad, "fourteen, fifteen—ah! there were sixteen yesterday," so he says; he thinks: How long until I have only fourteen, and who will be the next man to quit *la gamelle*?

We thought of all these things during the day, and we noted, more with anxiety than relief, that for us there were no drills or fatigues. My company was, indeed, warned to be ready to relieve the Turcos on guard at eight o'clock in the evening, but we were allowed to lounge about our quarters and talk with one another all the day. The different squads kept to themselves; a grave crisis either dispels all squad distinctions or accentuates them, and it was the latter that took place on this occasion. We ate our meals in gloomy silence, but in the intervals between them we speculated incessantly on what the colonel meant by saying that when the commandant had punished us he would take care to punish us too. Though we thought of everything that might occur, yet we were not satisfied; the indefiniteness of the threat was its chief terror. If one knows with certainty the worst, why, one can prepare to meet it, but when some fate, terrible but not tangible, certain but not understood, hangs over a man or a number of men courage is apt to ooze out at the finger ends. Talk of the sword of Damocles, that was nothing; —it simply meant death at some uncertain time—why, we all have such swords over our heads, and yet we eat and drink and sleep, we pray and curse, we laugh and weep, we hurt or help our neighbour, we gain or spend, as if life were the one thing safe and sure, safe and sure for ever. No one thinks much of his future beyond the grave; it is the future on this side of the Styx that we most earnestly dwell on. Why, even the man condemned to death thinks far less of what may happen to his soul, if he believes that he has a soul, when it leaves the body, than of the years of gladness and fellowship with men that the law is about to take from him. The uncertainty and the suspense united made us discontented and gloomy; we spoke to one another, it is true, but not in the old and pleasant way. There was not much cursing or swearing—we had gone beyond such solace or relief—but there was plenty of morose ill-humour, and as for *bonne camaraderie*, there was less of it in a company than there had been the day before in a single squad.

After the evening soup Nicholas nodded to me to come over to him. I was not sorry to go across the little space between us; he was the first who had even been commonly polite to me that day. When we were together he spoke in a low tone and in English—I may remark here that Nicholas was very well educated and spoke at least half-a-dozen languages with purity and ease—asking me what I intended to do.

"Nothing," I replied. "I see nothing that I can do."

"Nothing?" he queried.

"Nothing. And you?"

"Oh! I," said he, "do not intend to stay in Algeria any longer; my physician orders me to a warmer climate somewhere in the East."

"Yes," he went on; "I fancy that Tonquin will suit my present ailment; anyway, better see life along with the others who are now campaigning there than stagnate in a desert hole."

"You do not mean——" I began, but he interrupted me.

"Yes, I do mean it; and I know that they will be only too glad to get such volunteers as we are."

"They" (by "they" he meant the military authorities) "know very well that we shall be trying to escape from the fire to the frying-pan, and that we shall have only two things to depend upon to get us out of the latter—valour and good conduct. So we shall be the very best of soldiers, because, while others have merely to keep their good reputation, we shall have to earn ours over again. Trust me, they will be glad to accept us as volunteers for the war, and, listen, I know these French, when we volunteer they will almost altogether forgive us. They are very hard and strict, especially with us, and they are too nice about their honour, and they stand overmuch on ceremony and punctilio, but they are really generous, often more generous than just. When they find us trying to retrieve our good name they will give us every opportunity to do so. We shall have many vacancies in the ranks, it is true, and many a good comrade will not answer at the evening roll call, but it will be well with the survivors. In any case, I am tired of soldiering here. Why should I not see the world, not as I saw it before," he smiled sadly, as I thought, when he said this, "but as millions of men have seen it—a nameless unit in a crowd? After all, many of Cæsar's legionaries had happier lives than Cæsar."

When he ceased speaking there was silence between us for some moments. Then he asked:

"And you, young one, what will you do?"

"I will volunteer," I answered; "there surely cannot be worse fighting in Tonquin than there was here at Three Fountains a short while ago."

He smiled, and said: "Was it not good practice for war? Was it not better than all the drill in the world?"

"Yes," I replied; "if someone got a thousand francs every week, we should be the finest fighting men on the earth. I mean those of us who did not go out there," and I nodded towards the mound on the eastern side of the camp. He shook his head. "Say nothing about that; it is all over now. I do not mind your saying what you think to me alone, but do not, I ask you, speak too freely to our comrades. They will soon forget everything, if they are not constantly reminded of things."

After some further conversation we separated.

I said nothing to the others about our resolve, as I wished that the Russian should be the first to explain matters to our comrades. I had more than one reason for doing this. In the first place, Nicholas, as he was known in the corps—what his real name and rank were we never learned—was my senior in age and experience; in the second, he was a man of infinitely greater influence than I or any other in the company, partly on account of his money and generosity, but still more because of his manner, bearing, and unconscious air of authority; moreover, he was the clearest and most convincing speaker I have ever heard. Again, he had brought us into trouble and had done a good deal to get us out of it; to him, therefore, all looked for further deliverance. I felt sure that, when he told the rest of his intention, all of ours, and probably all of No. 4 Company, would volunteer along with him. It would be much better for us if companies volunteered instead of merely men or squads or sections. The greater the number going of their own accord to the war, the more lenient would our officers be; and, furthermore, no man would be likely to be sent amongst strangers—we should probably all soldier together. Should Nicholas and I go out by ourselves, we should be transferred with bad reputations to a company already in Tonquin, and for that neither he nor I had any liking. If all volunteered, we might still remain an unchanged unit, even though in a new battalion, and one must never forget that when a man has been for some time living and working and fighting, yes, and looting, and perhaps doing worse, along with certain companions, he has a feeling of *camaraderie*, of yearning for their society, which makes it very hard for him to leave them, though it must be acknowledged that a soldier easily makes new friends and new attachments wherever he goes.

Nicholas did not ponder long before he announced his intention of volunteering for Tonquin. I don't think it took the others much by surprise, perhaps because recent events had prepared them for anything, perhaps because the Russian's acts, no matter how strange they might appear in another man, were only ordinary, natural, and to be expected in him. Any way they merely nodded or smiled, and at first no one asked for an explanation. This, however, the Russian gave of his own accord.

"You know, *mes camarades*," he began, "that the colonel is very angry with us and that he has it in his power to make things very uncomfortable for those who have displeased him. Now I do not care to stay under his command if I can get away from it, and there is but one course, as far as I know, by which I can avoid his anger and perhaps regain the reputation of being a good soldier and one not likely to disgrace the flag. There is, as we all are aware, a war against savages going on at this moment in Tonquin. I mean to volunteer to go thither; it will be easier to campaign against Black Flags, who will kill me if they can and whom I will kill if I am able, than to suffer in a camp of hell in the desert, where one cannot resist nor even complain. Better, far better, will it be to march and fight, even to starve and die, like a soldier in an enemy's country than to live a life worse than a convict's in some one of those awful cantonments where even the native soldiers are discontented and restless. You all have heard, as I have, of the woes of poor soldiers in such places. The officers and sub-officers are hard enough here—I mean no offence to our own corporal, he has always been good comrade to his squad—but there they are veritable demons, there they carry revolvers by day and by night, and, if a sergeant should lose his temper and shoot a simple soldier, there is no redress, there is no punishment, unless the dead man's comrades themselves take a just vengeance on the murderer. And then there will be executions and deprivation of pay, and the last state of the company will be worse than the first. Again, in those places, where not even our poor amusements and relaxations are possible, where one can enjoy neither wine nor the society of women, men go mad and men commit suicide, and men deliberately break the laws in sheer despair, and, worst of all, men die lingering deaths from settled melancholy, thinking always, as they cannot help thinking, of home and former friends and the pleasant, happy days of youth. But I, for my part, will not, if I can avoid those places, go thither to starve, to mope, to rot alive, and to die—hopeless, friendless—for there men are not friends but only associates—with a curse upon my lips and heavy anger with God and man in my heart. No; rather will I volunteer for Tonquin. There I shall be, if no better, at least no worse than thousands of others who are fighting bravely, and are ready, if need be, to bravely die."

When Nicholas stopped speaking an Alsatian said : " I too will volunteer." That was all ; Alsatians are not inclined to talk much, but they are good, hardworking, steadfast men in action. If you are fighting and an Alsatian is your comrade, your rear-rank man let us say, don't be a bit afraid to go forward, the Alsatian will be always there, backing you up. They are not men who are anxious to lead a bayonet charge, but they won't refuse to follow, and where they go they generally stay, for just as they don't begin an advance they won't, on the other hand, begin a retreat. Put a Parisian, a Gascon, or a Breton at the head of a company of Alsatians and you have practically resurrected a company of the Old Guard.

There was some confused talking after this. Nicholas, the Alsatian, and I kept out of the conversation, smoking our pipes in quiet contemplation of the rest; the corporal of the squad was seated on his camp-cot, a cigarette between his lips, looking with a cynical smile at the Russian. At last it was decided—all the squad would volunteer. As soon as the corporal found that we were unanimous he seized his kepi and ran out of the hut without uttering a word save: *Bons soldats, bons camarades.* We learned afterwards that he rushed straight off to the captain and told him of our decision. This was welcome news, as all the officers were chafing and fuming because they had not been selected for the front. I may here mention that our corporal was the first to gladden the captain's heart and bring him some hope of gaining glory and promotion, and, when the captain got the chance of giving promotion, our corporal exchanged the two red chevrons on his sleeve for the single gold one of a sergeant.

Well, when the others heard of this, there was much earnest conversation and still more earnest gesticulation in the little camp. All were excited; the desire to get away from the punishment stations, the eager wish for change, the natural impulse of soldiers to put into practice the teaching of the drill-ground and the manoeuvres, all combined to render the men anxious to follow the example of our squad. Before we went on duty that night my company had volunteered to a man, and, when we dismounted guard in the morning, we were not a whit surprised to find ourselves relieved by native troops, for that told us that we had guessed aright and that No. 4 Company, our friends and erstwhile foes, had thrown in their lot with us and would be our *compagnons d'armes et de voyage*. We were very glad of that. Together we were a half battalion, a weak one, it is true—the mound on the east and the hospital held so many of our comrades—but still strong enough to demand and command respect.

While we were enjoying our morning soup the officers of the company came round. How different everything was then compared with the day before! The captain, a bronzed, heavy-moustached man, whose military career had not been very successful—he was a good soldier and a good officer, but he had made the great mistake of falling in love, as a *sous-lieutenant*, with his colonel's wife, and the colonel, now a general, had not forgotten—was in great good humour. He remembered our crime, only to laugh at it, and said that the men who could give so good an account of themselves against the heroes of No. 4 were just the soldiers he wished to lead into action. He told us to be very careful. If we misconducted ourselves again the company might be distributed amongst the four battalions of the other regiment of the Legion, and that would be bad for us and bad for him as well. "Let us only be allowed to remain together," he said. "We shall all go out to Tonquin, and then there will be plenty of excitement, and promotion must come." He was thinking, I suppose, of his own disappointments. It must be very hard on a man to be passed in the race by others who were boys at school when he was wearing a sword ; why, the commandant of the battalion was younger than he. The other officers were also pleased ; the lieutenant a handsome fellow of twenty-five or so, was anxious to get his company; the sub-lieutenant, a stern, hard-featured man of forty, who had risen from the ranks, was quite satisfied to go to a place where he might have a chance of picking up unconsidered trifles. Ah! *ces vieux militaires* are the quietest and most thorough-going pillagers in the world. Nothing comes amiss to them—they could teach even Cossacks how to loot—and how they manage to keep this loot and get it safely home to wife or mistress—for they have always a woman on their private pay-sheet—I cannot for the life of me imagine. They do it, however, and they are not only in the Foreign Legion or in the French army—you will find them in every army, nay, in every regiment in the world.

Well, the sergeants and corporals were well pleased too. They kept us for all that under strict discipline until the day we found ourselves aboard the transport at Marseilles. But I am anticipating.

At about five o'clock in the evening both companies were paraded and inspected just as on the day before, but there was a great change in the colonel's manner. He was not over friendly with us, but he did not abuse or threaten. He called us sharply to attention, and then said: "Every man in the front rank who wishes to volunteer for Tonquin will march one pace to the front; every man in the rear rank who wishes to volunteer for Tonquin will march one pace to the rear. Volunteers, march!" At once the ranks separated. All in front stepped one pace forward; all in the rear took one pace backward. He walked down between the ranks, saw that all had volunteered, took up his former position in front of us, and ordered us back to our original formation. "All have volunteered. I am well satisfied. Dismiss the parade, monsieur le commandant."

For some time after we were busy getting ready to leave Three Fountains, and no one was sorry when we presented arms to a detachment of zephyrs that came to take our place. As soon as they had returned the compliment we fell into marching array in columns of fours, wheeled to the left, passed by the flank of the zephyrs, saluted the Turcos of the main guard at the gate, and stepped out on our first march northward. Truly, we were glad to leave behind the cantonment of Three Fountains and its associations. Always fond of change, we dropped our sadness, the sadness which one cannot choose but feel when leaving behind for ever even one's temporary home. Before we had finished the first league spirits were as high, laughter as gay, jests as plentiful as on my very first march, when with the other two hundred recruits I went from the depot to the battalion. Normally the two companies should be about five hundred strong, but death and the doctor detained so many that I do not believe we were quite four hundred all told. However, at the depot, which we reached in good time, doing a fair day's march every day, we received additions to our numbers—self-styled recruits, really men who had learned more than a little of soldiering in other armies, and whom ill-luck or bad character or desire of French citizenship had driven or induced into the Foreign Legion.

At the depot we received our outfit for the East. The kepi was exchanged for the white helmet, lighter underclothing was served out to us, all clothing and footwear was renewed, and I may say without boasting that when, fully five hundred strong, we paraded for the last time before entraining for Oran, in order to hear the farewell address of the depot commandant, we presented as smart and soldier-like an appearance as any commanding officer could wish to see. The depot commandant made a short speech, shook hands with our commanding officer, wished him and us *bon voyage et prompt retour*, and then, with the band at the head of the column, we marched out of the gate, saluting the guard as we passed, amidst the ringing cheers of the veterans and recruits left behind. When we were safely in the train all discipline was at an end: we shouted, cheered, laughed and sang, and so began our journey to the land where more than half my comrades lie—as quiet as the Greek and the Portuguese under the little mound on the eastern side of the mud huts of *Trois Fontaines*.

CHAPTER X

ON a beautiful summer morning we marched down to the quay to join the transport that was to carry us and five or six hundred others to our destination in the the East. All was bustle, excitement, and confusion for some time, but matters quickly arranged themselves, and, when the last of the stores had been safely stowed away, we marched in single file up the gangway and stood to attention by squads on the deck. Each squad was led off by its corporal to the place assigned to it, and in a short time our quarters looked for all the world like a barrack on shore, save that one saw no bed-cots there. Our rifles and equipments were put in their proper places, the roll was called below for the last time, we were reported "all present and all correct," and then we were allowed to troop up on deck, to get our last glimpse of the land that many of us would never see again. As the ship cast off, we raised a cheer which was responded to by the people on the quay, a band ashore struck up the Marseillaise, the Frenchmen first, and then we others of the Legion took up the refrain, and thus amid cheering, singing, and waving of helmets and handkerchiefs we started on our voyage to Tonquin. There were not many friends of those aboard weeping on the quay; we legionaries had none, and the Frenchmen were zephyrs—that is, men of bad character who had been assigned to convict battalions, and their friends, no doubt, were not over sad about their departure. There were some ladies and children who were affected, but they belonged to the officers—the sub-officers and the men had no friends, no relations, no home, one might say, save the barrack, the cantonment hut, the tent, or, as at the time, the troopship. Well, so much the better: having nothing to lose but life, and that as a rule a wretched one, we should be the more reckless when recklessness was needed, and the French generals took care that we, the zephyrs and the legionaries, were put in the fighting line as much as possible and that the good men, the respectable soldiers, should only come into the fray when the burden of the fight was over and when we others were so spent with toil that reliefs were absolutely necessary. Let no one misunderstand me. I do not wish to convey that the French soldier or officer shirks danger; on the contrary, I believe Frenchmen to be amongst the most daring soldiers in the world and the most cheerful under hardships, but the generals did not see any good in putting worthy citizens, future fathers of respectable families, into the most dangerous positions when they had ready to their hands men who bore so bad a reputation as the zephyrs and the legionaries gathered from every country under the sun. They were quite right in this, but all the same we might sometimes, just once in a while, have been allowed to dawdle along with the reserve instead of being continually on the jump where the bullets were. Of course, though we grumbled, we were proud too that the most difficult and most dangerous work fell to our share.

For the first couple of days out I was very sea-sick, but the horrible *mal-de-mer* in the end passed off, and I was able to take an interest in things around me as before. I don't mean to say much of the life aboard. Such a tale would be only a recital of troubles and grievances, but troops on a transport cannot expect a very pleasant time. One thing we were glad of— there were no women and children aboard. The veterans told us why we should rejoice at this, and any man who has travelled on a troopship with women and their babies will easily guess the reason. The worst part of the voyage was while we were going through the Red Sea. There one loathed his morning coffee and growled at his evening soup. The dull, deadly, oppressive heat in that region almost killed us. We lay around, unable almost to curse, and the soldier who finds himself too weak to do that, must be in a very bad way indeed. Only once in the Red Sea did we show signs of life. It was when a French troopship passed us on her way home with sick and wounded from the war. The convalescents crowded on her deck and raised a feeble shout. We cheered heartily in reply, and we kept up the cheering until it was impossible for them any longer to hear. We pitied them, poor devils. How they must have in turn pitied us, going as we were to the wretched land where they had left behind health and many good comrades, and where we too should pay our quota of dead and receive our quota of wounds and illness. Anyway the sight of them roused us for a time, but we quickly fell back into the languor induced by the excessive heat.

Here let me make a remark which may be of interest to many. We legionaries had men, as I have already said more than once, from every country in Europe, and from some outside of it, and one might imagine that men of different nations would be differently affected by the heat, aggravated, as it was, by cramped quarters and wretched food. Well, I cannot single out any country whose natives endured the discomfort better or worse than the others, but there were undoubtedly two classes of men aboard, one of which was far more lively, far less given to grumbling, and altogether possessed of more buoyancy and resilience of temperament than the other. These were the men of fair complexion. All the fair-haired, blue-eyed soldiers seemed to be able to withstand bad conditions of living more easily and better than their dark-complexioned comrades. I offer no explanation of the fact, but I noted during the voyage for the first time, and afterwards I had many opportunities of confirming my original impression, that fair men are superior to dark ones in endurance and in everything connected with war except the actual fighting; with regard to that, complexion does not count. I have noticed in fever hospitals that the black moustaches far out-numbered the reddish ones; in a field hospital there was never such a disparity. I cannot say that other observers agree with me. I merely put on record a thing that I noticed and that produced a deep impression on me, but I never mentioned it to my comrades, nor shall I now write down the various speculations with regard to men and nations that I was led by it to indulge in. All I say is: I thank my stars that my moustache is rather red—that seems to me a token of endurance, if not of strength.

In due time we arrived off Singapore, and put in there. I must now mention a few incidents of our stay in that harbour; they were, indeed, the chief events of the voyage.

The reason why we put into Singapore was that coal had run short, and the captain of the troopship did not like to go on to Saigon with the small supply left. Those of us who did not know that Singapore belonged to Great Britain soon learned the fact, and more than one eagerly desired to get clear of the ship to land, and thus regain his freedom. Now, I am no apologist for desertion. I think it a mean and cowardly crime, but, if there be any excuse for it, surely many of ours must be held excused. Remember that we were foreigners in the French service, that many of ours had had good reason to flee from justice in their own countries, that we all had a bad reputation with our officers and our French comrades, and, above all, that recent events—the fight at Three Fountains and the morbidly suggestive mound at the east side of the camp there; the ugly fear of a horrible desert station and the intolerable heat of the Red Sea—had made many men think anxiously, constantly, longingly of getting away, at a stroke as it were, from ugly memories and gloomy forebodings begotten of them. Men don't desert from their colours without grave reason. Even the most flighty man will think twice and thrice before taking the risk of the court-martial that awaits detection or recapture. Moreover, in our case sentries with loaded rifles were on duty at all points; one would imagine that not even a rat could leave the ship unnoticed.

Well, the vessel was brought near the wharf and two gangways were run out, one for the coolies carrying in the full baskets, the other for the coolies going out with the empty ones. These coolies carried their baskets on their heads, as you often see women carrying loads in other countries. As each one passed the bunker he tipped the contents of his basket in, and then went under a little archway, and crossed out by the second gangway for a new load. Now there was one man of my company—a Bulgarian—who was under confinement for some slight offence against discipline, and, as the heat was almost unbearable, he had been brought up by the guard—acting with the commandant's permission, be it well understood—and allowed to sit under this archway during the heat of the day. I was the nearest sentry to him, being placed at the outgoing gangway, and one of my orders was to watch this man. Like many other orders I remembered this one only in order to be able to repeat it to the officer of the day, and never imagined that there was any necessity of caring more about it. I was mistaken.

As the coolies passed under the archway, a good deal of coal dust accumulated there. This dropped from the baskets, which they often carried mouth downward in their hands, when empty. The prisoner had a vessel of water, and this he carefully mixed with coal dust until he had enough to stain all his body black. I must mention that part of his little apartment was screened off from view by a half-partition, and while in this recess he could be seen only by the coolies as they passed through. Here he undressed and carefully blackened his person, and then, watching a favourable opportunity when my attention was completely taken up by a dispute on the quay, he throttled a coolie passing through, forcibly seized his basket, gave him —as payment, I suppose—a knock-down blow on the point of the jaw, and started for the gangway. This he gained unperceived by me. Half-a-dozen steps carried him ashore, and once on British soil he was safe from all arrest. He flung the basket on the ground, and at once ran at his utmost speed towards the town. A cry from those on shore called my notice to the running man, and I knew at once, by his size and carriage, that the Bulgarian had escaped. The moaning of the coolie, who was rapidly coming to after the sudden and savage assault on him, was another intimation that I had of the escape. I was put under arrest at once, and kept in close confinement until we reached Saigon, but the officer in command did not punish me further. The ingenuity displayed by the deserter was so evident, that no one blamed me very much for being taken off my guard and allowing a wrong man to go ashore, and, moreover, as we neared Tonquin, all thought more and more of the fighting and less and less of punishing a man who was not flagrantly in the wrong. Of course, there was no chance of recapturing the Bulgarian; he had reached foreign soil, and there is no act of extradition affecting men guilty of merely military offences. It was well for him, however, that my eyes were turned towards the dispute on the quay; all the blackening would scarcely have deceived me, and I should have shot him dead on the gangway before he could have time to reach the land. For all that I was glad that he got safely away, for, though a man will do his duty no matter how disagreeable it may be, yet he is not at all sorry when he misses the chance of doing such duty as mine would have been, had I noticed the runaway in time. Further on I shall have occasion to mention the case of another deserter, a man who deserted from a certain European army to French soil, and it was strange—oh, very strange—that neither the French nor the other sentries could hit him at less than a hundred yards' range, while he was making a desperate rush across the strip of undefined territory that marked the frontier.

Some other incidents occurred at Singapore, but, as I was under arrest, I can only speak of them as I heard about them from my comrades. After the Bulgarian's escape a far stricter watch was kept—double sentries were posted—but to a determined man nothing is impossible. More than one was found absent at morning roll call, and at last it became evident that, in some cases at least, connivance on the part of a pair of sentries had permitted the escape. If a man once got down into the water, he was practically free. Certainly a shark—and sharks do abound in these waters, and especially in the harbours, where they pick up all sorts of garbage—might cross his path, but there was not much danger, as the distance to the land was so small. No one of ours, as far as we could know, was caught in such a way. One, however, was caught by something almost as bad, but I must give a new paragraph to describing the hero of the tale before I begin the story about him.

The man I refer to I have already mentioned in connection with the negotiations between the companies after the fight at Three Fountains. He was the Italian that held the same leading place in the deputation from No. 4 Company as Nicholas the Russian did in ours. Without education—I don't believe that he could write his name—he possessed a fund of shrewdness and a faculty of quick observation that made him more than the equal of scholars—and many men of good education were in our ranks. Not at all desirous of a quarrel, he was pre-eminently one to avoid fighting with, for in a row he forgot all about his own safety and seemed not to care what hurt he received so long as he hurt his enemy, and any weapon that lay at hand would be used by him without hesitation at the time or remorse or shame afterwards. A smart, clean, active soldier; yet he was always getting into trouble and disgrace, now with his corporal, at another time with the sergeant of the section, but never with the officers. Fellows said that he belonged either to the Mafia or the Camorra, but opinions were divided as to whether he came to the Legion to avoid arrest by the Italian Government for crimes committed in the course of business or punishment from his association for treachery or some other offence against their laws. Anyway he was with us, and though not liked, still respected; though we did not fear him, yet we took good care to let him alone. He was not a man—to his credit be it said—who interfered with others. Why, then, should others interfere with him? About five feet five in height, of carriage alert rather than steady, with quick, black eyes, dark complexion, small, black moustache, regular features and even, white teeth, he was certainly one to attract anyone's attention, especially a woman's. He was very cynical with regard to the sex, not valuing woman's fondness much, but, all the same, so long as he was a girl's lover he allowed no poaching on his preserves. He sang well—French songs as well as Italian—and played on more than one musical instrument, his favourite one being a small flageolet, and with this he lightened more than one weary hour for us on shipboard. He never told anyone, I believe, of his intention to desert. I fancy he was too cautious for that. When he did go, no sentry connived at the business, for, even had our men been doing duty, not one of us cared so much for the Italian as to risk a court-martial for his sake.

I must here remark that the legionaries had been relieved of sentry duty, as so many of them had gone away without even bidding good-bye to anyone. The

French soldiers, the zephyrs, were now doing all this duty; and they did it so well, I must admit, that no man got clear away while they were on the watch— at least until the Italian left the ship—but his absence was not a long one. All our coal had been taken in, and the vessel had moved away from the wharf out into the harbour, so that it lay about 200 yards from shore. The sentries must have thought that no man would be so mad as to attempt to swim such a distance, since the water was full of sharks, and in all probability their vigilance had decreased. The morning after the ship had moved out the Italian did not answer at roll call, and it was at once assumed, and truly, that he had escaped, and, as no cry from the water had been heard by the men on duty, that he had got safely to land. Before the hour of departure the French consul came off in his own boat, to see the officers of the ship and of the troops. This, of course, was natural, but everyone was surprised to see him, as soon as he gained the deck, rush forward with malicious joy in his eyes to greet the commandant.

"Ah, mon commandant, I have a present for you."

"Thanks, thanks, my friend; how you are good!"

"A most charming present. I bring you a friend whom you most earnestly desire to see."

Leaning over the side he shouted out some orders to his sailors, and they, going under an awning at the stern, carried out the Italian bound hand and foot. How the commandant cursed him; how the Frenchmen smiled and jeered; how we, his comrades, felt sad that our worthy comrade should have been caught almost on the threshold of liberty! *Camaraderie* overcame all other feelings, and we pitied the poor wretch, for we guessed that a court-martial would have little mercy on a soldier, especially a soldier of the Legion, captured in the act of deserting from his company while on the way to the seat of war. As for the Italian, he was calm and collected, but, if he were free and had a knife and were within striking distance of the commandant, that officer would surely have had an end put to his cursing on the spot. In a moment the Italian was brought aboard and at once sent down to the prisoners' quarters, where he found several comrades, myself among the number, eagerly speculating on the noise and confusion above.

As soon as the guard had gone away someone asked the Italian what the noise on deck was about. He answered sharply:

"About a better man than you—about me."

None of us cared to put any further questions; Cecco was in very bad humour indeed. However, in about ten minutes he told us all, saying he had slipped over the side of the vessel when four sentries had come close enough to chat—this, you must remember, meant only the approach to one another of two posts, as all sentries had been doubled—that he had been in the water for about three minutes when he came close to a boat, which he boarded; that, like a fool, he made himself and his intention known before he found out the character of his hosts; that he was at once seized, and was told, when bound, that the boat belonged to the French consul and therefore he was still on French territory. "The rest you know," said he, "or can guess." We were sorry, and told him so. He thanked us graciously enough, and hoped we might have better luck in our enterprises than he had had in his, and, in reply to a question as to what he thought would happen, he said at first that he did not know and he did not care, but he would dearly like to have the commandant at his mercy just long enough to kill him. "Listen carefully," he went on. "I shall be shot in all probability, but they will give me a chance of saying a prayer and making my confession before I die. The commandant will also be shot, but he will get no notice, and, unless he be very lucky indeed, no priest will be present to send him absolved from sin into the presence of God." For the rest of the voyage the Italian and we got on well together. He got the best of the dinner, not that he thanked us or that we wanted thanks; he knew why we did it, and we should have been very bad soldiers indeed if we did not do a little to keep up the spirits of a man doomed, as we knew him to be, to a sudden and early death.

Let me anticipate once more. After our arrival at Saigon, Cecco was court-martialled, openly insulted the officers composing the court, was sentenced to death, and shot the following morning. And the commandant was shot in the back in a little skirmish in Tonquin—a brilliant little affair that would have brought him promotion had he lived. It may have been an accident, but there was at least a dozen Italians in the company immediately behind him, and in the heat of action bullets do occasionally go astray. How do I know that he was shot in the back? Well, I don't *know*, but I suspect for two reasons: first, there was a sort of investigation, which naturally led to nothing; and, secondly, the Italian's words came back to my mind directly I heard of the commandant's death. After all, is it not bad enough for an officer to punish a man or to get him punishment? Why should he swear at the poor devil and abuse him as if he had no spirit, no sense of shame, no soul? Any man will take his punishment fairly and honestly, if he believes that he has deserved it; no man will stand abuse without paying in full for it when he gets his chance, for abuse is not fair to the man who is waiting for his court-martial. But all, or nearly all, officers are either fools or brutes.

Another thing that happened at Singapore Le Grand told me afterwards. In the early days of desertion a fellow—I think he was a Belgian—came to Le Grand and proposed that they should go away together.

"I am," said the Belgian, "a baker by trade; you speak English well and can teach me. Let us go together. You will interpret for me and I will work for both. We shall get enough of money in six months to carry us to the United States, and there we shall separate as soon as I know enough of the language to make myself understood."

"No," replied Le Grand; "I volunteered for the war, and I mean to see what fighting means in Tonquin. Moreover, if I went away now, no one I care about would ever have any respect for me again. It is bad enough with me as it is; I will do nothing to make it worse. The most people can allege against me now is folly; no one shall ever be able to charge me with cowardice as well."

Many times the baker renewed his entreaties to Le Grand to go away. Le Grand would not: he knew that hardships—perhaps sickness or wounds or death—lay before him, but better anything than self-reproach and loss of self-respect. Le Grand was right in his own way, because he was, and is (for he is still alive and in a good position), a gentleman; the Belgian baker was wise too in his generation and according to his own lights. He slipped off before the Frenchmen were ordered to supply all the guards. No one knows whether he fell a prey to the sharks or not, and, I may add, no one—not even Le Grand—cares.

The only other important thing that was told to me was that our fellows and the zephyrs became rather dangerous to one another. From the beginning we were not too amiable, but when the commandant put us— at least the other legionaries, for I was at the time in the prisoners' quarters on account of the Bulgarian's escape— to do most of the duties about the ship and put Frenchmen only on sentry, so that no more men of the Legion might desert, things rapidly came to a head. The commandant was lucky in two respects—the voyage to Saigon was short, and a French war vessel accompanied the transport. Had there been a twenty days' voyage without an escort the decks would have been washed red with blood, for, be it remembered, though the average

French soldier can conduct himself with propriety in almost any place, the zephyr is a military convict pure and simple. No matter how bad we were, the zephyrs were worse. Well, let me put it in another way: the zephyrs aboard were the bad characters of the French army; we others, the legionaries, were the bad characters of all the other armies of Europe. They, the zephyrs, had no chance of regaining their characters in their own country, where their misdeeds were known; our fellows had started, each with a clean sheet, on joining an alien army. Thus our reputation as a body was bad, but no man had any very ugly charge against his name; the zephyrs were bad by man, by squad, by company, and by battalion. However, they are really amongst the finest fighting men in the world; some people, indeed, say that the zephyrs are second only to the legionaries.

There was no fight. The big war-vessel lay not so far away, and all knew what its shells could do. Strange that we met these very zephyrs afterwards, and our companies and theirs, certainly aided by others, did a hard afternoon's bayonet-work together. We were friends after that, so much so that I believe that one battalion, and that a battalion of zephyrs, is the only one of the French army to speak with liking—all, of course, speak with respect, unless at a distance—of the Foreign Legion. But everything to its own place.

At last we reached Pingeh—a fine harbour. I was set free, as well as all other prisoners save the Italian, and we disembarked, happy again at the change, to take our share in the war against the Black Flags, thinking more of the relief from the cramped quarters than of any dangers that lay before us.

CHAPTER XI

WHEN we arrived at Pingeh, the port of Saigon, the zephyrs disembarked first, and we followed. Straightway most of us were marched off to a camping-field where tents and other impedimenta were awaiting us, and in a short time we had formed a fairly creditable camp. Those of ours who were kept behind on the quay were employed in sorting out our baggage as the coolies carried the troopship's load ashore. Considering that all except the officers carried their belongings on their backs, this was not hard work, and most of them were satisfied, but the dozen or so left on guard over the ammunition cases brought out by the transport were not at all lucky, as they got no meal, not even a cup of coffee, for fully twelve hours. That's always the way. Your ordinary officer can't understand why everybody is not satisfied when he is. If the captain has a good lunch and a better dinner, the simple soldier may tighten his belt and put a bit of tobacco between his teeth—that is good enough for him. Well, there are officers who care for their men, but they are so few that, if you know a hundred captains, you may easily reckon the good ones on the fingers of a hand. Some are inclined to be good, but though physically brave they are morally cowards; they cannot stand the sneering of those who look upon the men as mere instruments for gaining decorations and promotion, and it is so very easy to acquire the habit of doing as most of your equals do. It is wrong—oh! I who have felt it know how wrong it is!—for a man who has rank and a better lot than others to forget the responsibility attached to his position, to let the men under him understand hour

H   113

by hour and day by day and week by week how little he cares for their comfort, to swear at the sick, to sneer at the wounded, to order the dead to be thrown any way into a trench, and to abuse the burial party because they did not cover the carcasses quickly enough. War is war, as an Alsatian in my company used to say ; but why should a man, or rather men, come into camp for the night after a long march, and perhaps a sharp fight, to be sworn at and abused by the officers who, for their own sakes even, should try to make things cheerful for all? But again I am digressing.

We spent about a week at Saigon, under canvas all the time. Of course, we got our share of inspection ; first the chief officer—I forget now who he was, not that he was at all worth remembering—then the medical officer, then a quartermaster—the best of all, for he supplied deficiencies in clothing. I must say this : when a French soldier goes on campaign he is well fitted out —they took from us every article that showed any signs of wear, and a new one was at once issued. At first we thought that we should have to pay out of our scanty means for the new supplies. We were only too glad to find that, instead of taking our money under false pretences, as they do in other armies, our pay was increased, and we were told, and truly told, that the increase would last while we were on active service. Take my word for it, no matter how bad the officers may be, the French Government is the best in the world to its troops on active service. If men suffer, it is not the fault of those in Paris ; put the blame rather on the underlings—I mean the commandants and the captains. But, remember, what I have just said I have said only of the Republic—of the monarchy and the empire I know nothing.

Another reason for this delay was that the French, if they can by any chance do it, keep men quiet on land for some days after a voyage. This is very sensible. No man gets what I may call his land legs until some time after he has come ashore from a transport, where space is small and men are many, where food is wretched, and water mawkishly warm and suspiciously sweet. The rest did us good; the new clothing and the extra pay put us in good humour. When at last we put on our knapsacks for the march into the interior, we were altogether different from the 500 semi-mutinous scarecrows who had landed from the troopship only six or seven days before.

Every man had 150 rounds of ball cartridge in his pouch; all rifles were loaded; we were evidently to be kept on the *qui vive* from the earliest possible moment; talking in the ranks was often stopped without any visible cause; the sentries were visited half-a-dozen times a night; discipline was in all respects as strict as it could be; and we were made to understand, as if we had learned nothing in Algeria, that we were in front of a cautious, skilful, and sometimes daring, enemy, and that every man was responsible for his own and his comrades' lives.

Now I have no intention of writing a history of the war in Tonquin. I shall merely give details of the most important events of my life there, and of these the first in order was the battle of Noui-Bop.

We had not been long in the East, and were by no means acclimatised, when the battalion to which our two companies had been sent was ordered to join a mixed force of French soldiers and natives under the command of a distinguished French general, whose name is of no importance to my narrative. This general was operating against a large force of Black Flags, and, as a result of his operations, there was every prospect of a hot engagement, and this was exactly to our taste. Ever since we had joined the battalion we had been looked upon with suspicion by the officers, for the news of the fight between the companies at Three Fountains had travelled to Tonquin, and many believed that it was a foolish thing to allow both companies to soldier together,

as there might be at any moment a renewal of the fray.
Even our comrades of the two other companies in the
battalion at first thought that we might again fall out,
but very soon they saw what the officers could not, or
would not, see—that No. 4 and ours were as friendly as
possible to each other and that there was not the
slightest chance of ill-feeling showing itself between us.
Thus we were anxious to be in a big battle ; we trusted
in ourselves, and every man was determined, by showing
reckless bravery in the field, to wipe away the disgrace
which we knew attached to us, partly for our little fight
and partly for the desertions at Singapore.

After a good deal of manœuvring, of which we bore
our share, at last it was evident that the eventful day
had come.   Some chasseurs d'Afrique who were with
us had located the Black Flags and their allies, many of
whom were regular soldiers of the Chinese army, in a
strong position at a place called Noui-Bop.   Our native
scouts confirmed this, and also reported that there were
several white officers amongst them—these we guessed
to be English or Prussians, or a mixture of both.   We
knew that the enemy had good rifles and plenty of
ammunition, that they held favourable ground, that
there was no chance of outflanking them owing to their
superiority in numbers and the nature of the country,
and that the frontal attack should be pushed well home
if it were to succeed.   Well, so much the better, we said
to ourselves.

On the morning of the battle we were aroused a little
after sunrise.   This was because, in the East, it is best
for European soldiers to get the work of the day done
before the sun becomes too hot.   After breakfast my
battalion was ordered to leave knapsacks, greatcoats,
blankets—everything, indeed, save our arms and the
clothing we stood up in—in the quarters which we had
occupied during the night, and about fifty men were
told off to see that there was no looting of their comrades' belongings while the fight was going on.   Then

we went forward, and took up our position in the centre of the fighting line. On our right there were Annamite tirailleurs, backed up by some French soldiers, I think zouaves; on our left a half-battalion of a French regiment of the line—if I do not mistake, the 143rd. We waited and smoked awhile, some laughed and joked, others puffed at their pipes in silence, the officers were talking and looking always to the rear. At last a dull booming was heard—the guns were beginning behind us—we could see the shells passing over our heads and bursting more than a thousand yards away in our front. Pipes were put up, but still we sat quietly on the ground, listening to the roar of the guns and watching the shells as they searched the line where our enemies lay. A staff officer galloped up to our commandant, and we all got up without waiting for the word of command. After a short colloquy the staff officer galloped back to the general, the orders came clear and abrupt from commandant and captains, and before we could well understand what we were doing No. 4 Company and mine were extended in skirmishing order, with the other two companies of the battalion behind us in support.

We had not advanced very far in this formation when a man, five or six files on my right, flung up his arms and came to the ground with a groan. Just then we began to fire, our firing being kept strictly under control by the officers and sub-officers, who saw no use in allowing us, as soldiers naturally do, to blaze away all our ammunition at too long a range against a well-protected enemy. We went along almost too well; not alone had the officers to control our fire, they had also to work hard to keep us in hand as we went forward in the attack. All was well. A man fell here and another there, but the losses were not enough to speak about until we came to the dangerous zone.

Now let me explain what is meant by the dangerous zone. I did not understand it at the time, but I afterwards learned all about it, and many a time I thanked my stars when the order came to fix bayonets, for then I knew that I was safely through the ugly place and that most, if not all, of the chances were in my favour.

The Chinese—at least those of them whom we were fighting—never put the rifle to the shoulder as Europeans do when about to fire. Instead, they tuck the rifle-butt into the armpit and try to drop the bullet, as it were, on the attacking party. They cannot well do this until the attack comes within five hundred yards of the defence, nor can they do it when the enemy is within two hundred yards of their line, but they succeed fairly well — that is, well for such clumsy shooters — while the fighting line of the advance is between five hundred and two hundred yards of their position. This was pointed out to us by our officers, and we could easily see for ourselves that what they said was true. Looking back—of course, when the battle was over—we saw only scattered bodies lying for the first three or four hundred yards of our advance, then a comparatively large number in the dangerous zone, after that few, for, as we closed with the bayonet and were practically at point-blank range, the Black Flags wavered and fired at the sky rather than at us.

Well, we had got along fairly until we came to within about five hundred yards of the enemy's trenches. Then the men went down fast, and the officers, sergeants, corporals, and veterans shouted out to us neophytes to run. And we did run; we covered about three hundred yards of heavy ground—we were attacking through rice fields, you must know—as quickly as men ever did before or since. I was pretty blown when I heard the order given to lie down, and down we lay, with bullets flying overhead, until we regained our breath. Above us the shells from our guns were shrieking, in front they were exploding; it gave us all—at least it gave me—a feeling of heartfelt gratitude that the big guns were on our side. After some time we were ordered forward again. We ran a bit, fired a round, ran again a little way and fired another cartridge, not at the foe, for as yet we could see no men in our front, but at the long line of smoke that overhung the trenches where the Black Flags and their allies, the Chinese regulars, were waiting for our charge.

In this fashion we managed to get to within about eighty yards of the enemy's trenches, and were then ordered to halt, lie down, and fire as often as possible at the heads and figures that we were now beginning to distinguish where the little puffs of smoke arose. A light breeze was sweeping down the battlefield, and this lifted the blue-white clouds, so that men on both sides could easily make out their enemies. An officer sprang up about twenty yards away from me, waved his sword, and shouted out something which I could not hear, so incessant was the rattle of musketry. I saw the others fixing their bayonets, and I reached round to my left side to pluck out mine. As I did so, I saw the supporting companies of ours running up to join us. Very soon they were at our side, and the four companies, nearly a thousand strong, poured in a hot fire for a minute or two. Then we heard the clear notes of the charge. In a second, commandant, officers, sub-officers, and simple soldiers were all racing for the trenches like madmen, shouting: "Kill, kill!" How I got there I do not know. I was in, anyway, if not amongst the first, certainly not amongst the last, and when there a horrible scene lay before my eyes. On all sides were dead and dying men, some of the dead quiet and calm in appearance, as if only sleeping, with just a little spot of red on the forehead or staining the breast; others torn to pieces by the deadly shells. Some of the wounded were quite passive and resigned; others were crying out, I suppose for mercy. But it was not of them we thought, our business lay with a large body of men, led by a big chief in yellow tunic and wide yellow trousers, who met us with bayonet, sword, and spear and tried to retrieve the fortunes of the day. Our officers—bad as they were, they were brave—rushed straight at this band. We followed like wolf-hounds rushing at wolves. Their hoarse cries and imprecations soon died away as with bloody bayonets we thrust and dug our way through them from front to rear. Once more the Asiatic went down before the European, and in five minutes from the time our foremost entered the trenches we had left not a single Black Flag or Chinese regular standing on his feet. Some of the wounded fired at us as they lay upon the ground ; that work, however, was very soon stopped.

Meanwhile the half-battalion of French troops of the line had gallantly carried their part of the entrenchments, but on the right the native troops, the Annamite tirailleurs, were in trouble. Some Frenchmen were with them, but these were too few of themselves to make head against the enemy, who thronged like bees to flowers where they saw a good chance of throwing back the attack. My captain, a good soldier and a bad man, hastily collected about a hundred of his men, and getting us into some sort of order gave us the word—and the example too, indeed—to charge. We fell upon the exposed flank of the barbarians. In a couple of minutes we drove it in upon the main left of the enemy, and very soon the Annamites, taking their courage in both hands, returned to the attack. Some of ours again went round and charged the enemy in the rear, and then the game was up—the battle was over. I wish I need say no more about the fighting, but many would not surrender, and these, of course, were promptly shot or bayoneted where they stood. Some wounded also suffered, but I must say that when a white man, zouave or legionary, put a wounded enemy out of pain it was only after the savage had tried to shoot or stab a passing soldier. Well, if a wounded man will try to kill there is only one thing to do—put it as soon as possible out of his power to do serious damage. I don't blame the savages much for firing or cutting at our fellows ; as they never gave quarter to whites, they naturally believed, I suppose, that whites would give no quarter to them.

Some of the Annamite tirailleurs did, I am afraid, a little unjustifiable killing. Well, it's the way with these people; they think as little of killing a wounded man as a hungry legionary would of killing a providentially sent chicken. We must make allowances; but I am very doubtful about the wisdom of European nations in supplying arms and teaching modern drill to the yellows, the blacks, and the browns. You may make any of these very good imitations of white soldiers, but the leopard cannot change his spots, and the effects of centuries of cruelty cannot be eradicated in a day. The Annamites had one excuse—they were merely doing to the Black Flags what the Black Flags would have done to them and to us had the issue of the fight been different. This is a poor excuse, I admit, but then any excuse is better than none at all. The white officers attached to our native levies did their best to keep their men in hand, but orders are not always minded, even by the very best soldiers, in the heat of action or the flush of victory.

No one must assume that what I have written is a full account of the battle of Noui-Bop. I merely tell what happened under my own eyes. I know nothing whatever of the events that occurred in other parts of the battlefield, nor must it be considered that the troops I have mentioned were the only attacking ones. There were others advancing far away to the right and to the left—we were only the centre of the advance—and when I speak of right and left, I mean right and left of the central attack, not extreme right and left of the firing line.

When we had cleared the Black Flags and their comrades out of the entrenchments, we had a short rest under arms. Very soon, however, we received orders to advance, but cautiously, so as not to get too far in front of the rest. In our rear we could see the artillerymen bringing up their guns to new positions. Occasionally a gun would be unlimbered and a shell or two thrown into a part of the enemy trying to re-form. These shells did not do much damage to the enemy, but they did a great deal of good to us; it was so pleasant to watch the projectiles hissing through the air and to know that our friends the Black Flags were also watching them, but with very different feelings. One of our fellows, a happy-go-lucky Andalusian, called the shells *lettres d'avis*—warning notices that we were coming and that it would be best for the barbarians to be "not at home." Only twice in this advance had we to make a regular attack, and in each case the men who opposed us did not wait to allow us to get to close quarters; they fled with a hail of bullets about their ears before we got within two hundred yards. The French advance on the extreme right seemed to have more difficulty. I fancy an attempt was made to take them in flank. Anyway, we heard a continuous roll of musketry, with the heavy booming of guns, for about ten or fifteen minutes, and then only a dropping fire, when the attack had evidently been repulsed. On the left no trouble was experienced; our comrades there swept forward, driving the men opposed to them like sheep. About eleven o'clock we were halted. The native levies were sent on in pursuit, as they were better able than European soldiers to follow up a retreating enemy in the heat of the noonday sun. We lay down and rested, happy in the thought that our first fight in Tonquin was over and won. We were not allowed to remain long at our ease after the fight. First two companies, and afterwards the other two, were sent back to get the knapsacks and other impedimenta left behind by the general's order before the advance. About half-past four in the afternoon we got some bread and soup, and a little after five, when the great heat of the day was over, we set forward on our march in the track of the retreating enemy and the pursuing tirailleurs. We kept on until nearly nine o'clock at night, occasionally halting for a rest. In spite of the Annamite levies being in front of us on this march we took all possible precautions against a surprise; we had a section of a company in front, and, in advance of that again, one of its squads. Other squads were out far to the right and to the left. These precautions may seem unnecessary, as our own friends were in front, but, indeed, they were very useful for several reasons. In the first place we saw that, no matter how triumphant our arms might be, there was to be no relaxation of precaution or of discipline; in the second, it was possible that our irregulars might have allowed a large body of the enemy to slip in behind them, and these might ambush us; again, all the men of the main body felt a sense of security, and consequently their nerves were not kept constantly strained—a material advantage in warfare. It is a good maxim to put all the watchfulness on a few and to allow the main body to rest or march in security; so an officer will have better soldiers in action. The best men in the world can't help feeling worried and depressed by constant expectation of an attack. A battle is nothing—very often it is, indeed, a relief—but always waiting and always speculating on an attack, and always wondering from what side it will come, will wear out the strongest nerves. Then come dogged sullenness, loss of interest in one's work, carelessness in duty, and slovenliness in the little things that all soldiers take pride in, and in the end disaster.

That night we lay about fifteen or sixteen kilometres from the place where we had rested the previous night. It was lucky that it was not my turn for guard; I felt so sleepy after the morning fight and the evening march. I had scarcely rolled myself up snugly in my greatcoat and blanket when I fell into a heavy, dreamless sleep, and I could almost swear that I had not had two minutes' rest when the reveille went in the morning. I felt very hungry, and that made me get up quickly from the spot of hard ground on which I had been sleeping, to help the others to light the fire for the squad's morning coffee. Nicholas the Russian asked me how I felt.

"Hungry, my comrade, hungry," I replied. And everyone, even the captain, who was passing at the time, laughed as if I had said a good thing. Soldiers are very like schoolboys; the simplest thing said or done by one they know far surpasses anything said, no matter how brilliant, anything done, no matter how renowned, by those they do not know. On active service they are even more easily amused. We often laughed heartily at sayings that, considered calmly by me now, show not the slightest trace of humour.

When the tale of dead and wounded was made up it was seen that our battalion had suffered more than any other corps in the fight, and that of the four companies constituting it mine had the greatest number of losses. This was not bad for me. For some reason or other the captain made me a soldier of the first class, and I was very glad indeed that Nicholas the Russian and Le Grand were also promoted to wear the single red stripe on their right sleeves. We laughed heartily as we thought of our advance in rank and of what we should have got instead of promotion if all were known about the quarrel at Three Fountains. Well, what people don't know won't trouble them.

For some time after this our battalion was always on hard duty. We on some days marched only ten or twelve kilometres; on others, in pursuit of a band of marauders, we covered as much as twenty-five or thirty. Remember, we had to do all this in a country where roads are bad and travelling over fields almost impossible, with heavy packs on our backs, and never less than a hundred rounds of ball cartridge in our pouches. Then no matter how pleasant the greatcoat and the blanket might be at night, they were no light load during the day, and especially between the hours of eleven in the forenoon and four in the afternoon, when we had to go forward if there was the slightest chance of catching up with some or other band of scoundrels. Moreover, when soldiers are on flying duty, they seldom get enough to eat, and what they do get is not the very best or nicest food in the world. One day we came in at the hour of evening soup to a little camp where some zouaves and marine fusiliers were. They were very good to us indeed; the soup they had just prepared for themselves they gave to us, and they took, good fellows that they were, the dry bread and unboiled rice that we had in our haversacks. They were decent men, these French soldiers; they saw that we had been on tramp for some time, and they hesitated not a moment to give us the savoury soup when they saw the hungry longing in our eyes and the convulsive twitch of nostrils, as the grateful odour was perceived. They did more; they gave us some wine and native spirit, and I do not know whether we were more pleased with the gifts or with the free, generous dispositions of the givers. Well, we did as much afterwards for Frenchmen.

This victory at Noui-Bop gave the French control over a large strip of country. Moreover, many new recruits joined the Annamite tirailleurs, for the Asiatic, like all others, wants to be on the winning side. There were promotions, of course, but the only ones I was at all interested in were those that gave the single red chevrons to Nicholas, Le Grand, and myself. We had got to like one another very much, and I believe that the promotion of one gave more pleasure to his comrades than to himself. I may say here that Nicholas and Le Grand afterwards refused further promotion; I, a boy and fool, took it when offered, but I must tell how that came about in another chapter.

CHAPTER XII

I WILL not weary the reader with an account of our marches to and fro, hunting straggling bands of marauders. This work soon became monotonous, and the recital of our doings would, I am sure, prove monotonous as well. Only one thing impressed itself strongly on my mind at the time, and this was that a man who fell out of the ranks had no chance of getting mercy from the Black Flags. Occasionally, we came across the horribly mutilated body of a French soldier or an Annamite tirailleur, and the sight was sickening. One circumstance, which I must now relate, made our blood boil over and, if we learned to give no quarter, the enemy had no one to blame but themselves.

We arrived at a small village one morning about nine o'clock, having been on the march continuously since five. Here we rested during the heat of the day, and one of the men of my squad and I went to a little shop to buy tobacco. We saw some fruit there—I don't know what kind it was—and my comrade purchased some and gave a share to me. We ate it, and thought no more about the business, but the fruit cost my poor friend his life.

When we were on the march that afternoon, I felt very sick. My comrade—I forgot to mention that he came from Lorraine and was serving with us in order that, when his time was up, he might become a French citizen—was even worse, and both of us had to fall out of the ranks. However, we again caught up with the company, but a second time we were compelled to stay behind, and this time the captain ordered our rifles and ammunition to be taken from us and carried by our comrades.

"The Black Flags," he said, "may get you if they like, but they sha'n't have your arms or ammunition."

I don't blame the officer, he was quite right. The same thing was done with every man who showed signs of weakness or weariness, for we had no ambulance in these hurried pursuits, and the abandoned soldier kept only his bayonet for defence against the human wolves that hung on our flanks and rear. Not much good that, for the cowards used to overpower the poor devils with stones, and, as soon as they were beaten to the ground, the brutes would seize them and execute their horrible tortures on their bodies before death came—a merciful release. Again, however, we struggled back to the company. Nicholas, who was carrying my rifle and ammunition in addition to his own, said : "Cheer up, my good friend ; keep on a little longer ; we shall soon be in camp." Le Grand, who was in the squad immediately behind mine, got permission to carry my knapsack, another man took my greatcoat, and still another my blanket, but, in spite of the relief thus afforded me, it was with the utmost difficulty that I kept on. The Lorrainer was similarly aided, but he was too unwell, and had for the third and last time to fall out. He never rejoined the company, and we could at the time only speculate upon his fate, but very soon we were to learn the truth.

Helped on by my comrades, I managed to stagger into the little collection of huts where we were to pass the night. Nicholas and Le Grand foraged for me, and got somewhere and somehow a supply of native spirit. Le Grand made me a stiff glass of boiling hot punch, and this I was compelled to drink, though my stomach rebelled at all things. I fell asleep soon after, and woke in the morning, qualmish, indeed, and weak, but completely rid of all the bad effects brought on by indulgence in the fruit. Nicholas insisted on my taking some of the spirit in my morning coffee, and also filled my water bottle with coffee containing about a glass of the fiery stuff, so that I might have medicine on the march. All the others of the squad were sympathetic, and Le Grand, though not of my squad, came over to our hut to inquire about me. Nobody minded this—it was no breach of squad etiquette, as we were both Irishmen— but, of course, it would not do for us to be too much together—we remembered the punishment given to the Alsatians.

Some information received by our officers made us return by the route passed over on the previous day. When we came near the place where the unfortunate Lorrainer had fallen out, a great cloud of birds rose up from the ground and flew, crying hoarsely, away. Very soon we learned the meaning of this. The captain of my company, who was riding in front, suddenly shouted out: "Halt!" and dismounting, gave the reins to his orderly and crossed into a rice field that bordered the way. What he saw there seemed to fill him with disgust and horror. He called out to the other officers to come and see; then the sergeants and the corporals were summoned; finally we private soldiers went by fours to view the sight. What a horrible thing met our gaze! On the ground lay the dead body of the Lorrainer, hacked and mutilated in a fashion that I cannot describe. We were almost sickened by the sight. Often before we had seen mutilated bodies, but never one so savagely disfigured as this, and, moreover, this was the body of one who had been our good comrade only the day before.

"Ah," said the captain to me, "was it not well that you struggled on?"

"My captain," said Nicholas, speaking before I could get out a word, "I will never again give mercy to a Black Flag. As they do to us, let us do to them."

The captain answered nothing to this, but sent us back to our ranks. Before we left the spot we buried the poor Lorrainer.

All that day we spoke of nothing but the horrible

sight we had seen in the morning.   We were angry; we made resolutions to take a sharp and speedy vengeance for the death of our comrade and the indignity shown to his corpse; we encouraged one another in the desire for revenge; we spoke of what might happen to any one of us who fell faint or wounded on the way; we were gloomy and sullen, not with despair, but with the gloom and sullenness of incensed men.   Had we met any enemies that day, not even the commander-in-chief of the army in Tonquin could have prevented us from treating them as they had treated our poor comrade, and, when we did get the chance, we took a bloody vengeance on the barbarians—such a vengeance as even in the Legion was spoken of with bated breath.

Now at this time the battalion had been divided into three parts—two companies held a depot of stores and ammunition, the remaining two were out as small flying columns through the country.   It was our turn to go into garrison and rest a while, and two days after burying our unfortunate comrade we marched into the depot.   The day after our friends of No. 4 Company came in, and the two companies, Nos. 1 and 2, that we relieved started off on a ten days' trip through the country, seeking the enemy but, as a rule, not finding them.   While we were resting in garrison we told the story of the Lorrainer's sad fate to the men of No. 4, and we also made them acquainted with our determination to have satisfaction at all costs for the brutality of those who had tortured to death a poor, sick soldier, to all intents and purposes unarmed, and then disfigured his body in so revolting a manner.   I give no details of the mutilation here, but we described it fully to our comrades, and they too were filled with horror and anger.   The two companies had got a strange sort of liking for each other, arising out of the fight at Three Fountains, and we could not have met men more willing to back us up in our resolve than they were, and fate sent us other allies almost as good too.

I

A few days before our turn came to go out on the tiresome tramp after quickly disappearing enemies, two companies of Frenchmen came into our little camp. To our surprise, and, indeed, at first to our disgust, they were the two companies of zephyrs that had come out with us in the transport. We had not lain alongside of them since we parted at Saigon, and then our feelings towards one another were not at all friendly. However, if soldiers quickly fall out, often they become friends again as easily, and so it happened with us. The zephyrs were not a day in camp before they knew all about the Lorrainer and our desire to avenge him, and, since they considered the people of Lorraine as their own flesh and blood, they felt almost as angry as we did. Very soon we all were, if not friends, at least allies for the purpose of obtaining vengeance on the Black Flags, and it was tacitly understood amongst the soldiers of the four companies that, when next we went into action, no quarter was to be given and that the commands, even the entreaties, of our officers to show mercy were to be disregarded. As soldiers we all recognised that it would be impossible to punish so many men, and we saw also that, if we took a terrible vengeance, the officers would do their best to hide the fact, and, though it might become known throughout the army, yet there was no chance of the general giving it official recognition by giving us official punishment.

Now the two companies of zephyrs numbered at the time about 300 men and No. 4 and mine about 350; the rest were in the hospital or the grave.

When No. 1 and No. 2 Companies of my battalion came into camp, the zephyrs and we others marched out. At the end of the first day's march we picked up a couple of companies of Annamite tirailleurs, weak ones they were, and angry, as they had had a couple of fights recently with the Black Flags and got by no means the best of the fighting. Another weak company of native levies joined us the next day, so that altogether our commandant had at his disposal about 650 Europeans and about 300 Asiatic tirailleurs. There were no guns with us, but we did not mind their absence, this time we meant to depend solely on the bayonet.

I have often wondered whether or not our officers knew of our resolution. Certainly the corporals and sergeants did, but these *sous-officiers* were too experienced to say anything to us about it; they might as well have tried to turn back Niagara as to change our minds. That they knew, and they knew also that we were dangerous men to cross when united and feeling strongly about anything. Bullets don't always fly towards the enemy. Many a man with a private grudge against sergeant or corporal might be only too glad to salve his conscience, or what stood for his conscience, by saying to himself that he was merely executing justice on behalf of his section or his squad. If the officers knew, they kept silent, but one thing was certain, however it came about: we were the quietest and most subdued force, to all appearance, in the world. The officers and sub-officers were strangely easy with us; we in the ranks dropped all the boisterous gaiety that usually distinguishes soldiers; we were well behaved, respectful, attentive to our duties—in short, for the time being we were model troops.

One evening our scouts brought in word that a fairly large body of the enemy, from two to three thousand strong, lay within two hours' march of our encampment. These were evidently the men who had driven back the Annamite tirailleurs, and our yellow friends were quite well aware of what had happened to their wounded, whom they had been compelled to abandon on the field. "So much the better," whispered we to one another; "the native levies will be our very good brothers this time."

Next morning we were aroused without sound of bugle, and after the morning meal had been disposed of, every man received a ration of wine. Some fellows drank this at once, most of us, however, put it into our water bottles for use during the day. Soon we were on the march, due precautions being taken against a flank attack or a surprise, and about eight o'clock or half-past we arrived within sight of the enemy. They were not disposed to stir on our account, and we were quite satisfied. We had begun to despise them—I mean when we met them in fair fight. That is the way with all Europeans; a white man gets to know his yellow brother only to despise him.

Towards nine o'clock the regular advance began. No. 4 Company of legionaries attacked on the right, my company being in support, with half-a-section, supported by some Annamite tirailleurs, flung out to guard against a flank attack on the part of the enemy; on the left a company of zephyrs were extended, the second company of Frenchmen doing the same duty on the left as mine did on the right; in reserve were the rest of the Annamite tirailleurs.

Our men advanced in the usual way until they came within charging distance of the enemy's entrenchment. At this time a slight diversion was caused on the left by a feeble attempt to outflank and throw into confusion the white soldiers and native levies advancing in support. This attempt failed, and, just as we knew that it had failed, a similar one was made on us. We quickly put an end to it, pouring in a heavy fire at short range, and when these attacks were repulsed a considerable body of the Black Flags left the field. But the firing line in front had still to reckon with the soldiers manning the trenches, and these certainly fought with admirable spirit and determination. Better for them had they run away!

When the time came, in the commandant's opinion, for the charge which was to end the fight, one section of my company was ordered forward to join No. 4, the other section, the one to the right, with about 100

Annamite tirailleurs, to overlap the enemy in that direction and, if possible, to take them in the rear.

As we ran along we heard first the heavy, continuous firing that always precedes the bayonet charge, and then the hoarse roar of "Kill, kill!" that told us that our comrades were going up with the bayonet.

We redoubled our exertions, slaughtered to a man a small body of Black Flags that tried to block the way, and very soon we were clear past the end of the entrenchments and were moving inwards—that is, to the left—to catch the savages in the rear. We just succeeded. The enemy, driven out of the entrenchments by the frontal attack, were pouring out in hundreds along their line of retreat. We rushed at them with cries of exultation and revenge, and as we drove back the fugitives on one side a section of zephyrs and some natives drove them back on the other. We had now completely hemmed them in. Roughly speaking, on the south were a company and a half of legionaries and a company and a half of zephyrs, with a few Annamites who had come up from the reserves; on the north, half a company of legionaries, half a company of zephyrs, and about a hundred and fifty native tirailleurs; between these two forces about six or seven hundred Black Flags and their allies. It was now a game of battledore and shuttlecock: our comrades on the south drove the savages on to our bayonets; we sent them yelling back again. Once more our fellows attacked and pushed them towards us; we, who had re-formed the ranks, again closed and used the bayonet mercilessly until they tried to break away. This went on for some time, but every charge brought the opposed lines of white soldiers closer, and thus diminished the little space in which the Black Flags could move. At last we were all a dense crowd, in the centre a mob of savages so closely packed together that they had scarcely room to thrust or cut, around this a circle of maddened men stabbing furiously and crying out:

"Vengeance for our comrade; kill, kill!" By scores the central mob went down. At last not more than fifty or sixty were left, and these were on their knees or thrown prone upon the ground crying out for quarter. We opened our ranks and let all the Annamites through; in three minutes not a Black Flag was left alive.

In plain words, this was a massacre—of that there can be no doubt. It is only fair, however, to put the responsibility on the proper shoulders. Therefore I say that it was meditated upon and carried out by the simple soldiers; the officers and sub-officers merely fought well while there was any show of resistance. It would be unjust to the men to say that the officers led us, for we were far too anxious to get to close quarters to require leading, but when the resistance had ceased the captains and lieutenants vehemently ordered, and, when orders were disregarded, begged of us to stop. The sergeants and the corporals asked us to refrain from killing, but they were not over-earnest about it—they understood us better than the leaders of higher rank— and they knew quite well that our desire of vengeance could be appeased only by blood. The corporal of my squad said to us afterwards:

"No doubt it was wrong, but perhaps it was necessary."

But, it will be asked, were there no leaders in the affair? Yes; there were leaders—indeed, the very best leaders that could be found for such a deed. You must understand that we had in our ranks men of education and refinement; gentlemen, let me say, who had gone astray. These were of many nations and of various crimes. I have already mentioned Nicholas the Russian. I could also tell you something of a Prussian ex-lieutenant of hussars; of an English infantry officer, son of a high official in the Colonies, who had sent in his papers after a five minutes' interview with his colonel; of the Austrian *beau sabreur* who loved women better than their honour and pre-ferred cards to his own; of many others who came to the Legion as a means of committing social suicide, and who—unhappy rascals that they were—were yet good, honest, fighting men, and not bad comrades if one only put a guard upon his tongue. Two of them could not live in the same squad, and the authorities knew it. Every one of them was a second corporal, so to speak, and really, to take the case of the man I knew best, Nicholas was far more respected amongst us than our authorised superior, and the corporal was as well aware of the fact as we. Well, these were the leaders. When the officers and sub-officers, who thought only of victory and perhaps promotion, would have had us show mercy when the fight was over, these men, born and trained leaders, encouraged us to slay and spare not, and showed us an example of fierce brutality which we, angry on account of the murder and mutilation of our comrade, only too faithfully followed. We should certainly have done some unfair killing in any case, but we others should not, I believe, have been guilty of such excesses were it not for the ruined gentlemen who for once saw a chance of giving vent to their long pent-up feelings of anger with all the world—especially their world—that had for ever cast them out. Long ago there was an Italian proverb: "Inglese Italianato e diavolo incarnato," and I believe it to have contained a good deal of truth at the time. Nowadays the "devil incarnate" is the gentleman by birth and breeding who has been rejected by his natural society because he has been so unlucky as to be found out.

Well, the fight was over, and we, having cleaned our bayonets, rested quietly on the field. Nobody in the ranks said a word; the sergeants stood apart from us and from each other; a little knot of officers gathered together and spoke in whispers. The commandant rode up and spoke in a low tone to them, then he went away, and the sections were ordered to fall into ranks. The zephyrs and we were marched a little way from the place, and were ordered to prepare a small encampment; the Annamite tirailleurs were sent out scouting while this was being done; there was not the slightest thought in any man's mind of pursuing the flying enemy. Indeed, pursuit would have been useless; those who had got away had too long a start, and we were very tired and in no mood for further fighting that day. About two hundred legionaries and some zephyrs were after a short time sent out to bury the dead. I should mention that our wounded had been first carried to the place where we were forming the little camp. I was glad that I was not with the burial party; those who formed it had no stomach for their evening soup. Towards nightfall all things necessary had been done—the wounded cared for, the dead buried four deep in a long trench, this for the Black Flags, and two shorter trenches, one for the legionaries and the zephyrs, the other for the Annamite tirailleurs. The camp was very quiet; the men not on guard or outlying picket lay about smoking, but with very little conversation; the officers of all detachments had assembled in the centre, and were talking earnestly about the events of the day.

Nothing was ever said to us about this ugly affair. It was over and done with; there was no use in talking about it. In any case, how could eight or nine hundred men—that is, including the Annamite tirailleurs—be punished? Cæsar could decimate his legions —the day is gone by for such punishment; moreover, even if special soldiers were selected for trial by court-martial their comrades would surely have revenge on the officers, the sergeants, and the corporals. It is dangerous—take my word for it, very dangerous—to go too far with any regiment in any army. With us it would be even worse, for no one, not even the general in chief command, would be safe from our bullets if only a chance arose. I believe that we were at once the worst used and the most feared corps on the face of the earth.

Not long afterwards No. 4 Company and mine rejoined our comrades of Nos. 1 and 2. We parted from the zephyrs in a very friendly way; they told us that they liked us very much, and we paid them a similar compliment. Often afterwards we heard from other legionaries that a certain corps of zephyrs had shown them singular friendliness In a short time the story went round about the affair, and people began to understand why this battalion of zephyrs was so well able to get on with the soldiers of the Legion. Our fellows were good comrades to them, just as they were good comrades to ours. If the zephyr had money, the legionary had a share; if the legionary had money, the zephyr did not find himself without wine and tobacco and the other things that money procures. Frenchmen of other corps did not mind. After all, it was none of their business; besides, the zephyr as well as the legionary had a rather ugly camp reputation; both were too ready to fight with men of other regiments on the slightest provocation.

In a short time we received some recruits, and the four companies of the battalion were brought up to a fairly respectable strength. Every company now numbered more than two hundred men, and at long last promotion came in the ranks. The sergeant of my section had died of wounds soon after the little affair I have just mentioned. My corporal was promoted in his stead. It will be remembered that the corporal of my squad had given the first intimation to the captain that we were about to volunteer for active service; the captain now took the opportunity of rewarding him for bringing the joyful news. There were only two soldiers of the first class in the squad—Nicholas the Russian and I. Nicholas, as the older and better soldier, was offered

the rank of corporal.   He refused it, as was natural.
It was all right to become a soldier of the first class,
because that rank saved him from many disagreeable
duties, but the idea of one who had commanded a
company accepting the control of a squad and receiving curses and abuse from the company officers when
a soldier got into trouble was not to be entertained
for a moment.   The second chevron was then offered
to me.   I accepted it on the spot, and by none was
I more heartily congratulated than by Nicholas.   He
went further than mere compliments and good wishes:
he asked me if I wanted money to pay for some drink
and tobacco for the men.   Luckily, I had a few francs
saved out of my scanty pay, and so I was able to decline his generous offer.   At the same time I assured
him that, if I wanted the loan of money from any man,
I would rather be in his debt than in another's.   And I
paid him the further compliment—its truth pleased him
—that I was, indeed, corporal on parade but that he was
corporal in camp, and that I should find it hard to prove
superior rank to his in a fight.   I knew—everybody knew
—that Nicholas had more influence than any corporal or,
for that matter, than either of the sergeants.   He was
glad that I openly admitted it to him, and a more loyal
soldier never helped a sub-officer when help was really
needed than he.   I, probably the youngest corporal in
the army—not yet seventeen—had a more orderly and
well-disciplined squad than any other corporal in the
service.   Partly, I believe, this was due to my own desire
to give fair play to all the men, but chiefly, I know, to
the thorough-going way in which Nicholas supported
me in everything.   Every man under me felt that I
would do my best to screen him if he broke the regulations, to save him as much as possible if he were brought
before the captain or the commandant by sergeant or
sergeant-major.   Often I deliberately shut my eyes to
things that were wrong in themselves but dear to the
heart of the soldier, and one day I went so far as

warmly to defend before the captain a man charged by the sergeant-major with a serious military offence, though everybody knew that the man's sole claim to be helped by me was that he was a member of my squad. Nicholas told me that I had acted imprudently. "The sergeant-major," he said, "will be your enemy; but there is one consolation, the squad is more than pleased. The Austrian, however," he went on, "had no right to get himself into such trouble and, as it were, compel you to save him from the consequences of his own guilt. We will punish him; get permission to go outside the camp this evening, and leave him to us." I understood. I got permission to be absent for four hours—from seven in the evening until eleven. When I came back the Austrian was lying on the floor of the hut with a blanket thrown over him, dead.

"It was an accident, my corporal," said Nicholas.

"Yes; an accident," said a Belgian; "we did not mean to break his neck."

I examined the body. It was quite true that he was dead; already his jaw had fallen, and a coldness and rigidity had seized upon his limbs. I thought for a minute. The lights were out, only a feeble ray of moonlight shone through the door.

"Is there anything to be done?" said I to Nicholas.

"Yes," he replied; "if we are all true comrades."

The others swore that they would be loyal to the death; as for me, there was no need of asseveration: if I tried to save the men of the squad, it was sink or swim for me with all.

"Let us bring him out," said Nicholas, "and put him outside the camp. Then let nobody know anything of him save that he lay down at the usual hour. You, corporal, must say that he was present when you came in; I will give the rest of the evidence."

We had some difficulty in getting out the dead body, but when Nicholas had interviewed a sentry we managed the rest easily enough. We left it about two hundred paces from the camp, fully dressed, and with a bayonet in the right hand. In the morning the nearest sentry called out for the sergeant of the guard. He on coming up recognised the body as that of a French soldier. It was carried to the guard-hut, and there lay awaiting identification. I reported the absence of the Austrian when the sergeant came round, and soon afterwards I was ordered to go to the guard-hut. There I identified the body. All the squad and myself were examined about the matter. Nicholas was the only one who knew anything, and his story was that, lying awake at night, he had heard the Austrian getting up, and asked him was he unwell. The Austrian had said: " A little, not much; don't disturb anyone about me." He had then gone out, and Nicholas had fallen asleep. Everyone believed that he had left the camp to visit some female friend, and that he had been suddenly fallen upon by natives and beaten to death. Such a little thing was quickly forgotten, and we of the squad took particular pains to avoid even mentioning his name.

After this event the squad would do anything for Nicholas and for me. That was why it was so good a squad. Why, the captain looked surprised when a man of mine was brought up before him. Well, if I were good to them, they were good to me, and I had the pleasant consciousness that no man would try to shoot me in the back when the bayonets were fixed for the charge.

I kept aloof from the other corporals, and was rather distant with the men—that is, with all except Nicholas. To him I never hesitated to confide my thoughts, and many a time he gave me advice well worth the having. He had read much and had travelled and mixed constantly with men, and all the worldly wisdom he had gained was at my disposal; indeed, I often felt secretly pleased that the Prince, as we sometimes called him in his absence, was so frank and free with me. He had, I knew, been exiled by the Tsar, or at anyrate compelled by circumstances to leave his country. I knew of some things he had done—and they were guilty deeds —but he was so clever, so superior to us others in manner and bearing, so generous when he had money, and, best of all virtues in a soldier's eyes, so loyal to his comrades, that a far more experienced man than I might have easily fallen under his influence.

I shall have more to say of the Russian in the next chapter, and soon after that he will disappear for ever from these pages. I shall not anticipate, however, but let the tale unfold itself in its proper order, making but one more observation here—namely, that when the account of the last fight which I have mentioned went through the Legion, and I believe I may say through all the army, it, coupled with the story of the fight at Three Fountains, gave No. 4 Company and mine a most unenviable reputation. In a way this was good; nobody felt inclined to quarrel with us, and a most unusual calm and quietness prevailed in every camp where we lay. At the same time the generals gave us our fill of fighting—more than our share, indeed—but these things will come in their own place afterwards. And so I close this chapter—the chapter of the slaughter.

CHAPTER XIII

THE next important event of my life in Tonquin was the first battle of Lang-Son. This was, to put it bluntly, a defeat for our troops and a really creditable victory for our enemies. Of course, reasons are given by the beaten side for every mishap. "Rank bad luck," for instance, unknown and unforeseen difficulties of country, unsuspected numerical superiority of the victors —anything and everything except a fair and straight admission of an honest beating in open warfare. Now these are all nonsense. Why should a general talk of "rank bad luck"? If he ascribes a defeat to this, may not people fairly ascribe his victories to good luck, and that alone? As for saying that the lie of the land was not known, that is merely a confession of ignorance, and worse—of carelessness in using his mounted men and his scouts. That an enemy may succeed in massing a great number of men at a given point without the knowledge or even suspicion of his opponent is quite conceivable ; is it not what every general who knows his business tries to do? Read the history of any campaign and you will find that all the decisive actions were won by a swift and secret concentration of troops against an important place held by comparatively weak numbers. If I were a general, I should try to divide my enemy's forces and concentrate my own. Ah, when a man is beaten let him say so honestly ; let him point out, if he wishes, how his opponent out-manœuvred him ; and let him, in the name of all the gods, say nothing about luck, and, above all, be discreetly silent about anything that might hint at his own carelessness or the worthlessness of his scouts.

Now, let me try to show how our defeat came about. But first let me again say that the enemy beat us fairly and squarely in the engagement; that we retreated is good enough proof of that. Well, in the first place, the generals and the other officers firmly believed that the Black Flags and their allies would never be able to stand up against either our rifle fire or our charge. They had good reason, I admit, for assuming this. Unfortunately, they never reckoned on having to fight regular troops, officered and disciplined by Europeans, and it was these regular troops, well armed, well drilled, well led, and showing an amount of courage and staying power which one does not usually attribute to Asiatics, that drove us off the field. There were Black Flags and other barbarians in the fight, but these we could have easily first stalled off with the rifle and afterwards cut to pieces with the bayonet: it was really the men in uniforms who won the fight.

In the second place, we soldiers had learned to depend implicitly on our commanders. They had led us so well that we had as much confidence in their foresight and military skill as they had in our courage and steadfastness. The day before we were driven from Lang-Son no man even dreamt that our generals could be ignorant of anything occurring within a radius of a hundred miles; that a numerous and well-appointed army was within striking distance without their knowledge seemed, or would seem, if such a thing entered our minds, the fancy of a fool or the vain imagining of a coward. When the fight was going on we were surprised at the gallant manner in which our foes stood up against us. After a time, when more than once we had hurled them back with the bayonet, we recognised that we were dealing with the most formidable force that we had yet encountered. They gave us bullet for bullet, thrust for thrust. They were good men, and when the bayonets crossed they fought quietly and earnestly, and died without a murmur, almost without a groan. They could never hold out long against us in a charge—they were too light—and, another point to be noted, though the Asiatic will face death by the hands of the executioner with far more stoicism than the European, in the press of the battle the white man's enthusiasm is infinitely better than the yellow man's contempt of death. But in the firing they more than held their own, they were more numerous, their ammunition was evidently plentiful, and, to tell the plain truth, in spite of our bayonet charges they fairly shot us off the field.

To put the matter in a nutshell: we were defeated because our generals did not know the kind and the number of troops opposed to them. Let me add, our overweening confidence in our own prowess gave way to something very different as we saw ourselves slowly but surely forced back, and noted that the bayonet was not used to gain ground for a fresh advance but merely to drive back for a moment a too closely pressing enemy. At the same time it is but justice to admit that the defence was a good one. We retired, undoubtedly, but we showed no confusion beyond that certain amount that always shows on a battlefield, nay, even at a peaceful review.

I must now go on to my own part in the unlucky fight. After the first repulse my battalion had been constantly engaged in covering the rear of the retreat. On our right flank some French line regiment was busy in the same way. All the other troops, as far as I could judge—but a corporal sees very little of a battle outside the part borne in it by his own company—had been withdrawn, and were hard at work getting ready a new line of defence, while we who were just in front of the enemy kept them back in order to gain time. At last we could scarcely hold them at bay, and the order was given that our battalion should retire by companies. Nos. 2 and 4 quickly left the firing line; No. 1 was the next to leave, and my company poured in as hot a fire as we could until the order was given to run at top speed to the rear. I, as luck had it, had just loaded. I fired deliberately at a white man I saw about three hundred yards away cheering on the enemy, and saw him fall. I then turned and ran as fast as I could after my comrades. These were now some distance in advance, but as I went along I saw a good path leading slightly away from the point where the company would naturally fall into ranks again for another volley or two at the enemy and to allow the men time to regain their breath. This path, though slightly diverging from my route, at any rate would bring me away from the enemy, and I could, when at a safe distance from the Chinese, cut across country to rejoin my squad. I was running through rice-fields, and I knew that I could vastly increase my speed on the path. My one object at the time was to get away; I had no desire to fall, wounded or unwounded, into my pursuers' hands. I therefore turned and fled along the path, which ran by the side of a small stream.

As I ran, I noticed that the ground on the other side of the path gradually rose and at length formed a fairly high mound. This, however, I did not mind; every step took me further from the savages. I gradually slackened speed as my breath gave out, and instinctively flung away the cartridge, that I had fired at the white officer and put my hand into the pouch at my right side for a fresh one. Just as my thumb and forefinger closed on a cartridge, a sudden apparition met my gaze. I was rounding a corner, and there, not twenty yards away, was a Chinaman, evidently as astonished as I at the rencontre. I have never been so frightened in my life as at this totally unexpected meeting with an enemy in such a place. I had no power to take the cartridge from the pouch and fit it into the rifle. I was thunderstruck; I felt an awful horror of impending death. The Chinaman—he seemed a giant in my eyes —hastily tucked the butt of his gun into his right armpit and fired. I ducked instinctively, and at once

K

knew that he had missed. The awkward way he fired and the sudden movement on my part had saved my life. In a second I had a cartridge in the rifle and the rifle at my shoulder; the Chinaman dropped his weapon and fled. Now the pathway was quite straight and level for a distance of about two hundred yards. There was no means of making a hasty escape to one side or the other; on the right ran the stream, on the left stood up a mound about eight or nine feet high. I saw, therefore, that I could let my man go a good distance without firing at him. This I desired, for my rifle kicked a little. When he was about a hundred and fifty yards away I aimed carefully at the back of his knee, pulled the trigger, and probably took him fairly in the small of the back. He flung up his arms, reeled, and fell face downwards in the water, and lay there quite still. I was satisfied. I felt a natural and yet an unreasonable anger with the man who had sought to take my life—natural, because every man hates those who attack him; un-reasonable, because why should not he try to do to me as I should have tried to do to him were the positions changed? But soon my anger gave place to caution. I reloaded and clambered up the bank, de-termined to leave the path, as I could not know that other Chinese might not stop my way with better success than the first. After crossing through some low shrubs and brushwood the sound of volleys quickly repeated led me to the company. I fell into my proper place. Nobody said anything except the captain—a new man not with us a month—who sarcastically asked if I had seen a ghost.

We gradually fell back towards the new line of defence. The regulars attacking wasted no time, and pushed us rather rapidly along. At last a staff officer came with a message to our captain, and we hurriedly poured a heavy fire into the advancing enemy, then we all turned and ran towards the point whither the captain led us. We got a good start and covered the ground quickly; at a little line of small trees and underwood lay safety. As we straggled into this we were ordered to face about and lie down. We saw the Chinese regulars coming along with hoarse cries of joy, not extended in skirmishing order, but in dense masses of men, who pressed and struggled to the front.

A bugle call rang out, and suddenly a horrible rattle of musketry began. The enemy were fairly caught. Every rifle of ours was blazing away at about two hundred yards' range at the easy target they presented. In a moment, as it seemed to me, the attack withered away. Where a minute before were triumphant soldiers rushing in pursuit of a fleeing foe, one saw now nothing but prostrate bodies on the ground. Many, no doubt, flung themselves down as the first shots rang out, but the vast majority must have been swept into eternity by our fire. But this was not all. Our guns began, and even those who were a thousand yards away felt staggered in their advance. For ten minutes we heard nothing but the rattle of musketry, the booming of the guns, the noise of the shells as they hurtled through the air, and then the explosions a thousand yards away. The cries and shrieking of the wounded were unheard and unheeded. If the enemy had driven us from the field and could fairly claim a victory, we in the end taught them such a lesson surely as defeated never before taught their conquerors. That last firing more than equalised losses, and, better still, gave us the bitter-sweet of vengeance, and restored the old feeling of self-confidence that had been so rudely shaken on that day.

This was really the close of the battle. In various parts firing still went on, but an attack in force by either side was manifestly impossible. The Chinese regulars had been too much cut up towards the close of the fighting; as for us, there was only one course to be taken—retreat towards our base in order to prevent being outflanked. The new line of defence had served its purpose. It was not strong enough, nor were we numerous enough, to withstand an attack in force on the morrow, especially as our opponents were strong enough to hold us in front while flanking columns got round even to our rear. After an hour's rest, which we badly wanted, the order was given to retire, and for seven hours we struggled on, angry, weary and hungry. At last we formed a little camp; some rice and brandy were served out—we had no soup or coffee —and so, in bad humour with ourselves, the enemy, and our rations, we lay down on the ground to forget in sleep discomfort and defeat.

Luckily, the enemy did not press their advantage as they should. We were soon reinforced, and when we had recovered from the fatigue of the fight and the retreat, we again tried conclusions with them with better success. The story of the second battle of Lang-Son will be told in due course. I must now narrate an incident that occurred between the battles, while we were still retreating and somewhat pressed by the foe.

First, it must be understood that my battalion formed part of the rear-guard. There were French soldiers of several corps and native levies as well, and I may say here that the Frenchmen showed as much steady courage in retiring before overwhelming masses of the enemy as they usually show of gallantry and *élan* in a charge. I can never again believe that the Frenchman is good only when advancing; given capable officers, he is a perfect soldier at all points. This retreat proved the fact. We were half starved; there was the continual fear of being wounded and left to the merciless Black Flags; for all that, while the legionaries were furious and occasionally downcast, though doing their duty like brave men, the men of the line, the zouaves, the marine fusiliers, the chasseurs—and I believe the rear-guard had men of all these—were, after the first feeling of anger and disappointment, cheerful, making light of difficulties, almost gaily prophesying a speedy revenge.

Now one evening my battalion halted after a weary, heartbreaking tramp during the day. We had had little food, and that unsuitable, for some time. In my squad was a man whose country I have good reasons for not mentioning; suffice it to say that he came from a land lying on the eastern frontier of France. I shall call him Jean, though that was not his name. All the day he was saying: "Quelle misère, quelle misère!" until we were sick of the words, and I told him, rather roughly I am sorry to say, to keep his troubles to himself. When we came into camp great precautions were adopted to prevent surprise, and I may detail these so that everything may be quite plain. Moreover, they will show how careful our officers were.

Now, as I have often mentioned, a battalion has four companies. Normally a company has two hundred and fifty men, but at this time the strongest company of my battalion numbered only about a hundred and sixty. In the camp the battalion lay in square, so that each company had one side of the square to protect in case of attack, and had to furnish all the guards and out-lying pickets on that side. My company lay on the side nearest the enemy, or, as I should rather say, nearest the quarter whence an attack would most probably come.

When the company was halted and faced outwards, a corporal and his squad—say seventeen all told—were detached to furnish the inner sentries. Of these eight men were posted at intervals about fifty paces from the main body; the corporal and the eight reliefs lay half-way between them and the company. Thus every soldier was on sentry for two hours at a time, and then had two hours to rest as well as he could on the bare ground. This squad constituted the guard.

Now two squads with their respective corporals, having an officer or sergeant in chief command, formed the outlying pickets of the company or, if you wish, of one side of the square encampment. Half of each squad acted as sentries about seventy-five yards from the inner line of watching men ; between the two lines of sentries the reliefs of the outlying pickets rested. The sentries of the guard stood up, the sentries of the outlying pickets lay down; no glint of buckle or bayonet was allowed to show. It was next to impossible to surprise the camp, even if the darkness should prevent the outer line of sentinels from seeing the approach of an enemy, by placing their ears to the ground they could easily hear the tread of any considerable body of troops, and it would require a very considerable body of men to surprise effectively—that is, to annihilate—about six hundred good soldiers, who knew how useless it was to ask for quarter from such enemies. I hope I have made this matter clear: military men, I know, will understand, and I hope that others may be able to comprehend it too.

My squad was for outlying picket that night, and as it contained only fifteen men I had to borrow one from the corporal of the next squad for duty. This happened to be the one in which Le Grand was, and I asked for him. My request was granted, and Le Grand was attached for twelve hours to my little party. The sub-lieutenant of the company was in charge of the picket, and having led us out to our places he ordered the other corporal and me to post the first sentries. I posted eight men, amongst them Jean, who was still suffering from melancholy, and returned to the spot where the reliefs were to lie. Nicholas, Le Grand, and I lay near one another on the ground and began a whispered conversation in English, a language that the Russian spoke with great purity and ease. In the course of this I mentioned to Le Grand the strange way in which Jean had been speaking all the day, and Nicholas volunteered to tell us the poor fellow's strange story. I can only give the merest outline of it. I wish

I could tell it just as I heard it that night, but Nicholas was a born storyteller; indeed, he was clever in all things.

I must try to give it in my own words.

Jean had been a light cavalryman in the army of his own country, which bordered on France. He was, in his own words, a *mauvais sujet*, always getting into trouble. He could not resist the charms of female society, and many a dreary hour he passed in prison for staying away from his duties because he could not tear himself away from some newly-found angel. Things in the end came to such a pass that his life in barracks became unbearable, as his comrades had now turned against him. A cavalryman's horse must be attended to, and if the rider be absent his comrades have to do extra work. Now extra work is merely a cause of extra swearing when the proper man for the duty is ill or absent on leave, or even absent without permission once in a while, but when a man is continually staying out and then getting sent to cells the affair is altogether different. In no army will soldiers stand that. It is quite enough, men say, for each to groom and feed his own charger, but it is very unfair that a soldier, his own work done, should be ordered to do the work of another who is away enjoying himself or paying for his pleasure in the guard-room. So Jean had been rather roughly disciplined by his fellow-soldiers, and this punishment did him so much more good than any inflicted by the officers that for nearly two months he was a fairly steady soldier. Seeing this, the other fellows became again friendly with him, never, indeed, having borne malice, and only desiring that he should do his share of the work.

Well, one night a big gamble was carried on in the barrack-room. Some recruits had come in for training, and two or three of these were fairly well off. The old soldiers thought that card-playing would tend to a more equal distribution of the money, and preparations were accordingly made for a wakeful night. A few bottles of brandy and wine were smuggled in, and when all the lights were out blankets were judiciously placed over the windows, the lower edge of the door, and even the keyhole, so that by no accident might the game be interrupted. Then some candles were lit, and after the men had been cordially invited to drink, some game or other was begun, and, as was natural, the more equable distribution of the money began. Now Jean was a very good card-player, and the little pile of silver and coppers at his corner of the table steadily increased, and when the little party broke up at reveille, his head was heavy with sleep and his pockets with money. He got through the duties of the day as well as he could, and when evening came dressed to go out, just merely, as he said to Nicholas afterwards, for a walk and a glass of wine. Of course, he took all his money with him : that was an obvious precaution.

Soon after passing through the gate he met a lady whose acquaintance he had made some time before. She was pretty and clever, knew how to dress, and was by no means averse to the society of a handsome light cavalryman whose pockets were well lined and whose reputation for generosity in his dealings with the fair sex was so well established as our friend's.

The pair had ever so much to say to each other, and Jean admitted that he had a little money, sent to him by a rich aunt, he said, who would some day die and leave him a nice little property—oh, merely a few thousand shillings a year. (I use the word shillings as it gives no clue to Jean's country.) "How good she was !" said the pretty girl. "And I," she went on ; "oh, you would never guess what I am doing now." Jean guessed, and guessed, and guessed again. It was all no use ; he had to pay for a pair of gloves before his curiosity would be gratified. Then she told him that a certain rich bachelor, a Government official, had gone for a cure to some watering-place and had left her in sole charge of his domicile until his return.

"Oh," said Jean, "I guessed the rich man, and yet I had to pay for the gloves."

"True, my friend, very true indeed," she answered; "but you did not guess the visit to the baths, and is not that, my handsome fellow, the most important thing?"

There was no denying this. Surely it must rejoice youth and health to find age and pain so careful, so thoughtful, for self and others!

Jean was generous; he could well afford to be, as he had won a large sum, for a soldier; the girl, to give her her due, was not too exacting. An idyllic life was lived by both in the beautifully furnished house of Dives Senex for almost a week. Jean went out only at dark, and then merely for a walk around the unfrequented parts of the town for an hour. As he wore the old man's clothes, which fitted fairly well, there was little danger of his being recognised. At last the dreaded morning came when Jean should leave the house. He knew that sharp punishment awaited him at the barracks, but he had made up his mind to make a bold bid for liberty. This time he feared the anger of his comrades more than a court-martial, for he had been guilty of the unpardonable sin of winning money and spending it without the aid of the other troopers, while all the work of barrack-room and stable was left to them. He knew very well that the consequences would be ugly, and he determined to desert from his corps, more from fear of the squad court-martial than of the regular one presided over by an officer. Of course, his desertion was nothing— that is common in all armies—but Jean's plan of deserting was unique. I at least have never heard of a similar case.

Now the town in which Jean's regiment lay was not very far from the French frontier. At this place there was a debatable ground about a hundred yards wide, and on each side a line of sentries, French on the west, Jean's countrymen on the east. Jean had quite made up his mind to cross to French territory; he believed that, if he could only get there and get a few kilometres away from the frontier, the French authorities would not trouble themselves to capture him and send him back. Moreover, desertion, as I have already had occasion to mention, is not an extraditable offence. The difficulties were to get to the frontier, to cross it safely, and to travel some distance into France.

Well, Jean knew that at a certain hour that day his regiment would be out of barracks for cavalry drill. He also knew a way of getting into his quarters without passing any men of his own regiment on duty. An infantry guard lay at a certain gate. They would in all probability let him pass; he could then cross the infantry parade ground, go under an archway or through a gate—I am not quite certain about this— and enter the cavalry barracks. Once there he would act as circumstances required.

To make as certain as possible of passing the guard, he bought a blue envelope, put a sheet of paper inside, fastened the edges, and wrote the address of some high officer upon it, and then placed the seemingly official document between his belt and tunic. Anybody would thus mistake him for an orderly carrying a despatch, and so no one would think of interfering. Thus prepared he easily passed the infantry guard, nodding genially to some of the men, and made his way across the parade ground to the entrance to the cavalry quarters. Here he was in luck; no one was about except a couple of recruits doing sentry duty—one at the stables, the other about fifty yards away. Jean was not recognised by either, and, going to his room, put on his sword, and dressed himself as if for general parade. He then went down to the stables, saddled his charger, which was the only animal in the place, mounted, and rode back the way he came. Again he passed without suspicion the infantry guard at the gate, and soon found himself smartly trotting towards the frontier. He was in high spirits. Everything had gone so well, surely luck would not desert him now.

As he neared the frontier he trotted towards a guard-house on the side of the road. The sentry near the door looked carelessly at him as he came up, the sergeant did not condescend to come forward to meet him : he was evidently only a light cavalryman sent with some ridiculous message or other from the town. When only a few yards from the guard-house, instead of pulling up and delivering the blue envelope which he now held in his hand, he flung it on the ground, and driving the spurs into his horse's sides he passed the astonished sentry and galloped into the debatable land. A gap in the hedge allowed him into the fields that bordered the road. He heard as he went through the report of a rifle behind, but the sudden turn saved him. He now went towards the French line at a spot about equi-distant from two French sentries, and as he did so he lowered his head to his horse's neck. The French sentries also fired and missed. You can scarcely blame them ; their surprise must have been so great when they saw a presumably mad light horseman invading single-handed the sacred soil of France. In less time than it takes to tell Jean was through the second line of guards and careering wildly across country, taking hedges, streams and ditches like the winning jockey of the Grand National. A few scattered bullets whizzed about his ears, but rider and horse were untouched. He was now safe from the fire of his fellow-countrymen, and the French sentinels probably did not want to hit him ; his escapade, serious though it might be for the others, was only a good joke to them. Moreover, a private soldier must be very bad-minded indeed when he tries to shoot another private, though of a different army, who has evidently got into trouble and is seeking to escape. Certain things excite compassionate feelings amongst men of all armies—amongst the simple soldiers, I mean. As for the sergeants and corporals, the thoughts of the chevrons they have and those they hope for make them dead to all feelings of pity for a man in trouble.

After some time Jean began to feel somewhat at ease. He pulled up under cover of a small wood and began to consider his next move. If he could only get rid of the uniform he fancied he should be comparatively safe. This had to be done quickly, as he was not more than three miles from the frontier, and the French cavalry would soon be on his track. While he was thinking he glanced around to see if he were observed, and saw an old man, evidently of the farming class, looking at him with surprise. Jean determined to appeal for aid, and going towards the peasant frankly told his story. The peasant smiled at first and then laughed heartily.

"My good friend," said he, "take off the saddle and bridle and put them here," at the same time pointing to a place where the underwood was very thick. Jean did so, and the old man carefully concealed them.

"Now lead your horse by the mane to that field where you see the cows grazing, and return."

Jean obeyed.

"Now come to my house"—he pointed it out—"in ten minutes: no one will be within. You will find clothes on a chair, but be sure to take away again your uniform, belts and sword—they would be of no use to me; hide them where they will not be likely to be found."

Jean did as he was told. He found some old clothes on the chair just inside the door; on a table were some bread and milk. He drank the latter and pocketed the former when he had put on the disguise, and then flung all his military clothing and equipments into a stagnant pool. On that day he did not travel far, but found a secure hiding-place until the darkness should allow him to go his way in safety. During the night he tramped about twenty-five kilometres, keeping his eyes and ears on guard, but only once was he in danger. He heard the footfalls of horses at a distance and left the road. Two mounted gendarmes passed, and after a short interval Jean resumed his journey. At daybreak again he sought and found a hiding-place, and there slept for some hours. When he awoke he felt hungry and thirsty, and resolved to try to buy something at a farm-house that was visible about five hundred yards away. As Jean spoke good French he anticipated no difficulty on the score of language, and, having some silver in his pockets, there surely ought to be no difficulty in the way of obtaining supplies. When he went to the farmhouse he was met by an old woman, who at once pitied the tired wayfarer with the handsome face and the ragged clothes; she gave him bread and meat and a glass of wine, refusing all payment. She was so good and looked so trustworthy that Jean told her his story, omitting, however, all mention of women, and explaining that his desertion was due altogether to the tyranny of the officers. The good old woman pitied him the more for his sad tale; she even gave him a suit of fairly good clothing belonging to her son, at the time serving with his regiment. How the women of Europe love and honour the soldier and pity his misfortunes! There the army has hostages from all homes. She even pressed money on him, but this he refused to take. He had money enough in his pocket to carry him a good way towards Paris, and, even if he had to tramp a bit of the way, with his new clothing he felt independent and free from care.

In the end Jean entered Paris, and immediately volunteered for the Foreign Legion. At once he was accepted, and after a short time in Algeria was sent to Tonquin. There he was taken into my battalion, and handed over to me to help to make up the number of the squad. And now he was amongst us, calling out every moment the unlucky words: "Quelle misère, quelle misère!"

Nicholas took up a longer time in telling this story than I, but you must remember that the Russian was very clever and had the story at first-hand. I have only given the general outline; most of the details have been forgotten by me after so many years.

Well, at last the sub-lieutenant in charge of both squads of the outlying picket ordered the reliefs to be posted. I took Nicholas the Russian, Le Grand the Irishman, and six others of various nationalities to relieve the half-squad that had done sentry duty for the previous two hours. I remember I put Le Grand in place of poor Jean. When we—that is, I, the corporal, and the eight men relieved—came back to the lying-down place I dismissed quietly the men, of course only from duty, not from the place, and lay down on my back, shut my eyes, and began to muse. Almost before I felt it I was in a half-doze, when suddenly the report of a rifle caused me to jump up. As I opened my eyes I saw, so quickly did the alarm arouse me, the falling body of a man. I hurriedly called out the names of the reliefs—the men relieved were now the reliefs—all answered except Jean.

"I think, my corporal," said an Alsatian, "that he has shot himself."

The whole camp was roused; the sub-lieutenant ran down and called me to account for the alarm. I went over to the prone figure, passed my hand across the face, and found it at once warm and wet. Poor Jean, as we saw when dawn came, had blown away the top of his head. There was no enemy, it was true, but I fancy the legionaries did not sleep any more that night; a dead comrade in the camp is worse, a thousand times worse, than a living foe outside.

Now I won't moralise over this. Jean, as I have called him, was a good comrade, especially when he had money; he was fickle, but so were all, amongst the women; he chose to shoot himself, that was his business and not mine. And that is all that I, his corporal, have to say.

CHAPTER XIV

A LITTLE time after the suicide of Jean we found
ourselves in a position to attempt the recapture of
Lang-Son. We went forward cautiously, doing at most
ten kilometres a day. Then even at the end of a day's
march we were in fit condition for a battle, in case the
enemy elected to attack us in the evening or during the
night. As we again went forward our spirits rose. We
were extremely glad to have done with the constant
retirement in front of the enemy; of all things in the
world the most disheartening is a withdrawal after a
defeat. A victory means hard work, and a pursuit
harder, but a retreat is the hardest of all. I am not
speaking of the glory of victory or the disgrace of
defeat. Like most soldiers I think only of my private
troubles and the troubles of my comrades, and I can
assure the reader that, when a battalion is falling back
on the base, supplies are bad and insufficient, anxiety
on the part of all is heart-breaking, an attack in force is
always to be expected, and no one can safely say that
those who have beaten his side once may not do so
again and more decisively. Even in a pursuit, when the
rations are short, one feels that the enemy is suffering
more than himself, and the thought that the battalion is
pressing on their rear, giving them no peace or ease
or quietness, adds a zest to the bad and scanty food
which makes it palatable and satisfying. Let no one
run away with the idea that we simple soldiers did not
feel the sting of defeat—indeed, we felt it, and sorely
too—but while one can forgive himself for a disaster,
he finds it very hard to forgive the enemy for following
it up. It is bad enough to be driven off a stricken field;

it is infinitely worse to be harassed afterwards. War is like gambling: if you win first, even though you lose afterwards, you like to keep on playing the game; but if you lose in the beginning, you will at once imagine that the game is not worth the candle. The young soldier who in his first battle tastes the bitterness of defeat and endures the hardships of the hurried march, the wakeful rest under arms, the wretched food, the dirt and worse than dirt, the continual strain upon the nerves, and all things else which are the portion of the conquered, will see war divested of all its seeming glory; his voice at least will never be for war.

The Black Flags and their allies, the Chinese regulars, gave us very little trouble on our march towards Lang-Son. What little fighting did take place on the way cannot be described by me, as my battalion had nothing to do with it. Annamite tirailleurs with some French soldiers and legionaries formed the first line of the advance. They easily overcame all the opposition offered to them; it was only when the grand assault in force had to be made that we others came into the fighting line. While advancing rations again were both good and sufficient; occasionally too we got an allowance of wine or brandy, and these extra rations pleased us very much, for it is wonderfully easy to make soldiers happy. Our guards and pickets were just as well set and kept as ever—our officers were taking no risks—and God help the man of ours who slept at his post. We acquiesed cheerfully in this; and in any case we were so accustomed to exact discipline and perfect precautions against surprise that constant guard and picket-mounting seemed as natural as getting one's morning coffee or evening soup. Since we did not march much any day there was always a fairly long time in camp, and when we entered camp in the evening, the men who had been up the night before lay down and rested while the others, who had had, thanks to their comrades' watchfulness, a good night's rest, lit the fires and cooked the evening meal

L

and performed all the other duties that soldiers have to do in the field. This had a good effect upon all ; it was just as if one man said to another : "You watched last night while I slept in safety, I will now work while you rest in comfort and wait for your soup." The officers, I am sure, noted this and were glad : anything that makes soldiers better comrades tends also to make them better fighting men.

At last the day came when we were within striking distance of the enemy. All ranks were satisfied. We knew that very soon the disgrace of the last action would be wiped away, and we in the ranks were just as eager to clean the slate as our officers. I do not think that many were thinking of gaining promotion or distinction in the fight. The important thing was to show to all the world, or at least to that part of it which was interested in the campaign, that our reverse was but an accident of war and its effects only temporary. Again, we all desired satisfaction for the torments and annoyances of the retreat ; these were too recent to be easily forgotten.

The battle was begun, as usual, by the artillery. They, however, were not long the only men engaged, for very soon after the cannonade had begun the long lines of infantry were extended to right and left. My company was in the right attack, and we went gaily forward in skirmishing order until a man or two fell. Then we opened fire at a pretty long range at the place where the cloud of smoke told us that our friends the enemy lay. This firing did not delay the advance. On the contrary, it hastened it, for now we fired and ran forward, fired again and made another dash towards the front. Indeed, our officers and sergeants had a good deal of work to keep us from going along too quickly, and in the end we corporals were commanded to cease firing and to devote our attention exclusively to keeping our squads well in hand, so that the line might advance evenly and the men be brought up in sound wind and condition to the point where the bayonets would be fixed for the final charge. Of course, I know you will say that the corporals should have been doing this from the very outset, but it is very hard for a man to carry a rifle and cartridges without making some use of them. Why, I have seen officers, and those of high rank too, take the rifle of a dead man and half-a-dozen cartridges from his pouch in order to have the satisfaction of firing a few shots at the enemy. It is human nature, or rather the nature of soldiers in a fight; one likes to feel that he is doing something on his own account to help his comrades and to hurt the foe.

Well, the officers and the sub-officers worked well together, and the men, to give them their due, obeyed orders willingly, especially when the excitement of the first firing had passed away and they had settled down to the steady work of the advance. When we came within about four hundred yards of the entrenchments the rushes succeeded one another more rapidly, and men went a greater distance between shots. Thus we gradually approached, until finally we were all ordered to lie down and fix bayonets. As we did so the supports joined the fighting line—they were somewhat blown with the last race forward—and so we lay about eighty yards or less from the enemy's position, firing as quickly as possible. The Chinese regulars and the Black Flags were not remiss either in their volleys. A hail of bullets crossed the zone between us, but their fire slowly slackened, especially as a very storm of shells was falling towards their rear. Their supports, we saw, could not easily come up. At length the guns in our rear ceased shelling the position; at the same time the fire had greatly diminished in front. The commandant saw that the time had come, and at the sound of the charge we sprang up, ran at the regulation *pas gymnastique* towards the trenches, and, when about twenty yards away, rushed at the top of our speed, with the usual charging cry of "Kill, kill," at the fortifications, which had been already so badly damaged by the guns. In a few seconds we were in and using the bayonet with deadly earnestness and a grim determination to wash away in blood the memory of our recent defeat. The Black Flags flung down their weapons and ran out at the back of the entrenchments, but the Chinese regulars fought very well indeed. Well as the Chinese fought they could not long stand up against us. I have already mentioned that they are very light; indeed, I doubt if the average weight is much more than seven stone and a half. Then they can stand bayoneting without shrinking, but they are by no means quick in using the bayonet themselves; again, if a Chinaman gets you on the ground he will drive his weapon home six or seven times more than are needed, and will never notice your comrade coming along, quietly, with lowered head and levelled bayonet to attack. It seems to me that the Chinese go into a fight with something ugly to foreigners to meet, but altogether unlike what we Europeans call courage; they just go in, they kill, they are killed, and that is all there is about it. Yet they are not cowards; if they are, why did they not run like the Black Flags? And they will charge wounded men with spirit, if I may use the word in that connection; and with just as much steady calmness they will await the onset of the foreign devils when they rush the mound, get into the ditch and slay, and, not yet slaked with blood, rush out at the rear of the entrenchments with bloody bayonets, and loot and murder and rapine in their minds.

We got in, and in a few moments not a man was left standing up in the trenches. We looked around. What was the next thing to do? " No. 1 Company, remain here," shouted the commandant as he tried to staunch the blood that ran down the left side of his face from an ugly sabre slash on the temple; "the other companies advance." We three companies got out at the rear of the field fortifications and awaited orders again. "Go up that hill, captain"—this to my captain from the commandant—"and help the soldiers of the line to carry it." "Yes, my commandant," said the captain. We turned towards the right and looked at the little hill. It was about three hundred yards only from level ground to crest; the top was fortified, but only slightly; the soldiers of the line were half-way up on their side, but they were meeting with a very gallant resistance. The rifles above showed no signs of slackening; a heavy, dense smoke covered the crest of the hill; midway down you saw the spirts of flame and little smoke clouds where the French were going up. That smoke quickly disappeared, for the men never fired twice in the same spot. We ran at first up the hill, and were not noticed; very soon we went more easily, as the hill grew steeper and the rifles above began to pay us attention. Then we fired upwards in return, but our bayonets were fixed, and we knew very well that in these alone lay any chance of success. How could we hit men above us whom we could not see? It was impossible, but we could, and did, send bullets so near their heads that aiming down was almost as fruitless for them as aiming up was for the soldiers of the line and ourselves.

As we went along an officer ran up almost to the top, waving his sword, and crying out to the men to follow. We went a little more quickly. Just as he reached a point about ten paces from the outer face of the entrenchments he fell, shot through the heart. A great cry arose from us; we sprang up, disregarding all cover, and madly raced for the summit of the little hill. Volley after volley was fired at us, but with little damage. Take my word for it, when the Asiatic sees the European charging with bayonet on rifle-barrel his aim is not quite so good as usual, and in any case his best is not much. So we rushed, and when we came to the little fortification we had small difficulty in getting in; by that time the French soldiers of the line had crowned the height on their side and were over the entrenchments. We were almost shoved back by the fugitives running from the Frenchmen, but we steadied ourselves and gave them the bayonet, until at last they were all down, and the soldiers of the line and the legionaries alone stood facing one another on the little hill with ugly curses and bloody steel. Not that they cursed us or we them; only when you are using the bayonet, and for a while afterwards, your language is a real reflex of your thoughts.

It was the Frenchmen who really carried the hill; we had only come in towards the end to their assistance. So we left them on the ground that they had so gallantly won, and, going down the side nearest the remnants of our opponents, we looked for more work more excitement, more glory, and more revenge. And we found them all very soon.

We had scarcely reached the bottom of the hill when a crowd of Chinese regulars, with some Black Flags who had not run away, charged us with loud cries and imprecations. We met them fairly and squarely, and pushed them at the point of the bayonet a few yards back. They were reinforced, and by sheer weight of numbers made us for a time give way. Our officers fought like devils; truth to tell, though we did not like them, we could not help admiring their courage in a fight. The captain was down, so was the sub-lieutenant, the lieutenant had been wounded at the beginning of the battle; the one sergeant who was left took up the command and led us back from a short retreat in an ugly rush against the enemy. I saw a Black Flag carrying a standard in his left hand, while he cut all around at our fellows with the sword in his right. I determined to have that flag, or at least to make a bold try for it, and went with levelled bayonet at the barbarian. He cut down a man of ours as I came, and had not time to parry my thrust with his sword, and failed to do so with the staff of the banner. He took the point fairly in the left side, and I had only just time to get my weapon back when he delivered a furious slash at my head. Receiving this on the middle of the rifle-barrel I thrust a second time, and sent him fairly to the ground. Reversing my rifle—that is, holding it at the left side instead of the right—I stabbed straight down, and pinned his right hand to the ground. Pressing then on the rifle with my left hand, so that he could not free his sword arm, I plucked away the banner with my right. Nicholas at the time shouted out: "Look out, corporal, look out." And, looking up, I saw half-a-dozen Black Flags coming straight at me. I flung the banner on the ground, pulled my bayonet out of the savage's hand, and, just in time, got into a posture of defence. The first man I stopped with a lunge in the face just between the eyes, but the others would have killed me were it not that now the squad came to my assistance. Nicholas and the others soon finished the half-dozen who had attacked me, but others came up too, and very soon about a dozen of us were desperately resisting a desperate attack. They outnumbered us by about four to one, but we were heavier, steadier, and, above all, quicker with the bayonet. All the same, man after man of ours went down till half our number lay dead or dying on the ground. Luckily, Le Grand noticed our difficulty and, calling together six or eight men of his own squad, came to our assistance. Le Grand and his comrades took the Black Flags in the flank; the new assailants overwhelmed them; they gave way sullenly at first, but in the end broke and fled, leaving more than half their number on the field. I was happy in retaining the banner, but I almost at once learned how dear that banner was to me. A cry from Le Grand made me turn round, and I saw Nicholas lying on the ground and a wounded Black Flag cutting at him with a sabre, while the poor Russian did his best to ward off the blows with his hands. As I looked, a Spaniard of Le Grand's squad drove his bayonet up to the rifle-muzzle three times in quick succession into the body of the wounded savage who was trying to kill our good comrade. I ran to Nicholas and, laying down rifle and captured flag, asked him how he felt, was he badly wounded, and without waiting for an answer began to bind his wounded arms and hands. He shook his head sadly.

"It is no use, my comrade; I have got worse than that."

Indeed he had, for his left side was torn open. Nicholas nodded his head towards a dead Black Flag, and we saw at once the weapon that had inflicted so horrible a wound. It was shaped somewhat like a bill-hook, but could be used for thrusting as well as cutting, about four inches of the end being shaped like a broad-bladed knife, the remainder of the steel rather resembling a narrow-bladed hatchet. The poor Russian, in spite of the severe wound, had managed to kill his enemy. I am glad he did so, for, had the barbarian been only wounded, I should have been sorely tempted to finish the work, and though one may kill a helpless man without pity when " seeing red " or to avenge a friend, yet afterwards the thought of such slaughter is unpleasant. After some time we stopped the bleeding, and were glad to be able to give him a good long drink, and then to refill his own water bottle with the few drops still remaining in the bottoms of ours. We left him only when we had to rejoin the company. The sergeant who now commanded it asked me gruffly where I had been. I showed him the captured banner, and in a few words told of the desperate fight made by the Black Flags to regain it. He seemed satisfied, and asked how many men I had lost.

" Nine," I replied.

He counted us, and said : " Nine lost and nine left; that is rather serious ; a banner is not worth so many men."

But you may be sure that it would have been worth a whole section in the sergeant's eyes, had he taken it.

There was little more fighting to be done that day. All along the line the French had been successful, and already linesmen, chasseurs, zouaves, legionaries, and tirailleurs were bivouacking in Lang-Son. My battalion searched out its wounded and brought them to an appointed spot; you may be sure that poor Nicholas was carried as gently as possible to the place. I went back for him before I thought of looking for anyone else, even an officer. He was lying quietly where we had left him, and I found that already he had drunk all the water in the bottle. Luckily, as I was going back, I passed the dead body of a white officer of our opponents; he was dressed in a yellow tunic and trousers, with tan boots; his white helmet lay a foot or so from his head; a heavy, fair moustache curled outwards on both cheeks; his jaw had fallen, and his wide-open blue eyes were staring upwards at the sky; at least a dozen gashes showed red upon the body, and a bloody sword in one hand, an empty revolver in the other, were evidence that his death had been amply paid for. A white man fights well when he knows that there is no quarter for him. Luckily, as I have said, I came across this body, for slung round the right shoulder and resting at the left hip was a leather bottle. I took this, and was glad to find that it was more than half full of brandy and water.

"A share, corporal," said a comrade.

"No," I answered; "all for Nicholas."

"Pardon me, corporal; I forgot."

Nicholas thanked me with a glance and a nod. With some rifles and a couple of greatcoats we made a fairly good litter, and bore him to the quarter where the surgeons were working in their shirt sleeves. There we left him with the attendants and went out to bring in others. When I was leaving the hospital, if I may call it so, for the last time, as every wounded man had been brought in, Nicholas beckoned to me. I went over, and he whispered:

"I am dying. I make you the heir to all I possess. Very little—but still all; here it is."

He pressed a small bag into my hand. I said:

"Not at all, good comrade; you will want it when you recover, or at least to get better attendance and a few delicacies in hospital."

"No, my friend; I am leaving *la gamelle*. Take it and I shall be pleased. Try to see me in the morning; to-morrow evening it will be too late."

He forced the little bag again into my hand. I had to take it, but I resolved to see him in the morning and to return it if he were still alive, though I could not help feeling an ugly presentiment that my poor friend was really dying and that the best friend I had in the little world of the Foreign Legion was about to leave me for ever.

After soup had been served out to all the men the sergeant, who still commanded the company, told me that I was wanted at the hospital. I, thinking only of Nicholas, said that I should go thither at once.

"Do you know, corporal," said he, "where it is?"

"Certainly, yes," I answered. "Did I not help to bring many wounded there to-day?"

"Of whom are you thinking?" he asked.

"Nicholas, the prince, you understand. Do you not remember Three Fountains?"

"Very well—too well, indeed," the sergeant replied; "but it is not the Russian who desires to see you, it is the captain." Calling to a hospital attendant passing at the time he inquired if the man were going to the officers' hospital. He was not going there, but would pass it on his way to his own destination.

"Go with him," said the sergeant to me; "he will show you the place. Ask for our captain."

I went away with the hospital orderly, and was shown the officers' hospital quarters by him. On giving name, company, and battalion—they saw my rank upon my sleeve—I was told to wait until the surgeon-in-charge could be told that I wished to see a patient. Very soon the surgeon came. He asked me quite abruptly whom I desired to see. I told him with military directness, but respectfully, and he said that I might be brought to where the captain lay. I went there with an orderly. The captain had a wound on the right arm not of much account; it certainly did not keep him in hospital, but, as he had been knocked down and stunned by a blow of a musket-butt on the left temple, the surgeons would, and did, detain him for awhile. Several times while I was with him he put his hands to his head and swore a little. But, of course, that was none of my business. He asked me about the banner I had taken—"not, you must remember," said he, "that that was very useful or very creditable."

I told the story, and especially laid stress on the facts that poor Nicholas had warned me of the first attack and that he was now dying in the simple soldiers' hospital.

"You are sorry?" he queried.

"Very; he was my good comrade."

"Had he much money?"

"He gave me all." And I showed the little bag.

"How much?"

I counted, and replied:

"One thousand four hundred and fifty francs, twenty or thirty piastres."

"You are rich."

"My captain, he will share with me if he lives, and if he dies I am the poorer by a friend."

"Pouf! a sergeant does not want friends amongst the simple soldiers."

"No, my captain, nor enemies; but I am not a sergeant."

"You are; the commandant will announce it to-morrow. He was with me an hour ago."

"Thanks, my captain; I did not see a ghost this time."

"Ah, you remember! What made you look so pale that day?" I told him, and his only remark was:

"It might have frightened a man, and you are only a boy. How old are you?"

"Oh, in truth," I said, "not yet seventeen."

"But you are over eighteen in the records."

"That, my captain, is my official age."

"Very well, very well; it has nothing to do with me."

After awhile the captain said:

"Who was Nicholas? What was he?"

I answered truly that I did not know—that nobody knew—that he had often plenty of money, and was a good comrade.

"We could not fail to see, my captain," I went on, "that he had been in a high position once; there is, indeed, a story that he commanded a company of Russian guards at Plevna, but no one knows with certainty. He did not tell, and we did not like to inquire." Then I asked the captain for permission to leave the company for half-an-hour in the morning.

"Why do you ask that?"

"I want to see Nicholas; he will be disappointed if I do not go to see him."

"Perhaps he will be dead."

"I think not so."

"Perhaps he will ask for his money."

"I mean to offer it to him."

The captain smiled, and said:

"You are a strange legionary; you do not care for money."

"On the contrary, my captain, I do like money and what it buys; but Nicholas is my friend."

"You may go; stay away an hour if you like. Tell the sergeant that I, the captain, have given you permission."

"A thousand thanks, my captain."

After some further questions and answers the captain ordered me to go. I saluted, and was just turning to leave when he called me back. Pointing to a cigar-box on a rickety table, he told me to give it to him. I did so. He opened it and took out two cigars.

"Give that to monsieur the prince, with his captain's compliments, and keep this for yourself. Tell him, sergeant"—he laid stress upon the word—"that I am sorry for his misfortune and proud to have had such a man in my company. Say to him exactly what I have said to you."

"Yes, my captain," I answered, saluted again, thanked him for the cigars, and went away. Let me say here, though it does somewhat anticipate events, that the captain was my good friend afterwards, and more than once broke my fall when I got into trouble. The death of Nicholas deprived me of a good comrade. By it I gained a friend in a higher position, but I would any day have surrendered the captain's good will if by so doing I could regain the companion of the barrack-room and the canteen.

When I got back to the company, I reported my return at once to the sergeant. He asked me what the captain wanted me for, and I told him that the officer had questioned me about the affair of the banner and about Nicholas. I said nothing of the money or the cigars.

"Did he tell you anything?"

"Yes; he said that I was to be sergeant to-morrow."

"Indeed," said the sergeant.

"I suppose, sergeant, I may thank you for a favourable report about to-day's fight."

"I only told the truth," said the sergeant, "and I always liked you when I was corporal of the squad."

Then I told him about the captain's permission to me to absent myself for an hour in the morning so that I might pay a visit to Nicholas.

"You must tell that," he replied, "to the sub-lieutenant in charge; an officer has been sent to us from another company."

"Very well," said I. "Where is he?"

He brought me to the sub-lieutenant's quarters. I told the officer of my permission; he was satisfied. Before I went he asked about the captain's wounds and a few questions of curiosity about Nicholas. I told him all I knew about the captain and almost nothing about my comrade. As I was leaving, the sergeant drew my attention to the fact that I had omitted speaking about my promotion.

"You captured a flag, you say?"

"Yes, sir; and there was a hard fight to retain it."

"And the commandant will promote you sergeant to-morrow?"

"Monsieur le capitaine said so, sir."

"Very good, very good; somebody must be sergeant, I suppose, and why not you as well as another? You may withdraw."

As we went away I asked the sergeant if there were any place where I could get a drink of wine or brandy.

"Certainly, yes—if you have money, my comrade."

"Come then," I said, "let us go there together."

He brought me to a small hut, where I had to pay a stiff price for his brandy and my wine, and when he saw that I had plenty of money he unbent and congratulated me more than once on my promotion. He ended by borrowing twenty francs, which I willingly lent; of course, he forgot to repay me.

The next morning on parade the commandant praised me a little and ordered me to take over the duties of No. 1 section. The sergeant who had borrowed the twenty francs from me the day before was appointed sergeant-major, and the corporal of a squad of No. 2 was made sergeant of that section. When we were dismissed, I reminded the new sergeant-major of my permission to visit Nicholas. He remembered the money I had shown the evening before and promptly brought me up before the sub-lieutenant in temporary command of the company, in order that I might report my intention of taking advantage of the leave given me by the captain. The sub-lieutenant offered no opposition. As I was going away the sergeant-major, no doubt remembering that I was comparatively rich—that is, rich for a sergeant of legionaries—told me that he would take care that my section was all right during my absence.

"Many thanks," I said; "perhaps monsieur le sergent-majeur would wet the promotion in the evening."

"But yes, but yes, with pleasure. Do not hurry, you will be back in good time; sometimes the sergeant-major is a better friend than a simple sub-lieutenant." He was right, and we both knew it.

I went across as quickly as I could to where the field hospital for the wounded of the right attack lay. I had little difficulty in finding Nicholas; he visibly brightened at seeing me, and, when I tried to shake hands, he put his finger on my sleeve, where the single gold chevron was that a sergeant of a section wears.

"It pleases me," he whispered; "but don't be too ambitious, other men have lost all through ambition."

I said nothing. I was glad that he was pleased, but I cannot tell how sorry to see him weak, worn out, and, as one may say, with the dews of death already gathering on his forehead. He could not speak, even in a low tone, he could only whisper; I had to bend down to catch his words.

He asked about a few men of the squad, and I told him who were dead, who dying, who still in the ranks. He was anxious too about Le Grand, and was very glad to hear that the latter had gone through the fight without even a scratch, though he had had one narrow escape.

"Le Grand," I said to Nicholas, "had to take a dead man's helmet."

"Why, why?" he eagerly whispered.

"Because his own was cut in two by a sabre-stroke. Had the cut been downwards, Le Grand would be alongside you to-day."

"I am glad he escaped so well; I like him."

After a little more conversation I was told that my visit must end.

"Who is chiefly with you, Nicholas?" I asked.

He nodded towards an attendant. I went to this man and gave him a hundred francs.

"Be good to my comrade," I said.

"Yes; yes," he replied, astonished at such a gift from a mere sergeant of legionaries; "I will do all I can, but that, alas! is little."

"I know," I answered, "there is no hope; but smooth the way for him as well as you can to Eternity."

He promised with many oaths that he would do so. I don't know whether or not he kept his word, but I really do think that the unexpected money, and still more the unexpected amount of it, made him a good friend to the last to my poor comrade.

So Nicholas the Russian passes out of my story. I never saw him afterwards, for that evening my company left Lang-Son for an outside station about ten miles from the place. Some time afterwards a legionary of No. 2 Company told me that he had been in hospital with Nicholas, and that the Russian had died about four o'clock in the afternoon of the day I visited him, and was buried in the evening of the same day. He is out of the turmoil of the world now, and I wonder, had he in early youth understood life as he learned it in the Foreign Legion, would he have "played the game" in the same way? One never knows. Perhaps he would have lived and died that wretched nonentity, the respectable member of society—the Pharisee who has neither courage to do evil nor heart to do good—but who lives his life out in constant endeavour to equate God and the devil, to balance, for his own benefit of course, his duty to his fellow-man and his so-called duty to himself; perhaps he unknowingly thought at the end as the Dying Stockrider spoke:

" I've had my share of trouble, and I've done my share of toil,
  And life is short, the longest life a span,
I care not now to tarry for the corn or for the oil
  Or the wine that maketh glad the heart of man.
For gifts misspent, and chances lost, and resolutions vain
  'Tis somewhat late to trouble : this I know—
I would live the same life over if I had to live again,
  And the chances are, I go where most men go."

Anyway, whatever he was to others, he was good friend and good comrade to me, and if no one else regrets, I regret.

Amice mi, vale, vale, vale!

M

CHAPTER XV

ONE evening the sergeants and corporals were ordered to forewarn the men that the battalion would leave the neighbourhood of Lang-Son early the following morning. Where we were going we did not know; indeed, I believe that even the commandant himself was unaware of our destination when he ordered the battalion to hold itself in readiness for a march. When the morning parade had been inspected—we, of course, paraded in full marching order—the commandant ordered us to stand at ease. While thus waiting in the ranks, an officer of the staff came and gave a written paper to the commandant. Shortly afterwards the staff-officer went away, and we were marched off in column of fours for some place or other, where, we—sub-officers and men—knew not, nor did we care. Restlessness is the chief characteristic of the soldier; he stagnates in garrison, or, if he doesn't, he avoids *ennui* by illegitimate amusements—excitements, I should say, that sooner or later get him into trouble.

I am ashamed to confess that I was as happy as the others as we tramped along. Of course, I was sorry for Nicholas, and as I spent the money he had left me with the other sergeant and the sergeant-major of the company, I felt that all the fun and gaiety that money can produce cannot make up for the loss of a good comrade. I took care to do as Nicholas would wish me towards my late associates, the corporals, and my former associates, the simple soldiers—they were not forgotten when the money was spent. Of course, I did not go outside my section, and I took good care that my former squad, the squad I had soldiered in ever since I was sent from the depot to a battalion, first as soldier of the second class in the little trouble with the Arabs in Algeria, in the big trouble at Three Fountains, in the troopship, at Noui-Bop; then as soldier of the first class till the end of the vengeance at a place I have not named—you may be sure it gets scant mention in the official records; then as corporal in the defeat at Lang-Son and the retreat afterwards, and at the second battle, when we recaptured the town:—oh no, I did not forget the men who were what Xenophon would call my table-companions; for their part, they thanked me but little, but we all understood.

There is no use in detailing our life for the next few weeks. We were always marching, now to the north, anon to the west, then a sudden turn to east, perhaps, or south or back towards the north again. It was all one; we looked for the enemy; we did not find him. At last a momentous order came for us. We were much reduced in strength, and the general commanding-in-chief determined to send most of the battalion to the sea coast and, if the doctors should recommend, back to Algeria. I don't think that we mustered six hundred of all ranks at the time, possibly we did not exceed five hundred. When I tell you that we were constantly receiving batches of fresh men—almost every troopship brought out a hundred or two hundred soldiers of the Foreign Legion—you will be surprised at this; but then the country is bad for Europeans, and we were always in the fighting line of the battles and on tramp here, there, and everywhere between them. Anyway, the commandant asked for volunteers to form a company to be left behind, and officers as well as men were asked to come forward.

"First," said the commandant, "I want a captain."

All the captains stepped out. He selected mine. I forgot to state that my captain had been sent back to duty, as soon as the surgeons found that the blow on the head had produced only temporary ill-effects.

"Now," said the commandant, "a lieutenant."

Forward stepped every officer of that rank. The sub-lieutenant—now a lieutenant—who had come out with my company, the *vieux militaire* who had risen from the ranks, the man who was good at fighting and better at pillage, the man who could overlook much if you were a good looter and handed him over a decent percentage of your gains, the man with the piercing eye, the hooked nose, the spike-like grey moustache was taken on the spot. I believe this selection gave the old soldier immense pleasure. "Ah," I can fancy him saying to himself, "the commandant knows better than to take boys fresh from school." Everybody under forty was to him a boy fresh from school, except, be it noted, Nicholas. He did not understand Nicholas, but he was too old a soldier, too experienced in the Legion, not to know the ruined nobleman, the dangerous man, when he met him. A sub-lieutenant was selected in turn, a mere boy who had been sent to us for some little peccadillo, some little indiscretion, probably in connection with a senior officer's wife. Then a sergeant-major was taken, an Alsatian from No. 3. The sergeants were now called on for volunteers, and, just as we all stepped forward, a French officer of chasseurs approached the commandant to speak with him.

"Select your own sergeants and corporals, captain," the commandant cried out to my captain; "the doctor will select the men, for I assume that all will volunteer."

The captain promptly selected the two sergeants of his own company. I was delighted. I, a boy of less than seventeen, as the captain knew, though in the records of the battalion I was approaching nineteen, found myself senior sergeant of a company that was evidently to be a separate unit for some time. How I mentally thanked the officer of chasseurs for his timely intervention, for I felt sure that the commandant would not have selected me. The corporals were quickly chosen, as the captain took all his own corporals who had not been seriously wounded and who did not show signs of breaking down, the others were taken by him from corporals of other companies after a hasty walk down the line of volunteers. He was a clever man, that captain of mine; all the outside corporals he selected were fair-haired. I have already mentioned that such men can stand hardships better than the black-haired ones.

When the commandant had finished his chat with the chasseur, he said:

"All men in the front ranks"—we were drawn up in column of companies—"that wish to volunteer, step one pace to the front; all men in the rear ranks that wish to volunteer, step one pace to the rear. March."

All stepped forward or backward, as the case might be; the commandant went down the right flank and saw all the companies opened out.

"Very well, *mes enfants*, since you all volunteer, the doctor will make a selection."

The doctor examined every man. As he marched down the ranks he cast out almost half, one glance told him that these could not be accepted, wounds and disease and semi-starvation and hardship had worn them out; the rest he carefully examined in the afternoon, and, to cut the matter short, next morning the commandant and other officers and other sub-officers and other soldiers said good-bye to a fairly strong company—we were more than two hundred and twenty all told—and started on their march to the coast. We felt sad as our comrades went away. In twenty-four hours we had forgotten them, as, undoubtedly, they had forgotten us. Wrong! you say; well, the soldier who can't forget will die of brooding over his memories.

In a day or two a few Annamite tirailleurs and eight or ten French engineers had came into camp. The chief officer of the tirailleurs brought a message for our captain, and in accordance with this we pushed forward about seventy or eighty miles and seized a strong position, right, as one may say, in the heart of the enemy's country. This we proceeded to fortify, the engineers superintending, the legionaries working, and the Annamites out on all sides to give us notice of any movements against our little post on the part of our foes. These, however, allowed us to finish the little fortification in peace; once it was finished, we cared not a jot for them. We had brought along a good deal of supplies; more of every kind that the country produced were collected from all sides; ammunition was plentiful, so why should we care?

This was my captain's first separate command, and he had a nice little force to help him to keep the post. First, there were the legionaries, two hundred and twenty seasoned soldiers; then about a hundred and eighty native levies under French officers; last, a really admirable demi-squad of engineers. No artillery, of course; but who wants artillery when he has enough of rifles? My captain did not, and he was really a clever man. Not that guns and gunners have not their uses—oh, they have—but they are wanted with brigades and divisions for big battles; they are useless, they are worse than useless, to small parties on the trail of the enemy or holding some out-of-the-way position which may have to be abandoned at a minute's notice. In a retreat, when you are burdened with guns, one or two things must be done—destroy the artillery, and so produce a bad effect on the men; keep it, and by so doing slow down your march in swampy ground. We were all glad that no guns had been sent to us. We were quite confident that we could maintain our ground with the rifle alone; then, if we really had to withdraw, we felt more confident of cutting our way through with steady bayonet fighting than if we had to depend on the spasmodic assistance of artillery in a retreat.

When the little fortification was finished to the satis-faction of the captain and the sergeant in command of the engineers, the little force was divided into four parts. Every part had a special duty every day. If No. 1 were employed guarding the camp for the twenty-four hours, No. 2 would be out in the day gathering stores of all kinds and getting information; No. 3 would be cooking and doing the other work of the camp, except guarding it; and No. 4 would be quietly resting. Thus every part had three days' work for one day of rest, but, be it well understood, every man was on guard-duty only one night in four. Every party, I may mention, had one-fourth of the legionaries and one-fourth of the Annamite tirailleurs. As for the engineers, they examined the fortifications every day, and did nothing then but cook and eat, mend and wash their clothing, and lie about and smoke. The officers commanding the parties were the lieutenant and the sub-lieutenant of the legionaries, the lieutenant and the sub-lieutenant of the native levies, while the captain exercised a general supervision over all, especially the entrenchments, the engineers, and the stores.

Things went on well and pleasantly for some time. In fact we were all getting tired of the monotony—that is, all except the Annamites, who were quite satisfied—and we sergeants and corporals especially were desirous of some excitement. This we got, and in full measure. That everything may be understood I must give a brief description of the post—the fortified encampment I may call it.

The main post was almost rectangular in shape, but a little way out from one corner stood a block-house, its nearest angle pointing towards an angle of the fort. This block-house was built with the intention of protecting the portion of the camp nearest to it, and also in order to prevent the enemy from taking up a commanding position within less than half musket-shot of our quarters. Furthermore, it dominated a spring from which a stream flowed in close proximity to the main fortification. This was very necessary, for the Black Flags have no compunction about poisoning "foreign devils." The block-house had two storeys, and was generally occupied by about twenty men, detached, of course, from the party on guard for the day. It was rather exposed on the two sides away from the main position, but being well and solidly built no one dreamed that it could ever be in any great danger. Well, it was; but that came afterwards, and will be dwelt on in due course. As for the big position being in danger, everyone scouted the thought. Ah, it's well for men that they are generally fools!

Well, the time came at last when the Black Flags came to visit us. The first token of their arrival in force was given by the cutting off of a squad of Annamite tirailleurs; the second, firing at long range on a party of legionaries; the third, the burning of a couple of villages. I suppose they thought that the people in these hamlets were friendly to us; they were, indeed, friendly, but so they would have been to any men who carried arms. The poor people who remain quietly at home and take no part in fighting always suffer most. We took their property and paid them for it, at least our officers did; the Black Flags came, took their money, their women, and often their lives, and then set fire to their wretched habitations. In war both sides live very much, if not altogether, on the country. You can imagine how pleasant that is for the cultivators and others who seek to continue the occupations which can be profitable only in time of peace. Well, cowards sow and brave men reap.

After the burning of the villages we scouted much more cautiously. Up to the first appearance of the Black Flags the Annamites were often by themselves, but afterwards we never went in smaller parties than thirty, of whom two-thirds were legionaries. So long as we had the natives, we could not very well be surprised; and so long as they had us with them, they knew that they would not be asked to bear the brunt of the fighting, if the enemy only showed himself in force.

One day I was in command of a small party that cautiously felt its way towards the north-east, where a village had been seen burning the night before. I had two weak squads of my section and a dozen natives, in all we were about thirty-five rifles. As we went slowly on, the corporal of the tirailleurs gave me to understand that there was danger ahead. I did not thank him for the information—I knew as much myself—but, as the ground was fairly open, I determined to push on a little farther. At the same time I took the precaution of sending a couple of men to reinforce the little party guarding each flank, and four to the corporal of legionaries who commanded the advance-guard. Scarcely had these soldiers reached their respective destinations, when heavy firing began in front, followed almost at once by scattered shots on the right. The Annamite tirailleurs came back at once, the legionaries did not retreat so quickly; they fired as they retreated, and showed no signs of panic. I steadied the natives by telling them very plainly that the man who moved without orders would be at once shot. When they understood this, they stood up to their fight fairly well.

As the outlying squads closed on my command, I asked the corporal who had led and the legionary of the first class who had commanded on the right, what they thought of the attack. The corporal said it seemed serious; the soldier of the first class, that we ought to move off to the base at once, as many men were trying to creep round to our rear. Now both of these might be depended on. The corporal was a man of much service; the other a Prussian who had found life in his own country too exciting, but who was a good soldier in all respects on active service; in garrison, of course, it was different. I fell back, therefore, showing a bold front, keeping the Annamites and six legionaries together—the latter to hold the former—and leaving all the other legionaries to fight in skirmishing order as we went away. A few of ours were wounded, and these the natives had to carry, but we managed to withdraw for more than half-a-mile without any serious casualty. Then a legionary was shot through the heart; an Annamite was sent for his rifle and ammunition, and the retreat went on as before. Once only did the enemy attempt to rush us. I hurried to the right with tirailleurs and legionaries when I saw them nearing for the charge, but our rifle fire was so effective that no man reached our bayonets.

Not very long afterwards the lieutenant of my company came up with about forty men, two-thirds of whom were legionaries. He at once took over the chief command, and had little difficulty in getting us all back to camp. I fancy, however, that the Black Flags could have done a great deal of harm to us if they had tried more resolutely to come to close quarters, for they outnumbered us certainly by six to one. They made only faint-hearted attempts to rush us, and every time they tried that game, we concentrated our fire on the men concentrated for the charge. They made a great mistake in massing themselves together, for our bullets could not fail to find a man or men amongst them in the too close formation they assumed. We, on the contrary, kept a very open formation in the firing line, but behind there were always two little squads ready to hurry up to the part where there was any danger of a serious attack. For my part, I was glad to see that the lieutenant practised the same tactics as I; in the first place, it was a sort of compliment to me; and in the second, no one could blame the sergeant for doing what the officer, a most experienced fighter, did. To end this portion of my story, I may say that the little party got back safely to the fortification with the loss of three legionaries and one Annamite tirailleur killed and about seven or eight wounded severely enough to go into hospital. There were other men wounded, but their wounds did not count—they were only bullet-grazings or flesh wounds.

When we were safely inside the little post, the captain ordered us to see first to our wounded and then to hold ourselves in readiness to go to any part of the defence where we might be required. The Black Flags, however, did not press the attack ; evidently they were only part of the enemy who meant to assault our position, probably a few hundred sent out for raiding purposes.

Nothing of any importance occurred for two or three days. We knew that the Black Flags were closing round us ; in fact, we could not go five hundred yards from the camp without being fired on, but that gave us no uneasiness. Ammunition and stores were plentiful, the block-house made our water supply safe, our friends were only a hundred miles away, and we guessed that very soon a general or other high officer would come to inspect the post, and, of course, such people are always accompanied by at least a couple of thousand men. A gold-laced cap and an escort are not a sufficient outfit for a general ; you must, to satisfy his *amour propre*, give him an army as well. One thing must be noted here. Though the block-house commanded the spring from which arose the rivulet that ran by the outer side of the fortification, yet the captain was not satisfied. He feared that in spite of all vigilance the well might be poisoned or polluted, so that orders were given that no water was to be taken into camp until four hours after sunrise. By that time all poisons that might have been deposited in the spring during the dark hours would be washed away, and a fatigue-party would have examined the stream carefully for dead bodies of men or animals. As I shall not allude to this again, I must tell here that on several occasions we found putrid bodies in the stream. We always took them out on the spot, and the men would take no water from the parts below where they were found for at least twenty-four hours. If the carcasses were got in the spring itself, a couple of engineers and two or three legionaries went out and cleansed it.

At last we recognised that regular siege was being laid to our position. The Black Flags, assisted by a fair number of Chinese regulars—we knew these by their uniforms—had possession of every natural vantage-point around the camp. In some places, the nearest enemies were fifteen hundred yards away from the outer face of the entrenchments, in one or two the ground permitted them to come with safety as near as six or seven hundred yards. The average distance between the opposing forces was, I believe, about a thousand yards. They did not carry round a big fortified line—that would be too much trouble and would require a large number of soldiers to man it at all points—but they selected six or eight places of natural strength, erected forts upon them, and crowded these forts with defenders. The intervals between these were held by constantly moving bands, numbering anything from half-a-dozen to a hundred.

For some time the fighting was desultory. We did not fire at them unless they came within easy range, for there was no use in throwing away ammunition, and, besides, it would be a good thing if they would only learn to despise us. They knew our strength to a man. If they saw or believed that we were short of cartridges, they would surely reckon us a certain prey. At the same time they would be doubtful of the success of a mere blockade, as our stores were plentiful, and any day might bring a relieving force. As for us, we eagerly desired a grand attack. We had enough of men to provide all parts of the entrenchment with a sustained rifle fire, and even if they did get up to our fortifications we trusted to our bayonet work too much to have any fear of the issue. Moreover, since the second battle of Lang-Son and our selection to remain behind when our comrades went down to the coast, we had conceived, unconsciously, I believe, a very high idea of our prowess both as individual soldiers and as a company.

The grand attack which we had been expecting and praying for—I mean that we should have prayed for, if we ever prayed—was delivered at last. For a couple of days and nights the enemy kept up a brisk fire, giving us no rest. To this we made but little reply. The Black Flags became bolder every hour, and on the second day of the fusilade some were so contemptuous of our fire that they crawled up to within less than two hundred yards of the entrenchments to burn their powder. Our arrangements for the second night did credit to the captain. He divided his little force into two parts. The first of these kept watch and ward from sunset until half-past one in the morning; the second, which had been resting with rifles by their sides, took up guard duty in turn until six. Thus, along the entrenchments half the men, clad in greatcoats, were standing up, looking out for any movement of the enemy, while the other half, wrapped up in greatcoats and blankets, lay down only a yard away from their watching comrades. Thus half the rifles in garrison were ready for instant use; the remaining half could be in action in thirty seconds. Our captain was clever— I have always said so, and I will always assert it; other captains are creatures of routine, and will do the same thing in a fortified post in the enemy's country as they were in the habit of doing in a quiet town in the heart of France. Routine, so admirable in time of peace, is a thing rather to be neglected in time of war.

The moiety to which I was attached lay down just behind the men on guard from sunset to half-past one. Then we were called to take our turn of duty. I had only dozed off once or twice while lying down, but for all that I was as wakeful as if I had slept for a week, when I turned out of the blanket and stood up

in my greatcoat in the chilly air. Very soon I had
the men under my charge at their posts. First, the
lieutenant came round to ask in an undertone if all
were ready within and if all seemed right outside;
then the captain visited me and bade me pass the
word up and down my command that the attack, if
made at all, would be made within an hour, or an hour
and a half at most, and that all should be thoroughly
on their guard, for on every man's rifle a good deal
depended.   I, standing at the centre of my section,
told the men on my right and left what the captain
had said, each of them whispered the message to his
next man, and so the words went down the ranks.
After this all was quiet; the men seemed like so many
bronze statues, but one knew that every eye was peering
out intently into the blackness and that every ear was
straining to catch the lightest sound.   As for me, I
looked now to the front, then to the right, and then
towards the left; I neither saw nor heard anything which
could betoken the approach of an enemy.

We were nearly an hour so waiting, watching, and
listening, and the constant strain had just begun to
tell upon the nerves, when from the eastern side of the
camp a report of a rifle came.   Almost at once this
was followed by a constant fire, not firing by volleys,
be it well understood, but a well kept-up fire on both
sides, never ceasing, but swaying, as it were, up and
down, as now the reports came almost all together,
now they came in twos and threes, or in dozens and
in scores.   The eastern side was not engaged long
when the northern and southern ones joined in.   A
moment afterwards the red spirts came to us out of
the darkness of the night.   We replied, and a hot fusilade
was well maintained without and within.   The block-
house garrison was also hotly engaged.   They had little
trouble with two faces, for the fronts of them were swept
by the fire from the nearest angle of the fort, but on
the other faces their work was far harder than ours.

As was obvious afterwards, when the light came and gave us the advantage, the Black Flags had tried to catch the main position unawares, if possible, but at least to give its garrison enough to do. The chief object was to win the block-house; that captured, we others could be poisoned out. I afterwards learned that in the block-house there were two engineers and twenty-one legionaries, the whole being commanded by the sergeant-major I spoke of, the Alsatian who came from No. 3. They were good men; one engineer and seven legionaries, all simple soldiers, were killed; almost all the others were wounded, but even wounded men who could stand remained at their posts, and those others who had to stay out of the fight loaded their rifles and the rifles of the dead, and passed them to the fighting men, so that two shots often went through a loophole when, in the Black Flags' minds, only one should be expected. They were good men; I am proud of having soldiered with such.

But one attempt was made to rush the fort. This occurred at the angle where the fire from the two sides swept the ground in front of two faces of the block-house. I don't believe that the enemy dreamt of taking our place by storm, but one thing was certain, the attack in force took away all aid for the block-house from the main position and made the men outside dependent altogether on themselves. That the determined attack on the little garrison outside, weakened as it was by death and wounds, did not succeed was due, first to their determined resistance, and secondly to the fact that, just as the attack became fiercest, the light became good enough for us to see our foes, to reckon their strength, and then to allow our captain to withdraw men from the two sides that were but feebly fired at to the others where the firing was practically point - blank. The sudden reinforcement overpowered the attack. A rapid and unexpected sally by fifty or sixty legionaries with fixed bayonets relieved the pressure round the block-house. The little garrison received from the sortie party a dozen men as reinforcements, the rest returned, and that really finished the engagement. A few shots still continued to be exchanged, but the firing after the sally was of no account—a man killed or wounded on either side "did not count in the tale of the battle."

After this we had a little peace. We buried our dead outside the ramparts, but we left no mounds to afford shelter to enemies. All the earth that would in ordinary cases form heaps above the graves was taken to strengthen our defences; the plain outside was left as level as before. Was he not a clever captain? As for the enemy's killed and wounded, the uniformed men amongst them took them away under a flag of truce. We never allowed more than twenty-five to be engaged on the work within a hundred yards of the outer face of the fortifications, because we never trusted the Chinese. One thing else we did, we sent out the Annamites to gather all the weapons and ammunition of those who had fallen near the camp. These were of no use to us, but we deprived the enemy of them. Some of the wounded fell out with the Annamite tirailleurs; well, it was so much the worse for the wounded.

When the burials were over and the wounded were going along well, we began to look forward to another attack. The Chinese regulars evidently took the business in hand this time, for there was no attempt to carry the main post or the block-house by assault; now we had to contend with mines. It was very well for us that there were engineers in the garrison; without them we should in all probability have seen most of our defences blown into the air. As it was, the Chinese mined and our engineers countermined. At first the mining was comparatively simple, as far as we were concerned. The Chinese had not the skill of the French sappers, and the result was that we always found out where they were boring, before they even imagined that we could know anything about their operations, but after we had destroyed a few mines, and with them a certain number of men, the underground attack became more skilful and more concealed. On more than one occasion both parties of tunnellers discovered each other at the same time, and the earth was quickly put back by both; we did not want a communication between mine and countermine, for that might give passage to a couple of thousand Chinese and Black Flags into our camp; the enemy did not want to come to close quarters with us, for more than once they had learned that, bayonet to bayonet, the Asiatic stood no chance against the European. I shall not say much about the underground operations, as I am not an engineer; moreover, my duties as sergeant kept me almost always above ground; we allowed the military engineers to direct everything below. Of course, it will be understood that the legionaries, and sometimes the Annamite tirailleurs, furnished the working parties; the regular engineers chiefly concerned themselves with planning the works first and overseeing them afterwards. There is a story of one countermine which, however, I must narrate, as it intimately concerned myself.

Our fellows had cautiously dug forward for a considerable distance. No sound of tunnelling on the side of the Chinese had been heard; as the *dénoûment* proved, they had been as cautious as we. The working party was tearing down the earth with the sharp edge of the pick, not striking with all their strength. Thus very little noise was made, and, besides, it was enjoined on all who were at work in the mine that talking could not be allowed. The men loyally obeyed orders, even if they had not felt inclined to do so through the spirit of discipline, the knowledge that the others were doing their best to tunnel under the fortification and then blow part of it to pieces prior to a grand attack with rifle and bayonet, would have made them obedient

N

enough. I had gone down into the mine, more out of curiosity than because I had business there; my excuse was that I wished to get the names of the men of my section working in the pit. When I went down, I stayed for a moment or two. While I was holding a whispered conversation with a sub-officer of engineers, a cry from a worker drew our attention. In a moment the engineer saw what had happened, and cried out: "Les Chinois, les Chinois!"

As a matter of fact, the Chinese miners and we were separated only by a thin wall of loose earth; a blow or two struck by I know not which party tumbled this down, and we were all mixed up together, French and Chinese, in the tunnel. All struck out at random. I drew my bayonet, which, of course, I always wore, and dashed the point in the face of a yellow man from outside.

The lamps were extinguished in the struggle that ensued; we were all striking blindly about with pick-axe, shovel, and bayonet; no man knew who might receive his blow. It was a horrible time. In the darkness I heard the cries and oaths and groans; I shoved forward my bayonet, it met something soft; I drew it back and lunged again; again it met the soft, yielding substance, or perhaps the blow was lost on empty air. If I struggled forward, I tripped over a body; if I went back, surely a miner would knock my brains out with his pick. This went on for a short space that seemed an eternity. At last hurrying footsteps and shouts of encouragement and a welcome gleaming of lights told of the arrival of aid. When our comrades came up, we found that all the Chinese able to flee had fled; fourteen of them, however, and eight or nine men of ours, were lying pressed against and on top of one another in a narrow space. All, dead and wounded alike, were carried out; the place was blocked up at once, and the countermine that had taken so much time and work on our part was filled in. When the dead and wounded were examined two legionaries and two engineers were found dead, four legionaries and an Annamite tirailleur wounded, ten Chinese killed outright, four just alive. An ugly list for the small place in which the fight was, but it was the darkness that caused so heavy a casualty list amongst comparatively few combatants. It was a most unpleasant struggle. After that experience I shall never care to fight again in the dark.

For some time afterwards the siege went on in a less exciting way. The enemy had evidently resolved to starve us out. We had, as we thought, enough of stores in the beginning to last until relief came, but when the relief did not make its appearance at or after the time expected, the captain began to have serious misgivings for the future. We were utterly shut off from all communication with the outside world; for all we knew, another disaster might have befallen the French troops, and, if that were the case, there could be no hope of relief in time. A full fortnight had now elapsed since the date that we had confidently set for the coming up of reinforcements; we were all asking one another the reason of the delay. Other questions also arose. Would our comrades come soon? If they did not, would our provisions hold out? Should we be able to fight our way through, in case the post had to be abandoned? There was no thought of surrender, for all understood that it was better to die fighting than to give ourselves up to the diabolical tortures inflicted by the Black Flags and their allies on unlucky prisoners of war.

One day rations were reduced by one half. In some way to make up for this an allowance of native spirit was served out every afternoon, but the brandy and the wine were carefully kept for the use of the sick and wounded. These were by no means few, and when the dead were added to the ineffectives the total reached almost fifty per cent. of the original force. Indeed,

after we had been on half-rations for a time, we legionaries formed a skeleton company of skeletons ; we were
so few and so reduced in weight. But through all we
were resolute and, nearly to the last, cheerful. Certainly when the half-rations were further diminished,
our spirits markedly sank, but no one expects starving
men to show much gaiety.

The soldiers were kept constantly on the alert both
by the enemy and by us, their sub-officers. The
captain told the sergeants and corporals that the men
were to be always engaged in some work or other, as
he did not wish to give them time to annoy themselves
by thinking. This instruction made me a busy man.
I was always on the look-out for little duties for my
section, at the same time taking care not to overwork
the men, and I tried to be as cheerful as possible with
them. My fellows and I got along well together on
the whole. I never brought a man before the captain
if I could help it, and I let the corporals of the section
understand that the squads were not to be sworn at more
than was absolutely necessary. At the same time all
knew that an order once given had to be at once
obeyed.

Things had been going on in this fashion for some
time when the enemy again plucked up courage to
attack. We were very glad of this, because it showed
that they feared the arrival of a French force before
they could reduce us to extremity by a mere blockade.
The second big fight was a replica of the first one,
only that on this occasion the assault on the block-
house was more determined than before. It lasted
longer too, for we were too few in number to risk fifty
or sixty men in a sortie, but, in spite of all, the defence
was successfully maintained. Two days afterwards
some Annamites captured a Chinese. He was in a state
of abject terror when brought before the captain, and
on the promise that his life would be spared and liberty
given him, he soon told us all he knew of the French

movements. We learned then that a strong force was approaching and might he expected almost at any moment; we were also told that a third and last attack was in preparation. This attack, however, and the relief of the post will be told in the next chapter, as they deserve a chapter to themselves.

CHAPTER XVI

IT was quite evident that the block-house would have to stand the brunt of the attack this time as before. Now we were rather weak in numbers for the adequate defence of the main position, yet not a single man could be withdrawn from the little garrison of the outside post. Even with the full number of rifles allowed to it the block-house might be taken—taken, that is, in the event of the death or the rendering ineffective of all its men, and that this was by no means an impossibility was proved by the losses in the last fight. Out of twenty-two sub-officers and men only seven were unscathed, and of the others three were slightly, five severely, wounded, and seven killed. With a more desperate and better sustained attack upon more exhausted troops, might not the Chinese fairly hope for complete success?

To make up in some degree for the anticipated loss of the outpost the captain gave orders that all vessels in camp should be filled, that, as these were emptied they should be refilled, and that no soldier should drink out of any vessel except his own water-bottle. All the rest, filled as they were, were placed in a central position in the camp, and this place all were forbidden to approach under pain of death. The sentries on guard had strict orders to allow no one to go near the precious stock of water. The captain said:

"If you do not shoot or bayonet the trespasser, I will drive you forth unarmed to become the prey of the Black Flags."

If their own brothers had dared to approach the water, the sentries would have shot them after hearing that.

A strong party was sent to the block-house, for there was a chance that it might hold out, and in any case the captain resolved that the enemy should not have it for nothing. The lieutenant of my company was in command. I was second; there were two corporals, one an Alsatian, the other a Lorrainer, and twenty men. This was as many as could be conveniently accommodated in the small space. We were all well supplied with ammunition; we carried, every man, three days' provisions. When we paraded before going out, the captain told us that we should hold our ground as well and as long as we could; if we managed to repel one assault, only one, our lives would be saved and the honour of the corps maintained.

Our small party took up its quarters, relieving the others, who were, you may be sure, not sorry to be relieved, and was at once divided into three parts. I commanded one, a corporal each of the others; as for the lieutenant, he was over all, and seemed to be ever watchful and absolutely incapable of feeling fatigue. While one party watched, the rest lay down and slept or tried to sleep. There was no cooking to be done, as our provisions were of the cast-iron pattern—baked bread and cooked meat; as for drink, we had a small allowance of native spirit and as much water as we should want for three days.

For twenty-four hours we were undisturbed, except when once the door was opened and a man looked out. Then a regular fusilade of shots came towards us. We saw that we were fairly cooped up, and that the only chance of our ever leaving the block-house alive lay in the arrival of French troops. We fancied, but this was perhaps imagination, that we could hear firing in the distance; this gave us hope and renewed our courage. Early in the evening of our second day on duty a strong attack was made not only on our post, but on the main position as well. At first this was confined to a hot fire, and four of ours, one the Alsatian corporal, were shot at the loopholes. As night came down, the enemy approached to short range, and even in the dark we were a splendid target for them. All the night they fired, and twice they set the block-house on fire, but volunteers quickly put out the flames, though at a fearful sacrifice of life. As the first beams of the rising sun illuminated the battlefield, the Chinese regulars, followed by a crowd of Black Flags, tried to storm the post. They succeeded in breaking down two upright beams on one side and tried to pour in, but our bayonets soon piled up a heap of bodies in the narrow entrance that they had made. We got a short respite now, and heard with feelings of indescribable joy a steady, well-sustained firing outside the position held by the enemy. Once more, however, the Chinese attacked. With battering rams of wood tipped with iron they broke down a clear half of one wall. Some of the superstructure fell and delayed them for a time, but this they quickly tore away, and the remains of the little garrison, having no longer power to hold the fort or hope of escape, sallied desperately forth, to sell their lives as dearly as possible. The lieutenant leading fell shot between the eyes; the rest of us rushed straight at the Chinese and bore them back. They rallied and again attacked. We fought with the courage of despair. We could make little head against them, but for all that we steadily piled up a rampart of bodies in our front. I heard as I fought the familiar war cry of the legionaries; I shouted out in reply. Just as a Chinese lifted his musket to fell me to the earth, I saw the advancing line of reinforcements. There was a sudden shock, and then came darkness on my eyes, and, when I came to, the block-house, now on fire, was blazing in the sunlight, and I felt a terrible agony in head and limbs and body. But the post had been held and relieved; the enemy were scattered in all directions, with hundreds of pursuers at their heels; there were no more short rations to be dreaded, no more night attacks, nothing now but rest and peace and warm congratulations.

Let me tell the fate of the little guard of the block-house. The lieutenant, both corporals, and eighteen soldiers were dead; two soldiers and I, the sergeant and second in command, were wounded. Both the soldiers died that night; I, the sole survivor, was promoted sergeant-major and recommended for the military medal. Had I been a Frenchman, I should have got the cross and a commission; as it was, I was more than satisfied, for did not I get the rewards won by my comrades as well as by me? For a few days I lay in hospital, and the doctors feared that I might suffer from concussion of the brain as a result of the heavy blow dealt me by the Chinese. However, all bad effects passed away quickly, and I returned to duty on the day that my promotion to the rank of sergeant-major was confirmed. The captain visited me in hospital; he would not allow me to talk, and merely said that he was glad I had survived, and then laughingly told me that "the devil's children had their father's luck." He could be sarcastic on occasion, but I did not mind; I can take a joke as well as another.

After the post had been relieved the remains of the original garrison were transferred to the sea-coast. The march down was exactly similar to all the other marches, except in one important matter, we did not have to break camp hurriedly and run after rapidly vanishing enemies. No; our daily marches were not too long, our nightly rest was unbroken, and, as we approached the coast, we got better quarters and better supplies. The men too had the proud con-sciousness of a dangerous and difficult duty well done. The other soldiers whom we met used to cook our soup and prepare the camps for us; that's the soldier's way of offering congratulations, and these were the com-pliments we liked.

When we marched one afternoon into Saigon, I was

in very bad health.   The reaction after the siege, with
its reduced rations, its constant watchfulness, and all
the little annoyances that beset a poor devil of a
sergeant trying to keep the men of his section content
under difficulties, together with the fatigue of the
march, made me feel very ill by the time we came to
the base.   Moreover, I was troubled about the accounts
of the company.   The sergeant-major who preceded
me, and who was killed in the last attack, had left the
company's accounts in an unintelligible state; no one
could tell whether any man had or had not been paid
a piastre since the beginning of the siege, nor could
you find out who had drawn occasional rations of wine
and extra tobacco.   The captain knew nothing; he
had been too busy with fighting and looking after
stores.   I went to him and said that it was not fair
to ask me to make up a dead man's accounts.   He
agreed with me, and asked me what the devil I was
going to do about the affair.

" Let the clerks at headquarters settle all," I replied ;
" it ought to be their business and not mine."

"Very well," said the captain; "but how will you
throw the work on their shoulders?"

"Easily enough," I answered; "I need but refuse
to accept the books until they are set right."

"But suppose you are ordered to take them and to
set them in order yourself?"

"Very well, sir; I will then claim money for every
man, dead or alive.   When the clerks point out to me
that a certain man is dead, I will withdraw his name:
in that way I shall give them more trouble than if
they were to make up the accounts themselves."

"Do what you like," said the captain; "only pay the
survivors—the dead may rest."

I took the hint, and made out the accounts in such
a way, that it appeared that all the dead had been paid
in full up to the day of death, and that none of the
survivors had obtained a centime for months.   The

paymasters grumbled, and I was called on more than once for an explanation. I could only say that I knew nothing about the men's accounts beyond what they told me.

"But how do you know," asked a commandant one day, "that the dead men were paid in full?"

"I don't know it, sir," I answered; "but I have marked them as paid because I cannot afford time to look for their heirs."

Everybody laughed at this—the idea of a legionary leaving legacies to his relations was too ridiculous. In the end, however, we survivors got nearly all the money we claimed, and everybody was satisfied.

It was easy to see that most of our company were unfit for further duty at the time. Many were in hospital, and those of us who remained in camp were listless and easily fatigued. The medical officers did not like our looks, and it became a current report that we should all be very soon sent back to Algeria. The transport was in harbour on which we were ordered to embark for transportation home—that is, to the legionaries' home, the wastes and sands of Northern Africa. Yet to us these very places seemed like heaven compared with Tonquin: we, were all tired of the harrassing warfare, the starvation, the marches, and the constant watchfulness. It was fated that I should not return in this vessel, as, only two days before it sailed, I had to go into the military hospital, a place dreaded above all others by soldiers. There I lay with an attack of fever, but my naturally strong constitution shook this off, and in a few weeks I was ready to embark in a hospital ship, with a few hundred others of all ranks and regiments, for Marseilles. I had a relapse while in the Red Sea, and thought for the first time that there was no longer hope for me. What made it worse was that every day a dead body went overboard, and, though the officials tried to keep this fact from us, sick men are too clever and too suspicious to be easily imposed upon. One morning I saw the cot near me empty—a poor marine fusilier had occupied it the day before. I had known that he was sinking rapidly, but still the fact of his death gave me a great shock. I got up with difficulty from my couch and made my way on hands and knees to the companion-ladder, ascended this in the same posture, and at length gained the deck unperceived. I felt the cool breeze of the Mediterranean on my face, and thanked Heaven that I was out of the horrors of Tonquin and the almost worse horrors of the Red Sea. I remember no more until I woke up to find myself back in my cot, with a couple of doctors and an orderly or two around me. The doctors spoke in a friendly way to me, and asked me why I had gone up to the deck. I said that I was restless, and scarcely knew what I was doing, but that the fresh breeze above had done me much good. They then said that very soon we should be at Marseilles and that I should be better off there. I thanked them, promised not to leave my cot again, and they withdrew. As they went, however, I over-heard one say—so sharp are sick men's ears: " He will come up again, probably to-morrow." I wondered vaguely whether he doubted my word or whether he was merely alluding to my probable death, but after a time I thought of other things. I made no further attempt to go up on deck ; even had I not promised to stay quietly below, I had not strength enough to climb the companion-way again.

A few days after we arrived at Marseilles and were carefully transferred to a large hospital on land. There, I must admit, we received excellent treatment. Not only were the doctors and the orderlies kind and atten-tive, but the ladies of the town were also extremely good to us. Chaplains also came round the wards frequently, and, of all the places in which I have ever been, the military hospital at Marseilles was one of the best. I could thoroughly appreciate the kindness then, for my health came back quickly from the day I landed from the hospital ship.

One day when I was allowed to get up and go to a convalescent ward for a few hours an orderly came into the room, in a great hurry apparently, and called out my name. I said:

"Here I am. What do you want?"

He replied: "Monsieur le général will be here soon."

"Does he come to tell me that I have been appointed his aide-de-camp?" I inquired, laughing at my own little joke.

"No, my fine fellow," cried a corporal of some line regiment in a corner; "he has come to ask you to be so kind as to marry his daughter, who has a fortune of only one hundred thousand francs."

"Ah," said a cuirassier—I forget his rank, "the request is that our friend the sergeant-major will consent to act as the general's second in a duel with the Tsar of Russia."

A chasseur believed that that was not true, as he had learned from a morning paper that I was to be ambassador to His Holiness the Pope, "who knows," he went on to say, "how moral and virtuous are the lives the legionaries lead, they being, in fact, monks in uniform." This settled the matter; nobody could invent a more improbable—let me say impossible—reason for the general's visit. I was asked continually afterwards how the Pope was. Did he still hold the idea of asking France to give him the sanctified legionaries as a new army? If we went to Rome, should we have to soldier with the Swiss and other guards? And a number of other questions were asked, all of which I answered to the best of my ability, trying in every case to give a "Roland for an Oliver," and often succeeding. I told the chasseur one day that the Pope would not take us of the Legion as his guards; he preferred the chasseurs: by converting them to decent practices he would gain

greater glory in heaven. The cuirassier learned that
His Holiness would soon send him the shield of faith—
he already had the breastplate of caution. The cuirassier did not like this. He indignantly protested that
he would rather fight in his shirt sleeves.

"Very well," I answered. "Do as the Austrians do—
take off your cuirass in time of war."

He asked me how I knew that. I replied: "Easily
enough. I have many Austrian comrades, but I have
no French ones. We legionaries are seemingly in the
French army, but not, in real truth, soldiers of it."
Truth to tell, I was getting a little angry, because
all wished to unite against the solitary soldier of
the Legion in the room. I let the rest see that I
was tired of their jokes, and afterwards they left me
alone.

Well, the general came in a short time into the room
and called out my name and rank. I stepped forward
and stood to attention.

"You the sergeant-major?" he asked, in a tone of
surprise.

"Yes, sir."

"Why, you are only a boy. How long have you
been in the Legion?"

I told him. Then he asked me a number of questions
about my service, to all of which I answered clearly and
respectfully.

"You are a young sergeant-major—very young." And
he turned to speak to a surgeon. Both looked at me
often during this conversation. I maintained always
the stiff, erect attitude of the soldier in front of his
superior officer.

"You have been recommended for the military medal,"
at last the general said.

"Yes, sir; my captain told me that he would recommend me for the decoration."

"The recommendation has been confirmed," said the
general, "and I have come to give you the medal. I

thought," he went on, "that I should meet a veteran, and I find a schoolboy."

I said nothing; indeed, I did not know what to say.

"It does not matter about your age or the length of your service," the general continued; "you have won rank and distinction, and I wish you a prosperous career."

"Thanks, my general."

"Is there anything you want?"

"Yes, my general."

"What is it?"

"A Little Corporal to lead a schoolboy sergeant-major, that is all."

He drew back and looked at me. A susurrus of approbation went through the room. Very little more was said. The general gave me the medal that I had won, paid me a compliment or two, and went away. But the story went round, and what would be hurtful to a Frenchman, who was at once soldier and citizen, was a cause of no offence in a legionary, who was only a soldier. But what I said was liked, and many a present I received afterwards. The French know that the legionary is a soldier pure and simple—well, not always pure, and very seldom simple—and they know that the soldier of the French army who gives up for life the clothes of the pékin and who dreams of nothing except fighting and promotion looks on Napoleon the Great as a terrestrial Archangel Michael. Him would we follow, him would we serve. God grant us another like him, and then—— And the legionaries understood, and wished as warmly as any Frenchman for the advent of another ideal restless man and restless man's idol. The Little Corporal when he was the great commander was bad, let us admit, to many, but he was never bad to the man who served him well. It was not birth or wealth that brought promotion under him but courage and devotion to duty. True, he made mistakes, and these great ones—the imprisonment of the Pope, the

invasion of the white Tsar's frozen land, the too early
return from Elba were such—but in his mistakes even
he was colossal, unapproachable.

It was after this visit and the receipt of the military
medal that the jesting conversations began amongst us.
However, I have told of them already, and there is
no use in going back upon a told story. That does
very well in conversation, especially when the glasses
are filled and the pipes going merrily, but in writing
it is of no account.

Very soon after this I was strong enough, the surgeons
said, to cross to Algeria. All the men whose acquaintance I had made were good enough to say that, though
they were glad I was able to leave hospital, yet they
were sorry to lose my companionship. I thanked them
all, told them that I had had a pleasant time, and hoped
to meet them again. In this I was sincere. I have very
pleasant memories of the hospital, but all the same I
wanted to get back to my own comrades.

Shortly after the surgeons had put my name on the
outgoing list I left the hospital for the troopship. I
was brought to Oran, and there sent again to hospital,
but only for a few days. Here I was treated very well
indeed by those in charge, and I made a few casual
acquaintances, whose comradeship helped very much
to pass the dreary time of waiting until the principal
surgeon should order me to be sent back to the regiment. I think they kept me longer than was absolutely
necessary, and this for two reasons—my youth and the
military medal. The surgeons were quite as curious
as my hospital companions to hear my story, to learn
all about my country and why I left it to join the
Legion, how I liked the French service, and every
other thing that they could think of. For the first
time in my life I was made much of as a man of
good service and tried valour; if I gave somewhat
exaggerated accounts of the perils I had passed who
can blame me? There was no sneering now at the

Foreign Legion; oh no! we were in Algeria, *la patrie des légionnaires*.

At last the surgeon-in-chief told me that I should soon leave the hospital. I thanked him for the information, and said that the only cause of regret at leaving was that I should leave so many good comrades behind.

"Have you been well treated here, sergeant-major?" he asked.

"Very well, sir; so well that I have lost the simple soldier's fear of the hospital."

He laughed, and said: "I am glad. Take the advice of a friend, always seek the surgeon when you are ill or wounded. The old prejudice was, in its time, a just one; nowadays things are different."

I promised that I would do so. At the same time even to-day I fear the surgeon's knife more than an enemy's bayonet or sword or even lance, and the lance is what the infantry man most dreads—that is, of course, of weapons. However, I have not since the day I left the hospital at Oran ever been the occupant of a bed in one, and I sincerely hope that I may never see, as a patient at least, the whitewashed wall of a hospital again.

From Oran I was sent to the depot at Saida, where I remained for some time. I did ordinary duty there as sergeant-major of a company of recruits during the illness of the regular sub-officer, and so learned a good deal more of my new duties than I knew when leaving Tonquin. I was very glad of this, especially as the officers were very decent to me. I was a different man now—a sergeant-major without a moustache but with the military medal—from the young recruit who was sworn at and abused every day by the drill instructors. No swearing or abuse now, only compliments and flirtation and general friendliness. A happy time indeed, too happy to last, as I learned before I was many months older.

I must now tell about my love and my sorrows and

o

how I came to leave the Legion for ever. Truly, I cannot say that I am sorry; truly, I cannot say that I am glad. If the service of the legionary was a hard service, yet it had its consolations; if you did wrong nobody minded—that is, so long as you broke only the ten commandments. Of course, military regulations and the rules of our society were very different things; the first had to be kept if one did not wish for punishment, you had to respect the second, or else lose the respect of your associates, and though boycotting is a comparatively new word yet it denotes an old and universal practice.

And now to tell of my *grande passion*, its course and its results, the story of which was at one time, and may be even still, a classic tale of the Legion.

CHAPTER XVII

I LEFT the depot one morning with a large party of recruits for a battalion in the inland parts of Algeria. We were about a hundred and eighty strong, and as a lieutenant was the only officer I ranked as second in command. We had two sergeants and eight or nine corporals to help to maintain discipline, but the men acted in a very good way on the march. I can recall no incident worth relating, but I remember one circumstance that made the march very pleasant. As the lieutenant had no brother officer to speak to and was naturally talkative, he had to associate very much with me. It must not be supposed that this diminished the respect in which I was bound to hold his rank; on the contrary, since he made the time pass agreeably for me, I felt more and more disposed to render him all outward signs of honour; and if I did address him as " my lieutenant " as we marched 20 paces ahead of the party, when others were within earshot I fell back on the more respectful "sir." I am sure he noted this, but he said nothing about it. This officer was a most entertaining talker; he was naturally clever, had received a good education, and was full of stories of Paris which were well worth hearing. He saw that I enjoyed his tales of life there, and thus had the best of all incentives to story-telling—a good listener. On the other hand, I told him more than he, as an officer, could learn of the Legion and the men who were in it. I did not trouble about the Alsatians and Lorrainers, who had enlisted solely to gain the rights of French citizens, but I let him know the life-history of more than one of

211

the Russians, Austrians, Germans and Spaniards who filled our ranks. I did more. I allowed him to see the trend of thought in the corps; I told him of our traditions, our jealousies, our loves and our hates; by the time that we arrived at our goal he understood better than most officers the character of the men whom he would have under his command. So the lieutenant and the sergeant-major were good comrades.

When we came to the battalion at the borders of the Great Desert the recruits were distributed amongst the companies, the sergeants and corporals were appointed to sections and squads, the lieutenant took the place of an officer who had died of fever, and so all were settled in the new battalion except myself. The commandant did not know what to do with me; he had enough sub-officers of my rank already, and yet he did not like to put me to any duties except those of the rank I held. This was on account of the military medal. If I had not had that, I should very soon have found myself acting as simple sergeant of a section. However, a way was found out of the difficulty—a way which led me into many sorrows— though these I have never regretted, counterbalanced as they were by so many joys.

There was a woman in the place who kept a canteen. She always remained with this battalion, and where others might starve she waxed wealthy —that is, wealthy for a *cantinière*. Her husband had been a sergeant of the third company. He had fallen fighting bravely in an obscure skirmish at some desert village, and when he fell he left a wife and baby daughter to the care of his comrades. The story of the pair was never fully known. They were Italians, and both of evidently gentle birth. When I heard about them first I thought of a Romeo and a Juliet giving up all for love, leaving behind family animosities with family riches, and seeking security from all search in the safest retreat in the world—the "legion of the lost ones." All the men saw and admired the heroic self-sacrifice of the gently-nurtured lady who left all to follow the chosen one in such a career, and I am proud to be able to say that during her husband's life and after his death no man ever said in her hearing anything that would bring a blush to her cheeks; in her presence even the most hardened rascal put on the semblance of a gentleman. People say that even the best man has some fault or imperfection of nature. It may be so. At anyrate even the worst man has some good, some respect for virtue and honour, even though he possesses them not himself.

After the death of her husband the widow opened a small shop, in which she sold wine, tobacco, and other things that soldiers spend their money on. The officers of the battalion stocked this for her, but in a short time she was able to pay them back, and she insisted on their accepting the money though they did not at all desire repayment. The regimental convoys were allowed to bring her goods as she required them, and the legionaries of her dead husband's battalion loyally spent most of their scanty pay in her canteen.

Whenever anyone received money from friends or relations in Europe her stock would be all cleared off at once, and so by the exercise of a little frugality she was able gradually to put by some money for the little daughter whom she idolised. At the time when I came to the battalion this girl was about fifteen years of age, slight, graceful, lively, bright-eyed, the pet of the battalion. Everyone jested freely with her, she jested freely with everybody, but no one ever thought of saying anything which her mother, a model of virtue, would not like to hear.

I had been but two or three days in my new quarters when an alarm of fire was raised one night, and we all turned out promptly as the cry went around. There was no danger for us, as the huts were one-storeyed and did not contain more than a squad each, but there might be sôme for the officers, whose quarters were more elaborate, and who, of course, were more isolated. A dozen or a score of men in a hut will all get clear, because some at least will be aroused, and these can pull out their suffocating comrades; a single officer may be smothered in his bed before even the watchful sentry realises the outbreak. When I came out of my quarters, in shirt and drawers, I glanced around, and saw at once that all the cantonment was safe. Then I heard a cry from the direction of the main guard-house that the village was on fire, but this was afterwards proved to be false. I flung on my clothes hurriedly and ran to the guard-house, for I had no assigned place on the parade that was now rapidly forming on the parade-ground, not being sergeant-major of any company, and asked the sergeant of the guard where the fire was.

"Madame's canteen," he replied; "twenty or thirty men have already gone to put it out."

"May I go to help?" (Of course, though I was of higher rank, he was the man in charge of the guard, and could prevent me, if he wished, from going out.)

"Certainly, my sergeant-major."

"Thanks, comrade, thanks." And I ran out and went to the widow's canteen. There I found the whole a mass of flames, and I saw at a glance that there was no hope of saving even the smallest portion of the house or its contents, especially as there was a sad lack of water. I asked a man if the woman and the girl had been saved. He told me that the girl had discovered the fire and awakened her mother, that both had made good their escape, and that then the widow had run back to recover her little store of money, the hiding-place of which no one else knew. "Then," he went on, "the daughter tried to go into the blazing house to bring back her mother, but she was forcibly prevented by some soldiers, and one or two of the legionaries who tried to enter were driven back, severely burned, by the fire and smoke." The flames, indeed, were terrible, all the wine barrels and spirit casks were blazing fiercely; there was no hope of life for anyone in such a hell. The poor widow fell a victim to her desire to regain for her daughter the money she had hoarded with so much anxious care, and nothing remained of her except a few charred bones, which were reverently gathered up and decently interred on the morrow. As for the money, it must have been chiefly in paper, for very little metal could be found in the ashes, and so the poor daughter was left completely alone in the world, without relations, at least as far as she knew, without means, and with only the friendship and the pity of the battalion to look to for aid.

The Italian girl was taken charge of by a sergeant's wife—one of those few noble women, few, I mean, comparatively speaking, who will go anywhere with their husbands, and who furnish in the most abandoned communities examples of unselfish heroism and exalted virtue, which make even men whose knowledge of the sex is confined to its most vicious members have some respect for purity and some doubts as to their favourite axiom : A man may be good, but a woman cannot be. The officers proposed that she should continue as *cantinière* in place of her mother, and generously offered to put her in a position to do so. As for us sub-officers and simple soldiers, our duty was plain : as soon as she was in a new home and shop, to go there, and there only, with the constant copper, the occasional silver, the God-sent gold. She knew this, the officers knew it ; we made no resolutions ; and said scarcely anything about the matter amongst ourselves, but all understood that it would be bad for the legionary who bought his wine or brandy elsewhere.

The commandant sent for the four sergeant-majors of the companies and for me, the supernumerary. He asked us how much it would cost to erect a new house. We said that it would cost nothing; the soldiers would build one in their spare time.

"Very well, my friends, very well. How much will it cost to put in a new supply."

We did not answer this at once, but after some time we all agreed that 2000 francs would put in a fairly good stock—that is, if carriage cost nothing.

"Oh, the carriage will be settled; I will see to that," said the commandant. "Now, sergeant-major," he went on, turning to me, "you have no company whose accounts you must make up, will you undertake to look after this business for Mademoiselle Julie?"

"I will do my best, sir, in this matter if you wish it."

"That will do," he replied; "you shall be sergeant-major of the canteen company. Is it not so?"

Every other sergeant-major laughed at me. They were glad that I had been sent to some duty, for a sergeant-major with the military medal is not long employed as simple sergeant, and each man, so long as I was unemployed in my proper rank, would fear for himself and his own position. Thus I became sergeant-major responsible for a canteen and the curious crowd assembled there. Some time afterwards, when the new quarters had been built by the legionaries and the little stock of *eau-de-vie*, wine, tobacco, and cigars had arrived, there was a grand opening. All the men had been saving up for awhile, and more than half the stock was sold at a good profit on the first evening. The girl was asked to do nothing except to take the money; four men willingly acted as assistants, pouring out the wine and the *eau-de-vie*, and, indeed, now and then tasting them too, for "you must not muzzle the ox treading out the corn," nor ask a man to help others to good things without occasionally helping himself as well.

One of them took so much brandy that I had to turn him out, a couple of comrades brought him away to his hut, and nothing was said about it, as the poor little *cantinière* begged him off with tears in her eyes. Just as things were becoming almost too lively the commandant and the other officers came down and entered the little shop. The first intimation we inside had of their arrival was the silence of the men who were laughing, singing, and carousing outside. The commandant put down a couple of gold pieces and asked for two bottles of wine. He and the others took each a sip of this and wished mademoiselle a prosperous business. Then the commandant gave me a strong hint that enough of business had been done for that day, and I promptly shut up shop after his departure. When all had left Giulia and I counted the money. We had a little gold, a good deal of silver, and a great quantity of copper—altogether over fourteen hundred francs. I congratulated her upon the successful evening's trading, and then we went to reckon up the supply still left. We found that at the same rate of sale the two thousand francs would be changed into at least two thousand six hundred, and that surely was excellent profit in an out-of-the-way camp of legionaries where money was rather scarce.

Then Giulia asked me to take a glass of wine and a cigar. I did not refuse. What legionary, what man, indeed, would, when pressed by so lovely a girl? Of late I had seen her constantly, as my management of her affairs and my continual reports about the progress of her new house brought me daily into her society. We always got on well together—fifteen and seventeen don't usually fall out—and my rank and medal brought me favour in her eyes. Moreover, I was very respectful in my words and demeanour. I pitied her misfortune, and my pity was not lessened by the sight of her beauty, and, before I had been three days attending to her affairs, I took more interest in them than I could by any chance take in the accounts of a company. We were very good friends and companions, but there was not a hint, not a suspicion, of love on either side. She was pretty and in trouble, and, therefore, had my sympathy. I was kind and attentive to her, and she was grateful. *Voilà tout !*

Before I drank the wine I made her put her lips to the glass, which she did, prettily and with a blush.

"You must never ask me to do that again," she said.

"Why, it is the custom of the Legion, ma camarade," I replied. "You are now a legionary; surely you will do as your good comrades do?"

"Well, at least not in the presence of others."

"Very well," I answered; "but always when we are alone?"

"Yes," she whispered; "when we are alone. I trust you." And she put her little hand out to me. I took it, and by a sudden impulse kissed it.

"You may always trust me," I said—"always."

A question now arose as to the disposal of the money. There was no danger from natives, as the new house was inside the lines; there was not much, indeed, from soldiers, as there were sentries near. At the same time I told Giulia that it would be safer to transfer it to some other place. "Can you not," I suggested, "take it to the woman in whose quarters you live?"

"No, no," she replied; "I will take some to give to her—she has been very good to me—but you are in charge, you must keep the greater part."

"I?" I said in astonishment.

"Yes; if you do not, I will leave it here."

"But, Mademoiselle Julie, there are very bad men in every battalion, and someone may break in and steal all."

"Let the sentinels keep watch."

"Ah! a sentinel may be glad to get half."

"I do not care; you are my sergeant-major"—as she said this a rosy flush came up over neck and face and ears—"and it is your duty to keep my money for me. Besides, did I not say that I trust you?"

In the end I had to take twelve hundred francs,

though with many misgivings. Giulia told me that she would give two hundred to the sergeant's wife, the rest she would keep herself. Then we locked up the place and departed to our separate quarters, after having made an appointment to meet in the morning, to inspect the stores and see if anything had been touched during the night. Giulia wanted me to take the keys as well as the money, but this I refused to do.

I could scarcely sleep that night on account of the money. I occupied a small room in a long, low-roofed building, given up to the accommodation of sergeants whose domestic arrangements did not include a woman. I barricaded the door, put a glass on the window, so that anyone trying to enter that way might knock it down on a tin basin placed just below, and put a naked bayonet and the box containing the money under my pillow. For all these precautions I spent a wakeful night, and rose in the morning, restless, anxious, and unrefreshed. After the morning coffee I felt better, and laughed to myself at my fears of the night. Who would take the money? surely not one of the sergeants. I did not, I could not, suspect them, but I certainly should not like to trust every man in the battalion; the Legion contains more than a due percentage of desperate ruffians, and our battalion had its fair share of the bad ones.

As I went across the parade-ground to keep my appointment with Giulia at the door of the canteen I met the captain of my company, or at least of the company to which I was attached, though I seldom paraded with it. He noticed the box and asked me what it contained. When I told him he laughed, and said that many a man would be pleased to be so trusted, especially by so beautiful a girl as Mademoiselle la Cantinière. I answered that the trust was pleasant but the responsibility too great; I did not wish to have the safe keeping of twelve hundred francs. "You cannot help it now, my sergeant-major of the canteen, you must undertake all the duties of your position." Then he told me to present his compliments to Mademoiselle Julie, and went away.

I met Giulia at the door. She looked annoyed at having to wait, but when I made her acquainted with the delay caused by meeting the captain her face cleared.

" I thought, mon ami," she said, " that you had forgotten your duty."

" That might be possible ; but, Mademoiselle Julie, how could I forget you ?"

She curtsied at the compliment, and I noticed the grace of her figure, the beauty of its curves, the wonderful arch of the instep ; and I must have looked my admiration, for when she lifted her eyes to meet mine, again the rosy flush came up over her neck and cheeks. " Let us see that all is right within," she said, and opened the door. When we were inside we saw at a glance that everything was as we had left it on the previous evening. " Now let us count the money," I said. In a second Giulia flew into a rage, she stamped her foot upon the ground, she cried out that I wished to insult her, that I thought her mean and suspicious, and finally burst into tears. I laid my hand upon her arm and wished to know what had vexed her ; she flung it off with an indignant gesture and bade me go away. I was thunderstruck. I could not tell how I had offended, and was beginning to feel aggrieved. Why should I be told that I had insulted her whom I would not pain for all the world ? The more I thought of my conduct towards her, the less reason I could see for her anger and tears. I was wise enough, however, to let her have her cry out : when she had done with weeping she would be reasonable. I was not mistaken.

When she had dried her tears, I asked how I had offended her. She looked, calmly enough now, at me, and said : " Did I not tell you yesterday that I trusted you ?"

"Yes," I replied.

"And yet to-day you ask that I should count the money. How can I do so and trust?"

I took off my kepi, bowed, and said: "Pardon me, I was wrong."

"You will never offend me again?"

"Never. And you, you will forgive?"

"Yes; once, but not a second time."

Again she gave me her hand, again I kissed it, then she put her hands upon my shoulders, and said: "My dear friend, if I did not trust you more than you think, I would not be alone with you here."

She asked me to take a glass of wine, voluntarily put the glass to her lips, and then handed it to me. I deliberately turned it round, so that my lips should touch where hers had touched, and drained it to the bottom, looking the while over it at Giulia. She smiled and looked pleased, and then turned away to get some cigars. I had more sense than to offer money. I took the cigars, and said:

"You are a good comrade, Giulia."

It was the first time I had called her by her name. She hesitated a little, and then answered:

"And you too, you will be a good comrade, will you not, Jean?"

"Oui, ma belle." And I bit off the end of a cigar, while she struck a match to light it for me.

Just as I began to smoke there came a knock at the door. I shouted out "Entrez," and the commandant came in. I put down the cigar and stood to attention.

"Everything goes well, is it not?" he asked.

"Yes, monsieur le commandant," Giulia replied; "I can soon repay some of the money advanced by you and the other officers."

"No, my child," the commandant said; "you are the daughter of the regiment now. The battalion must be father and mother to you; we cannot accept repayment."

"But my mother paid back the money given to her by the officers."

"Yes, my dear child; but your mother was not born in the regiment, and though we lent to her we give to you. We gave it, indeed, and did not expect to be repaid. I was a sub-lieutenant then, and I remember all. She insisted, and we were compelled to accept. With you it is different; we will insist, and you must not refuse. How do you like the sergeant-major of the canteen?" he went on. We all laughed at the queer title; no one had ever heard of such a rank.

"Very well, monsieur le commandant."

"Yes, yes; I think he will be good; if he is not, tell me." With that he went away.

"I must be good, Giulia?" I said, as I lit the cigar again.

"Yes; very good, my comrade; you must never offend me again."

"Ah! you do not forget—perhaps you will never forget—and then, what is the good of being forgiven?"

"I will forget; yes, I will never remember, unless you force me to."

I promised that I should never offend her again, and she smiled and said that she believed me.

"Nobody will enter here during the day," I told her, "and I will leave the box here; if I do not I must carry it everywhere with me, and that will be inconvenient."

Giulia asked me why I should carry it about with me, and I told her that I should have no peace or ease of mind while it was out of my sight unless it was in the canteen, which was near so many sentinels. I also mentioned my fears for its safety the previous night and the precautions that I had taken. She was very sorry that I had been so restless, and advised me to leave it in future in the canteen. To this I demurred. I told her that if the box were there, I should be getting up at all hours of the night to come and look at the place, and perhaps I might be shot by a sentry. "But can we not find a hiding-place—some place that nobody could find even in broad daylight?" The idea struck me as a good one. We searched in all directions, and finally decided on an empty box half-full of straw that had contained bottles. By leaving this, of course, without the money, in full view of everybody during the day, no man who might enter at night would dream of searching it. Then I proposed that we should put only the money there every evening and that I should take away the empty box.

"No, my friend, you shall not. Something might happen if the bad ones thought that the box was full; better lose the money than a good friend's life."

"As it pleases you, my comrade; I will obey orders, then I cannot offend."

That evening the canteen did a good trade, so good, indeed, that we—that is, Giulia and I—determined on sending for more wine and *eau-de-vie*. I went to the commandant in the morning and told him how affairs stood. He was glad to hear my report, and ordered me to make out the order and give it to him to be forwarded. I brought him the written order to a merchant in Oran and handed over eighteen hundred francs in cash. He had the money counted by a clerk, and then told me that he would see that Mademoiselle Julie's order and money were safely transmitted. I saluted and went away.

As day after day passed Giulia and I became all the better friends. We openly showed our liking for each other. We were constantly meeting, sometimes by accident it is true, but oftener by unexpressed design, and, whenever we met, we always stopped to speak. I, being unattached to any company for battalion duties, had plenty of time on my hands; Giulia, of course, had nothing to do until evening, as I took good care that her place was swept and cleaned every morning by legionaries, who were only too glad to do this work for a glass of brandy and an ounce of tobacco apiece; thus we, as it were, could not help meeting so frequently. The others noticed and said nothing; it was tacitly understood at the time through the battalion that we were lovers, and yet we had never even spoken of love, and I had kissed her hand only twice. We were happy together, and that, for the moment, was enough for both.

CHAPTER XVIII

WHEN Giulia and I met next morning at the canteen we found money and goods untouched. She did not ask me to take a glass of wine this time but filled it out, put it to her lips, and gave it to me. I drank the wine, lit a cigar, and asked her if she had any orders. We laughed at this, then she in her pretty way insisted that I was the sub-officer in charge and that her duty was to listen and obey, mine to command. I objected, saying that the lady's wishes had to be considered first. A good deal of harmless chat followed. I smoked the cigar, she deftly rolled a cigarette and lit it from my cigar, our faces were close together, and I told her it was well that cigarette and cigar were between us and also kept our lips engaged. But this was all fun, we had nothing to do; the men of the battalion, at least three companies of them, were out marching with knapsacks and pouches full, the fourth company was up to its eyes in work, some on guard, some cooking, some doing the necessary duties of a camp; I honestly believe that we two were the only idle, careless ones in the cantonment.

As she flung away the end of a cigarette she said: "I have resolved to live here after a few days."

"What!" I cried, "you to stay here alone, beautiful and with money?"

She smiled back, as it were triumphantly, and replied: "Why not?"

"But you are beautiful."

"Thanks, my comrade."

"And there will always be money in the house."

"It is true."

"And beauty and money, what will they not tempt men to do?"

"I shall have a protector."

This was a blow to me, and she must have seen it, for she said quickly, putting her hand on my arm, that the sergeant and his wife whom she had been staying with since her mother's death would keep house for her.

"Oh," I cried, "I am so glad and I was so sorry."

"I trust you, Jean," she answered; "will you not trust me?" I was not allowed to reply; she put a pretty finger on my lips, and said:

"Yes, I know you trust me; why say to me what I know?"

What pleasant days we had together! What fun and jesting and pretended rebukes! When the sergeant and his wife were installed in one of the rooms over the canteen, I used to stay until the call went for "Out lights," and then I groped my way in the darkness back to my quarters, challenged by every sentry on the road. Soon the battalion got to understand that *le jeune* was always to be found going to his quarters at a certain hour, and the sentries used to look out especially for me. I, of course, had to answer their challenges and to give my reason for being out at night. I always said:

"Visiting Sergeant M——." As I passed the scoundrels used to say: "Sergeant M——, is he married? Has Madame M—— a friend at her house?" And I dared not say anything in reply, because if I did all the battalion would be laughing at me and somebody else next day.

You must not think that the men wished to hurt anyone's feelings. No; bad as they were, forgetful as they were of the ten commandments, they had no intention, not even the slightest, of offending Giulia or me. Giulia was the pet. Many envied me, I am sure, but they envied me because they thought things; had they known that Giulia and I were merely good friends, good comrades, and that no word of love had ever been said by either of us they would have laughed, and said: "Oh, boy and girl to-day, lover and mistress to-morrow," but that was because, with a lingering taste for good, they had quite given up expecting it here or hereafter. One thing I must say, the legionaries were very quiet in the canteen. They called for their drinks and went outside at once, and there smoked, drank, and sang as best pleased each. Sometimes a man would have no money and would wish for a drink in the morning or a pipeful of tobacco at night. He came to me, and said:

"I want it, my sergeant-major; will you give it me?"

"I can't give it," I used to say, "but I'll ask for it for you, and if you don't pay when you have money I shall have to pay instead and I'll never ask for you again."

They did not always pay, but that was because a man's money was stopped—he was in hospital, perhaps, or in jail—but Giulia and I never minded that; the men who could pay did.

To say the truth, no battalion in the world was so good or so comfortable as ours at that time. The men never drank out of the lines, therefore those who went too far could be easily carried away to bed. There was very little fighting, for no man, indeed, would strike a blow in Mademoiselle Julie's canteen, and if a blow is not struck soon, soldiers forgive and forget easily; moreover, if a man had no money he could get his bit of tobacco and, perhaps, his glass of *eau-de-vie* without begging for it. Giulia never wrote down the name of a man she gave credit to; she said always: "It is not my honour, but yours, that is at stake." That phrase with us was worth all the ledgers in the world.

One evening I was sitting on the edge of the counter talking about something or other to a corporal who had dropped in for a glass of wine and had asked me to join him in the drink. In spite of the difference in rank I consented, for I knew quite well that the social position that the corporal used to hold was very much higher than my own; as a matter of fact, the man had at one time a commission in the British army, and his father draws to this very day a big pension from the British Government. But that is by the way. As we chatted Giulia listened and was interested; we spoke of some affairs of the battalion, and Giulia knew as much as we did of such things. We three were the only persons in the canteen. I had just told Giulia to refill the glasses, and she was about doing so when a man entered, a simple soldier. I did not know him at the time; I found out afterwards that he was a Hessian and bore the reputation of being taciturn and unsociable, thereby rendering himself an object of dislike to all. He called for a glass of brandy and drank it, then for another, which he sipped slowly, and tried to enter into conversation with Giulia. The corporal and I resumed the conversation interrupted by the Hessian's entrance, and Giulia evidently preferred to listen to us rather than to the new-comer. As he noted this he became rather angry, and made some remark about his money being as good as another's, and that canteen girls should be obliging to all customers. Giulia, who had a hot temper, told him at once to finish his drink and to take himself and his money elsewhere. The Hessian drank his brandy, and as he was leaving said that she knew the difference between a simple soldier and a sergeant-major, and if someone had no chevrons on his sleeve he would soon be taught that it was unmannerly to sit on a counter in the presence of a lady. My temper had been gradually rising and this was too much for me. I jumped down from the counter, took off my belt and bayonet, which I handed to Giulia, stripped off my tunic, and told the scamp that there were no chevrons on my shirt. He was astonished, and almost before he could put himself on his defence I had given him in quick succession right and left fists in the eyes. I followed up the attack vigorously, and in less than three minutes all the insolence was taken out of him and he begged for mercy. Then I kicked him out of the canteen and told him never again to enter it, put on my tunic and sat down, this time on a chair.

"I must apologise," I said to Giulia; "I should not have sat on the counter; in one sense he was right. I will not ask pardon for quarrelling, for he offended you too."

"You may sit where you like, my sergeant-major," Giulia replied; "I shall not be offended."

"But I should not sit on the counter."

"Sit where you wish," she repeated; "I shall be satisfied."

"Même sur vos genoux, mademoiselle," said the English corporal, with a smile. Giulia blushed, laughed, and shook her head.

I may finish here about the Hessian. The story was told by him that I had committed an unprovoked assault. When the commandant heard this, he sent for me. I told the truth, and my version of the affair was corroborated by Giulia and the corporal. The commandant would take no official notice of the affair, but he privately admonished me that it was very wrong to take off my belt and tunic. "You should not have undressed, even partially," he said, "in the presence of a lady and an inferior." But he gave me no blame for the beating I gave the Hessian.

Here I must explain the military meaning of being undressed. If a man is on duty and wearing a belt and bayonet, he is undressed if he takes them off. Should he be supposed to wear white trousers and white gaiters, he is undressed if he wears red trousers with black leggings. So one can understand that, when the commandant admonished me for being undressed in the presence of Giulia and the corporal, he referred quite as much to the taking off of my belt and bayonet as he did to the taking off of my coat.

Soldiers have to be very particular about their clothing and equipments; this is quite right, as it tends to good discipline and order.

When the canteen closed for the evening Giulia and I smoked our cigarettes as usual, while I sipped my glass of wine. We were rather silent, for I was thinking of the quarrel and its probable consequences; what Giulia thought of I cannot tell. At last I finished my cigarette, carefully extinguished the end for fear of fire, and drained my glass. I rose to go. Instead of shaking hands with me across the counter — for she had been sitting inside all the time, whilst I occupied a seat outside — Giulia came round to where I was and for the first time asked me what I thought would happen.

"Oh, nothing, nothing," I replied; "what can happen? I had to do as I did; I surely could not allow any man to misconduct himself here?"

"Yes, yes; but you took off your belt and tunic."

"Oh, that will never be mentioned; why should the scoundrel talk of that?"

"Yes; but he will talk of it, and there will be trouble —trouble for you on my account."

"Well, if there is to be trouble for me I shall not mind it, since it will be on your account; were it on account of any other I should be vexed."

"But you may lose your rank," she insisted.

"I shall not mind, so long as they leave me on duty in the canteen."

"But they may not leave you here; another may come."

"That is true," I answered, "and that is the only thing I am afraid of."

"You would like to stay here with me?" said Giulia, blushing as she spoke.

"Always, always with you," I replied, and, putting my kepi on the counter, I took her in my arms and kissed her full upon the lips.

Then we forgot all about the Hessian and thought only about ourselves. I have no mind to write all about our love story; people who have loved will understand, and those poor wretches who have never known what it is to love passionately and to be as passionately loved could never comprehend, were I to write till Doomsday about Giulia and myself.

At last the time came for parting. Giulia told me that she should not sleep for thinking of what might happen as a result of the quarrel, but I succeeded in calming her fears. "Trust me," I told her; "I took the wisest course, though I did not think of that at the time. If I had allowed the rascal to go away unpunished, the commandant would call me a coward and say that I was unworthy to wear the military medal, and all the officers and men would agree with him. Now the worst that can be said is that I lost my temper and forgot my rank. Even that too will be pardoned, since they will easily see that I could not allow myself to be insulted in your presence without taking instant vengeance for the affront." She grew more composed as I spoke, and I felt more at ease; in comforting Giulia I comforted myself.

I did not get the message that the commandant wished to see me until about three o'clock in the afternoon of the next day. All the morning I had enough to do to prevent Giulia from breaking down; her eyes showed that she had spent a restless night, a night of tears, but as the morning wore on she almost forgot her anxiety in my cheering words and more than cheering kisses. When a sergeant told me that I was wanted at the officers' quarters Giulia broke down completely. I kissed her once more, bade her be of good courage, and gave her over to the sergeant's wife, whose kindness and tender sympathy were of inestimable value to us both. The sergeant's wife was a good woman and deserved a better fate than that which was her lot afterwards; but then, what will you?

It is only the good who suffer in this world; the bad are always to be found at the top of the wheel.

Well, the commandant received me as I have already told, and after a kind admonition—how kind these officers that men fear so much can be when they like!—sent me away. I saluted, turned, walked a pace or two, and then set off running at the top of my speed to the canteen. I burst in the door, ran up the stairs, taking three steps at a time, and bounded with a loud cry of joy into the room where Giulia was weeping. I could say nothing, nothing intelligible at all events, but Giulia understood. So did the sergeant's wife, for she discreetly went away and left us to ourselves and our happiness.

Things went on badly for the Hessian. He was always an ill-liked comrade, but this last affair was too bad indeed. All sympathised with Giulia and myself, and the sympathy was not merely on account of the chance a man had of getting tobacco and a glass of spirits when his pockets were empty. Oh no; the legionaries were glad that they could get a little credit, but then they always paid—that is, all paid except the poor devils whose money was stopped for some reason or other—and they were pleased with the canteen, pleased with Giulia, who had been born in the battalion, and I think they were not discontented on account of my position, for was not I a legionary like themselves? So the Hessian was not spoken to, or only spoken to to be cursed; if he replied he was beaten; if he complained, there were plenty to prove that he was a bad comrade and that it was impossible to soldier with him, and, unfortunately for himself, he had been known as an unsociable fellow for a long time. The end was that he volunteered for Tonquin, where there were some of ours still, and his captain was by no means sorry to be rid of him, for one can never know what may occur when a man is deservedly unpopular in the Legion and has not grace or tact enough to get back to favour with his comrades.

As for Giulia and me, life was idyllic. We did not mind the laughing jests of our comrades; they never went too far. There was a leaven of the gentleman in the battalion, and this leaven leavened all the mass. Then the really bad ones were afraid; the example of the Hessian was too fresh in their minds. But, indeed, all were kind and agreeable. That Giulia and I should be lovers had been obvious to all others long before we ourselves thought of being such to one another, and when the legionaries noticed that she lived for me alone, just as all my thoughts were alone hers, they kept their coarse jokes to themselves and were as polite to us as if we were far higher than they in social position. Some of the songs were not of a moral kind, but as the evening concert always took place outside the canteen Giulia was not supposed to hear, and, indeed, when she did hear she did not always understand. When she did comprehend she said nothing; one cannot be a *cantinière* in the Legion and a prude.

At this time Giulia and I were always together. Certainly while the canteen was open I was outside the counter, often making one of a party of sergeants who came to drink in comrade-like fashion with one another; at other times merely going around to see that there was no disorder—well, no more disorder and abandonment than are reasonable in a canteen where belts are off and tongues wag freely. I very seldom had any trouble, most of the legionaries kept within bounds, and those who felt disposed to give a loose rein to the desire of ardent spirits were prevented from doing so by a constant lack of money. Sometimes, however, when some Russian or Prussian or Austrian had received money from Europe there was a little danger of a free fight, and I, who had been in the encounter at Three Fountains, did not like these things.

I had told Giulia about that trouble and she was just as concerned as I, but she was concerned for my safety and my rank, while I was anxious about her shop and herself. Any man can start a row—oh, it is quite easy, I assure you—but it is not every man that can stop one. Besides, I remembered how the huts were torn down at Three Fountains and the Russian's advice to the old soldier sutler: "Take your goods and madame away." The advice about madame seemed especially applicable to Giulia, and yet I knew she would stay by me, and it was my duty to stay by the canteen.

One day the English corporal whom I have mentioned came to the canteen and asked Giulia to take care of some money for him. Giulia refused point-blank, but said that he might speak to me. When I learned what he wished me to do I at once saw the reasonableness of the request, inasmuch as no man would like to keep so large a sum of money as the corporal had in his own possession in a hut. The Englishman had just received from home a Bank of England note for £100, and many a simple soldier would kill him for such a sum. But, one may object, how negociate such a billet in such a place? Oh, no one could do that except the owner, or someone like Giulia, who would change it for him in the regular way of business; but many a man was nearing the end of his five years' service, and a Bank of England note could be easily hidden for a time and in the end changed in Paris. One hundred pounds!—twenty-five hundred francs!—why, it was a fortune.

I said that I would take the note and give him a receipt for it, and that, as he drew money from Mademoiselle Julie, he could give receipts until the full amount was withdrawn. He thanked me, gave me the note, took a receipt, and immediately applied to Giulia in my presence for a hundred francs. She gave him the money at my request and he gave me an acknowledgment. That evening his squad was merry; he had given them fifty francs to spend, the other fifty he spent with his brother corporals.

On the following day he asked me about the stock in the canteen. I told him that there was not at the time enough to justify him in giving a spree to a section, but that in less than a week he could stand treat to the battalion if he liked.

"Oh no ; not the battalion, only the company."

"I understand," said I ; "I know that you cannot go outside your own company, but I spoke of the battalion merely to show you Madèmoiselle Julie's resources."

"I see," the corporal replied ; "well, tell me when you are ready, and my comrades shall enjoy an evening's carouse."

Let me now tell about the money. Of course, it was Giulia's, not mine, and she kept it in her money box, which was snugly hidden in her own room in a place that no one knew of except ourselves. Even the sergeant's wife did not know it. She never entered Giulia's room except on invitation. Giulia herself kept the place as it ought to be, sweeping it, dusting the furniture, and having everything as neat and clean as it could be in a palace. Once a week she gave me the key. I went there with a couple of privates — of course, she then took the box away—the legionaries with me removed everything to another place and washed out the room and left it with windows and door open for a couple of hours. They then returned, replaced the furniture, got a couple of drinks, a couple of cigars and a franc, and went away satisfied. But this is mere domestic economy.

Giulia also kept the receipt for the hundred francs. But, one will say, why not transact the business without troubling me ? Well, the amount was so large and the money was so strange that she wished me to settle everything for her, as I was, in her opinion, the one man in the world who knew everything and was always right. Again, she knew how much I prized her trust, and so was glad to pay me a delicate compliment.

Moreover, we were so closely united to each other now that it would seem to so gentle and confiding, yet high-spirited a girl as she was a breach of faith for her to engage in such a transaction without my knowledge and consent. Yet when I asked Giulia why she had not taken the money from the corporal at once, she only answered: "I don't know; but I would not." Then she kissed me, and said: "I will never take anything, unless you know about it and are satisfied."

What a sum of happiness the events, even the very words, of our lives made at this time! Ah, well! the sum was soon to be added up, and the total not exceeded, for ever.

About five days after my last conversation with the English corporal the new stock arrived. It had cost altogether about two thousand francs, and we—that is, Guilia and I—were sure to make at least five or six hundred francs profit. When we ordered the stuff we expected that it would last for some time, but now, knowing the corporal's resources and intention, we settled that it would all be sold within a week. We were not disappointed; in fact, the day after it arrived we had to send an order for a similar quantity to our agent at Oran.

"I see that the new goods have arrived," said the Englishman to me as I met him on the parade-ground.

"Yes," I replied. "I have been looking for you. If you tell me now how much you want I can get it, and you can write out the receipt."

"Thanks, my sergeant-major; but you are a man of experience in these things. You were at Three Fountains; is it not so?"

"Yes," I answered, laughing.

"Then will you tell me how much I ought to have for the entertainment of my company?"

"Oh, five hundred francs will do well, but seven or eight hundred will really be a generous amount to spend."

"Let me be very generous then ; get me a thousand."

"Very well ; but remember there will be change left. Let your squad understand that they will have the spending of that, so shall you have sentries guarding your sleep."

"You are right, my sergeant-major, you are right ; I am obliged to you for the hint. Will not Mademoiselle Julie give us a glass of wine, so that we may clink our glasses together ?"

"Oh, certainly. Nobody amongst the officers troubles about the canteen. One can generally get a glass of *eau-de-vie* or *vin ordinaire* at any reasonable hour. The commandant knows that no man is given more than he can safely bear, and what is the use of being strict in such a place as this ?"

The corporal knew this. If a man wanted a drink at any hour when the canteen was supposed to be shut, he could speak to me and I could get it for him. He did not, however, enter the canteen ; he had to take it, and that quickly, at a window at the back. As a rule, men only wanted a glass of brandy in the morning —about half-a-dozen at most ; these were the men who had had too much drink the evening before and who possessed or borrowed the necessary coppers in the morning.

As the English corporal and I took our drinks together at the little window, I told him the true story of Three Fountains. Giulia listened with interest, though she had heard all about it before. Once I asked her to refill the glasses. She said : "Do not continue until I return ; I wish to hear it all again." Of course, I waited for her return and then proceeded with my tale. When I had finished, I said that I hoped there would not be any such work here.

"Oh no," replied the corporal ; "not if I can help it."

"You must not make them drunk," said Giulia.

"No, no, Madame Julie ; I give you my word of honour."

It was the first time that she had been addressed as madame. She blushed a rosy red, turned her head aside for a moment, and gave me one swift glance of—— Oh, I knew well what it meant and how it pleased me, but I will say no more. The corporal was a gentleman and went away at once. He finished his drink, raised his kepi, and said adieu.

There was a good deal of boisterous mirth that evening at the canteen and around it. A couple of men did strike each other, but before any serious damage was done, I had both under guard and on the road to the guard-room. The rest took the hint; they saw that fighting meant loss of the drink and fun of the evening, and a night in the guard-room and punishment in the morning. A few men who were evidently overcome, or nearly so, by the effects of the liquor were carried away to bed by their comrades, and, taken all in all, the evening passed away satisfactorily. Next morning, however, nearly a hundred men turned up for *eau-de-vie*, and all had money. The corporal had been judiciously generous; everyone was pleased.

The Englishman gave one more spree, three nights after, to his company, but this second one did not cost him more than four hundred francs. Then he spent two hundred francs one evening with his section; what was left was kept for his squad. In acting as he did he followed the custom of the Legion, but I have already said enough about that.

As he was drawing the last fifty francs I said to him in Giulia's presence.

"Monsieur le caporal, you have spent your money as it should be spent, but it may be a long time until you are rich again. Do not hesitate if you want a litre of wine or some brandy or tobacco and have no money. There has been a great profit in a short time; whenever you feel inclined come and have your share of it."

"Yes," said Giulia; "you will be always welcome, whether your pockets are full or empty."

"I thank you both," the Englishman replied, "and I like and respect you too much not to take advantage now and then of your generous offer."

"Come as often as you like," I said; "you will always find a welcome, and that not merely on account of the profit."

"Yes," said Giulia; "that is true."

"I will come," the corporal answered, "but not very often; such a welcome is too good to be worn out." He lifted his kepi to Giulia, bowed, and went away.

He did not come very often without money, only now and then, as he had said, but, you see, he was very proud.

CHAPTER XIX

SOON afterwards some important changes took place in the battalion. We were ordered to prepare a draft of four hundred officers and men for the East, and in lieu of these we received a corresponding number of recruits and veterans sent home. The changes in the officers were many, for, in addition to those who went as a matter of course with the draft, others volunteered for foreign service and were accepted. As far as I was concerned, the officer most to be regretted was the adjutant. The man who went was always kind and had ever a pleasant word for Giulia and for me; the one who replaced him was destined to be our greatest enemy. We could not guess this at the time, and naturally thought that all things would go on as usual, but it was not long before we were cruelly undeceived.

The new adjutant was a stout, thick-set man of about thirty-five years. He had seen a good deal of service both in Algeria and Tonquin, and was undoubtedly a very smart soldier and a most capable man for performing the duties of his rank. That is all one can say in his favour. He was harsh, even tyrannical; he never spared a man's feelings, and his tongue could cut like a whip-lash. All the legionaries, from sergeant-major down to simple soldier, feared and hated him; before he had been in the battalion a fortnight we, who had been the most joyous and careless fellows on earth, every man pleased with himself and with his comrades, became the most sullen and dogged lot in the world. There was just as much drinking as ever, but the singing, the *camaraderie*, the easy give-and-take feeling that used to prevail, were all gone. Moreover, the men drank more brandy and less wine, and, as I pointed this out to Giulia, I said :

"Carissima, there will be bad work soon ; somebody's blood will flow, and then there will be an execution."

She shuddered as she replied : "How I wish that that bad man were sent away ! Before he came we were all happy, now I, even I, am gloomy and troubled ; I am oppressed by some foreboding that I cannot understand."

I could enter into her feelings, for I too had anxious thoughts, not for Giulia or myself, indeed, but for the other legionaries. I felt that an outbreak of some kind would occur, but the chief trouble was to persuade myself that it would be merely a rash act on the part of one man, who would free all from tyranny and take the punishment by himself, but as the days wore on I, who knew the Legion by heart, could see that there was a far greater chance of a number of men being concerned in the *émeute*. One thing delayed action, the newcomers and the rest had not sufficiently fraternised — four hundred strangers are too many for any battalion to assimilate quickly.

One morning half-a-dozen men were having a nip of brandy each at a little window at the back of the canteen ; I was standing a little apart, and Giulia was passing out the glasses. Suddenly the new adjutant came round the corner and sternly asked the meaning of giving out drink at such an hour. Nobody could reply. We all knew that the commandant winked at the business, we all knew too that the canteen should not be open at that time, but then no harm had ever come of it, no man ever got more that one *petite verre*, and surely that would rather help a man than hurt him if he wanted it. But how could I, the one chiefly addressed, say all that ? Oh no ; I had to be silent and take my abuse as best I could, and truly the adjutant was abusive. He was still speaking like a brute when

Q

Giulia, with flushed cheeks and sparkling eyes, broke in, and said:

"The sergeant-major has nothing to do with it, it is I alone who am to blame."

The adjutant saluted her politely and replied that he understood that I was in military charge of the canteen, but, even had I nothing to do with it, I was acting in a most disgraceful fashion when I allowed these pigs to get drunk so early in the morning.

"The soldiers are not pigs," answered Giulia, "and they are not drunk; no man ever gets more than a *petite verre* at this hour."

"Then it is usual to supply drink so soon," the scoundrel said; "ah! the commandant must hear of this."

Then he took my belt and bayonet and sent me to my own room, to remain there under arrest; as for the others, he merely wrote down their names and ordered them away. When they had gone—it was long afterwards that I learnt this—he tried to begin a conversation with Giulia, but he had scarcely uttered an endearing word when she put down the window and walked away. She was right, and the scoundrel was wrong, but he made her and me suffer for it.

Just as I was expecting my morning coffee, I heard a tap at the door, and cried "Come in." Giulia entered carrying a tray with coffee and rolls and butter. I took the tray from her and put it on the floor. There was no table, of course; in a bachelor sergeant's room nothing, indeed, but the camp-bed and a shelf or two for my equipments. Then I kissed her, and said:

"You spoke bravely this morning; I am glad of it. I should like to say what you said, but they would punish me."

"Are you pleased?" she asked.

"Yes, carissima mia; and all the battalion will be pleased when they hear about it."

"I do not care about the battalion if you are content."

"Yes, yes, ma belle; I am very content. Is he not a rascal?"

"Oh," said Giulia, "I hate him; all the trouble comes from him; somebody must kill him or we shall never again have peace."

"Somebody will kill him," I answered; "you may rest assured of that."

"But not you, not you," she cried; "promise me, not you."

"Certainly not," I replied; "why should I kill him when there are so many others who have more grievances than I? Moreover, I have no desire to be shot; I am too happy here with you to wish to leave you. Heaven for me is here."

She was satisfied with this, and insisted on my tasting the coffee.

"Is it nice?" she asked.

I smiled, and said that it was very nice.

"Does it taste well?"

"Oh yes; I never drank any coffee I liked so well."

The truth is, Giulia had put a glass of *eau-de-vie* into the coffee, and I felt that I wanted it after the scene in the morning. How kind, how thoughtful she was! I told her so over and over again before she left, and when she did go, she said with a pretty way of command that she had:

"Expect me in an hour, and do not lose your temper with anyone until I come back; there is trouble enough already."

I promised and she went away.

Giulia, as she had promised, came back in an hour. She brought me a little wine, for she knew that very soon I should be in front of the commandant, and a glass of wine does summon up one's courage. A glass of wine before an interview, a glass of brandy before a battle—that is sound sense. Very soon a couple of soldiers of my own rank came for me. I gave them the remainder of the liquor, and they were very pleased.

"I hope you won't get into serious trouble," said the Alsatian.

"Not at all," chimed in the Spaniard; "he'll get off, but there must be no more drinking out of hours."

"I will take care of that," said Giulia; "will you tell your companies?" They promised to do so, and we three went away, I in the centre without belt or bayonet, and Giulia followed, after locking the door of my room. When we came before the commandant one of the escort took off my kepi. The adjutant was present, looking as stiff and unimpressionable as a block of wood. When the accusation was read out I was asked if I had anything to say. I replied that I had not. The commandant considered and considered and considered. He walked up and down for a few moments, then stood still for a second or two, and resumed his walk. After about five minutes he said:

"You are young, you have the military medal; I do not like to punish you." Here the adjutant interposed and asked permission to make a statement. When this was granted, he raked up the whole story of the quarrel at Three Fountains, as if everyone did not know about it. He laid stress upon the fact that I had been one of the ringleaders in that affair, and ended by asking was such an one as I fit to look after a canteen. Then the commandant said:

"When you came first to the battalion there was a sergeant-major in every company, and I could not find a place for you. Most commandants would have made you simple sergeant of a section. Will you now consent to give up one chevron and become sergeant? If you do, I will say no more about this affair." I jumped at the offer, the more readily as nothing was said about taking me from the society of Giulia.

"Very well," said the commandant; "present yourself here to-morrow morning with only one chevron on your sleeve."

My kepi, belt and bayonet were returned to me. Having put them on, I saluted and walked away a free man again.

Giulia was waiting for me a short distance off. I told her all about the matter as we walked towards my quarters. When we arrived there I said:

"Get your scissors and cut off the chevron."

"No, no," she cried; "I will never cut it off."

"Then give me your scissors and I will do it."

But she would not give her scissors for that purpose. So I had to take off my tunic, and with the point of a little Spanish knife which I used for cutting tobacco —these Spanish knives are very handy little things, for one cannot always wear a bayonet, and one never knows how trouble may arise—I ripped the upper chevron from my sleeve. I laid it on my camp-bed. Giulia took it, kissed it, and put it in her bosom.

"I would not cut it off," she said, "but I will sew it on again, when the time comes." That time never came.

Giulia went away to see about some things in the canteen. In less than five minutes she was back again, looking as angry as a tigress at bay. When she grew a little composed, she told me that the sergeant who stayed with his wife in the room over the bar had been appointed to the charge of the place and that I was to be assigned to his section in No. 4 Company in the morning. This was most unpleasant news, but I comforted her by saying that it really made no difference, except that I could not now go to see her at the canteen except during the hours when it was open, but that I should do my best to see her as often as possible outside duty hours. "They cannot separate us anyway," I said; "you are all in all to me and I am all in all to you." So she relieved her sorrow by a good cry, and then sat, quite quiet, on my lap. After all, the great thing was that nobody could part us altogether.

Next morning things turned out as Giulia had said. I was posted for duty to the first section of No. 4 Company instead of the sergeant whose wife had given shelter and protection to Giulia after her mother's death, and he was assigned to look after the canteen. I very soon fell into the routine duties of a sergeant. The section was handed over to me in first-class order and temperament save for one thing—the soldiers were discontented with the tyranny of the adjutant. This did not affect me much, as they were more or less inclined to look upon me as a martyr, and my reduction in rank was a fresh source of ill-humour, showing, as it did, another proof of the mischievous malevolence of the adjutant. I took, or pretended to take, the matter easily. I did my duty as it should be done during what one may call business hours, but when the work of the day was over I was good comrade to all. It was lucky that I made so many friends at the time; I wanted them—every one—very soon.

While I was acting as sergeant, the adjutant made several attempts to get into the good graces of Giulia, but she repulsed him on every occasion. At last he asked her point-blank why she would not even acknowledge his salute, and she told him bluntly that she disliked him and that she wished him in Tonquin or in his grave—anywhere, so long as he was out of the battalion. Now Giulia was passionate even for an Italian, and as she spoke she raised her voice, unthinkingly, indeed, and some soldiers going with a corporal to relieve the sentries heard what she said as they passed by. The adjutant saw that they heard; he knew that he was hated by all, and he felt that in a couple of hours the whole battalion would be secretly enjoying his rebuff. With a curse he turned on his heel. Afterwards he neglected Giulia but paid more than enough of attention to me. He cursed me openly on parade, he found fault with every man in my section, not a buckle was bright, not a strap was clean, the greatcoats were badly folded, the bayonets were dull and the rifles were foul. In short, every fault that a man can find was found by him, but, be it well understood, only in the absence of the captain and other officers of the company. When the adjutant had charge of the parade and the sergeants commanded the companies, then the men of my section knew that a bad quarter of an hour awaited them. The other legionaries noted this too. They were glad, because it was quite obvious now that the majority of the battalion might endure the adjutant's harshness patiently, for were not the men of No. 1 section of No. 4 Company the really aggrieved ones? It was tacitly understood in the battalion that the avenger would come from us.

All this time Giulia and I met every afternoon just before the opening of the canteen, and afterwards for ten minutes or so when the canteen was closed for the day. While the place was open I was always to be found there, unless I was on guard or had some duty to perform that kept me away. The other sergeants had easy lives. Every extra piece of work was passed on to me by the adjutant, and let me say here that the adjutant is the worst enemy a sub-officer can have. It's bad to be disliked by the commandant, because he will block promotion ; the captain's enmity is hard to bear, because he can snarl three or four times a day; but the adjutant can play the very devil with a man in a thousand ways. Imagine asking a man who has made a slight mistake in making out the orders of the day:

" Can you read and write ? "

" Yes, sir."

" Well," comes the reply before more than a hundred soldiers, " take care in future to read and write correctly. Go back to your place, you stupid pig."

And as the man departs he is suddenly ordered to halt and face right-about, and then asked:

"Who promoted you sergeant?" And before he has time to answer, the remark is made, loudly enough to be over all the parade:

"There is not a man in the camp less fitted to wear the gold chevron than you. To your place, rascal!"

If Giulia happened to be passing through the parade ground it was worse. The abuse I received—and remember there is no redress in the Legion unless one settles matters for himself with an unexpected bullet or bayonet-thrust, and then there will be an execution—the abuse, I say, that I received made my blood often almost boil with rage. I could not have endured it but for the sweet company of Giulia; with her in the evening I forgot the wrongs and insults of the day. Truly there is no solace for a troubled spirit like the society of the loving and beloved one; her sweet sympathy more than makes up for all.

The sergeant of No. 2 section of my Company was a German Pole, a good-humoured fellow, ready for any fun, except when the adjutant's eyes were fixed upon him, but withal a good soldier. His time was nearly up, and he meant to go to Paris, and there make a living somehow, when he should be at last done with the Foreign Legion. He and I were on very friendly terms, and, indeed, I was oftener with him than with any other sergeant of the corps. One evening—it was almost his last evening with us—he drank more than was good for him, and awoke in the morning with a headache and a sick stomach. I saw that he could not drink his morning coffee, and asked him if he would not like a glass of *eau-de-vie*.

"Yes," he replied; "but one cannot get that now, this cursed adjutant has spoiled all."

"Never mind," I answered, "I will get it for you."

"Take care, my comrade, you will get into more

trouble, and are not things bad enough with you already?"

"So bad," I said, "that they cannot be worse." And I took my kepi and sallied forth. As luck would have it Giulia was sitting at the open window of her bedroom, and when I beckoned to her she came out on the cantonment square to meet me. I told her that a poor devil was ill and wanted some brandy.

"All right," she said, "I will get some and give it to you at your own quarters."

I returned, told the Pole that he should soon receive some medicine, and waited for Giulia at the door. Now either the adjutant must have observed all this, or some scoundrel must have told him about it, for just as I turned into the bachelor sergeants' quarters with the drink and Giulia went away again towards the canteen, the adjutant came running up at the top of his speed, crying out: "Halt, halt, sergeant; what have you got there?" I was forced to deliver up the little flask. He uncorked it, smelled, and said:

"Very well, very well, consider yourself a prisoner. Ah, Mademoiselle Giulia," he went on, "what excuse can your lover make now?"

"Go away, Giulia," I said.

"Silence; to your room, rascal!" roared the angry adjutant.

"Good-bye, my well-beloved," said Giulia. "Out of my way, pig" (this to the adjutant). And she walked across the square with the air and tread of an empress.

The adjutant gnashed his teeth and bit his moustache with rage; he hissed rather than said to me:

"You, rascal, shall pay for this, and this payment, understand well, is only the first; others are sure to come afterwards." I turned on my heel and entered my apartment.

The Pole was very sorry, and would, I believe, have told about his part in the affair, but I pointed out, as

others also did, that there was no use in his getting
into trouble, as by so doing he could not help me in
the least. Everyone saw quite plainly that I should
certainly be reduced to the rank of corporal, if not
lower, and all were, or professed to be, sorry for my
misfortune. To cut the tale short, I may as well say
at once that I got my choice of resigning my position
as sergeant of a section and becoming a mere corporal
of a squad or of going before a court-martial. Of
course I resigned, for the offence of obtaining liquor
at a wrong hour after the previous warning could not
be overlooked, and, as likely as not, a court-martial
might send me back to the ranks, a thing I had no
desire for. The first time I passed the adjutant with
the two red chevrons on my sleeve instead of the
single gold one he smiled with an unholy joy, but
the smile changed to a scowl as he saw the kiss of
welcome that I received from Giulia at the door of
the canteen.

It was well for all the other squads in the section
that I was reduced. They were now treated not worse,
certainly, than the rest of the legionaries, but my little
squad of sixteen men had to bear the brunt of the
adjutant's anger. I was very concerned at this, and
told Giulia. She—clever and good girl—at once found
out a means of in part compensating them, but she did
not tell me, and she strictly warned them not to tell me
either. They—poor devils—were only too glad to keep
her counsel, and it was by a mere accident that I learned
the truth afterwards. Her plan was this: She told the
men of my squad that they could come to the canteen
with or without money and that they need not be afraid
of a refusal on her part to supply them, as far as they
could reasonably expect, with drink and tobacco. Now
a legionary will stand a good deal of abuse during the
day if he knows that brandy and other comforts await
him for nothing in the evening; and, moreover, it was
evident to all that no one was especially aimed at except

me, and that, when No. 7, let us say, of the squad was told that he was a dirty pig, he was merely getting the benefit of remarks that were really meant for me. When the adjutant had done abusing the men one by one he gathered, as it were, all the abuse together and hurled it at my head, and often those rough legionaries, smarting as they were under their own vexations, used to feel for me more than for themselves. I said to them one day after the devil had left the hut, where he had kicked about our equipments, swearing that we did not know the meaning of good order, that I would never report any man for anything: "No matter how bad we may be," I continued, "we are abused and sworn at. We are all punished for the evil we do and the evil that we don't even think of."

"I hope," said a simple soldier, a Sicilian, "that the devil will be dead soon."

He looked significantly at me, and then at the others, but, as I said nothing, the implied proposal went by the board. But we all began to think seriously from that day forth.

Many a stolen interview I had with Giulia when all in the cantonments were asleep. I could rarely see her now, for the adjutant found me plenty of work for my leisure time, and I took care to be in the hut every evening lest there should be a fight amongst the comrades of the squad. One must not imagine that they were bad comrades to one another. On the contrary, they were very good indeed, but when men are angry at being abused and sworn at without cause and without mercy they will easily quarrel among themselves. So I watched the squad carefully, and more than once stopped a dispute that might have suddenly led to a general fight, and very soon the simple soldiers saw that I was taking care of them for their sakes as well as for my own. At first they were inclined to resent this, but common-sense prevailed, and they acknowledged—tacitly only, of course—that I was in the right.

One night about twelve o'clock I was speaking to Giulia at the little window at the back of the canteen. We had been talking for half-an-hour of various matters and the time had passed quickly for both. I was about kissing her good-night when I heard a step behind me. In a second I was out of Giulia's arms and had faced about. Instinctively my hand sought my left side, where the bayonet was.

"Who is there?" said the well-known voice of the adjutant.

"Caporal Le Poer de la quatrième compagnie, monsieur," I replied.

"What are you doing here? Why are you not with your squad? Who is in charge at the hut?"

I said nothing, for I had nothing to say. I almost felt the chevrons take flight from my arm. I had sense enough, however, to take my hand from the hilt of the bayonet. Things were bad enough as they were.

The adjutant marched me to where a sentinel was on duty. He gave me in charge to this man and went to the guard-hut. Very soon a corporal and two men of the guard arrived, and I was taken to the prisoners' quarters, to rest as well as I could on a plank bed until morning. When I was brought before the commandant the charges were read out against me of having been absent without leave or necessity from the hut where my squad lay, of having left no one in charge while I was away, and of going to the canteen in the middle of the night. The commandant looked very serious, and, I daresay, so did I. What I had done was good to do, but bad to be charged with doing. Any other officer coming upon me as the adjutant had come would have passed on and not minded; even the commandant, I am sure, would pretend not to see. But when the charge was made and its truth admitted, then discipline compelled that proper notice should be taken of it. I was not sent before a court-martial. I was permitted to resign both chevrons, and so I went back to my company a simple soldier of the second class.

I said to Giulia as we talked that evening at the end of the counter in the canteen—the other legionaries, I must mention, were decent enough to keep out of ear-shot—that I should be very careful now, as I had no more chevrons to lose, and an ugly punishment was sure to follow the next charge. "But for you, carissima," I went on, "I should volunteer again for Tonquin." Giulia at this began to weep quietly, but I soon reassured her. I told her that I would never go anywhere willingly unless she came with me, and then she quickly dried her tears.

"You must take good care, Jean, of everything, and above all things, you must never allow yourself to lose your temper. Yes," she continued, "no matter what is said to you, no matter how hard it may be to bear, control yourself and all will be well. Come every evening, and I will comfort you for all the troubles and insults of the day."

I promised faithfully to follow her advice, and though oftentimes it was hard to keep my temper, yet the remembrance of my promise and the thought that every minute that passed brought the time of our next meeting nearer made me feel, if not supremely happy, at least well content to endure with outward equanimity the curses, epithets and abuse that were my daily lot. I had one other consoling thought, some day surely the devil would be struck down by an irritated man, and he would in all probability be taken away in the midst of his sins. That was the constant prayer of the legionaries of the battalion. May he die, and die soon, and may he go safely home to his father, who is in hell.

Now that I was as low as I could be in the Legion, the adjutant, sergeants and corporals led me a terrible life. There was no work too hard or too dirty for me; I did twice as much camp-cleaning as any other; my spare time was encroached upon; and I found myself almost every night a prisoner in the guard-house. The adjutant had the right of making me what one may call a prisoner at large for a week, and longer, at a time. All he had to do was to pretend to find fault with me for laziness, though I was an active soldier; for dirt, though I was a clean one; for carelessness, though I, for my own sake as well as for Giulia's, was the most careful soldier in the battalion. Then, when all the day's duties were over I could not go, as others went, to the canteen. I had to report myself at the guard-room and enter the prisoners' quarters, where I might stretch myself on the plank bed in the clothes which I had worn all the day, until the call went next morning to summon me to another dreary round of hard work and hurtful words. No one must wonder that the sergeants and corporals ill-treated me; the adjutant would have ill-treated them, if they had shown me any signs of favour or even of fair-play. Moreover, it's the way of the world to kick the man that's down, and human nature is the same in the Legion as elsewhere.

I should have become quite reckless but for the love and kindly sympathy of Giulia. With her I almost forgot my sorrows, and the firm assurance I had that nothing could lower me in her eyes, and that no man in all the world could steal her heart from me, was my great safeguard in the moments, and they were many, of temptation. The rest of the legionaries watched with interest the conduct of the adjutant; they felt that some time or other the crisis would arrive; it was agreed on all sides that I was the predestined avenger.

CHAPTER XX

THOUGH I did my best to keep out of trouble, still I could not help now and then breaking the regulations. Other soldiers broke them far oftener than I, but I knew quite well that the sergeants and corporals were all watching me in order to bring me up before the commandant on some charge or other, and so curry favour with the dreaded adjutant. Now it would not be fair to blame them for this, every sub-officer naturally preferred that the simple soldier should get into trouble rather than himself; and, moreover, the man who could get me punishment was sure to be left alone by the tyrant of the battalion. I certainly felt a bit sore about it at times, and Giulia, to whom I communicated my suspicions, was very angry indeed.

The first serious affair in which I was involved, as a simple soldier, occurred one evening in the hut where my squad lay. I was not a prisoner at large at the time, and so had not to go to the guard-hut, report myself for the night, and then take up my quarters in the cells where the prisoners were kept under guard. As I sat on the edge of my bed-cot, smoking and thinking, an Austrian came in, evidently under the influence of drink. This man was as pleasant a companion as one could wish for when sober, but when drunk—he was not often so, I must confess—his disposition underwent a change; he became violent, abusive and quarrelsome. The first person he laid eyes on when he passed the door was myself, and towards me he accordingly staggered. I cannot recall what he said first, but I know that I was angry and returned a very sharp answer. He then began to curse and revile me, and

255

I am afraid that my language in reply was as " frequent
and painful and free " as his. The corporal of the
squad came in as we were warming to our work and
saw how matters were going. He left the hut at once,
and, mean hound that he was, listened just outside the
door. Very soon he returned, and, ordering some other
soldiers to arrest us, marched us both to the guard hut,
and left us there for the night in charge of the sergeant
of the guard. In the morning the Austrian, who had
slept off the effects of the drink, was very sorry.
I told him that it was a pity he had not fallen out
with someone else, as I was certain to get a heavy
sentence.

"You know," I went on, "the corporal will put the
affair in as bad a light as possible for me, because by
doing so he will have the adjutant as his good friend;
and, besides, I have been up before the commandant
so often of late and have been reduced in rank so much
that he will consider me a soldier of very bad character
and will punish me as such. In any case you are a
soldier of the first class, and at most he can only take
away your chevron."

" That is true, my comrade; I am very sorry, that
cursed brandy made a fool of me."

" Well, it can't be helped now," I said; " I bear no
malice."

" Thanks, my friend, thanks," the Austrian replied;
" but Mademoiselle Julie, she will never forgive me."

" So much the better," I told him; " then you will
get no more brandy, and so will keep out of prison."
He sighed heavily and said no more: I could see
that he was really sorry at last.

At the usual hour all the prisoners made their appearance before the commandant. The Austrian and
I were the last to be tried, and we could see that our
judge was in bad humour that morning and unsparing
of abuse and punishment alike. When our turn came
we presented ourselves before him, bareheaded, without

belts, and guarded by an armed escort. When the charge had been read out the corporal and some men gave evidence in support of it, and we were asked, the Austrian first, as he was a soldier of the first class, what we had to say in reply. Neither could say anything, and truly, unless we had a very good defence indeed, it was best to say nothing, for the commandant, a good man in many ways, was very short-tempered, and was evidently in a rage that morning. The Austrian was condemned to lose his chevron, and then the officer turned to deal with me.

"You have been here often of late," he said, very mildly to all appearance, but I knew what that sudden mildness meant. I said nothing.

"Can you not speak?" he almost roared.

"Yes, sir."

"You have been here often, very often—too often; is it not so?"

"Yes, sir."

"Do you think that I have nothing to do except to listen to complaints against you?" Again he spoke very quietly.

"No, sir."

"Then why are you here almost every day?"

"I cannot avoid it, sir."

"Well, well, it is necessary that you learn a lesson. Four hours *en crapaudine*. Remember, remember well, not to appear here again soon."

Now I have already described this punishment, and have said something about its effects, as I heard about them from others, and as I saw men when they were put in it, but I was now for the first time to feel them for myself. The adjutant did a very mean thing, and many men who would not mind seeing me *en crapaudine*, not through any dislike of me but simply because they were used to the sight of prisoners so placed, severely blamed him for it, and blamed him the more severely as they felt that this new system of punishment might

R

become the custom of the battalion. Everyone feared for himself, one may say.

Now it was usual to keep a soldier sentenced to this discipline in the guard-hut until the great heat of the day had passed and then to put him in a certain portion of the parade-ground trussed up like a dead fowl. The adjutant, however, did not allow this to be done with me. He came down to the guard-hut a little before noon, had me taken from the cells to the place of punishment, and there, my ankles being fastened together and my hands manacled behind my back, I was forced upon my knees, my body pressed back until the centres of both pairs of irons were joined as closely together as possible, and so every joint of my body put upon the rack. But this was not all. When I was safely *en crapaudine* the brute knocked my kepi off with his stick, and so I was left in a posture of agony, exposed with bare head to all the torturing rays of an African sun. Now one can understand why my comrades were indignant; now one can see why they dreaded punishment in the noonday hours, for even if the kepi were left on a man's head, he would in all likelihood cast it off by his own struggles, and be sure, be very sure, that no one would dare to approach to replace it. It was replaced for me, I grant, and replaced more than once, and other things were done that helped me in some sort to bear my punishment, but Giulia was not amenable to military law as we others were, and even the adjutant dared not fall out openly with her, for all Frenchmen, including even the commandant, naturally side with the woman in a quarrel, especially when the woman is *figlia del reggimento*.

I was not long *en crapaudine* before I realised to the full the awful agony that men endure when they are truly and literally on the rack. Pains were quickly felt by me at the knees and at the ankles and at the wrists. My hands, forced backwards into an unnatural position, dragged heavily upon my neck, and the pain, beginning there, travelled down gradually to the shoulder-joints, so that from neck to ankles there was not a joint without its share of torment. Soon afterwards the small of my back became involved in the general dislocation, and then it seemed to me as if a heavy weight had been placed upon my abdomen and was squeezing the lower part of my body out of all proportion. Then a tight band, as it were, was fastened on my chest; I seemed to feel my ribs crushed in upon my heart, my breath came and went quickly, and, to complete the agony, my forehead began to feel constricted, and shooting pains ran from temple to temple, as if some demon from the lower regions were thrusting and thrusting and thrusting again a red-hot knife through my brain. At this time I must have begun to cry out, or at least to groan, for I was suddenly aware of a rough hand grasping me by the head and another pulling down my underjaw, some hard substance was shoved into my mouth, and in spite of all the pain that I was enduring my senses for a moment came back fully to me. I knew that I was gagged and that the first part of my punishment was over, for men generally drift into insensibility when the gag is applied; there will be an occasional lifting of the eyelids, a spasmodic shaking of the head, and that is all.

I learned afterwards that Giulia had replaced my kepi more than once, and had even bathed my temples and forehead with cold water, but she was not allowed to remove the gag, though she begged and prayed that it might be taken away. The adjutant had wisdom enough to keep away; it was well known that Giulia, for her own protection in so strange a society, so remote too from civilisation, always carried a knife about her person, and very often a dainty little five-chambered revolver that would certainly kill at near range. But for all that he saw that I was bound and gagged to the last minute of the four hours, and the sergeant of the guard, as well as the sentry who stood near, knew very well the consequences of yielding to Giulia's prayers and entreaties.

"Oh no; anything in reason, Mademoiselle Julie; but you know as well as a *vieux soldat* that we cannot disobey our orders. Disobedience on our part would injure us and not save your lover in the least."

Giulia understood, and could only weep and pray that the time might fly with eagle wings. Alas! for her, even more than for me, time, had only leaden feet that afternoon in the little cantonment near the desert, and, worst of all, the sun blazed furiously in a cloudless sky.

At long last the fourth hour came to an end. Quickly the gag was withdrawn from my mouth, the irons were taken from my limbs, and I was lifted up to my feet. But I could not stand, I staggered and almost fell; Giulia was not strong enough to hold me up, but the sergeant caught me at the other side, and both lowered my body gently to the ground. One could easily see that it was impossible for me to reach without help the hut where my squad lived, and some legionaries who had been looking on with interest at the scene—poor devils, not one of them could tell when his own turn might come—came across from where they were standing and volunteered to carry me to my cot. Giulia gratefully accepted this offer, and I was borne as tenderly as possible to my hut. There some of my own squad took me, undressed me, and put me to bed, and left the hut to Giulia and myself. Giulia managed to get me to drink some brandy and water, and I gradually felt better, but as my senses returned I became more and more conscious of the awful pain in every joint of my body. There was but one thing to set me right again—rest, absolute, complete rest, rest without stir of limb, for every time I ever so slightly moved a terrible stabbing pain ran right from the part I moved through all my body.

That evening the canteen was kept open during the

usual hours by the wife of the sergeant who had replaced me in military charge of it. Giulia would not
leave me, and in some degree to make up for keeping
the others out of their hut, she gave money to those of
the squad who had not given evidence against me. The
corporal got none, neither did the Austrian ; as for two
or three others who had been summoned as witnesses
before the commandant, they got merely angry words,
mixed with contemptuous epithets. They did not stand
this long. They left the hut as quickly as possible
and kept away until nightfall, when an unpleasant surprise awaited them and the other comrades of the squad.
It seems that Giulia went away for a short time while
I was sleeping and made certain preparations for
spending the night in the hut. Consequently, when
the corporal and the soldiers assembled outside and
called to Giulia that all lights would soon have to be put
out, she told them plainly that the lights would not be
put out in that place, that she had candles enough to
last until morning, and that she meant to allow no man
to enter for the night.

"I stay here," she told them, "for the sake of my
lover. I will keep you out for the sake of my good
name. I have three loaded revolvers and plenty of
spare cartridges, if any one of you should attempt to
enter, I will kill him."

They tried to persuade her to go to her own quarters ;
they promised that they would take turn about to
watch me ; all was of no use. At last the corporal
went and told the adjutant. The latter saw no way of
settling the matter, knowing full well that he would
receive a bullet rather than a word from Giulia, so
he wisely resolved to tell the commandant of the affair.
The commandant, in good humour by this time, only
laughed and said that he would see about it. So he
came across, and, rapping at the door, asked Giulia for
the privilege of entering. Giulia opened the door, the
commandant saluted her with his customary courtesy,

and then inquired for me. I answered for myself, and with deliberate malice I told him that the four hours *en crapaudine* would have been easily endured if I had undergone the punishment in the evening, as was usual, but that the heat of the sun had hurt me severely, especially as the adjutant had knocked my kepi off with his stick. The commandant was indignant; he was only like all officers, who don't care what men suffer so long as the sufferings are not intruded upon their notice, but who, on hearing a specific case of unfair play, will virtuously condemn somebody and then forget all about the affair. That's the way in every army in the world; Sergeant X speaks harshly to Private Y to-day, the captain overhears, and speaks still more harshly to the sergeant for his abuse of the private; next day Private A, who has been soundly rated by Corporal B, seeks redress, and is told at once that he did not get half enough and that if he can only carry foolish complaints to his captain, as a little girl to her mother, he has no right to wear a uniform—he should rather wear a petticoat. Yes; officers are inconsistent in their conduct to the soldiers, so are rich people in their conduct to the poor: one day in the week kindness; six days in the week ugly names and cutting words and, worst of all, unveiled contempt.

Well, the commandant said that he would speak to the adjutant in the morning, and—I may as well finish with this now—he kept his word, and gave the brute as straightforward, pointed, and condensed a reproof as a superior officer ever gave to an inferior. He did it before witnesses of all ranks, and so the story was told through all the battalion, and even those who had no money were happy that day.

When the commandant volunteered to escort Giulia to her abode she refused point-blank.

"I will stay here," she said, "all the night, and I will fire on any man that tries to enter."

The commandant, pretty experienced—as most officers

are—in the ways of women, saw that she had quite
made up her mind, and, shrugging his shoulders, said :
" Very well ; but let the men take their greatcoats and
blankets away."

" Yes ; but you, monsieur le commandant, will wait
till all have departed."

" But yes, but yes." And he went to the door and told
the men that they were to come in, take their coats and
blankets, and leave the hut at once. Afterwards he
would dispose of them for the night. He managed well
enough by dividing them amongst the neighbouring
huts, where the poor, evicted fellows made each man
his bed as best he could upon the ground. Then he
told the sergeant of the guard that the lights in my hut
were not to be taken notice of by the sentries, and went
home to bed, proudly happy in the consciousness of
having acted kindly towards people, for all of whom—
Giulia, of course, excepted—he felt the most supreme
contempt when they were not on active service. You
must know that in front of the enemy we legionaries
were always addressed as " mes enfants," at all other
times any ugly name was good enough for us.

Giulia insisted on my staying in bed all next day,
and no one said a word about it. In the early forenoon
the lieutenant—with whom I got on so well in the
march to the cantonment and who was now in charge
of the company during the illness of the captain—came
and spoke very sympathetically to us both. He said
nothing about the lecture read by the commandant to
the adjutant, rightly judging that there were many who
would be very glad to give us all the news about that.
As he was going away he said something to the corporal
who was standing near the door. After the officer's
departure the sub-officer told me that I might stay in
bed another day if I liked. I thanked him, but declined.
The fact is, I knew my comrades were anxious to get
back to their quarters, as they were sure to be anything
but comfortable divided amongst so many squads. Con-

sequently, I told Giulia that evening that I was nearly myself again, and I asked her to bring across a couple of bottles of *eau-de-vie*, so that we might make some amends to the others for their eviction. Giulia brought more than I had asked for. She carried across from the canteen two bottles of brandy, three of wine, and a couple of pounds of tobacco. When the others saw the bottles and the packages they were more than satisfied; they drank her health that night, and swore often, and with vehemence, that they would all willingly die for her. What children soldiers are, and how easily they are pleased!

After this I had a fairly easy time for a few weeks. But I had become rather reckless now, and all Giulia's powers of persuasion were needed to prevent me from breaking down into a careless, slovenly soldier. What is the good, I often thought, of cleaning equipments when I shall be abused just as much as if they were really dirty? Where is the use of springing smartly at the word of command when I shall be called a lazy rascal and a stupid fool? What matters it whether I am idle or hardworking when I get the same reward every time? Since I am to be abused and punished let me at least deserve the abuse and the punishment, then I shall be more content. But Giulia would not hear of this. She was determined that I should continue to be a clean, careful, active soldier. She had a wonderful fund of hope, and she had one argument that I could not withstand. "Yes, yes, it is hard," she would say; "but remember, when you begin to deserve trouble, I shall begin to deserve it too." Now, though I could easily be reckless on my own account, I could not find it in my heart to be reckless when Giulia was certain to share the consequences along with me. She was too good, too true, too loving to be drawn by me, who loved her so much, into any rashness which would end bitterly for us both—more bitterly, I fancied, for her, who would survive, than for me, whose troubles would soon be over.

Nevertheless, I grew more and more morose every day. True, I was never morose in Guilia's society, but in the hut I was not a pleasant companion, and I am afraid that my comrades left me more and more to myself every day. The corporal did not seem to watch me any longer. I fancy he was getting to be a little afraid. He, as well as the rest, saw that it would take very little to make me lose my temper altogether. And when a desperate legionary, his mind full of real—as mine were—or fancied wrongs, does break out, he is more like the Malay who runs amok than the European who strikes a blow or two and then is carried—kicking, striking, biting, and cursing—to the guard-house. Another reason that the corporal had for not interfering with me was this, the other legionaries were not indignant with me for my moroseness and want of good-fellowship. Now, as a rule, the man who keeps aloof from the rest of his squad has a bad time. Men will not allow themselves and their society to be flouted by another not a bit better, not a bit higher, than themselves. In the Legion all are equal—the ex-prince and the ex-pauper, the man of good character and the man of bad. But when the men of a squad see that a comrade is in bad temper with his superiors and recognise that he has reason, then they will not mind aloofness or sharp answers or ugly words. On the contrary, they will sympathise, never knowing when their own turns may come for ill-treatment. So the corporal, seeing that the men were quite satisfied that I should live my life to myself and felt sympathy and not anger on account of my conduct, wisely left me alone. There were many ugly stories current in the Legion of what had been done by men driven to desperation, and, be it well understood, the sub-officer valued his chevrons a good deal less than he valued his life.

I got myself into trouble more than once about this time, but I was never afterwards put *en crapaudine* Twice I was buried up to the neck in the ground, or rather once to the waist and once to the neck. This was called putting a man *en silo*. It was a hard punishment, but not to be compared with the other. The worst of it was that one felt as if heavy weights were pressing him at all points, but this feeling of pressure was nothing compared to the straining and racking of the joints when one was *en crapaudine*. A good proof of this is that I was never gagged when *en silo*. I could easily enough stand it without a cry. It is of no account now why I was thus punished. I freely admit that the commandant was quite justified in making me suffer for my offences, but it must be remembered to my credit that there would have been no offences if I had been left alone. Ill-treatment made me act foolishly, that is the first point; I paid for my folly, that is the second; the third is, when a punishment is over the offence that entailed it ought to be forgotten.

I was now, to all intents and purposes, a man apart from his fellows. The other legionaries watched me curiously. They wondered, I fancy, how long I should stand the strain and how the certain result would actually come about. The adjutant was just as tyrannical as ever to the men of the battalion; he distributed his curses and abuse with perfect impartiality, but no one minded now. The officers were the only ones who did not understand, though they, doubtless, had heard of many tragedies in the Legion, yet they seemed to have forgotten all: officers really care only for their own pleasure and comfort, and every one of them, from commandant down to sub-lieutenant, felt quite satisfied so long as there was an appearance of good order and discipline. If I were an officer, I should remember that a troublesome, riotous battalion seldom furnishes materials for a tragedy; a quiet, well-behaved one, where the men speak in drawing-room tones and seem to be always looking out for something, has more elements of danger in it. In the Indian Mutiny it was the good soldier who gave the most trouble and took the biggest share of the beating; he mutinied because his conscience drove him to it, and his conscience would not allow him to surrender. When a bad soldier mutinies, any hound is good enough to bite him, and once bitten, he hands in his gun. To put the matter in a nutshell: the battalion was too good; it was so quiet and calm that any man of observation might see that there was something ugly underneath.

CHAPTER XXI

ONE day as I was crossing the parade-ground I saw the adjutant stop Giulia, who was coming to meet me, and speak, as I thought, earnestly to her. I knew that he admired her and that a good deal of my troubles arose from her avowed preference for me, but my mind was quite easy on that score. Dozens of men in the battalion would be very glad to replace me in her favour, but all were aware that she was true as steel, and though this knowledge probably made many more envious of my good fortune yet it certainly kept them from annoying Giulia with unavailing protestations of love. Indeed, Giulia and I often laughed together when a legionary after a second or third glass of *eau-de-vie* looked longingly at her for a moment and then sighed with love and liquor. At first she used playfully to resent my allusions to her conquests, but as soon as she understood my absolute faith in her constancy she entered into the spirit of badinage quite as freely as I. I never jested about the adjutant. When we spoke of him we were both angry—I for my disgrace and punishment, Giulia because at the time she understood better than I did the reason of his severity. Many times she told me that he had spoken in a more than friendly manner to her, but she always added that her answers were not the answers he wished for, and I had often heard from my comrades of scenes at or near the canteen when she spoke her mind openly to him and made him feel that worst of all tortures to a man of sensitive mind—words of utter contempt from the woman he adores. What must have made things worse for the adjutant was that he knew, as the others did, that his repulses were deserved, and the officer was especially punished in this—that the whole battalion rejoiced in his discomfiture, and men repeated over and over again in hut and guard-house and canteen the very expressions with which Giulia had cut him to the heart. I had never questioned her closely about his behaviour and attempts at love-making—I thought of him as an enemy, not as a rival—but when I saw him so deliberately stop Giulia as she was approaching me I resolved to ask her, not out of jealousy, be it well understood, but out of curiosity, what he had to say so important that he laid his hand upon her arm to detain her.

I could not speak to Giulia that day about this, as very soon after the adjutant had stopped her on the parade-ground I was sent on some duty or other that kept me busy until the canteen was opened, and then there was no chance of private conversation. Next day was Sunday, and I then could be with her for at least a couple of hours, so that I did not mind the delay. While I was in the canteen that Saturday evening, drinking a glass of wine with a couple of Alsatians, I asked Giulia to meet me at the main gate on the following day. She, of course, consented; my asking was only a matter of form, a compliment to the girl. She told me that she would bring a flask of wine and that she would also have a packet of cigarettes and a few cigars.

"Why do you tell me that, Giulia?" I asked. "When you bring me any present I accept and thank you, but you know I want nothing but your comradeship and your love."

"I know well," she replied; "but I want you to come out of the cantonment with me to-morrow. I want to tell you many things, and we shall be away for a long time. If I am not back in time to open the canteen the sergeant's wife will open it for the soldiers. But you and I, we must talk long and earnestly to-morrow.

Confide in me as I confide in you. I am true—I shall always be so—and you, I know, will be true as well."

To this I could answer nothing except that I loved her better than my life; that I trusted her more than any man had ever trusted woman; and that I was her own, her very own, for ever.

When we met next day at the main-guard Guilia, as she had promised, had a little parcel that made the sergeant of the guard, the sentry on duty, and the other legionaries lounging about, consider me a happy man in spite of all my misfortunes. I could see that, and I own it gave me pleasure. The lowest, as well as the highest, desires to inspire envy in the hearts of others. So long as they think him especially favoured, the sorrows and troubles, which he alone knows of and feels, seem to diminish, even almost to disappear. But I had more than the envy of my comrades to console me; Guilia, happy and smiling, came towards me as I approached, and the sight of her happiness at meeting me was more than enough to make me forget all my disgrace, all my punishment, the hard words which came as regularly as the bugle went for parade, the extra toil that I was condemned to as the tyrant's enemy, and all the incidental annoyances that were sure to come to one whom his fellows had already named " Pas de chance." Yes; that, as I now remember it, was the last of the happy moments. It seemed as if the gods were giving us an overtaste of happiness before the time of anger, strife, and utter wretchedness opened on our lives.

We passed out together through the gate, Giulia in her smartest dress, and I in the regulation Sunday attire, with belt and bayonet and gloves. In Europe people put on silk hats and frock coats on Sundays; we of the Legion merely wore gloves and bayonets, but even with these small additions to our usual costume we felt extra dressed. It was a warm day—that is, warm even for Algeria—and we walked rather slowly along. Once we passed through the gate I took the little parcel from Guilia, saying, with a happy smile: "I am robbing you ma belle."

"You cannot rob me of anything," she replied, "since all I have is yours."

Then I kissed her, forgetting all about the legionaries of the guard who were lounging about the gate. How they must have envied me, my good comrades.

We did not go far from the cantonment, merely about a quarter of a mile, to a place where we had spent many a pleasant hour together on former Sundays. It was not an ideal resting-place. It was certainly not a meadow pied with daisies, with a murmuring rivulet at hand, but there really was a little shelter, for a fairly big rock overhung the spot, and in the lee of this one could somewhat escape the fierce heat of the sun. None of the other soldiers came near it on Sundays. They would, of course, have no hesitation in disturbing me, but Giulia the imperious, Giulia who could refuse the blessed liquor even to a rich man if she wished, was not to be offended. A couple of legionaries, a Spaniard and a Greek, had on one occasion posted themselves in a position whence they could watch our love-making, and had carried back a report to their comrades that Giulia and me were not so much in love as people thought, and it was only two days afterwards, when they entered the canteen together and were sternly ordered out of it, that they found out that we had discovered them and would not provide amusement for spies. The other soldiers had no sympathy with either Greek or Spaniard, and so the corps could boast, as I told them one day, of at least two men who did not drink. It is all very well to be a teetotaller from choice, but to be one from necessity is a very different thing, especially to a soldier. And the lesson Giulia taught by refusing even a glass of *vin ordinaire* to the precious pair made all the rest desirous of leaving us our chosen resting-place to ourselves.

When we arrived and sat down Giulia took the little parcel from me and opened it. There were three or four cigars, a couple of dozen cigarettes, and a pint bottle of wine. Some sweets were also there, but I left these for Giulia.

"Very well," I said, "this is a real feast. We can live here for at least four hours with such supplies."

"Is it not good?" she asked.

"Very good," I told her; "you grow kinder every day; but I too have a little surprise for you, carissima."

"What! a surprise for me? What is it?" And she laid her pretty little hand upon my arm.

I bade her shut her eyes, and when she did so, I clasped a silver bracelet on her wrist—it had cost me more than two months' pay—and was amply rewarded for my gift by the childish joy she showed when she beheld it. How happy we were that Sunday!

But this story has little to do with happiness now that it approaches the end. When we had taken a little of the wine and were quietly enjoying our cigarettes I asked Giulia what the adjutant had said to her on the previous day.

"I will tell you all now," she said to me. "I can no longer keep it from you, though I do not wish to give you pain. You have always trusted me, as I have trusted you. Is it not so, dearest?"

"But yes," I answered; "no one could doubt you; you are too good and too true. Why, even the worst man in the battalion knows and acknowledges that."

"I am well content," Giulia said to me; "you have not erred. I have always been faithful, and I will be faithful for ever. But I cannot prevent anyone, not even the man I hate most, from loving me, and things have come to such a pass now that it is only right that you should know all."

Thereupon, seeing that the poor girl was in great distress, I flung away my cigarette, and taking hers from between her fingers flung it away too. Then I kissed her, and keeping her very closely in my arms, said :

"Tell me everything; but I must tell you one thing first: I am quite sure that, no matter what troubles we may have endured or may have to endure, neither will ever grieve the other by want of love or want of trust."

She sobbed for a moment quietly on my breast, and then began :

"It is all because of that adjutant—that devil who will not allow anyone to be happy. He has always, since he came to the cantonment, desired to take me for himself, and whenever he came with his unwished-for proposals I insulted him and drove him away. Then he threatened that he would take vengeance on you, and I warned you to be on your guard. In spite of all he injured you and nearly broke my heart, but I constantly hoped that he might leave the battalion with the next draft. The draft has gone and he re-mains ; there will be no new draft for months, and what hope is left now? When he stopped me on the parade yesterday it was to renew his unwelcome proposals, but this time he asked me to be his wife. I was angry, and told him that, were he even President of the Republic, I would neither let him kiss me as lover nor wed me as husband, and that, no matter what rank he might win, he would always remain the same—a tyrant to those beneath him, and a tyrant, I believed, was only slightly better than a slave. Then he swore with vehemence that he would have you shot before a month was over, and that is why I tell you." At this point she wept, and could not be comforted for a long time. When she became somewhat calm, I told her that now we knew the adjutant's intentions we could do at least some-thing to prevent their realisation, and that, in any case, if the affair should come to the worst it would be easy enough to have a little satisfaction before being punished. This did not seem very comforting, but it was the best

s

I could say. My mind was at the time even more full of hate of the adjutant than love of Giulia, and I think she must have noticed this, for she tried to turn my thoughts in a pleasanter direction. Almost in a moment she, who had but a moment before been hopeless and comfortless, dried her tears, smiled bravely into my eyes, and told me I thought more of my anger than of her love. I put aside at once all emotions save those of tenderness and affection, I petted and carressed her, I told her over and over again what women never tire of hearing : *Je t'aime, je t'aime, je t'aime.* If you can say " I love you " to a woman, and she feels that you say it with truth, you have made the most eloquent speech in the world to her ears—that is, be it well understood, if she is inclined to say the same words to you. If she cannot respond, why ! say good-bye and forget her. He is only a fool who cannot, even though it hurts, give up a love that meets with no response.

But there was no danger of lack of response on Giulia's part. In a pretty mixture of Italian, French, and English that we had taught each other she gave me assurances that were not the less valued because they were repetitions of ones that I had received from her many times before, and that fell upon my ears all the more pleasantly that I well knew them to be absolutely true. There can be no mistaking the love or the hate of an Italian girl ; the Southern warmth shows itself in both. As I had experience of one, so the adjutant had sorely felt the other.

While we were thus creating happiness for each other, a harsh voice fell upon our ears. It was the adjutant's. I stood up and faced round to meet him, all thoughts of love had now disappeared, only hatred of the tyrant filled my heart. I remembered the many insults, the unfair surprises, the more than devilish ingenuity with which he had hounded me down. I thought of my former rank and contrasted it in my mind with my then lowly condition ; I remembered my lost chevrons, my lost pay, my lost position, my lost chance of promotion, my lost friends, for what sergeant could associate with the reduced sub-officer in the ranks! I thought of Giulia's sorrows, her wakeful nights when she knew that I was tossing uneasily on a plank bed, her anxiety as the hour approached for my trial, her fear of some terrible result, the insulting proposals that she was compelled to hear and of which she dared not speak, and as all these thoughts surged through my brain I saw no adjutant, no superior officer of mine, but a man-wolf, a demon incarnate hot from hell. Yet I was outwardly calm; I said no word, nor for some moments did he speak, but I felt that the crisis had come at last. I was glad that we three were quite alone; the thought flashed upon my mind that it was Sunday, and that day I wore my bayonet.

At last he spoke: "Will mademoiselle kindly go away and permit me to speak alone to the soldier?"

"No," Giulia replied; "I will stay. Why have you come here?"

"I came," said the adjutant, speaking very slowly and impressively, all the while looking hard at me, "to make a proposition to this man."

"I can guess your proposition," I replied, stopping Giulia with a gesture, "and I give you the same answer as Mademoiselle Julie has already given. She does not give me up; I do not give up her. Did you think," and I spoke with deliberation equal to his, "that I would allow my darling to purchase an easy life and also promotion for me by giving you even one kiss, even one glance of favour! No," I went on, "Giulia's kisses and caresses and words of love are for me and for me alone; get some woman of the camp—she will be good enough for you."

The adjutant controlled himself with an effort. After a short delay, in which, I presume, he determined to make one attempt more to gain his object, for his desire was greater than his hate, he said:

"I have offered to marry her; you are not in a position to do so. When we are married I will get leave of absence and we will go away, and while away from the battalion I can arrange a transfer; then we shall never meet again. If she comes away with me as my wife, I will take care that she has a happy and comfortable life; if she does not marry me, and I ask her now for the last time, she cannot be happy here, for I will see that you at least will not be long her lover." Then, turning to Giulia, he went on: "If you really love him, save him now."

He held out his hands appealingly to her. As he stood so exposed I struck his cheek fair and full with the back of my right hand.

"Your answer, dog," I cried.

With an angry indrawing of his breath he turned to me, and his right hand felt for his sword. It was half out of the scabbard when I plucked my bayonet from its sheath, and driving it straight forward I pierced his right arm as it lay across his body. He did not let go his hold of the sword hilt in spite of the wound, but drew the sword and raised it to cut me down. As his right arm went up I pushed it back with my left hand and, coming to close quarters, plunged my bayonet into his body. He reeled, and again I drove my weapon home. He staggered away from me, and before I could get close enough to repeat the thrust fell heavily upon his back. He lay quite still. I mechanically wiped my bayonet clean, and then said to Giulia:

"I could not help it; he would have killed me if he could."

Giulia said nothing, but when I had put up my side-arm she came to me and, putting her dear arms round my neck, wept bitter tears of anticipation upon my breast.

There was nothing to be done except to go back to camp and wait for what might happen. Neither of us spoke of the result that each felt was certain. Though we were resolved to say nothing about the affair yet we made no attempt to divert suspicion from ourselves. The half-smoked cigarettes, the half-empty bottle, the paper and twine of the parcel, all were left behind in close proximity to the body of the adjutant. As we walked slowly back Giulia suddenly halted and faced me.

"They will kill you," she said.

"I think so," I answered.

"And I, I will not live when you are gone."

I pleaded with her for her own life. I used all the arguments I could think of about the wickedness of self-destruction; nought was of avail.

"But, carissima mia, your father was killed in battle, and your mother, who loved him fondly, did not kill herself."

"Ah, mon Jean, I was born at the time. Her baby made her live."

"And Giulia,"—I took her in my arms and kissed her,—"do you not understand? Is it not so?" She broke down into a flood of tears.

"O Jean, Jean, I must live, I must live, even though one half of my life goes out with you."

I caressed and comforted her—we were in full view of the gate, but we minded not. She grew calm at last, and looked at me with a new look in her eyes—a look that I had seen but once before, when the English corporal had called her madame, but then it meant rather bashful hope and half-afraid longing, now it showed knowledge and certainty and free confession.

"I am very happy now," I told her as we approached the gate where the men relieved from duty as sentinels were standing. "I care not now what may happen to myself, and for you half, and more than half, of my anxiety has left me. There is only one thing that I must do now, I must look for Père Michel at once. You will go to your quarters; he will come with me there. Tell the sergeant and his wife to expect us. Do not be afraid, they will not be surprised."

Giulia said nothing in reply; a closer clinging to my arm, one quick glance, a sudden heaving of the breast, these told me more than any words could tell.

We separated just inside the gate, Giulia going at once to her quarters, while I went towards the officers' building to find the chaplain. I saw him at once, and told him the more important facts on the spot; he shook his head, and told me that there was but one way to make reparation. He said that Giulia and I should both confess our sins, but I said:

"No; marry us now or marry us never."

Anxious to do his best, and knowing full well that many in the battalion were worse than I—he did not know about the adjutant's fate at the time, as I took care to keep that to myself—he yielded to my entreaties and went with me to the canteen. There we were married, the sergeant and his wife acting as witnesses. The good priest, he was a good and brave man, gave us some advice; he told us that he would always remember us in his prayers, and went away. Then the sergeant said: "I suppose there will be great rejoicing in the camp this evening," and looked astonished when Giulia utterly broke down. His wife drew him away, and we were alone together, the most utterly wretched bride and bridegroom that the world has ever seen. Giulia said to me:

"You are mine, all mine now; when they seek you they must find you here." I dreaded the effect of my arrest in her presence, but she insisted.

"I will show good courage, I will not give way to grief," she answered. "You shall see, and you shall not be ashamed."

After that we sat together on the side of the little bed. We said little, but our hearts were bursting; there had never been so perfect, so complete, so unutterable a sympathy between us. We knew then, as we never did, and never could, know before, the intense sweetness of love, which only exquisite anguish can bring forth.

After some time—I know not, nor shall ever know, how long—we heard the dull sound of a rifle butt upon the door below. It was quickly opened, and through the raised window we heard the words: "Is Mademoiselle Julie within?"

"No; but Madame Julie is," replied the sergeant, with a laugh.

"Is she alone?"

"No; her husband is with her."

"Ah, we want him; we must enter."

Giulia pressed more closely to my side. In a moment the rifle butt sounded on our door. "Entrez," I called out. The door was flung open and a sergeant appeared, two soldiers peering curiously over his shoulders.

"You are my prisoner."

"Very well, my sergeant; pardon me for a moment."

Then to Giulia: "My darling, I must obey orders."

Giulia said nothing. I kissed her, said: "Be of good courage," and walked to the door.

As the soldiers placed themselves one at each side I heard a loud cry. I would have turned back, but I was pushed headlong down the stairs. There was no use in resisting, so I went quietly to the guard-house, with an awful fear at my heart for my poor love in her agony and loneliness. As I entered the prison I heard a legionary of the guard say to his comrades:

"I knew how it would be; yes, long ago."

That night I slept little. The hard plank was nothing, I was used to that; the death of the adjutant was nothing in itself, for had he not deserved it? Its consequences, as far as they affected me, I could take without flinching, but the thought of Giulia, of her future, in which nought was certain save hopelessness and the sense of utter loss, made me wakeful and anxious through the silent hours. Three legionaries confined for some offence were my companions in the cell. They knew nothing of the affair, and when I was suddenly pushed through the door by the sergeant of the guard, these men eagerly asked what new misfortune was mine.

"Can you not guess?" I answered.

They looked at one another, the same thought was in the minds of all. The Sicilian said:

"You have done it! Yes, I knew you would. I am glad that he is gone, yet I am sorry for you, and still more sorry—" He stopped and shook his head.

"Yes," said a Pole; "that is the way, it is the woman always that suffers most."

The third, a Frenchman by birth, who found it better to be a Lorrainer in the Legion than to serve in his proper regiment in France, was the last to speak.

"It is done now, and we shall all be grieved at the loss of a good comrade, but the battalion will be happy once more. I salute," he continued, taking off his kepi, "the hero who has freed us from slavery."

We were silent for a time. Then the Frenchman asked me how it happened.

"I struck him, he drew his sword, and then I gave him my bayonet, voilà tout!"

"How often?"

"Three times."

"Very well," said the Sicilian; "then it must be all right. It is all right; the battalion must have a new adjutant now."

I refused my soup when it came and the Frenchman offered me his.

"If I cannot take my own, why yours?" I asked angrily.

"Mine is not soup, it is something better." It was, and I gladly took it. He had wine instead of soup. This was wrong, but a good comrade who has money can do a kindness to a prisoner. But he must be a very good comrade, and he must have more than enough to buy the wine.

They saw that I was disinclined for much speaking, and they went away to the other end of the cell. There they spoke and gesticulated freely. Yet very seldom did a word reach me; their voices were low, their heads close together, but I noted, half abstractedly as it were, the quick action of the shoulders, the eager motion of the hands. After some time they stopped the conversation and sat or lay down on the rough planks that served for beds. No other prisoners came in that night; sergeants and corporals were not thinking of making arrests, and the soldiers were too busy talking about the affair to quarrel. Yet there were many besides Giulia and me who were sorry for what would surely happen: the quick court-martial, and then the volley at the open grave.

CHAPTER XXII

NEXT morning the preliminary investigation was held by the commandant. He finished with all other work first, and then directed that I should be brought before him. I knew this, because the others were taken away to stand their trial, and I was left behind. When I was in his presence I saluted, and the commandant said with soldierly directness:

"The adjutant is dead; you are charged with killing him; have you anything to say?"

"Only this, sir," I replied, "he insulted me, then he insulted Mademoiselle Julie, who is now my wife; I struck him, he drew his sword, and I my bayonet. I was the quicker of the two, and wounded him; then he raised his sword to cut me down, and I repeated the blow."

"But there were three wounds; is it not so?" he said to the surgeon.

"Yes, monsieur le commandant."

"How do you explain the third wound?"

"Two," I answered, "were in self-defence, the third, sir, in passion."

"Ah; and how in self-defence?"

"The first, sir, on the arm as he drew his sword; the second on the body as he lifted it to strike; the third, sir, on the body in the anger of the moment."

"That will do," said the officer; "as the general is arriving to-day I will lay the matter before him. But I warn you, prepare for a court-martial and its result."

I saluted, and was led away.

There is no need to go through the preliminaries. The general received the same information from me as the commandant had got, and at once ordered a board of officers to try me for the offence.

"They will not have much difficulty in deciding, as the accused confesses his crime, so I will wait here to confirm the finding," he said to the commandant.

I heard this as I was facing about with the escort to return to the guard-house, and the last vestige of hope disappeared.

I gave no further evidence before the court-martial than I had already given to the commandant. I did not like to speak of the adjutant's animosity towards me, as that and its consequences would supply a motive for my act, and that I did not wish to impress upon their minds. Better let them think it was sudden, as, indeed, it was in one way, than deliberate and led up to by his own fault, as it was in another. One must understand that, but for my resentment and sense of wrong and oft-thought desire of his death, I should not have killed him; and one must also know that, were he passing quietly by, I should not have rushed upon him with my bayonet. My feelings were due to the injuries and insults he had heaped upon me; my sudden action to his threat about my life to Giulia, repeated, as it was, to me.

The result of the court-martial was that I was acquitted of the killing, as that was done in self-defence, but found guilty of striking my superior officer, and for that sentenced to be shot. This was duly confirmed, read out on general parade, and the execution was set for the following morning at eight o'clock. As I heard the words read out, standing bareheaded, without a belt, between two soldiers with loaded rifles and fixed bayonets, I felt that my last sun would set that night. Little I guessed of what would be accomplished by the wit and courage of a loving woman, by the unselfish chivalry of two legionaries, who had gone separately to Giulia, neither knowing of the other's design, and offered to help her and her husband, even at the risk of their lives. And yet both these men made light of their action at the time, and, were they in the land of the living to-day, would surely only claim the credit of having stood by a comrade in trouble and a woman in distress. They were the English corporal, whom I have already mentioned, and an Irishman—a simple soldier—let us call him Mac. When Giulia thanked the corporal he told her that, as he had lost his honour long ago, it did not matter if he lost his life now.

"Surely not your honour?" she queried.

"Well, I think not, indeed, but the world, unfortunately, does not agree with me."

Mac said he could not do less than try to rescue me, —"il est mon pays, n'est ce pas?"—and he, because he was an Irishman, could always get what he wished in the canteen. I did not know this. I found out, however, that Giulia often gave Mac, the only other Irishman in the battalion, brandy and wine and tobacco without payment, as he was my countryman, and I do not blame the poor devil for accepting, for he was always in trouble, his pay was constantly stopped, and a soldier can do easily without his dinner, but is ripe for mischief if he is deprived of his glass and of his pipe. Well, she did not lose in the end, as he said—but that must come in its own place.

Now the Englishman was corporal of the guard that night. I did not know anything definite about the plan for my escape, for when Giulia visited me at about six o'clock in the evening all she could tell me was to hope, to watch, and to be ready. I needed little advice about the last two matters; as for hoping, that was almost impossible. About eight o'clock the corporal visited me, as a matter of duty, to see that all was right. He ordered me, in a loud, rough voice, to get up from where I lay. As I stood in front of him he whispered: "After midnight," and departed.

At about twenty minutes past twelve I heard a low

voice calling to me at the window. This I had left open, so that there might be a means of communication if anyone could get to the other side. I had not much expectation of this, as a sentry was posted just there, and no legionary, I thought, would be such a fool as to risk punishment by permitting even Giulia to speak to me. When I went to the window I found Mac outside.

"Hurry, hurry," he said; "we must get these bars out quickly. We can lose no time if we are to succeed."

Now there were two iron bars fixed vertically in the mud of which the wall was built, and Mac, giving me a bayonet, told me to clear the lower end of one, while he cleared the lower end of the other. We said nothing more. We worked with a will. In a short time the ends were free, and then Mac, a powerful man, pulled the bars out, so that I could just squeeze my body through. I had, however, to take off my tunic to do so, and I passed this out first. When I got out I saw a body on the ground.

"You have his bayonet," said Mac, "take his rifle and belt as well."

The man lay quite motionless. I took his belt and put it on and then possessed myself of the rifle. I felt happy enough now. Now they could not shoot me like a dog; I could at least die fighting.

"Wait a moment," said Mac.

In a few minutes we heard the door of the guard-house opening, and then the voice of the corporal telling the sentinel in front that he would return in a quarter of an hour. The corporal came round to where we stood. He had his rifle, bayonet, and ammunition. He said:

"Is it all right?"

"Yes."

"Are you armed?"

"Yes, both; he has the sentry's weapons."

"Very good; let us go. When we are at a safe

distance from the guard-house we shall pretend to be
a visiting patrol."

In this way we passed the sentries at a distance from
the main-guard and marched boldly along till we came
to where a native cavalryman was on duty near the
horses.   He challenged, and received a satisfactory
reply.   As we passed him the corporal halted. us, and
ordered me to hold his rifle for a moment.   I took it,
and before I or the cavalry-guard could understand
the Englishman had the latter by the throat.   Mac laid
down his rifle and seized the unfortunate fellow's arms,
and in a few moments he was a corpse.

"Now," said the corporal to me, "you get the woman,
we will get ready the horses."

"Where is she?" I asked.

"Some place over there."   And he pointed with his
hand.

I went in the direction pointed out and soon met
Giulia.   She had been easily able to follow us, for our
steady tramp could be heard at some distance.   We
made no attempt to conceal our movements ; we were
to all appearance a visiting patrol.   As I came to her
side I whispered : "It goes very well, carissima.   The
others are getting out the horses."

Giulia flung herself into my arms.   I snatched a kiss
and led her to where Mac and the Englishman were
busy.   They had two horses already out, and were
saddling them with all despatch.   One must understand
that the saddles and bridles are always kept near the
chargers, especially in a place where at any moment
a raid from the desert may have to be repelled.   Soon
four horses were ready, and then we all mounted and
rode slowly towards a gate at the rear of the camp,
where a single sentinel was posted.   This man, luckily
for us, was a Turco.   When the corporal replied to his
challenge and told him that we were officers he believed
the story.   Then the Englishman and I dismounted,
taking only our bayonets, and approached the gate.

The sentry protested against our opening this, but I got behind him and flung my hands about his neck. At the same moment the corporal wrenched away the rifle and bayonet and buried his own steel in the Turco's heart.

We opened the gate as quickly and quietly as possible and went out. For ten minutes we walked our horses slowly and almost noiselessly away from the camp. Then we headed due south after a short consultation—the corporal leading, Giulia and I following, Mac bringing up the rear. We were now going straight for the Great Desert, where alone there was hope of safety. Had we gone north towards the Mediterranean, our freedom would not be worth twenty-four hours' purchase. As it was, we had a good chance of getting safely away from French pursuit, for our post lay at the extreme south of French territory in that part. But in the desert what were we to do? We did not know—we did not think about that. All our energies and thoughts were directed to getting clear away from the French and native cavalry. We knew that the escape would be soon discovered, but we fancied that no pursuit would be attempted until dawn, and it was our business to travel as far as we could from the cantonment in the short time that we had at our disposal. Moreover, if we could only put a fair distance between ourselves and our pursuers there was every likelihood that they would never catch up with us, because the native horsemen would not care to go too far into the desert, for they would get little quarter from the Arabs who infest it. Why, they would be killed for the sake of their horses, equipments, and arms, and the wild Arab does not fear the native levies as he does the Frenchmen, for two reasons—in the first place, the Arab is quite as good a fighting man, and he knows it, as the other African; in the second, it is only the white soldiers whose weapons kill from afar. As for us, we had to venture into the desert, as I have already said. We wanted, to use another phrase of mine, to get from the fire to the frying-pan—*du feu à la poêle*.

We kept steadily forward until the sun came up in the east with his usual suddenness. Then we halted, and began to consider our position. At best it was a bad one. We were four, with four horses; for ourselves, we had only a haversack of food and a flask of brandy that Giulia had been thoughtful enough to bring, for our horses we had nothing. As far as fighting power went we were better off, as we had three good rifles—*fusils Gras* we called them—and eighty rounds of ball cartridge per man. We had bayonets as well, and Giulia had a pair of revolvers and a stiletto, so that, given a fair chance, we were good enough for a dozen enemies. One must remember that we were desperate; nothing could be gained by surrendering to Frenchmen, since our lives were now forfeit; with a woman in the party we could not surrender to Arabs.

The English corporal, Mac and I, spoke in English.

"I want you to promise one thing," I said to them: "if two go down, let the third kill my wife."

"Oh, that's understood," said the Englishman.

"I hope it may not be my lot," said Mac, "but I'll do it all the same."

"Now," said the corporal, "we must go farther south and chance meeting with the Arabs. I don't know," he went on, "whether I am anxious to meet any or not. If we don't meet any we shall probably miss the wells; if we do meet them there will be a fight."

"It is better to fight," said Mac, "than to die of thirst in the desert."

"I think so too," I said.

"Well," asked the corporal, "shall we go straight on at top speed or rest?"

"Let us go on," I advised; "let us press on as far as we can, then if we meet any Arabs, or if the spahis ride up to us, we can halt and fight. Remember, without food or water for our horses we cannot run, we cannot make even a running fight; it must be a standing fight to a finish."

The Englishman and Mac agreed with me, and before we started again I said to Giulia in their hearing:

"N'aie pas peur, ma bien chère, tu ne seras pas prisonnière, plutôt tu seras tuée par le dernier protecteur."

"Je suis bien content," she replied, and, bowing prettily to the others, she murmured a word of thanks.

We rode on for about two hours, and then halted to rest our horses and to eat a little of Giulia's provisions. We did not drink, as brandy is not a good thing when one has nothing else. If we could only get our usual morning coffee we should have had a nip apiece, but we who had soldiered in Algeria and other hot climates were too sensible to touch fire-water without anything to qualify it and with the certainty of a hot day's march before us. After eating and smoking we got back into our saddles and rode on until the heat of the sun made us again halt for our own sakes as well as on account of our animals. In spite of our discomfort we felt fairly happy; we had made a good morning's march since the sun appeared, and though we had done very little in the darkness, yet we believed ourselves to be safe enough from pursuit. After a couple of hours' rest we resolved, in spite of the heat, to press on again, and, going rather slowly, we and our horses were not too hard pressed. About four o'clock in the afternoon we again halted, this time for about an hour, and then, as our horses did not seem to suffer overmuch from the want of food and water—they were desert horses, one must remember —we again mounted and continued our journey to the south.

It was, I should say, a little past five o'clock in the afternoon when Mac, who had halted for a moment to look to the north, shouted to us that the spahis were coming. We turned, and saw, a long distance away,

T

for the atmosphere was very clear, a party of mounted soldiers advancing on our tracks. There was no use in tiring our horses and ourselves by an attempted flight; we understood quite plainly that the native cavalrymen were certain to overtake us, and it was just as well to await them where we stood. We dismounted, hobbled our horses, and came together for consultation. The corporal said:

"We must stand at least ten paces apart from one another, unless they charge; in that case we must stand back to back."

"Give your orders, corporal," I said, "and we will obey."

"Yes," assented Mac; "there must be a commanding officer in every battle."

"Very good," said the corporal. "You, Mac, go ten paces to the right; you stay here, mademoiselle; you"—this to me—"go ten paces farther to the left; and I place myself at the extreme left, so we shall offer bad targets, especially for cavalry."

When we had ranged ourselves as ordered our enemies were close enough for us to note their numbers; they were a dozen in all.

"Why," shouted Mac, "it's only a corporal's squad; we're a corporal's squad ourselves, boys, and we're whites."

"As soon as you think you can hit a man or horse fire," commanded the corporal.

In a moment or two I heard a report on the right. Mac, one of the best shots in our old battalion, had fired, and the result was of good omen. A horse fell heavily in the advance, pitching his rider forward, a second stumbled over the first, staggered to the left, and brought down a third. We cheered as we saw this, and the rest of the little troop pulled up for a moment. As they did so the corporal and I fired. A man tumbled out of his saddle on their right; in the centre a horse, mad with the sudden shock and the pain of the bullet, suddenly ran away with its rider. They passed not more than fifty yards to our right, and Mac's rifle spoke again : the spahi flung up his hands and fell forward on his horse's neck.

"Well done, Mac," I shouted out, "we can easily whip them now."

As I spoke I dropped on one knee and levelled my rifle at the little knot of men and horses. The corporal and I fired almost together, and though no man or horse fell, yet we felt certain that some damage was done. We knew quite well, as every soldier knows, that a wounded horse will not always fall and that an Arab will sit in his saddle with more than one bullet in his body. One result our fire had, it caused the spahis to withdraw out of range, and this gave us a respite. One will ask : Why did not the cavalry return our fire? Well, it would do them no good. Our weapons killed at a much longer range than theirs; for two reasons—first, the rifle always carries farther than the carbine; and, second, our weapons were of later pattern and, therefore, better than theirs.

We could now reckon up our successes. To Mac's first shot three horses and three men had fallen ; of these two horses and one man remained on the ground. My first shot had sent a horse careering madly over the desert, and Mac's second had put his rider out of the fight. The corporal had also brought down a man, but this fellow had been carried away by his comrades. As for the last shots, there was no apparent result, but we believed that some damage had been done by them. Anyway three men and three horses were accounted for, and we who had driven back a dozen spahis had no fear of only nine, though we were not such fools as to imagine that these hot-blooded Arabs were more than temporarily discomfited by our success.

Very soon the Arabs again advanced, but in a different fashion. Instead of now coming forward in a bunch they separated widely over the plain, so as to form a great half-circle in our front and our flanks.

"Don't throw away a shot," commanded the corporal. And then, hesitating for a moment, he continued: "Let us draw closer together—this is the grand attack—if they don't come home now in their charge, they will never do it."

We all closed in on Giulia; we formed a lozenge or diamond in array. I looked straight towards the north, the corporal to the west, Mac to the east, and Giulia was just at my back, but looking past me at the quickly-moving spahis. Our bayonets were fixed. Suddenly one of the spahis, the corporal, I suppose, uttered a loud cry and charged. All the rest followed his example, and in a moment the nine were within long range. We fired and loaded, fired again and loaded again. I cannot say how often this occurred, but I saw a horse fall in my front to my second bullet, and soon afterwards I knew that two men at least were charging home. As they came with levelled lances I heard the corporal say:

"Mine are settled; I'm with you; Mac's all right; come out and meet them."

We went out together; as we did the corporal commanded:

"Go to the right; shoot your man if you can, if not, use your bayonet."

I fired and missed. I met the lowered lance with my bayonet, and, like a fool, turned it up; the spahi let it go and swung the heavy butt downwards and to his right rear. I could not avoid the blow; it took me fairly on the breast, sending me to the ground. As he pulled at the reins to get his charger back I heard a sharp report, followed by another: my enemy collapsed and fell. As I rose painfully to my feet, feeling as if a ton weight were laid upon my chest, Giulia caught me in her arms and asked with anxiety if I were hurt. "Not much," I answered: "but where are the others?"

I saw Mac a few paces away aiming at a retiring spahi; turning round I saw the English corporal wiping his bayonet; near him lay a dead soldier. On the plain at various distances lay men and horses; farther off than these the remains of the spahis had assembled —one mounted and three dismounted men.

"What happened to you, mon camarade?" said the corporal.

"Oh, I replied, "like a fool I turned the lance up instead of down; he then struck me with the butt, and Giulia shot him just in time to save me."

"It seems to me," said the corporal, speaking in French, "that Madame Julie is always saving your life."

"Yes," I replied, smiling; "and I would rather owe it to her than to anyone else."

We were now quite satisfied. It was absolutely impossible for the four survivors to attack us with any hope of success owing to our weapons. They were quite aware of this; in fact, they were in difficulties now, for the question arose for them: How were they to get back to the cantonment? Their horses were dead or wounded, for all we knew the men might be wounded as well, and the spahis could not by any chance like the prospect of meeting in the desert any of their co-religionists who had remained unsubdued.

One thing we had to do, and do quickly. This was to get away as far as possible from the remnants of the spahis. If we remained in their vicinity until darkness came we should lose all the advantage of our superior weapons, and we were well aware that the native troops are daring and skilful fighters with cold steel. Moreover, it is the Arab nature to lust for vengeance, especially on Christians, though our Christianity was of a rather shadowy nature, more than to love even his life, and these men had sufficient reason to hate us. Accordingly we mounted and turned our weary horses' heads again towards the south, going at an easy pace, and now and again looking back to see if there were new pursuers on our track. When we had gone some distance and had lost sight of the defeated spahis, the corporal said : "Let us turn to the right; if new men have come up to the others, they will go due south." The advice seemed good, so we went westwards for about two hours, and then halted to rest ourselves and our horses. We were very thirsty now, but Mac told us to our great delight that he had taken two water bottles from dead spahis.

"Why did you not tell us before?" asked the corporal.

"I thought it best to wait, and, besides," he answered, "I was thinking more about pursuit than about even the water."

We very soon half emptied one, Giulia getting the first and largest drink, and then we poured into this bottle the contents of the spirit flask that Giulia had brought.

"Now, madame," said the corporal, "you shall have the bottle of water for yourself, we will be satisfied with the other."

This was a very good arrangement. Giulia did not like *eau-de-vie* and we did; moreover, Giulia wanted more liquid in the desert than three veteran campaigners.

At about two o'clock in the morning we set out again, and travelled very slowly in a south-westerly direction. Our horses were beginning to show signs of failing, and we eagerly scanned the desert all around us after the sun had risen to try to discover signs of an oasis or even of a caravan. Our steeds would soon give up the struggle, that we knew, and we could scarcely hope to keep it up on foot for more than twenty-four hours. Now one must not imagine that we were hopeless. On the contrary, we felt that fortune, having befriended us so long, would not now abandon us. We thought of the difficulties surmounted in the escape and of the good fight which we had made against our pursuers, and with such recent memories our spirits could not be cast down. We had a little food, a little drink, good weapons, and enough of ammunition. We knew that every man could trust his comrades, and so, while our horses lasted, and for at least a day afterwards, we could laugh at Fate.

So we jogged along for some time after dawn, rested for an hour, and then pushed on again. About midway between sunrise and noon Mac, whose eyes were as keen as a vulture's, cried out :

"At last, boys, at last ; look yonder."

We looked, and saw a slowly-moving object. There was no doubt about what it was, our path would soon intersect that of a caravan. When the parties met one of two things would be our portion—safety or death— for, if we could not get water and food in hospitable fashion, we had no resource but to fight for them, and desert fights are serious.

CHAPTER XXIII

I SAID to the Englishman:
"Let us halt, eat, and drink; we shall then be better able to fight, if fighting should be necessary."

"That is right," replied the corporal; "we will finish all our provisions and all the water, even madame's."

"Yes," I said; "we shall soon have as much as we need, or we shall need nothing."

We dismounted, divided the scanty remains of the food into four equal portions, and all ate slowly and enjoyingly. Then we drank all the water left in Giulia's bottle, sharing it as fairly as we could when we had no measure and had to guess at the total amount and then at each one's share. As for the little stock of brandy and water, that, on Mac's suggestion, was to be kept until we were nearer the caravan and, therefore, nearer the fight that might ensue. Giulia would take none, but we others were very glad we had it, not that we wanted brandy to nerve us for the fray, but a little does one no harm just before the beginning of an engagement. After the meal we filled our pipes and lit them with one of the few matches that Mac had in his pockets when we came away from the cantonment, then we mounted again, and rode slowly towards the point where we had resolved to strike the path of the caravan.

As we went along we observed that it was not a large company, and this made us naturally glad. We only hoped now that there might be many women and children and slaves; if so, our chances of success either by fair means or by foul would be vastly increased. Very soon we saw a couple of camels with riders coming towards us, and we knew that we had been observed and that our friends of the caravan were curious to find out the meaning of our little party traversing the desert. The camelmen rode up to within easy range, but it was not our business to begin a fight. We did not even call out to them; it was better, as the corporal said, to let them go back and report, and then we should see what the main body would do. When the Arabs, for such they evidently were, had observed us closely for some minutes they turned and rode back upon their comrades. These had halted, and as we were now in full view we halted too. As we dismounted the corporal said:

"Now for the last drink."

"Not the last, I hope," said Mac.

"Oh, who the devil knows and who the devil cares?" answered the Englishman. Then, as if ashamed of showing any emotion, he went on: "I beg your pardon, I could not help speaking so hastily just now; I am irritable, but I promise you I shall be cool enough in the fight."

"Oh, it's all right," replied Mac; "I've often been a bit hasty myself."

Giulia, scarcely understanding, looked at me with a puzzled air. When I smiled at her she smiled back at me, her confidence restored.

When we had drunk the brandy and water I asked the corporal whether or not we should fight the desert Arabs as we had fought the spahis.

"Certainly yes," he replied; "we did well in the rehearsal, may we not hope to do even better now?"

"I think so," I answered; "you see it is no longer a plan; it is now, as it were, a piece of drill that we have learned."

"Yes," said Mac; "we can go through it now as a soldier goes through the bayonet exercise; yes, let us fight as we fought before."

"If the battle does not go well," said Giulia, "you must not forget me."

"But no," I answered her, "but no; that is the one thing that we others are always thinking about. You must be saved, even though safety lay only in death."

"But the work must be done thoroughly," she insisted.

"Madame need not fear," said the corporal, speaking in a low voice; "even were I in my death agony, I should have strength enough left to kill."

"So should I," said Mac, "but I'd be sorry all the same." I was about to speak, but Giulia put her finger on my lips, and said:

"I am well content, I am almost happy."

Very soon a number of men, some on camels, others on horses, rode out from the caravan towards us. Our horses were hobbled, as we preferred to fight on foot. We were infantrymen by training, and, even had we been of the cavalry, we could get no good from our chargers after the long journey without food or water. When we ranged ourselves in open order the oncoming Arabs halted, and evidently consulted together. After a few moments of deliberation they divided into two parties, each about half-a-dozen strong, and prepared to attack us on both flanks. When the party on the right came within long range Mac called out:

"Am I to fire, corporal?"

"Yes; when you think you can hit man or camel or horse," replied the Englishman.

Almost immediately afterwards Mac fired, but no result seemed to follow the shot. He fired a second time, and brought down a man who was riding on a camel somewhat in advance of the others, brandishing a lance. A hurried volley came towards us now, but the range was too great for their guns, and we did not even hear the whistle of the bullets. The corporal and I had already begun to fire on the party approaching our left, and very soon a hot fusilade was going on. Luckily for us our opponents did not attempt to charge; they foolishly depended on their fire arms, with the result that we had emptied three saddles before their bullets began to hiss past our ears. When at last their bullets began to be unpleasantly perceptible the nearest Arab was full 300 yards away, and not one of us had been touched. We were now warming to the work, and at such a range in so clear an atmosphere it was easy for our rifles to tell. Not more than a dozen shots had whizzed past our heads when the Arabs were forced to retire, leaving five men on the plain, while two camels sprawling on the ground and two horses standing shivering with hanging heads told us that the animals had suffered as well as the men. As the Arabs galloped away we fired once or twice at their backs, but it is very hard for a soldier to hit a horse or a man going away from him.

We came together for a council of war. We at length decided to give them half-an-hour to recommence the attack ; if they did not assail us again within that time, or if they should continue their journey, we were then to assault the caravan. The plain fact was that we had to get possession of the caravan ; if we did not, our horses would fail, and we, on foot in the desert, should have no chance of saving our lives. Moreover, we felt justified in acting as highway robbers, for the Arabs had deliberately halted, and then sallied forth to take our lives, so as to possess themselves of our horses and arms. For me there was another thought : if the fight had gone against us, as it might easily have done if the Arabs had had sense enough to scatter and then to come straight home in a charge, Giulia would have had to die. There was no other resource. We Europeans could not endure the thought that a woman of our own blood, of our own colour, of our own ideas, should become the slave of a Bedouin of the desert.

We did not have to wait long. Ten men, five on camels, five on horseback, rode out from the caravan and started in a headlong charge against us. They began to gallop at a very long distance off, and this was lucky for us, for when the horses arrived at our position they were quite blown. Our rifles spoke quickly and well. There was no aiming at individuals, all we tried to do was to put as many bullets as we could into the moving mass before it could reach our bayonets. We were in close order now, with Giulia in the rear. In spite of all our efforts the Arabs reached the spot where we were, but neither horse nor camel would come upon the steel. All swerved aside, and the Arabs, firing from the backs of their animals, tried to shoot us down. But our rifles were better, far better, and we were steady as rocks upon the ground. Moreover, Giulia's revolvers were emptied, all save one chamber, and that was kept for herself. I cannot tell about my comrades, except that each did his duty, but I can tell what happened to myself. An Arab mounted on a camel tried to reach me with his spear; I lunged at his camel's snout, and got my bayonet well home. The terrified animal drew back, and as it did so I shot its rider dead. A second Arab, who had dismounted, or whose horse had been shot, came at me with a scimitar. But it was of no use; the long rifle and bayonet got in twice—once, as I had been taught long before, on the face, the second time full in the region of the heart. That ended my fighting for the day. The attack was over. One Arab was galloping away, but not so fast that a bullet from Mac's rifle could not reach him; two or three wounded who were trying to go off were soon settled by the English corporal and myself. We had no mercy in our hearts; they would not give us quarter, and we would give none to them. Not a man of the ten who attacked us escaped, and had a hundred others been in our power at the time we should have slain them all.

It was now our turn to attack. We mounted our horses, having first freed them from their hobbles, and advanced as quickly as the poor brutes could move towards the place where the caravan lay. When we came within about 500 yards of it three or four Arabs opened fire. Mac and the English corporal dismounted and returned the fire with success. After a few shots two of the Arabs fell, and then the shooting ceased. An old man, evidently a sheik, came forward with his hands raised above his head and spoke to us in Arabic. The corporal knew a few words of the language, and told him that we wanted water and food. When the sheik heard this he offered us all that the caravan had of what we required, and begged us to spare the lives of all who surrendered. This we promised to do, and in a quarter of an hour we were furnished with four fresh saddle-horses and two others for burden, with enough of food to last a fortnight, and a fair supply of water. We left the horses that had hitherto borne us to the beaten party; they were worn out, and, besides, they bore the stamp of the French Government. We took clothing also from four of the dead men, and afterwards found an opportunity of changing our uniform—of course, only kepi, tunic, and trousers—for an attire more befitting the desert and, therefore, less noticeable in it. Even Giulia, the while we turned our backs, put on an Arab dress, and many merry compliments we paid her about it.

When we left the caravan we pushed south at full speed for half-an-hour. Then turning to the west we went on at a fairly quick pace for more than two hours. As we might by that time consider that we had reached a place of comparative safety we halted for a rest. We had made a good meal of dates, bread and water after seizing the caravan, and so felt no hunger, but we soldiers—pretended Arabs I suppose we ought to call ourselves now—were glad to fill our pipes and talk over the two excellent fights we had made, for liberty first, and then for life. But we did not halt long; we had still to go farther west, and then to turn our horses' heads north for Morocco. This dangerous way through savage Sahara and almost as savage Morocco was for us the one way of escape, the one way of safety, the one way that would bring us back to civilisation and to happiness. Yet, dangerous as it was, we were filled with high hopes of success. All our undertakings had prospered, somehow or other ; each one felt that there was no danger in the world that he and his good comrades could not overcome. And I am the sole survivor—but why should I anticipate ?

For three days we travelled due west, caring our horses and sparing our supplies. Then we came upon an oasis, at which we refilled our water bottles. Luckily, there was not a soul at it or in sight, for we had no desire, now that we were sufficiently well equipped with all that we wanted, to try conclusions again with the fighting men of the desert. Our only wish at the time was to travel without attracting the observation of any. Then we turned towards the north-west and went slowly and cautiously along. We knew that soon we should be in the land of the Moors, but we were not so foolish as to believe that we should find a settled government there. We were quite well aware that most of the tribes south of the Atlas Mountains yield obedience only to their own chiefs, but we had no fear of the agricultural people. The only ones likely to attack us were the nomadic Arabs, and most of these would be left behind by us along with the desert. One must remember that in the Sahara there is but one law, the law of force, the plunderer of to-day is often the plundered of to-morrow. Where all are robbers, robbery is no reproach. In Morocco, however, even south of the Atlas Mountains, people have settled down in villages, poor and dirty it is true, but still homes. Where men have houses, ploughs, and oxen they begin to be civilised, and one may generally pass along without molestation. One must pay his way, of course, and we had money enough to do that, as Giulia had taken all her savings with her. True, our money might excite their cupidity, but then we need never show much at a time, and we presented all the appearance of a party that could defend its possessions. The English corporal and Mac did look really formidable; their beards had not been shaved since we came away, and I in fun nicknamed Mac the "hirsute tiger" and the corporal the "shaggy lion." They laughed at the names and at one another, and when the jest was explained to Giulia she laughed too, but not, as I noticed, with the same heartiness as of old. Poor girl! she was not at all well. Her strength was reduced, and the troubles, the anxieties, the privations of her life in the desert, following upon her agony before and during my trial, were beginning to tell seriously upon her, and I could do nothing to spare her in the least!

As we were riding along together one day the corporal said—in English, so that Giulia might not understand:

"It is all very well for you, Jean—you ought to be happy because you have escaped death—but what are Mac and I to do if we ever escape from the desert?"

I did not say anything in reply, but Mac spoke.

"I am satisfied if I can get home to Ireland once more; once there I will think twice before again becoming an exile."

"Very good," answered the corporal; "but I have no home to go to."

"Can you not go to the United States," I asked, "and make a new home there?"

"Yes, yes, I have thought of that; but——"

He said no more, and we all rode silently on for a time.

That night, when Mac called me for my turn of guard, he said:

"Did you notice how queer the corporal was to-day?"

"Oh yes; and so did Giulia. She asked me if there was anything wrong, and I knew not what to tell her."

"Ma foi," said Mac, "I see trouble ahead. Believe me, there will be at least one more fight, and 'twill be for the corporal's satisfaction this time."

"I can't help it," I replied; "he fought for me, and if he wants me I'll fight for him."

"So will I," answered Mac. "Good night."

About two days afterwards we came to a little village, and boldly demanded food, water and lodging. We promised to pay for all we got, but we took care to drive a hard bargain, so that they might think us poorer than we were. People will tell you about Arabian and Moorish and Turkish hospitality, but then these have never been with Arabs or Moors or Turks; if they had been, they would know that such hospitality has its price and that the price is limited by two things only—the wealth and the cunning of the purchaser. Of course, we kept the usual watches that night; we thought we were safe, but one can never be safe enough.

Next morning we got ready to depart. Giulia, Mac, and I had gone slightly in advance, Mac and I leading the horses that carried our supplies. The corporal was last. Suddenly we heard a woman's cry, then a loud oath and a shriek, and, looking back, we saw the Englishman lifting an Arab, or rather a Berber, woman to his saddle. Just as he succeeded a native rushed at him with a spear and stabbed him twice in the side. The corporal let go his hold of the woman and tried to unsling his rifle, but was unable to do so before the Berber thrust at him again, and brought him heavily to the ground. I had meanwhile dropped the bridle of the horse that I was leading and turned back. My rifle was unslung in a moment, and I fired at almost point-blank range at the Berber, just as he was preparing to drive his weapon home again in the body of my prostrate comrade. He flung up his arms and stumbled forward, tripping over the corporal. I rode back to help the Englishman, but it was too late; he was dead. Meanwhile shots began to fly round us; all the villagers were aroused by the outcry and the report of my rifle. Mac shouted to me to come away; there was no hope save in instant flight. I turned again, and regained Giulia's side, only to find that the pack-horses had stampeded. Mac fired at the crowd of natives, with what success I know not, and then the three of us galloped away at top speed, followed as we went by a dropping fire.

When we had got about half-a-mile from the village we looked back, and saw we were pursued. Six or eight Berbers were on our trail, and were evidently determined to take vengeance on us for the corporal's rashness. Our horses were quite fresh, and we pushed on, as it would not do to fight too near their village, for then they might be so reinforced that all hope of success on our part would disappear. If we could only get the half-dozen or so that followed us sufficiently far away we could enter into a fight with confidence. We had the European's usual contempt for savages, and our two previous fights had given us a wonderful amount of faith in ourselves and our weapons. True our fighting power had been much diminished by the death of the Englishman, for the loss of one rifle was serious in so small a band; but, even so, Mac and I were quite sure that we could first stall off the grand attack, and then inflict such damage on our opponents that they, or what was left of them, would be glad enough to retire.

We had gone thus about five or six miles when Mac called to Giulia and me to pull up. "No," I shouted; "let us press on a little farther." Mac shook his head. I saw that he was very pale; the fear that another comrade was passing away took instant possession of my heart. When we halted the pursuing Berbers were not more than half-a-mile away; they were six in number, and kept close together.

"What is wrong?" I asked.

"I was hurt," Mac replied, "in the firing at the village, and I could not go farther at that pace."

U

"Where did you get it?"

"In the right side." And he held his hands pressed upon his body just above the right groin.

"It is all right," he went on. "I can get through this fight, but after——" He stopped, smiled feebly, and shook his head. In a moment I had taken off his belt, opened his clothes, and looked for the wound. It was a small one, just a little hole in the side, with scarcely any outflow of blood. This made me serious. I had often seen similar ones, and I knew, as all soldiers do, that the wound that does not bleed outwardly bleeds inwardly, and is the most dangerous for the sufferer and the most difficult for the surgeon.

"Never mind," said Mac; "you can do nothing—at least you cannot until we have beaten off these rascals. Do not weep, petite," he said to Giulia; "I now repay you for all your kindness to me when my pay was stopped."

This only made Giulia weep all the more. Poor girl, it was for her a morning of tribulation.

But the work had to be done. We all lay down close together, and as soon as the Berbers came within easy range Mac and I opened fire. The fight was like both the others, except that these Berbers, being village-bred agriculturists, did not try to charge us with so much resolution as either the spahis or the Bedouins. They fired upon us for some time, but Mac and I were too well armed to mind much the popping of their guns, and when we had shot three men and a couple of horses the survivors withdrew. Then Mac insisted that we should mount and go forward again, because, as he truly said, if others came up they might attack us in that place, but the sight of their dead comrades would scarcely impel them to pursue. Giulia and I could not deny this. It was apparent that the best chance of safety lay in leaving the field to the dead and making good our retreat before the Berbers learned that another man of ours had been placed *hors de com-*

bat. Nevertheless, it was with heavy hearts that we remounted. It pained Giulia and myself to see the changed look in our good comrade's eyes; his forced smile made us sad, for the thought crossed our minds that soon we should be alone together in a savage land, without a friend, and almost without hope.

CHAPTER XXIV

WE struggled on together for about half-an-hour. Then Mac said that he could go no farther, and Giulia and I lifted him out of the saddle and placed him tenderly on the ground. I asked him if he were in much pain; he said that he felt very little, but that his lower limbs were becoming numbed.

"The end cannot be far off," he went on, "and, when I am gone, take my rifle and cartridges, and put as great a distance as possible between yourselves and the Berbers."

"Do not think of us," I replied, "think of yourself; you have but a short time to make your peace with God."

He said nothing to me, but I saw his lips moving in quiet prayer. After some time he said:

"Good-bye, my good comrades; it is nearly over."

Giulia was weeping, and there were tears also in my eyes. I pressed his hand, and Giulia, bending down, kissed him on the forehead. A moment after he ejaculated: "O Lord, have mercy." And at the words his gallant spirit passed away.

We were now lonely indeed. In one morning Giulia and I had lost our two companions—the two men who did not hesitate to risk their lives, as they used to put it, for the comrade in trouble and the woman in distress. The outlook that had been so favourable the day before was now dark and gloomy. Two-thirds of our fighting strength had gone; but that was not the worst: we missed even more the ruined Englishman's stern manner and stout heart, the laughing Irishman's constant wit on the march and steady

308

earnestness in the fight. Both were good friends, of totally different natures, yet equally sympathetic; each made up for what the other lacked. One never minded the gloom that too often sat upon the corporal's brow in listening to the ceaseless jesting and careless laughter of the simple soldier; and when the fight came one felt that Mac would care, and care well, for his share of it, but that the Englishman, while working as a fighting man, was planning as our chief.

People will say: Oh, but you were once sergeant-major, and why did not you command rather than the corporal? Well, for two good reasons. First, if I had once been sergeant-major, he had once been captain. Second, somebody had to be close to Giulia in every fight, for reasons that may be guessed—and who had a better right to be at her side than I?

There was no time for us to bury poor Mac, even had I pick and shovel for the work. Anyway, no soldier thinks much about where his body will lie after death: no grave at all is as good as a place in a trench where hundreds of others are pressing and crowding around. When you have once seen a battlefield grave, where three or four hundred lie like sardines in a tin, you will find little, if indeed any, poetry in the words "God's acre." Not that the burial party should be blamed, be it well understood. Oh no! they must think of the living, especially the wounded, and in a hot climate quick burial is the only thing to prevent a pestilence of the sun.

Giulia and I managed to go about twelve kilometres farther on our road that day. I did not want to go so far, but she insisted. She knew, as I did, that she was not in a fit state to travel such a distance; but some fear of the Berbers who had killed our comrades had taken possession of her heart, and she would not, nay, she could not, rest until we were quite safe from further pursuit. But she could not hold out very long; at last even to sit her horse when going at a mere

walking pace was too much for her strength, and she
was compelled to yield to my entreaties and to dis-
mount and rest. Poor girl! she was very nervous
and excited, Even the struggles that ended in complete success had tried her too much, and now she felt
with tenfold anxiety and apprehension the death of the
two loyal, brave, and generous comrades who had been
so suddenly lost. And a woman always feels the loss
of a friend more than a man does, because a man can
easily get another, but a women must be always
suspicious of those who tender her friendship, lest
there be poison in the gift.

That night we could set no guard. Both of us were
weary in spirit and in body. There was no one to relieve me if I watched, and Giulia could not rest unless
I was so near that her hand could always touch me. I
thought of a plan: it was to picket the horses so that
there should be no danger of losing them, and then to
withdraw about four hundred yards from the spot where
they were placed. The horses might attract enemies
in the night, but if we were some distance away, we
ought to be in comparative safety. Giulia assented;
and when I had settled the horses for the night I
helped her to a spot a good distance from them, and
after a little interval, during which Giulia wept and I
comforted her as best I could, we lay down to rest in
the desert side by side. As I was sleeping, as a soldier
sleeps who has learned to rest with aching body or even
with aching heart, Giulia clasped me by the shoulder,
and brought me back to active thought and life.

"What! is there an attack?" And I tried for my
rifle in the dark.

"No, no! oh no! it is not that. I am ill; oh, what
shall I do!"

But I will not tell the story. The night wore on,
and when dawn came it was only to show me that
the best of all my comrades, the comrade who made
life happy and a thing of joy, the woman who had

loved and trusted, ever true, ever unchanging, was about to pass out of my life for ever. The end came shortly after the dawn. It was quiet, for poor Giulia was worn out with all that she had gone through, and, when all was over, Arab or Berber or robber of the road might take my life, and I should not resist. What was the good of life since I had lost my love?

All that day I stayed quietly by the dead body of my dear one. I forgot the horses; I forgot the danger of attack; I forgot all things save that I was at last alone, really alone, in the world. I thought of those whom I had loved and lost—Nicholas the Russian, the English corporal, Mac; but every moment my thoughts reverted to the greatest loss of all—the loss of her whose corpse, pale and bloodless, it is true, but with an indefinable beauty of feature and expression, lay quiet and still upon the sand.

In the evening I dug a grave with my bayonet, and gently, tenderly, laid there to rest the remains of her who had loved me with so great a love.

.   .   .   .

There is little more to be said. I had no difficulty in making my way to Tangier. I was not molested, nor did I molest anyone. The only thought in my mind was to get as far away as possible from Africa— the land for me of so many chances and changes, of exquisite love and still more exquisite sorrow. I was hopeless, heartless, not in the sense that I was heartless to others—I was heartless only for myself.

From Tangier I crossed to Spain, and there found a relation at Salamanca—one of those men who, studying for the priesthood, choose the foreign colleges rather than Maynooth. He helped me with money to reach Ireland, but from him, as from all others, I kept the true story, the story, I may now say, of "twenty golden years ago."

THE RIVERSIDE PRESS LIMITED, EDINBURGH

A CATALOGUE OF BOOKS PUBLISHED BY METHUEN AND COMPANY: LONDON 36 ESSEX STREET W.C.

CONTENTS

MARCH 1904

A CATALOGUE OF
MESSRS. METHUEN'S
PUBLICATIONS

Colonial Editions are published of all Messrs. METHUEN'S novels issued at a price above 2s. 6d., and similar editions are published of some works of general literature. These are marked in the Catalogue. Colonial editions are only for circulation in the British Colonies and India.

PART I.—GENERAL LITERATURE

Abbot (Jacob). THE BEECHNUT BOOK. Edited by E. V. LUCAS. Illustrated. *Demy 16mo. 2s. 6d.* [Little Blue Books.

Acatos (M. J.). See L. A. Sornet.

Adeney (W. F.), M.A. See Bennett and Adeney.

Æschylus. AGAMEMNON, CHOEPHOROE, EUMENIDES. Translated by LEWIS CAMPBELL, LL.D., late Professor of Greek at St. Andrews. *5s.* [Classical Translations.

Æsop. FABLES. With 380 Woodcuts by THOMAS BEWICK. *Fcap. 8vo. 3s. 6d. net.* [Illustrated Pocket Library.

Ainsworth (W. Harrison). WINDSOR CASTLE. With 22 Plates and 87 Woodcuts in the Text by GEORGE CRUIKSHANK. *Fcap. 8vo. 3s. 6d. net.* [Illustrated Pocket Library.

THE TOWER OF LONDON. With 40 Plates and 58 Woodcuts in the Text by GEORGE CRUIKSHANK. *Fcap. 8vo. 3s. 6d. net.* [Illustrated Pocket Library.

Alexander (William), D.D., Archbishop of Armagh. THOUGHTS AND COUNSELS OF MANY YEARS. Selected by J. H. BURN, B.D. *Demy 16mo. 2s. 6d.*

Alken (Henry). THE ANALYSIS OF THE HUNTING FIELD. With 7 Coloured Plates and 43 Illustrations on wood. *Fcap. 8vo. 3s. 6d. net.* [Illustrated Pocket Library.

THE NATIONAL SPORTS OF GREAT BRITAIN. With descriptions in English and French. With 51 Coloured Plates. *Royal Folio. Five Guineas net.* [Burlington Library.

THE NATIONAL SPORTS OF GREAT BRITAIN. With Descriptions and 51 Coloured Plates by HENRY ALKEN. *4s. 6d. net.*

Also a limited edition on large Japanese paper, *30s. net.*

This book is completely different from the large folio edition of 'National Sports' by the same artist, and none of the plates are similar. [Illustrated Pocket Library.

Allen (Jessie). DURER. With many Illustrations. *Demy 16mo. 2s. 6d. net.* [Little Books on Art.

Almack (E.). BOOKPLATES. With many Illustrations. *Demy 16mo. 2s. 6d. net.* [Little Books on Art. Nearly Ready.

Amherst (Lady). A SKETCH OF EGYPTIAN HISTORY FROM THE EARLIEST TIMES TO THE PRESENT DAY. With many Illustrations, some of which are in Colour. *Demy 8vo. 10s. 6d. net.* [Nearly Ready.

Anderson (F. M.). THE STORY OF THE BRITISH EMPIRE FOR CHILDREN. With many Illustrations. *Crown 8vo. 1s. 6d.*

Andrewes (Bishop). PRECES PRIVATAE. Edited, with Notes, by F. E. BRIGHTMAN, M.A., of Pusey House, Oxford. *Crown 8vo. 6s.*

Aristophanes. THE FROGS. Translated into English by E. W. HUNTINGFORD, M.A., Professor of Classics in Trinity College, Toronto. *Crown 8vo. 2s. 6d.*

Aristotle. THE NICOMACHEAN ETHICS. Edited, with an Introduction and Notes, by JOHN BURNET, M.A., Professor of Greek at St. Andrews. *Demy 8vo. 15s. net.*

Ashton. (R.). THE PEELES AT THE CAPITAL. Illustrated. *Demy 16mo. 2s. 6d.* [Little Blue Books.

MRS. BARBERRY'S GENERAL SHOP. Illustrated. *Demy 16mo. 2s. 6d.* [The Little Blue Books.

Asquith (H. H.), The Right Hon., M.P. TRADE AND THE EMPIRE. An Examination of Mr. Chamberlain's Proposals. *Demy 8vo. 6d. net.*

Atkins (H. G.). GOETHE. With 12 Illustrations. *Fcap. 8vo. 3s. 6d.; leather, 4s. net.* [Little Biographies. Nearly Ready.

Atkinson (T. D.). A SHORT HISTORY OF ENGLISH ARCHITECTURE. With over 200 Illustrations by the Author and others. *Fcap. 8vo. 3s. 6d. net.*
[*Nearly Ready.*

Austen (Jane). PRIDE AND PREJU-DICE. Edited by E. V. Lucas. *Two Volumes. Small Pott 8vo. Each volume, cloth, 1s. 6d. net.; leather, 2s. 6d. net.*
[*Little Library.*

NORTHANGER ABBEY. Edited by E. V. Lucas. *Small Pott 8vo. Cloth, 1s. 6d. net.; leather, 2s. 6d. net.* [*Little Library.*

Bacon (Francis). THE ESSAYS OF. Edited by EDWARD WRIGHT. *Small Pott 8vo. 1s. 6d. net; leather, 2s. 6d. net.*
[*Little Library.*

Baden - Powell (R. S. S.), Major-General. THE DOWNFALL OF PREMPEH. A Diary of Life in Ashanti, 1895. With 21 Illustrations and a Map. *Third Edition. Large Crown 8vo. 6s.*
A Colonial Edition is also published.

THE MATABELE CAMPAIGN, 1896. With nearly 100 Illustrations. *Fourth and Cheaper Edition. Large Crown 8vo. 6s.*
A Colonial Edition is also published.

Baker (W. G.), M.A. JUNIOR GEO-GRAPHY EXAMINATION PAPERS. *Fcap. 8vo. 1s.* [*Junior Exam. Series.*

Baker (Julian L.), F.I.C., F.C.S. THE BREWING INDUSTRY. *Crown 8vo. 2s. 6d. net.*
[*Books on Business. Nearly Ready.*

Balfour (Graham). THE LIFE OF ROBERT LOUIS STEVENSON. *Second Edition. Two Volumes. Demy 8vo. 25s. net.*
A Colonial Edition is also published.

Balfour (Marie Clothilde). FROM SARANAC TO THE MARQUESAS. Being Letters written by Mrs. M. I. STEVENSON during 1887-8 to her sister Miss JANE WHYTE BALFOUR. With an Intro-duction by GEORGE W. BALFOUR, M.D., LL.D., F.R.S.S. *Crown 8vo. 6s. net.*
A Colonial Edition is also published.

Bally (S. E.). A FRENCH COMMERCIAL READER. With Vocabulary. *Second Edition. Crown 8vo. 2s.*
[*Commercial Series.*

FRENCH COMMERCIAL CORRE-SPONDENCE. With Vocabulary. *Third Edition. Crown 8vo. 2s.*
[*Commercial Series.*

A GERMAN COMMERCIAL READER. With Vocabulary. *Crown 8vo. 2s.*
[*Commercial Series.*

GERMAN COMMERCIAL CORRE-SPONDENCE. With Vocabulary. *Crown 8vo. 2s. 6d.* [*Commercial Series.*

Banks (Elizabeth L.). THE AUTO-BIOGRAPHY OF A 'NEWSPAPER GIRL.' With Portrait of the Author and her Dog. *Second Edition. Crown 8vo. 6s.*
A Colonial Edition is also published.

Barham (R. H.). THE INGOLDSBY LEGENDS. Edited by J. B. ATLAY. *Two Volumes. Small Pott 8vo. Each volume, cloth, 1s. 6d. net; leather, 2s. 6d. net.*
[*Little Library.*

Baring-Gould (S.). Author of 'Mehalah,' etc. THE LIFE OF NAPOLEON BONA-PARTE. With over 450 Illustrations in the Text, and 12 Photogravure Plates. *Gilt top. Large quarto. 36s.*

THE TRAGEDY OF THE CÆSARS. With numerous Illustrations from Busts, Gems, Cameos, etc. *Fifth Edition. Royal 8vo. 15s.*

A BOOK OF FAIRY TALES. With numerous Illustrations and Initial Letters by ARTHUR J. GASKIN. *Second Edition. Crown 8vo. Buckram. 6s.*

A BOOK OF BRITTANY. With numerous Illustrations. *Crown 8vo. 6s.*
Uniform in scope and size with Mr. Baring-Gould's well-known books on Devon, Cornwall, and Dartmoor.

OLD ENGLISH FAIRY TALES. With numerous Illustrations by F. D. BEDFORD. *Second Edition. Cr. 8vo. Buckram. 6s.*
A Colonial Edition is also published.

THE VICAR OF MORWENSTOW: A Biography. A new and Revised Edition. With Portrait. *Crown 8vo. 3s. 6d.*
A completely new edition of the well-known biography of R. S. Hawker.

DARTMOOR: A Descriptive and Historical Sketch. With Plans and numerous Illus-trations. *Crown 8vo. 6s.*

THE BOOK OF THE WEST. With numerous Illustrations. *Two volumes.* Vol. I. Devon. *Second Edition.* Vol. II. Cornwall. *Second Edition. Crown 8vo. 6s. each.*

A BOOK OF NORTH WALES. With numerous Illustrations. *Crown 8vo. 6s.*
This book is uniform with Mr. Baring-Gould's books on Devon, Dartmoor, and Brittany.

BRITTANY. Illustrated by J. A. WYLIE. *Pott 8vo. Cloth, 3s.; leather, 3s. 6d. net.*
[*Little Guides.*

OLD COUNTRY LIFE. With 67 Illustra-tions. *Fifth Edition. Large Cr. 8vo. 6s.*

AN OLD ENGLISH HOME. With numer-ous Plans and Illustrations. *Cr. 8vo. 6s.*

HISTORIC ODDITIES AND STRANGE EVENTS. *Fifth Edition. Cr. 8vo. 6s.*

YORKSHIRE ODDITIES AND STRANGE EVENTS. *Fifth Edition. Crown 8vo. 6s.*

STRANGE SURVIVALS AND SUPER-STITIONS. *Second Edition. Cr. 8vo. 6s.*
A Colonial Edition is also published.

A GARLAND OF COUNTRY SONG: English Folk Songs with their Traditional Melodies. Collected and arranged by S. BARING-GOULD and H. F. SHEPPARD. *Demy 4to. 6s.*

SONGS OF THE WEST: Traditional Ballads and Songs of the West of England, with their Melodies. Collected by S. BARING - GOULD, M.A., and H. F. SHEPPARD, M.A. In 4 Parts. *Parts I., II., III.*, 2s. 6d. each. *Part IV.*, 4s. *In One Volume, French Morocco*, 10s. net.

Barker (Aldred F.), Author of 'Pattern Analysis,' etc. AN INTRODUCTION TO THE STUDY OF TEXTILE DESIGN. With numerous Diagrams and Illustrations. *Demy 8vo.* 7s. 6d.

Barnes (W. E.), D.D. ISAIAH. With an Introduction and Notes. *Two Vols. Fcap. 8vo.* 2s. net each. With Map. [Churchman's Bible.

Barnett (Mrs. P. A.) A LITTLE BOOK OF ENGLISH PROSE. *Small Pott 8vo. Cloth*, 1s. 6d. net; *leather*, 2s. 6d. net.
[Little Library.

Baron (R. R. N.), M.A. FRENCH PROSE COMPOSITION. *Crown 8vo.* 2s. 6d. *Key*, 3s. net.

Barron (H. M.), M.A., Wadham College, Oxford. TEXTS FOR SERMONS. With a Preface by Canon SCOTT HOLLAND. *Crown 8vo.* 3s. 6d.

Bastable (C. F.), M.A., Professor of Economics at Trinity College, Dublin. THE COMMERCE OF NATIONS. *Second Edition. Crown 8vo.* 2s. 6d.
[Social Questions Series.

Batson (Mrs. Stephen) A BOOK OF THE COUNTRY AND THE GARDEN. Illustrated by F. CARRUTHERS GOULD and A. C. GOULD. *Demy 8vo.* 10s. 6d.

A CONCISE HANDBOOK OF GARDEN FLOWERS. *Fcap. 8vo.* 3s. 6d.

Beaman (A. Hulme) PONS ASINORUM; OR, A GUIDE TO BRIDGE. *Second Edition. Fcap. 8vo.* 2s.

Beard (W. S.) JUNIOR ARITHMETIC EXAMINATION PAPERS. *Second Edition. Fcap. 8vo.* With or without Answers. [Junior Examination Series.

JUNIOR GENERAL INFORMATION EXAMINATION PAPERS. *Fcap. 8vo.* 1s. [Junior Examination Series.

EASY EXERCISES IN ARITHMETIC. Arranged by. *Cr. 8vo.* Without Answers, 1s. With Answers, 1s. 6d.

Beckford (Peter) THOUGHTS ON HUNTING. Edited by J. OTHO PAGET, and Illustrated by G. H. JALLAND. *Demy 8vo.* 10s. 6d.

Beckford (William). THE HISTORY OF THE CALIPH VATHEK. Edited by E. DENISON ROSS. *Pott 8vo. Cloth*, 1s. 6d. net; *leather*, 2s. 6d. net. [Little Library.

Beeching (H. C.), M.A., Canon of Westminster. LYRA SACRA: A Book of Sacred Verse. With an Introduction and Notes. *Pott 8vo. Cl.*, 2s.; *leather*, 2s. 6d. [Library of Devotion.

Behmen (Jacob). THE SUPERSENSUAL LIFE. Edited by BERNARD HOLLAND. *Fcap. 8vo.* 3s. 6d.

Belloc (Hilaire). PARIS. With Maps and Illustrations. *Crown 8vo.* 6s.

Bellot (H. H. L.), M.A. THE INNER AND MIDDLE TEMPLE. With numerous Illustrations. *Crown 8vo.* 6s. net.
See also L. A. A. Jones.

Bennett (W. H.), M.A. A PRIMER OF THE BIBLE. *Second Edition. Crown 8vo.* 2s. 6d.

Bennett (W. H.) and Adeney (W. F.). A BIBLICAL INTRODUCTION. *Crown 8vo.* 7s. 6d.

Benson (A. C.), M.A. A LIFE OF LORD TENNYSON. With 9 Illustrations. *Fcap. 8vo. Cloth*, 3s. 6d.; *Leather*, 4s. net.
[Little Biographies.

Benson (R. M.). THE WAY OF HOLINESS: a Devotional Commentary on the 119th Psalm. *Crown 8vo.* 5s.

Bernard (E. R.), M.A., Canon of Salisbury. THE ENGLISH SUNDAY. *Fcap. 8vo.* 1s. 6d.

Bertouche (Baroness de). THE LIFE OF FATHER IGNATIUS. With Illustrations. *Demy 8vo.* 10s. 6d. net.
A Colonial Edition is also published.
[Nearly Ready.

Bethune-Baker (J. F.), M.A., Fellow of Pembroke College, Cambridge. A HISTORY OF EARLY CHRISTIAN DOCTRINE. *Demy 8vo.* 10s. 6d.
[Handbooks of Theology.

Bidez (M.). See Parmentier.

Biggs (C. R. D.), B.D. THE EPISTLE TO THE PHILIPPIANS. With an Introduction and Notes. *Fcap. 8vo.* 1s. 6d. net.
[Churchman's Bible.

Bindley (T. Herbert), B.D. THE OECUMENICAL DOCUMENTS OF THE FAITH. With Introductions and Notes. *Crown 8vo.* 6s.
A historical account of the Creeds.

Binyon (Laurence). THE DEATH OF ADAM, AND OTHER POEMS. *Second Edition. Crown 8vo.* 3s. 6d. net.

Blair (Robert). THE GRAVE: a Poem. Illustrated by 12 Etchings executed by LOUIS SCHIAVONETTI, from the original inventions of WILLIAM BLAKE. With an Engraved Title - Page and a Portrait of Blake by T. PHILLIPS, R.A. *Fcap. 8vo.* 3s. 6d. net.
Also a limited edition on large Japanese paper with India Proofs and a duplicate set of plates. 15s. net.
[Illustrated Pocket Library.

Blake (William). ILLUSTRATIONS OF THE BOOK OF JOB. Invented and Engraved by. *Fcap. 8vo.* 3s. 6d. net.
Also a limited edition on large Japanese paper with India proofs and a duplicate set of plates. 15s. net. [Illustrated Pocket Library.

SELECTIONS. Edited by M. PERUGINI. *Small Pott 8vo.* 1s. 6d. net; *leather*, 2s. 6d. net.
[Little Library.

Maxland (B.) M.A. THE SONG OF SONGS. Being Selections from ST. BERNARD. *Small Pott 8vo. Cloth, 2s.; leather, 2s. 6d. net.* [Library of Devotion.

Bloom (T. Harvey), M.A. SHAKESPEARE'S GARDEN. With Illustrations. *Fcap. 8vo. 2s. 6d.; leather, 3s. 6d. net.*

Boardman (J. H.) See W. French.

Bodley (J. E. C.) Author of 'France.' THE CORONATION OF EDWARD VII. *Demy 8vo. 21s. net.* By Command of the King.

Body (George), D.D. THE SOUL'S PILGRIMAGE: Devotional Readings from his published and unpublished writings. Selected and arranged by J. H. BURN, B.D., F.R.S.E. *Pott 8vo. 2s. 6d.*

Boger (Alnod J.) THE STORY OF GENERAL BACON: A Short Account of a Peninsula and Waterloo Veteran. *Crown 8vo. 6s.*

Bona (Cardinal). A GUIDE TO ETERNITY. Edited with an Introduction and Notes, by J. W. STANBRIDGE, B.D. *Pott 8vo. Cloth, 2s.; leather, 2s. 6d. net.* [Library of Devotion.

Borrow (George). LAVENGRO. Edited by F. HINDES GROOME. *Two Volumes. Small Pott 8vo. Each volume, cloth, 1s. 6d. net; leather, 2s. 6d. net.* [Little Library. THE ROMANY RYE. Edited by JOHN SAMPSON. *Small Pott 8vo. Cloth, 1s. 6d. net; leather, 2s. 6d. net.* [Little Library.

Bos (J. Ritzema). AGRICULTURAL ZOOLOGY. Translated by J. R. AINSWORTH DAVIS, M.A. With an Introduction by ELEANOR A. ORMEROD, F.E.S. With 155 Illustrations. *Crown 8vo. Second Edition. 3s. 6d.*

Botting (C. G.), B.A. JUNIOR LATIN EXAMINATION PAPERS. *Fcap. 8vo. Second Ed. 1s.* [Junior Examination Series. EASY GREEK EXERCISES. *Cr. 8vo. 2s.*

Boulton (E. S.). GEOMETRY ON MODERN LINES. *Crown 8vo. 2s.*

Bowden (E. M.). THE IMITATION OF BUDDHA: Being Quotations from Buddhist Literature for each Day in the Year. *Fourth Edition. Crown 16mo. 2s. 6d.*

Bowmaker (E.). THE HOUSING OF THE WORKING CLASSES. *Crown 8vo. 2s. 6d.* [Social Questions Series.

Brabant (F. G.), M.A. SUSSEX. Illustrated by E. H. NEW. *Small Pott 8vo. Cloth, 3s.; leather, 3s. 6d. net.* [Little Guides. THE ENGLISH LAKES. Illustrated by E. H. NEW. *Small Pott 8vo. Cloth, 4s.; leather, 4s. 6d. net.* [Little Guides.

Brodrick (Mary) and Morton (Anderson). A CONCISE HANDBOOK OF EGYPTIAN ARCHÆOLOGY. With many Illustrations. *Crown 8vo. 3s. 6d.*

Brooke (A. S.), M.A. SLINGSBY AND SLINGSBY CASTLE. With many Illustrations. *Cr. 8vo. 5s. net.* [Nearly Ready.

Brooks (E. W.). See F. J. Hamilton.

Brownell (C. L.). THE HEART OF JAPAN. Illustrated. *Second Edition. Crown 8vo. 6s.* A Colonial Edition is also published.

Browning (Robert). SELECTIONS FROM THE EARLY POEMS OF. With Introduction and Notes by W. HALL GRIFFIN. *Small Pott 8vo. 1s. 6d. net; leather, 2s. 6d. net.* [Little Library.

Buckland (Francis T.). CURIOSITIES OF NATURAL HISTORY. With Illustrations by HARRY B. NEILSON. *Crown 8vo. 3s. 6d.*

Buckton (A. M.). THE BURDEN OF ENGELA: a Ballad-Epic. *Second Edition. Crown 8vo. 3s. 6d. net.*

Budge (E. A. Wallis). THE GODS OF THE EGYPTIANS. With over 100 Coloured Plates and many Illustrations. *Two Volumes. Royal 8vo. £3, 3s. net.*

Bulley (Miss). See Lady Dilke.

Bunyan (John). THE PILGRIM'S PROGRESS. Edited, with an Introduction, by C. H. FIRTH, M.A. With 39 Illustrations by R. ANNING BELL. *Cr. 8vo. 6s.* GRACE ABOUNDING. Edited by C. S. FREER, M.A. *Small Pott 8vo. Cloth, 2s.; leather, 2s. 6d. net.* [Library of Devotion.

Burch (G. J.), M.A., F.R.S. A MANUAL OF ELECTRICAL SCIENCE. With numerous Illustrations. *Crown 8vo. 3s.* [University Extension Series.

Burgess (Gelett). GOOPS AND HOW TO BE THEM. With numerous Illustrations. *Small 4to. 6s.*

Burn (A. E.), B.D., Examining Chaplain to the Bishop of Lichfield. AN INTRODUCTION TO THE HISTORY OF THE CREEDS. *Demy 8vo. 10s. 6d.* [Handbooks of Theology.

Burn (J. H.), B.D. A MANUAL OF CONSOLATION FROM THE SAINTS AND FATHERS. *Small Pott 8vo. Cloth, 2s.; leather, 2s. 6d. net.* [Library of Devotion. A DAY BOOK FROM THE SAINTS AND FATHERS. With an Introduction and Notes. *Small Pott 8vo. Cloth, 2s.; leather, 2s. 6d. net.* [Library of Devotion.

Burnand (Sir F. C.). RECORDS AND REMINISCENCES, PERSONAL AND GENERAL. With many Illustrations. *Demy 8vo. Two Volumes. Second Edition. 25s. net.* A Colonial Edition is also published.

Burns (Robert), THE POEMS OF. Edited by ANDREW LANG and W. A. CRAIGIE. With Portrait. *Third Edition. Demy 8vo, gilt top. 6s.*

Burnside (W. F.). OLD TESTAMENT HISTORY FOR USE IN SCHOOLS. *Crown 8vo.* 3s. 6d.

Burton (Alfred). THE MILITARY ADVENTURES OF JOHNNY NEWCOME. With 15 Coloured Plates by T. ROWLANDSON. *Fcap. 8vo.* 3s. 6d. *net.* [Illustrated Pocket Library.

Caldecott (Alfred), D.D. THE PHILOSOPHY OF RELIGION IN ENGLAND AND AMERICA. *Demy 8vo.* 10s. 6d. [Handbooks of Theology.

Calderwood (D. S.), Headmaster of the Normal School, Edinburgh. TEST CARDS IN EUCLID AND ALGEBRA. In three packets of 40, with Answers. 1s. each. Or in three Books, price 2d., 2d., and 3d.

Cambridge (Ada) [Mrs. Cross]. THIRTY YEARS IN AUSTRALIA. *Demy 8vo.* 7s. 6d.
A Colonial Edition is also published. [Nearly Ready.

Canning (George). SELECTIONS FROM THE ANTI-JACOBIN; with additional Poems. Edited by LLOYD SANDERS. *Small Pott 8vo, cloth,* 1s. 6d. *net.; leather,* 2s. 6d. *net.* [Little Library.

Capey (E. F. H.). ERASMUS. With 12 Illustrations. *Fcap. 8vo. Cloth,* 3s. 6d. *net; leather,* 4s. *net.* [Little Biographies.

Carlyle (Thomas). THE FRENCH REVOLUTION. Edited by C. R. L. FLETCHER, Fellow of Magdalen College, Oxford. *Three Volumes. Crown 8vo.* 18s.
THE LIFE AND LETTERS OF OLIVER CROMWELL. With an Introduction by C. H. FIRTH, M.A., and Notes and Appendices by Mrs. S. C. LOMAS. *Three Volumes. Demy 8vo.* 18s. *net.* [Nearly Ready.

Carlyle (R. M. and A. J.), M.A. BISHOP LATIMER. With Portrait. *Crown 8vo.* 3s. 6d. [Leaders of Religion.

Channer (C. C.) and Roberts (M. E.). LACE-MAKING IN THE MIDLANDS, PAST AND PRESENT. With 16 full-page Illustrations. *Crown 8vo.* 2s. 6d.

Chesterfield (Lord), THE LETTERS OF, TO HIS SON. Edited, with an Introduction, by C. STRACHEY, and Notes by A. CALTHROP. *Two Volumes. Cr. 8vo.* 12s.

Christian (F. W.). THE CAROLINE ISLANDS. With many Illustrations and Maps. *Demy 8vo.* 12s. 6d. *net.*

Cicero. DE ORATORE I. Translated by E. N. P. MOOR, M.A. *Crown 8vo.* 3s. 6d. [Classical Translations.
SELECT ORATIONS (Pro Milone, Pro Murena, Philippic II., In Catilinam). Translated by H. E. D. BLAKISTON, M.A., Fellow and Tutor of Trinity College, Oxford. *Crown 8vo.* 5s. [Classical Translations.
DE NATURA DEORUM. Translated by F. BROOKS, M.A., late Scholar of Balliol College, Oxford. *Crown 8vo.* 3s. 6d. [Classical Translations.

DE OFFICIIS. Translated by G. B. GARDINER, M.A. *Crown 8vo.* 2s. 6d. [Classical Translations.

Clarke (F. A.), M.A. BISHOP KEN. With Portrait. *Crown 8vo.* 3s. 6d. [Leaders of Religion.

Cleather (A. L.) and Crump (B.). THE RING OF THE NIBELUNG: An Interpretation, embodying Wagner's own explanations. *Second Ed. Crown 8vo.* 2s. 6d.
THE WAGNER CYCLE. In Three Volumes. *Fcap 8vo.* 2s. 6d. *net each.* VOL. I.—PARSIFAL, etc.

Clinch (G.). KENT. Illustrated by F. D. BEDFORD. *Small Pott 8vo. Cloth,* 3s.; *leather,* 3s. 6d. *net.* [Little Guides.
THE ISLE OF WIGHT. Illustrated by F. D. BEDFORD. *Small Pott 8vo. Cloth,* 3s.; *leather,* 3s. 6d. *net.* [Little Guides.

Clough (W. T.) and Dunstan (A. E.). ELEMENTARY EXPERIMENTAL SCIENCE. PHYSICS by W. T. CLOUGH, A.R.C.S. CHEMISTRY by A. E. DUNSTAN, B.Sc. With 1 Diagram. *Crown 8vo.* 2s. [Junior School Books.

Cobb (T.). THE CASTAWAYS OF MEADOWBANK. Illustrated. *Demy 16mo.* 2s. 6d. [Little Blue Books.
THE TREASURY OF PRINCEGATE PRIORY. Illustrated. *Demy 16mo.* 2s. 6d. [Little Blue Books.
THE LOST BALL. Illustrated. *Demy 16mo.* 2s. 6d. [Little Blue Books.

Collingwood (W. G.), M.A. THE LIFE OF JOHN RUSKIN. With Portraits. *Cheap Edition. Crown 8vo.* 6s.

Collins (W. E.) M.A. THE BEGINNINGS OF ENGLISH CHRISTIANITY. With Map. *Crown 8vo.* 3s. 6d. [Churchman's Library.

Colonna. HYPNEROTOMACHIA POLIPHILI UBI HUMANA OMNIA NON NISI SOMNIUM ESSE DOCET ATQUE OBITER PLURIMA SCITU SANE QUAM DIGNA COMMEMORAT. An edition limited to 350 copies on handmade paper. *Folio. Three Guineas net.* [Nearly Ready.

Combe (William). THE TOUR OF DR. SYNTAX IN SEARCH OF THE PICTURESQUE. With 30 Coloured Plates by T. ROWLANDSON. *Fcap. 8vo.* 3s. 6d. *net.*
Also a limited edition on large Japanese paper. 30s. *net.* [Illustratd Pocket Library.
THE TOUR OF DR. SYNTAX IN SEARCH OF CONSOLATION. With 24 Coloured Plates by T. ROWLANDSON. 3s. 6d. *net.*
Also a limited edition on large Japanese paper. 30s. *net.* [Illustrated Pocket Library.
THE THIRD TOUR OF DR. SYNTAX IN SEARCH OF A WIFE. With 24 Coloured Plates by T. ROWLANDSON. 3s. 6d. *net.*

Also a limited edition on large Japanese paper. 30s. net.

[Illustrated Pocket Library.

THE HISTORY OF JOHNNY QUAE GENUS: The Little Foundling of the late Dr. Syntax. With 24 Coloured Plates by ROWLANDSON. *Fcap. 8vo.* 3s. 6d. net.

Also a limited edition on large Japanese paper. 30s. net.

[Illustrated Pocket Library.

THE ENGLISH DANCE OF DEATH, from the Designs of THOMAS ROWLANDSON, with Metrical Illustrations by the Author of 'Doctor Syntax.' With 74 Coloured Plates. *Two Volumes. Fcap. 8vo.* 9s. net.

Also a limited edition on large Japanese paper. 30s. net.

[Illustrated Pocket Library.

THE DANCE OF LIFE: a Poem. Illustrated with 26 Coloured Engravings by THOMAS ROWLANDSON. *Fcap. 8vo.* 3s. 6d. net.

Also a limited edition on large Japanese paper. 30s. net.

[Illustrated Pocket Library.

Cook (A. M.), M.A. See E. C. Marchant.

Cooke-Taylor (R. W.). THE FACTORY SYSTEM. *Crown 8vo.* 2s. 6d.

[Social Questions Series.

Corelli (Marie). THE PASSING OF THE GREAT QUEEN: A Tribute to the Noble Life of Victoria Regina. *Small 4to.* 1s.

A CHRISTMAS GREETING. *Sm. 4to.* 1s.

Corkran (Alice). MINIATURES. With many Illustrations. *Demy 16mo.* 2s. 6d. net.

[Little Books on Art.

LEIGHTON. With many Illustrations. *Demy 16mo.* 2s. 6d. net.

[Little Books on Art.

Cotes (Rosemary). DANTE'S GARDEN. With a Frontispiece. *Second Edition. Fcap. 8vo. cloth* 2s. 6d.; *leather,* 3s. 6d. net.

Cowley (Abraham) THE ESSAYS OF. Edited by H. C. MINCHIN. *Small Pott 8vo. Cloth,* 1s. 6d. net; *leather,* 2s. 6d. net.

[Little Library.

Cox (J. Charles), LL.D., F.S.A. DERBYSHIRE. Illustrated by J. C. WALL. *Small Pott 8vo. Cloth,* 3s.; *leather,* 3s. 6d. net.

[Little Guides.

Cox (Harold), B.A. LAND NATIONALIZATION. *Crown 8vo.* 2s. 6d.

[Social Questions Series.

Crabbe (George), SELECTIONS FROM THE POEMS OF. Edited by A. C. DEANE. *Small Pott 8vo. Cloth,* 1s. 6d. net; *leather,* 2s. 6d. net. [Little Library.

Craigie (W. A.). A PRIMER OF BURNS. *Crown 8vo.* 2s. 6d.

Craik (Mrs.). JOHN HALIFAX, GENTLEMAN. Edited by ANNIE MATHESON. *Two Volumes. Small Pott 8vo. Each Volume, Cloth,* 1s. 6d. net; *leather,* 2s. 6d. net. [Little Library.

Crashaw (Richard), THE ENGLISH POEMS OF. Edited by EDWARD HUTTON. *Small Pott 8vo. Cloth,* 1s. 6d. net; *leather,* 2s. 6d. net. [Little Library.

Crawford (F. G.). See Mary C. Danson.

Crump (B.). See A. L. Cleather.

Cunliffe (F. H. E.), Fellow of All Souls' College, Oxford. THE HISTORY OF THE BOER WAR. With many Illustrations, Plans, and Portraits. *In 2 vols. Vol. I.,* 15s.

Cutts (E. L.), D.D. AUGUSTINE OF CANTERBURY. With Portrait. *Crown 8vo.* 3s. 6d. [Leaders of Religion.

Daniell (G. W.), M.A. BISHOP WILBERFORCE. With Portrait. *Crown 8vo.* 3s. 6d. [Leaders of Religion.

Danson (Mary C.) and Crawford (F. G.). FATHERS IN THE FAITH. *Small 8vo.* 1s. 6d.

Dante. LA COMMEDIA DI DANTE. The Italian Text edited by PAGET TOYNBEE, M.A., D.Litt. *Demy 8vo. Gilt top.* 8s. 6d. *Also, Crown 8vo.* 6s.

THE INFERNO OF DANTE. Translated by H. F. CARY. Edited by PAGET TOYNBEE, M.A., D.Litt. *Small Pott 8vo. Cloth,* 1s. 6d. net; *leather,* 2s. 6d. net. [Little Library.

THE PURGATORIO OF DANTE. Translated by H. F. CARY. Edited by PAGET TOYNBEE, M.A., D.Litt. *Small Pott 8vo. Cloth,* 1s. 6d. net; *leather,* 2s. 6d. net. [Little Library.

THE PARADISO OF DANTE. Translated by H. F. CARY. Edited by PAGET TOYNBEE, M.A., D.Litt. *Small Pott 8vo. Cloth,* 1s. 6d. net; *leather,* 2s. 6d. net. [Little Library.

See also Paget Toynbee.

Darley (George), SELECTIONS FROM THE POEMS OF. Edited by R. A. STREATFEILD. *Small Pott 8vo. Cloth,* 1s. 6d. net; *leather,* 2s. 6d. net. [Little Library.

Davenport (Cyril). MEZZOTINTS. With 40 Plates in Photogravure. *Wide Royal 8vo.* 25s. net.

Also a limited edition on Japanese vellum with the Photogravures on India paper. *Seven Guineas net.* [Connoisseurs Library.

Dawson (A. J.). MOROCCO. Being a bundle of jottings, notes, impressions, tales, and tributes, from the pen of a lover of Morocco. With many Illustrations. *Demy 8vo.* 10s. 6d. net. [Nearly Ready.

Deane (A. C.). A LITTLE BOOK OF LIGHT VERSE. With an Introduction and Notes. *Small Pott 8vo. Cloth,* 1s. 6d. net; *leather,* 2s. 6d. net. [Little Library.

Delbos (Leon). THE METRIC SYSTEM. *Crown 8vo.* 2s.

Demosthenes: THE OLYNTHIACS AND PHILIPPICS. Translated upon a new principle by OTHO HOLLAND. *Crown 8vo.* 2s. 6d.

Demosthenes. AGAINST CONON AND CALLICLES. Edited with Notes and Vocabulary, by F. DARWIN SWIFT, M.A. *Fcap. 8vo.* 2s.

Dickens (Charles).
THE PICKWICK PAPERS. With the 43 Illustrations by SEYMOUR and PHIZ, the two Buss Plates and the 32 Contemporary Onwhyn Plates. 3s. 6d. *net.*
This is a particularly interesting volume, containing, as it does, reproductions of very rare plates. [Illustrated Pocket Library.
[Nearly Ready.

THE ROCHESTER EDITION.
Crown 8vo. Each Volume 3s. 6d. With Introductions by GEORGE GISSING, Notes by F. G. KITTON, and Topographical Illustrations.

THE PICKWICK PAPERS. With Illustrations by E. H. NEW. *Two Volumes.*

NICHOLAS NICKLEBY. With Illustrations by R. J. WILLIAMS. *Two Volumes.*

BLEAK HOUSE. With Illustrations by BEATRICE ALCOCK. *Two Volumes.*

OLIVER TWIST. With Illustrations by E. H. NEW.

THE OLD CURIOSITY SHOP. With Illustrations by G. M. BRIMELOW. *Two Volumes.*

BARNABY RUDGE. With Illustrations by BEATRICE ALCOCK. *Two Volumes.*

DAVID COPPERFIELD. With Illustrations by E. H. NEW. *Two Volumes.*

Dickinson (Emily). POEMS. First Series. *Crown 8vo.* 4s. 6d. *net.*

Dickinson (G. L.), M.A., Fellow of King's College, Cambridge. THE GREEK VIEW OF LIFE. *Third Edition. Crown 8vo.* 2s. 6d. [University Extension Series.

Dickson (H. N.), F.R.S.E., F.R.Met. Soc. METEOROLOGY. Illustrated. *Crown 8vo.* 2s. 6d. [University Extension Series.

Dilke (Lady), Bulley (Miss), and **Whitley (Miss).** WOMEN'S WORK. *Crown 8vo.* 2s. 6d. [Social Questions Series.

Dillon (Edward). PORCELAIN. With many Plates in Colour and Photogravure. *Wide Royal 8vo.* 25s. *net.*
Also a limited edition on Japanese vellum. *Seven Guineas net.* [Connoisseurs Library.

Ditchfield (P. H.), M.A., F.S.A. ENGLISH VILLAGES. Illustrated. *Crown 8vo.* 6s.
THE STORY OF OUR ENGLISH TOWNS. With Introduction by AUGUSTUS JESSOPP, D.D. *Second Edition. Crown 8vo.* 6s.
OLD ENGLISH CUSTOMS: Extant at the Present Time. An Account of Local Observances, Festival Customs, and Ancient Ceremonies yet Surviving in Great Britain. *Crown 8vo.* 6s.

Dixon (W. M.), M.A. A PRIMER OF TENNYSON. *Second Edition. Crown 8vo.* 2s. 6d.
ENGLISH POETRY FROM BLAKE TO BROWNING. *Second Edition. Crown 8vo.* 2s. 6d. [University Extension Series.

Dowden (J.), D.D., Lord Bishop of Edinburgh. THE WORKMANSHIP OF THE PRAYER BOOK: Its Literary and Liturgical Aspects. *Second Edition. Crown 8vo.* 3s. 6d. [Churchman's Library.

Driver (S. R.), D.D., Canon of Christ Church, Regius Professor of Hebrew in the University of Oxford. SERMONS ON SUBJECTS CONNECTED WITH THE OLD TESTAMENT. *Crown 8vo.* 6s.
THE BOOK OF GENESIS. With Notes and Introduction. *Demy 8vo.* 10s. 6d. [Westminster Commentaries.

Duguid (Charles), City Editor of the *Morning Post,* author of the 'Story of the Stock Exchange,' etc. THE STOCK EXCHANGE. *Crown 8vo.* 2s. 6d. *net.* [Books on Business.

Duncan (S. J.) (Mrs. COTES), Author of 'A Voyage of Consolation.' ON THE OTHER SIDE OF THE LATCH. *Second Edition. Crown 8vo.* 6s.

Dunn (J. T.), D.Sc., and **Mundella (V. A.).** GENERAL ELEMENTARY SCIENCE. With 114 Illustrations. *Crown 8vo.* 3s. 6d.

Dunstan (A. E.), B.Sc. See W. T. CLOUGH.

Durham (The Earl of). A REPORT ON CANADA. With an Introductory Note. *Demy 8vo.* 7s. 6d. *net.*

Dutt (W. A.). NORFOLK. Illustrated by B. C. BOULTER. *Small Pott 8vo. Cloth,* 3s.; *leather,* 3s. 6d. *net.* [Little Guides.
SUFFOLK. Illustrated by J. WYLIE. *Small Pott 8vo. Cloth,* 3s.; *leather,* 3s. 6d. *net.* [Little Guides.
THE NORFOLK BROADS. With coloured and other Illustrations by FRANK SOUTHGATE. *Large Demy 8vo.* 21s. *net.*

Earle (John), Bishop of Salisbury. MICROCOSMOGRAPHIE, OR A PIECE OF THE WORLD DISCOVERED; IN ESSAYES AND CHARACTERS. *Post 16mo.* 2s. *net.* [Rariora.
Reprinted from the Sixth Edition published by Robert Allot in 1633.

Edwards (Clement). RAILWAY NATIONALIZATION. *Crown 8vo.* 2s. 6d. [Social Questions Series

Edwards (W. Douglas). COMMERCIAL LAW. *Crown 8vo.* 2s. [Commercial Series.

Egan (Pierce). LIFE IN LONDON, OR THE DAY AND NIGHT SCENES OF JERRY HAWTHORN, ESQ., AND HIS ELEGANT FRIEND, CORINTHIAN TOM. With 36 Coloured Plates by I. R. and G. CRUIKSHANK. With numerous designs on wood. *Fcap. 8vo.* 4s. 6d. net.

Also a limited edition on large Japanese paper. 30s. net.

[Illustrated Pocket Library.

REAL LIFE IN LONDON, OR THE RAMBLES AND ADVENTURES OF BOB TALLYHO, ESQ., AND HIS COUSIN, the Hon. TOM DASHALL. With 31 Coloured Plates by ALKEN and ROWLANDSON, etc. *Two Volumes. Fcap. 8vo.* 9s. net.

[Illustrated Pocket Library.
[Nearly Ready.

THE LIFE OF AN ACTOR. With 27 Coloured Plates by THEODORE LANE, and several designs on wood. *Fcap. 8vo.* 4s. 6d. net. [Illustrated Pocket Library.

Egerton (H. E.), M.A. A HISTORY OF BRITISH COLONIAL POLICY. *Demy 8vo.* 12s. 6d.

A Colonial Edition is also published.

Ellaby (C. G.). ROME. Illustrated by B. C. BOULTER. *Small Pott 8vo. Cloth,* 3s.; *leather,* 3s. 6d. net.

[Little Guides. Nearly Ready.

Ellerton (F. G.). See S. J. Stone.

Ellwood (Thomas), THE HISTORY OF THE LIFE OF. Edited by C. G. CRUMP, M.A. *Crown 8vo.* 6s.

Engel (E.). A HISTORY OF ENGLISH LITERATURE: From its Beginning to Tennyson. Translated from the German. *Demy 8vo.* 7s. 6d. net.

Erasmus. DE CONTEMPTU MUNDI. From the Edition printed by Thomas Berthelet, 1533. *Leather,* 2s. net.

[Miniature Library.

A Book called in Latin ENCHIRIDION MILITIS CHRISTIANI, and in English The Manual of the Christian Knight, replenished with most wholesome precepts, made by the famous clerk ERASMUS of Roterdame, to the which is added a new and marvellous profitable preface.

From the edition printed by Wynken de Worde for John Byddell, 1533. *Leather,* 2s. net. [Miniature Library.

Fairbrother (W. H.), M.A. THE PHILOSOPHY OF T. H. GREEN. *Second Edition. Crown 8vo.* 3s. 6d.

FELISSA; OR, THE LIFE AND OPINIONS OF A KITTEN OF SENTIMENT. With 12 Coloured Plates. *Post 16mo.* 2s. 6d. net. (5¼ × 3½).

From the edition published by J. Harris, 1811.

Ferrier (Susan). MARRIAGE. Edited by Miss GOODRICH FREER and Lord IDDESLEIGH. *Two Volumes. Small Pott 8vo.*

Each volume, cloth, 1s. 6d. net; *leather,* 2s. 6d. net. [Little Library.

THE INHERITANCE. *Two Volumes. Small Pott 8vo. Each Volume, cloth,* 1s. 6d. net.; *leather,* 2s. 6d. net. [Little Library.

Finn (S. W.), M.A. JUNIOR ALGEBRA EXAMINATION PAPERS. *Fcap. 8vo.* 1s. [Junior Examination Series.

Firth (C. H.), M.A. CROMWELL'S ARMY: A History of the English Soldier during the Civil Wars, the Commonwealth, and the Protectorate. *Crown 8vo.* 7s. 6d.

Fisher (G. W.), M.A. ANNALS OF SHREWSBURY SCHOOL. With numerous Illustrations. *Demy 8vo.* 10s. 6d.

FitzGerald (Edward). THE RUBAIYAT OF OMAR KHAYYAM. From the First Edition of 1859. *Leather,* 1s. net. [Miniature Library.

THE RUBAIYAT OF OMAR KHAYYAM. Printed from the Fifth and last Edition. With a Commentary by Mrs. STEPHEN BATSON, and a Biography of Omar by E. D. ROSS. *Crown 8vo.* 6s.

EUPHRANOR: a Dialogue on Youth. *Demy 32mo. Leather,* 2s. net. [Miniature Library.

POLONIUS: or Wise Saws and Modern Instances. *Demy 32mo. Leather,* 2s. net. [Miniature Library.

FitzGerald (E. A.). THE HIGHEST ANDES. With 2 Maps, 51 Illustrations, 13 of which are in Photogravure, and a Panorama. *Royal 8vo.* 30s. net.

Flecker (W. H.), M.A., D.C.L., Headmaster of the Dean Close School, Cheltenham. THE STUDENTS' PRAYER BOOK. Part I. MORNING AND EVENING PRAYER AND LITANY. With an Introduction and Notes. *Crown 8vo.* 2s. 6d.

Flux (A. W.), M.A., William Dow Professor of Political Economy in M'Gill University, Montreal: sometime Fellow of St. John's College, Cambridge, and formerly Stanley-Jevons Professor of Political Economy in the Owens Coll., Manchester. ECONOMIC PRINCIPLES. *Demy 8vo.* 7s. 6d. net.

Fraser (J. F.). ROUND THE WORLD ON A WHEEL. With 100 Illustrations. *Fourth Edition. Crown 8vo.* 6s.

A Colonial Edition is also published.

French (W.), M.A., Principal of the Storey Institute, Lancaster. PRACTICAL CHEMISTRY. *Part I.* With numerous Diagrams. *Crown 8vo.* 1s. 6d.

[Textbooks of Technology.

French (W.), M.A., and Boardman (T. H.), M.A. PRACTICAL CHEMISTRY. *Part II.* With numerous Diagrams. *Crown 8vo.* 1s. 6d. [Textbooks of Technology.

Freudenreich (Ed. von). DAIRY BACTERIOLOGY. A Short Manual for the Use of Students. Translated by J. R. AINSWORTH DAVIS, M.A. *Second Edition. Revised. Crown 8vo.* 2s. 6d.

A 2

Fulford (H. W.), M.A. THE EPISTLE OF ST. JAMES. With Notes and Introduction. *Fcap. 8vo.* 1s. 6d. net.
[Churchman's Bible.

C. G. and F. C. G. JOHN BULL'S ADVENTURES IN FISCAL WONDERLAND. By CHARLES GEAKE. With 46 Illustrations by F. CARRUTHERS GOULD. *Second Ed. Crown 8vo.* 2s.6d. net.

Gambado (Geoffrey, Esq.). AN ACADEMY FOR GROWN HORSEMEN: Containing the completest Instructions for Walking, Trotting, Cantering, Galloping, Stumbling, and Tumbling. Illustrated with 27 Coloured Plates, and adorned with a Portrait of the Author. *Fcap. 8vo.* 3s. 6d. net.
[Illustrated Pocket Library. Nearly Ready.

Gaskell (Mrs.). CRANFORD. Edited by E. V. LUCAS. *Small Pott 8vo. Cloth,* 1s. 6d. net; *leather,* 2s. 6d. net. [Little Library.

Gasquet, the Right Rev. Abbot, O.S.B. ENGLISH MONASTIC LIFE. With Coloured and other Illustrations. *Demy 8vo.* 7s. 6d. net.
[Antiquary's Library. Nearly Ready.

George (H. B.), M.A., Fellow of New College, Oxford. BATTLES OF ENGLISH HISTORY. With numerous Plans. *Third Edition. Crown 8vo.* 6s.

Gibbins (H. de B.), Litt.D., M.A. INDUSTRY IN ENGLAND: HISTORICAL OUTLINES. With 5 Maps. *Third Edition. Demy 8vo.* 10s. 6d.
A COMPANION GERMAN GRAMMAR. *Crown 8vo.* 1s. 6d.
THE INDUSTRIAL HISTORY OF ENGLAND. *Tenth Edition.* Revised. With Maps and Plans. *Crown 8vo.* 3s.
[University Extension Series.
THE ECONOMICS OF COMMERCE. *Crown 8vo.* 1s. 6d. [Commercial Series.
COMMERCIAL EXAMINATION PAPERS. *Crown 8vo.* 1s. 6d.
[Commercial Series.
BRITISH COMMERCE AND COLONIES FROM ELIZABETH TO VICTORIA. *Third Edition. Crown 8vo.* 2s.
[Commercial Series.
ENGLISH SOCIAL REFORMERS. *Second Edition. Crown 8vo.* 2s. 6d.
[University Extension Series.

Gibbins (H. de B.), Litt.D., M.A., and **Hadfield (R. A.),** of the Hecla Works, Sheffield. A SHORTER WORKING DAY. *Crown 8vo.* 2s. 6d.
[Social Questions Series.

Gibbon (Edward). THE DECLINE AND FALL OF THE ROMAN EMPIRE. A New Edition, edited with Notes, Appendices, and Maps, by J. B. BURY, M.A., Litt.D., Fellow of Trinity College, Dublin. *In Seven Volumes. Demy 8vo. Gilt top,* 8s. 6d. each. *Also, Crown 8vo.* 6s. each.
MEMOIRS OF MY LIFE AND WRITINGS. Edited, with an Introduction and Notes, by G. BIRKBECK HILL, LL.D. *Crown 8vo.* 6s.

Gibson (E. C. S.), D.D., Vicar of Leeds. THE BOOK OF JOB. With Introduction and Notes. *Demy 8vo.* 6s.
[Westminster Commentaries.
THE XXXIX. ARTICLES OF THE CHURCH OF ENGLAND. With an Introduction. *Third Edition in One Vol. Demy 8vo.* 12s. 6d. [Handbooks of Theology.
JOHN HOWARD. With 12 Illustrations. *Fcap 8vo. Cloth,* 3s. 6d.; *leather,* 4s. net.
[Little Biographies.

Godley (A. D.), M.A., Fellow of Magdalen College, Oxford. LYRA FRIVOLA. *Third Edition. Fcap. 8vo.* 2s. 6d.
VERSES TO ORDER. *Cr. 8vo.* 2s. 6d. net.
SECOND STRINGS. *Fcap. 8vo.* 2s. 6d.
A new volume of humorous verse uniform with *Lyra Frivola.*

Goldsmith (Oliver). THE VICAR OF WAKEFIELD. With 24 Coloured Plates by T. ROWLANDSON. *Royal 8vo. One Guinea net.*
Reprinted from the edition of 1817.
[Burlington Library.
Also *Fcap. 8vo,* 3s. 6d. net. Also a limited edition on large Japanese paper. 30s. net. [Illustrated Pocket Library.
Also *Fcap. 32mo.* With 10 Plates in Photogravure by Tony Johannot. *Leather,* 2s. 6d. net.

Goudge (H. L.), M.A., Principal of Wells Theological College. THE FIRST EPISTLE TO THE CORINTHIANS. With Introduction and Notes. *Demy 8vo.* 6s. [Westminster Commentaries.

Graham (P. Anderson). THE RURAL EXODUS. *Crown 8vo.* 2s. 6d.
[Social Questions Series.

Granger (F. S.), M.A., Litt.D. PSYCHOLOGY. *Second Edition. Crown 8vo.* 2s. 6d. [University Extension Series.
THE SOUL OF A CHRISTIAN. *Crown 8vo.* 6s.

Gray (E. M'Queen). GERMAN PASSAGES FOR UNSEEN TRANSLATION. *Crown 8vo.* 2s. 6d.

Gray (P. L.), B.Sc., formerly Lecturer in Physics in Mason University College, Birmingham. THE PRINCIPLES OF MAGNETISM AND ELECTRICITY: an Elementary Text-Book. With 181 Diagrams. *Crown 8vo.* 3s. 6d.

Green (G. Buckland), M.A., Assistant Master at Edinburgh Academy, late Fellow of St. John's College, Oxon. NOTES ON GREEK AND LATIN SYNTAX. *Crown 8vo.* 3s. 6d.

Green (E. T.), M.A. THE CHURCH OF CHRIST. *Crown 8vo.* 6s.
[Churchman's Library.

Greenwell (Dora). THE POEMS OF. From the edition of 1848. *Leather,* 2s. net.
[Miniature Library. Nearly Ready.

Gregory (R. A.) THE VAULT OF HEAVEN. A Popular Introduction to Astronomy. With numerous Illustrations. *Crown 8vo.* 2s. 6d.
[University Extension Series.

Gregory (Miss E. C.) HEAVENLY WISDOM. Selections from the English Mystics. *Pott 8vo. Cloth* 2s.; *leather*, 2s. 6d. net.
[Library of Devotion. Nearly Ready.

Greville Minor. A MODERN JOURNAL. Edited by J. A. SPENDER. *Crown 8vo.* 3s. 6d.

Grinling (C. H.). A HISTORY OF THE GREAT NORTHERN RAILWAY, 1845-95. With Illustrations. Revised, with an additional chapter. *Demy 8vo.* 10s. 6d.

Gwynn (M. L.). A BIRTHDAY BOOK. *Royal 8vo.* 12s.

Hackett (John), B.D. A HISTORY OF THE ORTHODOX CHURCH OF CYPRUS. With Maps and Illustrations. *Demy 8vo.* 15s. net.

Haddon (A. C.), Sc.D., F.R.S. HEAD-HUNTERS, BLACK, WHITE, AND BROWN. With many Illustrations and a Map. *Demy 8vo.* 15s.

Hadfield (R. A.). See H. de B. Gibbins.

Hall (R. N.) and Neal (W. G.). THE ANCIENT RUINS OF RHODESIA. With numerous Illustrations. *Second Edition, revised. Demy 8vo.* 21s. net.

Hamilton (F. J.), D.D., **and Brooks (E.W.).** ZACHARIAH OF MITYLENE. Translated into English. *Demy 8vo.* 12s. 6d. net.
[Byzantine Texts.

Hammond (J. L.). CHARLES JAMES FOX: A Biographical Study. *Demy 8vo.* 10s. 6d.

Hannay (D.). A SHORT HISTORY OF THE ROYAL NAVY, FROM EARLY TIMES TO THE PRESENT DAY. Illustrated. *Two Volumes. Demy 8vo.* 7s. 6d. each. Vol. I. 1200-1688.

Hannay (James O.), M.A. THE SPIRIT AND ORIGIN OF CHRISTIAN MONASTICISM. *Crown 8vo.* 6s.

Hare, (A. T.), M.A. THE CONSTRUCTION OF LARGE INDUCTION COILS. With numerous Diagrams. *Demy 8vo.* 6s.

Harrison (Clifford). READING AND READERS. *Fcap. 8vo.* 2s. 6d.

Hawthorne (Nathaniel). THE SCARLET LETTER. Edited by PERCY DEARMER. *Small Pott 8vo. Cloth,* 1s. 6d. net; *leather,* 2s. 6d. net. [Little Library.
HEALTH, WEALTH AND WISDOM. *Crown 8vo.* 1s. net.

Heath (Dudley). MINIATURES. With many Plates in Photogravure. *Wide Royal 8vo.* 25s. net.
Also a limited edition on Japanese vellum,

with the Photogravures on India paper. *Seven Guineas net.*
[Connoisseurs Library.

Hedin (Sven), Gold Medallist of the Royal Geographical Society. THROUGH ASIA. With 300 Illustrations from Sketches and Photographs by the Author, and Maps. *Two Volumes. Royal 8vo.* 36s. net.

Hello (Ernest). STUDIES IN SAINTSHIP. Translated from the French by V. M. CRAWFORD. *Fcap 8vo.* 3s. 6d.

Henderson (B. W.), Fellow of Exeter College, Oxford. THE LIFE AND PRINCIPATE OF THE EMPEROR NERO. With Illustrations. *Demy 8vo.* 10s. 6d. net.

Henderson (T. F.). A LITTLE BOOK OF SCOTTISH VERSE. *Small Pott 8vo. Cloth,* 1s. 6d. net; *leather,* 2s. 6d. net.
[Little Library.
ROBERT BURNS. With 12 Illustrations. *Fcap. 8vo. Cloth,* 3s. 6d.; *leather,* 4s. net.
[Little Biographies.

Henley (W. E.). ENGLISH LYRICS. *Crown 8vo. Gilt top.* 3s. 6d.

Henley (W. E.) and Whibley (C.). A BOOK OF ENGLISH PROSE. *Crown 8vo. Buckram, gilt top.* 6s.

Henson (H. H.), B.D., Canon of Westminster. APOSTOLIC CHRISTIANITY: As Illustrated by the Epistles of St. Paul to the Corinthians. *Crown 8vo.* 6s.
LIGHT AND LEAVEN: HISTORICAL AND SOCIAL SERMONS. *Crown 8vo.* 6s.
DISCIPLINE AND LAW. *Fcap. 8vo.* 2s. 6d.
THE EDUCATION ACT—AND AFTER. An Appeal addressed with all possible respect to the Nonconformists. *Crown 8vo.* 1s.

Herbert (George). THE TEMPLE. Edited, with an Introduction and Notes, by E. C. S. GIBSON, D.D., Vicar of Leeds. *Small Pott 8vo. Cloth,* 2s.; *leather,* 2s. 6d. net.
[Library of Devotion.

Herbert of Cherbury (Lord), THE LIFE OF. Written by himself. *Leather,* 2s. net. From the edition printed at Strawberry Hill in the year 1764.
[Miniature Library. Nearly Ready.

Hewins (W. A. S.), B.A. ENGLISH TRADE AND FINANCE IN THE SEVENTEENTH CENTURY. *Crown 8vo.* 2s. 6d.
[University Extension Series.

Hilbert (T.). THE AIR GUN: or, How the Mastermans and Dobson Major nearly lost their Holidays. Illustrated. *Demy 16mo.* 2s. 6d.
[Little Blue Books.

Hill (Clare), Registered Teacher to the City and Guilds of London Institute. MILLINERY, THEORETICAL, AND PRACTICAL. With numerous Diagrams. *Crown 8vo.* 2s.
[Textbooks of Technology.

Hill (Henry), B.A., Headmaster of the Boy's High School, Worcester, Cape Colony. A SOUTH AFRICAN ARITHMETIC. *Crown 8vo.* 3s. 6d.
    This book has been specially written for use in South African schools.

Hobhouse (Emily). THE BRUNT OF THE WAR. With Map and Illustrations. *Crown 8vo.* 6s.

Hobhouse (L. T.), Fellow of C.C.C., Oxford. THE THEORY OF KNOWLEDGE. *Demy 8vo.* 21s.

Hobson (J. A.), M.A. PROBLEMS OF POVERTY: An Inquiry into the Industrial Condition of the Poor. *Fourth Edition. Crown 8vo.* 2s. 6d.
    [Social Questions Series.

THE PROBLEM OF THE UNEMPLOYED. *Crown 8vo.* 2s. 6d.
    [Social Questions Series.

INTERNATIONAL TRADE: A Study of Economic Principles. *Crown 8vo.* 2s. 6d. net.

Hodgkin (T.), D.C.L. GEORGE FOX, THE QUAKER. With Portrait. *Crown 8vo.* 3s. 6d. [Leaders of Religion.

Hogg (Thomas Jefferson). SHELLEY AT OXFORD. With an Introduction by R. A. STREATFEILD. *Fcap. 8vo.* 2s. net.
    [Nearly Ready.

Holden-Stone (G. de). THE AUTOMOBILE INDUSTRY. *Fcap. 8vo.* 2s. 6d. net. [Books on Business.

Holdich (Sir T. H.), K.C.I.E. THE INDIAN BORDERLAND : being a Personal Record of Twenty Years. Illustrated. *Demy 8vo.* 15s. net.

Holdsworth (W. S.), M.A. A HISTORY OF ENGLISH LAW. *In Two Volumes. Vol. I. Demy 8vo.* 10s. 6d. net.

Holyoake (G. J.). THE CO-OPERATIVE MOVEMENT TO-DAY. *Third Edition. Crown 8vo.* 2s. 6d.
    [Social Questions Series.

Hoppner, A LITTLE GALLERY OF. Twenty examples in photogravure of his finest work. *Demy 16mo.* 2s. 6d. net.
    [Little Galleries.

Horace: THE ODES AND EPODES. Translated by A. D. GODLEY, M.A., Fellow of Magdalen College, Oxford. *Crown 8vo.* 2s. [Classical Translations.

Horsburgh (E. L. S.), M.A. WATERLOO: A Narrative and Criticism. With Plans. *Second Edition. Crown 8vo.* 5s.

SAVONAROLA. With Portraits and Illustrations. *Second Edition. Fcap. 8vo. Cloth,* 3s. 6d. ; *leather,* 4s. net.
    [Little Biographies.

Horton (R. F.), D.D. JOHN HOWE. With Portrait. *Crown 8vo.* 3s. 6d.
    [Leaders of Religion.

Hosie (Alexander). MANCHURIA. With Illustrations and a Map. *Demy 8vo.* 10s. 6d. net.

Howell (G.). TRADE UNIONISM—NEW AND OLD. *Third Edition. Crown 8vo.* 2s. 6d. [Social Questions Series.

Hughes (C. E.). THE PRAISE OF SHAKESPEARE. An English Anthology. With a Preface by SIDNEY LEE. *Demy 8vo.* 3s. 6d. net.

Hughes (Thomas). TOM BROWN'S SCHOOLDAYS. With an Introduction and Notes by VERNON RENDALL. *Leather. Royal 32mo.* 2s. 6d. net.
    [Nearly Ready.

Hutchinson (Horace G.). THE NEW FOREST. Described by. Illustrated in colour with 50 Pictures by WALTER TYNDALE and 4 by Miss LUCY KEMP WELCH. *Large Demy 8vo.* 21s. net.
    [Nearly Ready.

Hutton (A. W.), M.A. CARDINAL MANNING. With Portrait. *Crown 8vo.* 3s. 6d.
    [Leaders of Religion.

Hutton (R. H.). CARDINAL NEWMAN. With Portrait. *Crown 8vo.* 3s. 6d.
    [Leaders of Religion.

Hutton (W. H.), M.A. THE LIFE OF SIR THOMAS MORE. With Portraits. *Second Edition. Crown 8vo.* 5s.

WILLIAM LAUD. With Portrait. *Second Edition. Crown 8vo.* 3s. 6d.
    [Leaders of Religion.

Hyett (F. A.). A SHORT HISTORY OF FLORENCE. *Demy 8vo.* 7s. 6d. net.

Ibsen (Henrik). BRAND. A Drama. Translated by WILLIAM WILSON. *Third Edition. Crown 8vo.* 3s. 6d.

Inge (W. R.), M.A., Fellow and Tutor of Hertford College, Oxford. CHRISTIAN MYSTICISM. The Bampton Lectures for 1899. *Demy 8vo.* 12s. 6d. net.

LIGHT, LIFE, AND LOVE : A Selection from the German Mystics. With an Introduction and Notes. *Small Pott 8vo. Cloth* 2s. ; *leather,* 2s. 6d. net.
    [Library of Devotion.

Innes (A. D.), M.A. A HISTORY OF THE BRITISH IN INDIA. With Maps and Plans. *Crown 8vo.* 7s. 6d.

Jackson (S.), M.A. A PRIMER OF BUSINESS. *Third Edition. Crown 8vo.* 1s. 6d. [Commercial Series.

Jacob (F.), M.A. JUNIOR FRENCH EXAMINATION PAPERS. *Fcap. 8vo.* 1s. [Junior Examination Series.

Jeans (J. Stephen). TRUSTS, POOLS, AND CORNERS. *Crown 8vo.* 2s. 6d.
    [Social Questions Series.

Jenks (E.), M.A., Reader of Law in the University of Oxford. ENGLISH LOCAL GOVERNMENT. *Crown 8vo.* 2s. 6d.
    [University Extension Series.

Jessopp (Augustus), D.D. JOHN DONNE. With Portrait. *Crown 8vo.* 3s. 6d. [Leaders of Religion.

Jevons (F. B.), M.A., Litt.D., Principal of Hatfield Hall, Durham. EVOLUTION. *Crown 8vo.* 3s. 6d. [Churchman's Library.
AN INTRODUCTION TO THE HISTORY OF RELIGION. *Second Edition. Demy 8vo.* 10s. 6d. [Handbooks of Theology.

Johnston (Sir H. H.), K.C.B. BRITISH CENTRAL AFRICA. With nearly 200 Illustrations and Six Maps. *Second Edition. Crown 4to.* 18s. net.

Jones (H.). A GUIDE TO PROFESSIONS AND BUSINESS. *Crown 8vo.* 1s. 6d. [Commercial Series.

Jones (L. A. Atherley), K.C., M.P., and Bellot (Hugh H. L.). THE MINERS' GUIDE TO THE COAL MINES' REGULATION ACTS. *Crown 8vo.* 2s. 6d. net. [Nearly Ready.

Julian (Lady) of Norwich. REVELATIONS OF DIVINE LOVE. Edited by GRACE WARRACK. *Crown 8vo.* 3s. 6d.

Juvenal, THE SATIRES OF. Translated by S. G. OWEN. *Crown 8vo.* 2s. 6d. [Classical Translations.

Kaufmann (M.). SOCIALISM AND MODERN THOUGHT. *Crown 8vo.* 2s. 6d. [Social Questions Series.

Keating (J. F.), D.D. THE AGAPE AND THE EUCHARIST. *Crown 8vo.* 3s. 6d.

Keats (John), THE POEMS OF. With an Introduction by L. BINYON, and Notes by J. MASEFIELD. *Small Pott 8vo. Cloth,* 1s. 6d. net; *leather,* 2s. 6d. net. [Little Library.

Keble (John). THE CHRISTIAN YEAR. With an Introduction and Notes by W. LOCK, D.D., Warden of Keble College. Illustrated by R. ANNING BELL. *Second Edition. Fcap. 8vo.* 3s. 6d; *padded morocco,* 5s.
THE CHRISTIAN YEAR. With Introduction and Notes by WALTER LOCK, D.D., Warden of Keble College. *Second Edition. Small Pott 8vo. Cloth,* 2s.; *leather,* 2s. 6d. net. [Library of Devotion.
LYRA INNOCENTIUM. Edited, with Introduction and Notes, by WALTER LOCK, D.D., Warden of Keble College, Oxford. *Small Pott 8vo. Cloth,* 2s.; *leather,* 2s. 6d. net. [Library of Devotion.

Kempis (Thomas À). THE IMITATION OF CHRIST. With an Introduction by DEAN FARRAR. Illustrated by C. M. GERE. *Second Edition. Fcap. 8vo.* 3s. 6d.; *padded morocco,* 5s.
THE IMITATION OF CHRIST. A Revised Translation, with an Introduction by C. BIGG, D.D., late Student of Christ Church. *Third Edition. Small Pott 8vo. Cloth,* 2s.; *leather,* 2s. 6d. net. [Library of Devotion.

A practically new translation of this book which the reader has, almost for the first time, exactly in the shape in which it left the hands of the author.
THE SAME EDITION IN LARGE TYPE. *Crown 8vo.* 3s. 6d.

Kennedy (James Houghton), D.D., Assistant Lecturer in Divinity in the University of Dublin. ST. PAUL'S SECOND AND THIRD EPISTLES TO THE CORINTHIANS. With Introduction, Dissertations and Notes. *Crown 8vo.* 6s.

Kestell (J. D.). THROUGH SHOT AND FLAME: Being the Adventures and Experiences of J. D. KESTELL, Chaplain to General Christian de Wet. *Crown 8vo.* 6s.

Kimmins (C. W.), M.A. THE CHEMISTRY OF LIFE AND HEALTH. Illustrated. *Crown 8vo.* 2s. 6d. [University Extension Series.

Kinglake (A. W.). EOTHEN. With an Introduction and Notes. *Small Pott 8vo. Cloth,* 1s. 6d. net; *leather,* 2s. 6d. net. [Little Library.

Kipling (Rudyard). BARRACK-ROOM BALLADS. 73rd Thousand. *Cr. 8vo. Twentieth Edition.* 6s.
A Colonial Edition is also published.
THE SEVEN SEAS. 62nd Thousand. *Ninth Edition. Crown 8vo, gilt top,* 6s.
A Colonial Edition is also published.
THE FIVE NATIONS. 41st Thousand. *Second Edition. Crown 8vo.* 6s.
A Colonial Edition is also published.
DEPARTMENTAL DITTIES. A New Edition. *Crown 8vo. Buckram,* 6s.
A Colonial Edition is also published.

Lamb (Charles and Mary), THE WORKS OF. Edited by E. V. LUCAS. With Numerous Illustrations. *In Seven Volumes. Demy 8vo.* 7s. 6d. each.
THE ESSAYS OF ELIA. With over 100 Illustrations by A. GARTH JONES, and an Introduction by E. V. LUCAS. *Demy 8vo.* 10s. 6d.
ELIA, AND THE LAST ESSAYS OF ELIA. Edited by E. V. LUCAS. *Small Pott 8vo. Cloth,* 1s. 6d. net; *leather,* 2s. 6d. net. [Little Library.
THE KING AND QUEEN OF HEARTS: An 1805 Book for Children. Illustrated by WILLIAM MULREADY. A new edition, in facsimile, edited by E. V. LUCAS. 1s. 6d.

Lambert (F. A. H.). SURREY. Illustrated by E. H. NEW. *Small Pott 8vo, cloth,* 3s.; *leather,* 3s. 6d. net. [Little Guides.

Lambros (Professor). ECTHESIS CHRONICA. Edited by. *Demy 8vo.* 7s. 6d. net. [Byzantine Texts.

Lane-Poole (Stanley). A HISTORY OF EGYPT IN THE MIDDLE AGES. Fully Illustrated. *Crown 8vo.* 6s.

Langbridge (F.) M.A. BALLADS OF THE BRAVE: Poems of Chivalry, Enterprise, Courage, and Constancy. *Second Edition. Crown 8vo. 2s. 6d.*

Law (William). A SERIOUS CALL TO A DEVOUT AND HOLY LIFE. Edited, with an Introduction, by C. BIGG, D.D., late Student of Christ Church. *Small Pott 8vo, cloth, 2s.; leather, 2s. 6d. net.*
[Library of Devotion.
This is a reprint, word for word and line for line, of the *Editio Princeps.*

Leach (H.). THE DUKE OF DEVONSHIRE. A Biography. With 12 Illustrations. *Demy 8vo. 12s. 6d. net.*
[Nearly Ready.

Lee (Captain Melville). A HISTORY OF POLICE IN ENGLAND. *Crown 8vo. 7s. 6d.*

Leigh (Percival). THE COMIC ENGLISH GRAMMAR. Embellished with upwards of 50 characteristic Illustrations by JOHN LEECH. *Post 16mo. 2s. 6d. net.*

Lewes (V.B.), M.A. AIR AND WATER. Illustrated. *Crown 8vo. 2s. 6d.*
[University Extension Series.

Littlehales (H.). See C. Wordsworth.

Lock (Walter), D.D., Warden of Keble College. ST. PAUL, THE MASTER-BUILDER. *Crown 8vo. 3s. 6d.*
JOHN KEBLE. With Portrait. *Crown 8vo. 3s. 6d.* [Leaders of Religion.

Locker (F.). LONDON LYRICS. Edited by A. D. GODLEY, M.A. *Small Pott 8vo, cloth, 1s. 6d. net; leather, 2s. 6d. net.*
[Little Library.

Longfellow, SELECTIONS FROM. Edited by LILIAN M. FAITHFULL. *Small Pott 8vo, cloth, 1s. 6d. net; leather, 2s. 6d. net.*
[Little Library.

Lorimer (George Horace). LETTERS FROM A SELF-MADE MERCHANT TO HIS SON. *Tenth Edition. Crown 8vo. 6s.*
A Colonial Edition is also published.

Lover (Samuel). HANDY ANDY. With 24 Illustrations by the Author. *Fcap. 8vo. 3s. 6d. net.* [Illustrated Pocket Library.

Lucas (E. V.). THE VISIT TO LONDON. Described in Verse, with Coloured Pictures by F. D. BEDFORD. *Small 4to. 6s.*
E. V. L. and C. L. G. ENGLAND DAY BY DAY: Or, The Englishman's Handbook to Efficiency. Illustrated by GEORGE MORROW. *Fourth Edition. Fcap. 4to. 1s. net.*
A burlesque Year-Book and Almanac.

Lucian. SIX DIALOGUES (Nigrinus, Icaro-Menippus, The Cock, The Ship, The Parasite, The Lover of Falsehood). Translated by S. T. Irwin, M.A., Assistant Master at Clifton; late Scholar of Exeter College, Oxford. *Crown 8vo. 3s. 6d.*
[Classical Translations.

Lyde (L. W.), M.A., Professor. A COMMERCIAL GEOGRAPHY OF THE BRITISH EMPIRE. *Third Edition. Crown 8vo. 2s.* [Commercial Series.

Lydon (Noel S.). A JUNIOR GEOMETRY. With numerous diagrams. *Crown 8vo. 2s.* [Junior School Books.

Lyttelton (Hon. Mrs. A.). WOMEN AND THEIR WORK. *Crown 8vo. 2s. 6d.*

M. M. HOW TO DRESS AND WHAT TO WEAR. *Crown 8vo. 1s. net.*

Macaulay (Lord). CRITICAL AND HISTORICAL ESSAYS. Edited by F. C. MONTAGUE, M.A. *Three Volumes. Cr. 8vo. 18s.*
The only edition of this book completely annotated.

M'Allen (J. E. B.), M.A. THE PRINCIPLES OF BOOKKEEPING BY DOUBLE ENTRY. *Crown 8vo. 2s.* [Commercial Series.

MacCulloch (J. A.). COMPARATIVE THEOLOGY. *Crown 8vo. 6s.* [Churchman's Library.

MacCunn (F.). JOHN KNOX. With Portrait. *Crown 8vo. 3s. 6d.* [Leaders of Religion.

McDermott, (E. R.), Editor of the *Railway News,* City Editor of the *Daily News.* RAILWAYS. *Crown 8vo. 2s. 6d. net.* [Books on Business.

M'Dowall (A. S.). CHATHAM. With 12 Illustrations. *Fcap. 8vo. Cloth, 3s. 6d.; leather, 4s. net.* [Little Biographies.

Mackay (A. M.). THE CHURCHMAN'S INTRODUCTION TO THE OLD TESTAMENT. *Crown 8vo. 3s. 6d.* [Churchman's Library.

Magnus (Laurie), M.A. A PRIMER OF WORDSWORTH. *Crown 8vo. 2s. 6d.*

Mahaffy (J. P.), Litt.D. A HISTORY OF THE EGYPT OF THE PTOLEMIES. Fully Illustrated. *Crown 8vo. 6s.*

Maitland (F. W.), LL.D., Downing Professor of the Laws of England in the University of Cambridge. CANON LAW IN ENGLAND. *Royal 8vo. 7s. 6d.*

Malden (H. E.), M.A. ENGLISH RECORDS. A Companion to the History of England. *Crown 8vo. 3s. 6d.*
THE ENGLISH CITIZEN: HIS RIGHTS AND DUTIES. *Crown 8vo. 1s. 6d.*

Marchant (E. C.), M.A., Fellow of Peterhouse, Cambridge. A GREEK ANTHOLOGY. *Second Edition. Crown 8vo. 3s. 6d.*

Marchant (E. C.), M.A., and Cook (A. M.), M.A. PASSAGES FOR UNSEEN TRANSLATION. *Second Edition. Crown 8vo. 3s. 6d.*

Marr (J. E.), F.R.S., Fellow of St John's College, Cambridge. THE SCIENTIFIC STUDY OF SCENERY. *Second Edition.* Illustrated. *Crown 8vo. 6s.*

AGRICULTURAL GEOLOGY. With numerous Illustrations. *Crown 8vo.* 6s.

Marvell (Andrew). THE POEMS OF. Edited by EDWARD WRIGHT. *Small Pott 8vo, cloth,* 1s. 6d. *net ; leather,* 2s. 6d. *net.*
[Little Library.

Mason (A. J.). THOMAS CRANMER. With Portrait. *Crown 8vo.* 3s. 6d.
[Leaders of Religion.

Massee (George). THE EVOLUTION OF PLANT LIFE: Lower Forms. With Illustrations. *Crown 8vo.* 2s. 6d.
[University Extension Series.

Masterman (C. F. G.), M.A. TENNYSON AS A RELIGIOUS TEACHER. *Crown 8vo.* 6s.

Mellows (Emma S.). A SHORT STORY OF ENGLISH LITERATURE. *Crown 8vo.* 3s. 6d.

Michell (E. B.). THE ART AND PRACTICE OF HAWKING. With 3 Photogravures by G. E. LODGE, and other Illustrations. *Demy 8vo.* 10s. 6d.

Millais (J. G.). THE LIFE AND LETTERS OF SIR JOHN EVERETT MILLAIS, President of the Royal Academy. With 319 Illustrations, of which 9 are in Photogravure. 2 *vols. Royal 8vo.* 20s. *net.*

Millais. A LITTLE GALLERY OF. Twenty examples in Photogravure of his finest work. *Demy 16mo.* 2s. 6d. *net.*
[Little Galleries. Nearly Ready.

Millis (C. T.), M.I.M.E., Principal of the Borough Polytechnic College. TECHNICAL ARITHMETIC AND GEOMETRY. With Diagrams. *Crown 8vo.* 3s. 6d.
[Textbooks of Technology.

Milne (J. G.), M.A. A HISTORY OF ROMAN EGYPT. Fully Illustrated. *Crown 8vo.* 6s.

Milton, John, THE POEMS OF, BOTH ENGLISH AND LATIN, Compos'd at several times. Printed by his true Copies.
The Songs were set in Musick by Mr. HENRY LAWES, Gentleman of the Kings Chappel, and one of His Majesties Private Musick.
Printed and publish'd according to Order. Printed by RUTH RAWORTH for HUMPHREY MOSELEY, and are to be sold at the signe of the Princes Armes in Pauls Churchyard, 1645. 3s. 6d. *net.*
[Rariora.

THE MINOR POEMS OF JOHN MILTON. Edited by H. C. BEECHING, M.A., Canon of Westminster. *Small Pott 8vo, cloth,* 1s. 6d. *net ; leather,* 2s. 6d. *net.*
[Little Library.

Mitchell (P. Chalmers), M.A. OUTLINES OF BIOLOGY. Illustrated. *Second Edition. Crown 8vo.* 6s.
A text-book designed to cover the Schedule issued by the Royal College of Physicians and Surgeons.

'Mail (A.)' MINING AND MINING INVESTMENTS. *Crown 8vo.* 2s. 6d. *net.* [Books on Business. Nearly Ready.

Moir (D. M.). MANSIE WAUCH. Edited by T. F. HENDERSON. *Small Pott 8vo. Cloth,* 1s. 6d. *net ; leather,* 2s. 6d. *net.*
[Little Library.

Moore (H. E.). BACK TO THE LAND: An Inquiry into the cure for Rural Depopulation. *Crown 8vo.* 2s. 6d.
[Social Questions Series.

Morfill (W. R.), Oriel College, Oxford. A HISTORY OF RUSSIA FROM PETER THE GREAT TO ALEXANDER II. With Maps and Plans. *Crown 8vo.* 7s. 6d.

Morich (R. J.), late of Clifton College. GERMAN EXAMINATION PAPERS IN MISCELLANEOUS GRAMMAR AND IDIOMS. *Sixth Edition. Crown 8vo.* 2s. 6d. [School Examination Series.
A KEY, issued to Tutors and Private Students only, to be had on application to the Publishers. *Second Edition. Crown 8vo.* 6s. *net.*

Morris (J. E.). THE NORTH RIDING OF YORKSHIRE. Illustrated by R. J. S. BERTRAM, *Small Pott 8vo, cloth,* 3s. ; *leather,* 3s. 6d. *net.*
[Little Guides. Nearly Ready.

Morton (Miss Anderson). See Miss Brodrick.

Moule (H. C. G.), D.D., Lord Bishop of Durham. CHARLES SIMEON. With Portrait. *Crown 8vo.* 3s. 6d.
[Leaders of Religion.

Muir (M. M. Pattison), M.A. THE CHEMISTRY OF FIRE. The Elementary Principles of Chemistry. Illustrated. *Crown 8vo.* 2s. 6d.
[University Extension Series.

Mundella (V. A.), M.A. See J. T. Dunn.

Naval Officer (A.). THE ADVENTURES OF A POST CAPTAIN. With 24 coloured plates by Mr. WILLIAMS. *Fcap. 8vo.* 3s. 6d. *net.*
[Illustrated Pocket Library.

Neal (W. G.). See R. N. Hall.

Newman (J. H.) and others. LYRA APOSTOLICA. With an Introduction by CANON SCOTT HOLLAND, and Notes by CANON BEECHING, M.A. *Small Pott 8vo. Cloth,* 2s. ; *leather,* 2s. 6d. *net.*
[Library of Devotion.

Nichols (J. B. B.). A LITTLE BOOK OF ENGLISH SONNETS. *Small Pott 8vo. Cloth,* 1s. 6d. *net ; leather,* 2s. 6d. *net.*
[Little Library.

Nimrod. THE LIFE AND DEATH OF JOHN MYTTON, ESQ. With 18 Coloured Plates by HENRY ALKEN and T. J. RAWLINS. *Third Edition. Fcap. 8vo.* 3s. 6d. *net.*
Also a limited edition on large Japanese paper. 30s. *net.*
[Illustrated Pocket Library.

THE LIFE OF A SPORTSMAN. With 35 Coloured Plates by HENRY ALKEN. *Fcap. 8vo. 4s. 6d. net.*
Also a limited edition on large Japanese paper. *30s. net.*
[Illustrated Pocket Library.

Norway (A. H.), Author of 'Highways and Byways in Devon and Cornwall.' NAPLES: PAST AND PRESENT. With 40 Illustrations by A. G. FERARD. *Crown 8vo. 6s.*

Novalis. THE DISCIPLES AT SAIS AND OTHER FRAGMENTS. Edited by Miss UNA BIRCH. *Fcap. 8vo. 3s. 6d.*

Oliphant (Mrs.). THOMAS CHALMERS. With Portrait. *Crown 8vo. 3s. 6d.*
[Leaders of Religion.

Oman (C. W.), M.A., Fellow of All Souls', Oxford. A HISTORY OF THE ART OF WAR. Vol. II.: The Middle Ages, from the Fourth to the Fourteenth Century. Illustrated. *Demy 8vo. 21s.*

Ottley (R. L.), M.A., Professor of Pastoral Theology at Oxford and Canon of Christ Church. THE DOCTRINE OF THE INCARNATION. *Second and Cheaper Edition. Demy 8vo. 12s. 6d.*
[Handbooks of Theology.

LANCELOT ANDREWES. With Portrait. *Crown 8vo. 3s. 6d.*
[Leaders of Religion.

Overton (J. H.), M.A. JOHN WESLEY. With Portrait. *Crown 8vo. 3s. 6d.*
[Leaders of Religion.

Owen (Douglas), Barrister-at-Law, Secretary to the Alliance Marine and General Assurance Company. PORTS AND DOCKS. *Crown 8vo. 2s. 6d. net.*
[Books on Business.

Oxford (M. N.), of Guy's Hospital. A HANDBOOK OF NURSING. *Second Edition. Crown 8vo. 3s. 6d.*

Pakes (W. C. C.). THE SCIENCE OF HYGIENE. With numerous Illustrations. *Demy 8vo. 15s.*

Parkinson (John). PARADISI IN SOLE PARADISUS TERRISTRIS, OR A GARDEN OF ALL SORTS OF PLEASANT FLOWERS. *Folio. 30s. net.*
Also an Edition of 20 copies on Japanese vellum. *Ten Guineas net.* [Nearly Ready.

Parmenter (John). HELIO-TROPES, OR NEW POSIES FOR SUNDIALS, 1625. Edited by PERCIVAL LANDON. *Quarto. 3s. 6d. net.*

Parmentier (Prof. Léon) and Bidez (M.). EVAGRIUS. *Demy 8vo. 10s. 6d. net.*
[Byzantine Texts.

Pascal, THE THOUGHTS OF. With Introduction and Notes by C. S. JERRAM. *Small Pott 8vo. 2s.; leather, 2s. 6d. net.*
[Library of Devotion.

Paston (George). SIDELIGHTS ON THE GEORGIAN PERIOD. With many Illustrations. *Demy 8vo. 10s. 6d.*

ROMNEY. With many Illustrations. *Demy 16mo. 2s. 6d. net.* [Little Books on Art.

Pearce (E. H.), M.A. THE ANNALS OF CHRIST'S HOSPITAL. With many Illustrations. *Demy 8vo. 7s. 6d.*

Peary (R. E.), Gold Medallist of the Royal Geographical Society. NORTHWARD OVER THE GREAT ICE. With over 800 Illustrations. *2 vols. Royal 8vo. 32s. net.*

Peel (Sidney), late Fellow of Trinity College, Oxford, and Secretary to the Royal Commission on the Licensing Laws. PRACTICAL LICENSING REFORM. *Second Edition. Crown 8vo. 1s. 6d.*

Perris (G. H.). THE PROTECTIONIST PERIL; or the Finance of the Empire. *Crown 8vo. 1s.*

Peters (J. P.), D.D. THE OLD TESTAMENT AND THE NEW SCHOLARSHIP. *Crown 8vo. 6s.*
[Churchman's Library.

Petrie (W. M. Flinders), D.C.L., LL.D., Professor of Egyptology at University College. A HISTORY OF EGYPT, FROM THE EARLIEST TIMES TO THE PRESENT DAY. Fully Illustrated. *In six volumes. Crown 8vo. 6s. each.*

VOL. I. PREHISTORIC TIMES TO XVITH DYNASTY. *Fifth Edition.*
VOL. II. THE XVIITH AND XVIIITH DYNASTIES. *Fourth Edition.*
VOL. IV. THE EGYPT OF THE PTOLEMIES. J. P. MAHAFFY, Litt.D.
VOL. V. ROMAN EGYPT. J. G. MILNE, M.A.
VOL. VI. EGYPT IN THE MIDDLE AGES. STANLEY LANE-POOLE, M.A.

RELIGION AND CONSCIENCE IN ANCIENT EGYPT. Fully Illustrated. *Crown 8vo. 2s. 6d.*

SYRIA AND EGYPT, FROM THE TELL EL AMARNA TABLETS. *Crown 8vo. 2s. 6d.*

EGYPTIAN TALES. Illustrated by TRISTRAM ELLIS. *In Two Volumes. Crown 8vo. 3s. 6d. each.*

EGYPTIAN DECORATIVE ART. With 120 Illustrations. *Crown 8vo. 3s. 6d.*

Phillips (W. A.). CANNING. With 12 Illustrations. *Fcap. 8vo. Cloth, 3s. 6d.; leather, 4s. net.* [Little Biographies.

Phillpotts (Eden). MY DEVON YEAR. With 38 Illustrations by J. LEY PETHYBRIDGE. *Large Crown 8vo. 6s.*

Pienaar (Philip). WITH STEYN AND DE WET. *Second Edition. Crown 8vo. 3s. 6d.*

Plautus. THE CAPTIVI. Edited, with an Introduction, Textual Notes, and a Commentary, by W. M. LINDSAY, Fellow of Jesus College, Oxford. *Demy 8vo. 10s. 6d. net.*

Plowden-Wardlaw (J.T.), B.A., King's Coll. Cam. EXAMINATION PAPERS IN ENGLISH HISTORY. *Crown 8vo. 2s. 6d.*
[School Examination Series.

Pocock (Roger). A FRONTIERSMAN. *Third Edition. Crown 8vo. 6s.*
A Colonial Edition is also published.

Podmore (Frank). MODERN SPIRITUALISM. *Two Volumes. Demy 8vo. 21s. net.*
A History and a Criticism.

Pollard (A. W.). OLD PICTURE BOOKS. With many Illustrations. *Demy 8vo. 7s. 6d. net.*

Pollard (Eliza F.). GREUZE AND BOUCHER. *Demy 16mo. 2s. 6d. net.*
[Little Books on Art. Nearly Ready.

Pollock (David), M.I.N.A., Author of *Modern Shipbuilding and the Men engaged in it,*' etc., etc. THE SHIPBUILDING INDUSTRY. *Crown 8vo. 2s. 6d. net.*
[Books on Business.

Potter (M. C.), M.A., F.L.S. A TEXT-BOOK OF AGRICULTURAL BOTANY. Illustrated. *Second Edition. Crown 8vo. 4s. 6d.* [University Extension Series.

Potter Boy (An Old). WHEN I WAS A CHILD. *Crown 8vo. 6s.*

Pradeau (G.). A KEY TO THE TIME ALLUSIONS IN THE DIVINE COMEDY. With a Dial. *Small quarto. 3s. 6d.*

Prance (G.). See R. Wyon.

Prescott (O. L.). ABOUT MUSIC, AND WHAT IT IS MADE OF. *Crown 8vo. 3s. 6d. net.*

Price (L. L.), M.A., Fellow of Oriel College, Oxon. A HISTORY OF ENGLISH POLITICAL ECONOMY. *Fourth Edition. Crown 8vo. 2s. 6d.*
[University Extension Series.

Primrose (Deborah). A MODERN BŒOTIA. *Cr. 8vo. 6s.* [Nearly Ready.
PROTECTION AND INDUSTRY. By various Writers. *Crown 8vo. 1s. 6d. net.*

Pugin and **Rowlandson.** THE MICRO-COSM OF LONDON, OR LONDON IN MINIATURE. With 104 Illustrations in colour. *In Three Volumes. Small 4to. Three Guineas net.* [Nearly Ready.

"Q." THE GOLDEN POMP. A Procession of English Lyrics. Arranged by A. T. QUILLER COUCH. *Crown 8vo. Buckram. 6s.*

QUEVEDO VILLEGAS, THE VISIONS OF DOM FRANCISCO DE, Knight of the Order of St. James. Made English by R. L.
From the edition printed for H. Herringman, 1668. *Leather, 2s. net.*
[Miniature Library.

G. R. and E. S. THE WOODHOUSE CORRESPONDENCE. *Crown 8vo. 6s.*

Rackham (R. B.), M.A. THE ACTS OF THE APOSTLES. With an Introduction and Notes. *Demy 8vo. 12s. 6d.*
[Westminster Commentaries.

Randolph (B. W.), D.D., Principal of the Theological College, Ely. THE PSALMS OF DAVID. With an Introduction and Notes. *Small Pott 8vo. Cloth, 2s.; leather, 2s. 6d. net.* [Library of Devotion.

Rashdall (Hastings), M.A., Fellow and Tutor of New College, Oxford. DOC-TRINE AND DEVELOPMENT. *Crown 8vo. 6s.*

Rawstorne (Lawrence, Esq.). GAMONIA: or, The Art of Preserving Game; and an Improved Method of making plantations and covers, explained and illustrated by. With 15 Coloured Drawings by T. RAWLINS. *Fcap. 8vo. 3s. 6d. net.*
[Illustrated Pocket Library.

Reason (W.) M.A. UNIVERSITY AND SOCIAL SETTLEMENTS. *Crown 8vo. 2s. 6d.* [Social Questions Series.

Reynolds, A LITTLE GALLERY OF. Twenty examples in photogravure of his finest work. *Demy 16mo. 2s. 6d. net.*
[Little Galleries.

Roberts (M. E.). See C. C. Channer.

Robertson, (A.), D.D., Lord Bishop of Exeter. REGNUM DEI. The Bampton Lectures of 1901. *Demy 8vo. 12s. 6d. net.*

Robertson (Sir G. S.) K.C.S.I. CHITRAL: The Story of a Minor Siege. With numerous Illustrations, Map and Plans. *Fourth Edition. Crown 8vo. 6s.*

Robinson (A. W.), M.A. THE EPISTLE TO THE GALATIANS. With an Introduction and Notes. *Fcap. 8vo. 1s. 6d. net.*
[Churchman's Bible.

Robinson (Cecilia). THE MINISTRY OF DEACONESSES. With an Introduction by the late Archbishop of Canterbury. *Crown 8vo. 3s. 6d.*

Rochefoucauld (La), THE MAXIMS OF. Translated by DEAN STANHOPE. Edited by G. H. POWELL. *Small Pott 8vo, cloth, 1s. 6d. net; leather, 2s. 6d. net.* [Little Library.

Rodwell (G.), B.A. NEW TESTAMENT GREEK. A Course for Beginners. With a Preface by WALTER LOCK, D.D., Warden of Keble College. *Fcap. 8vo. 3s. 6d.*

Roe (Fred). ANCIENT COFFERS AND CUPBOARDS: Their History and Description. With many Illustrations. *Quarto. £3, 3s. net.*

Rogers (A. G. L.), M.A., Editor of the last volume of *The History of Agriculture and Prices in England.* THE AGRICUL-TURAL INDUSTRY. *Crown 8vo. 2s. 6d. net.* [Books on Business.

Romney. A LITTLE GALLERY OF. Twenty examples in Photogravure of his finest work. *Demy 16mo. 2s. 6d. net.*
[Little Galleries.

Roscoe (E. S.). ROBERT HARLEY, EARL OF OXFORD. Illustrated. *Demy 8vo. 7s. 6d.*
This is the only life of Harley in existence.

BUCKINGHAMSHIRE. Illustrated by F. D. BEDFORD. *Small Pott 8vo, cloth, 3s.; leather, 3s. 6d.* [Little Guides.

Rose (Edward). THE ROSE READER. With numerous Illustrations. *Crown 8vo. 2s. 6d. Also in 4 Parts. Parts I. and II. 6d. each; Part III. 8d.; Part IV. 10d.*

Rubie (A. E.), M.A., Head Master of College, Eltham. THE GOSPEL AC-CORDING TO ST. MARK. With three Maps. *Crown 8vo. 1s. 6d.* [Junior School Books.

THE ACTS OF THE APOSTLES. *Crown 8vo. 2s.* [Junior School Books.

THE FIRST BOOK OF KINGS. With Notes. *Crown 8vo. 1s. 6d.* [Junior School Books.

Russell (W. Clark). THE LIFE OF ADMIRAL LORD COLLINGWOOD. With Illustrations by F. BRANGWYN. *Fourth Edition. Crown 8vo. 6s.*
A Colonial Edition is also published.

St. Anselm, THE DEVOTIONS OF. Edited by C. C. J. WEBB, M.A. *Small Pott 8vo. Cloth, 2s.; leather, 2s. 6d. net.* [Library of Devotion.

St. Augustine, THE CONFESSIONS OF. Newly Translated, with an Introduction and Notes, by C. BIGG, D.D., late Student of Christ Church. *Third Edition. Small Pott 8vo. Cloth, 2s.; leather, 2s. 6d. net.* [Library of Devotion.

St. Cyres (Viscount). THE LIFE OF FRANÇOIS DE FENELON. Illustrated. *Demy 8vo. 10s. 6d.*

Sales (St. Francis de). ON THE LOVE OF GOD. Edited by W. J. KNOX-LITTLE, M.A. *Small Pott 8vo. Cloth, 2s.; leather, 2s. 6d. net.* [Library of Devotion.

Salmon (A. L.). CORNWALL. Illustrated by B. C. BOULTER. *Small Pott 8vo. Cloth, 3s.; leather, 3s. 6d. net.* [Little Guides.

Sargeaunt (J.), M.A. ANNALS OF WESTMINSTER SCHOOL. With numerous Illustrations. *Demy 8vo. 7s. 6d.*

Sathas (C.). THE HISTORY OF PSELLUS. *Demy 8vo. 15s. net.* [Byzantine Texts.

Schmitt (John). THE CHRONICLE OF MOREA. *Demy 8vo. 15s. net.* [Byzantine Texts.

Seeley (H. G.) F.R.S. DRAGONS OF THE AIR. With many Illustrations. *Crown 8vo. 6s.*

Sells (V. P.), M.A. THE MECHANICS OF DAILY LIFE. Illustrated. *Crown 8vo. 2s. 6d.* [University Extension Series.

Selous (Edmund). TOMMY SMITH'S ANIMALS. Illustrated by G. W. ORD. *Second Edition. Fcap. 8vo. 2s. 6d.*

Shakespeare (William).
THE FOUR FOLIOS, 1623; 1632; 1664; 1685.
Each *Four Guineas net.*

The Arden Edition.
Demy 8vo. 3s. 6d. each volume. General Editor, W. J. CRAIG. An Edition of Shakespeare in single Plays. Edited with a full Introduction, Textual Notes, and a Commentary at the foot of the page.

HAMLET. Edited by EDWARD DOWDEN, Litt.D.

ROMEO AND JULIET. Edited by EDWARD DOWDEN, Litt.D.

KING LEAR. Edited by W. J. CRAIG.

JULIUS CAESAR. Edited by M. MAC-MILLAN, M.A.

THE TEMPEST. Edited by MORTON LUCE.

OTHELLO. Edited by H. C. HART.

CYMBELINE. Edited by EDWARD DOWDEN.

TITUS ANDRONICUS. Edited by H. B. BAILDON. [Nearly Ready.

THE MERRY WIVES OF WINDSOR. Edited by H. C. HART.

MIDSUMMER NIGHT'S DREAM. Edited by H. CUNINGHAM. [Nearly Ready.

HENRY V. Edited by H. A. EVANS.

The Little Quarto Shakespeare. *Pott 16mo. Leather, price 1s. net each volume.*
TWO GENTLEMEN OF VERONA.
A COMEDY OF ERRORS.
THE TEMPEST.
THE MERRY WIVES OF WINDSOR.
MEASURE FOR MEASURE.
LOVE'S LABOUR'S LOST.
A MIDSUMMER NIGHT'S DREAM.
MUCH ADO ABOUT NOTHING.
AS YOU LIKE IT.
THE MERCHANT OF VENICE.
ALL'S WELL THAT ENDS WELL.
A WINTER'S TALE.
THE TAMING OF THE SHREW.
TWELFTH NIGHT.
KING JOHN.
KING RICHARD II.
KING HENRY IV. Part I.
KING HENRY IV. Part. II.
KING HENRY V.
KING HENRY VI. Part I.
KING HENRY VI. Part II.
KING HENRY VI. Part III.
KING RICHARD III.

Sharp (A.). VICTORIAN POETS. *Crown 8vo. 2s. 6d.* [University Extension Series.

Shedlock (J. S.). THE PIANOFORTE SONATA: Its Origin and Development. *Crown 8vo. 5s.*

Shelley (Percy B.). ADONAIS; an Elegy on the death of John Keats, Author of Endymion, etc. Pisa. From the types of Didot, 1821. *2s. net.* [Rariora.

Sherwell (Arthur), M.A. LIFE IN WEST LONDON. *Third Edition. Crown 8vo. 2s. 6d.* [Social Questions Series.

Sichel (Walter). DISRAELI: A Study in Personality and Ideas. *Demy 8vo. 12s. 6d. net.*

BEACONSFIELD. *Fcap. 8vo, cloth, 3s. 6d.; leather, 4s. net.* [Little Biographies. Nearly Ready.

Sime (J.). REYNOLDS. With many Illustrations. *Demy 16mo.* 2s. 6d. net.
[Little Books on Art.

Sketchley (R. E. D.). WATTS. With many Illustrations. *Demy 16mo.* 2s. 6d. net.
[Little Books on Art.

Sladen (Douglas). SICILY. With over 200 Illustrations. *Crown 8vo.* 5s. net.
[Nearly Ready.

Small (Evan), M.A. THE EARTH. An Introduction to Physiography. Illustrated. *Crown 8vo.* 2s. 6d.
[University Extension Series.

Smallwood, (M. G.). VANDYCK. With many Illustrations. *Demy 16mo.* 2s. 6d. net. [Little Books on Art. [Nearly Ready.

Smedley (F. E.). FRANK FAIRLEGH. With 28 Plates by GEORGE CRUIKSHANK. *Fcap. 8vo.* 3s. 6d. net. [Nearly Ready.
[Illustrated Pocket Library.

Smith (Horace and James). REJECTED ADDRESSES. Edited by A. D. GODLEY, M.A. *Small Pott 8vo, cloth,* 1s. 6d. net.; *leather,* 2s. 6d. net. [Little Library.

Snell (F. J.). A BOOK OF EXMOOR. Illustrated. *Crown 8vo.* 6s.

Sophocles. ELECTRA AND AJAX. Translated by E. D. A. MORSHEAD, M.A., Assistant Master at Winchester. 2s. 6d.
[Classical Translations.

Sornet (L. A.), and Acatos (M. J.), Modern Language Masters at King Edward's School, Birmingham. A JUNIOR FRENCH GRAMMAR. *Crown 8vo.* 2s.
[Junior School Books.

South (Wilton E.), M.A. THE GOSPEL ACCORDING TO ST. MATTHEW. *Crown 8vo.* 1s. 6d. [Junior School Books.

Southey (R.) ENGLISH SEAMEN. Vol. I. (Howard, Clifford, Hawkins, Drake, Cavendish). Edited, with an Introduction, by DAVID HANNAY. *Second Edition. Crown 8vo.* 6s.
Vol. II. (Richard Hawkins, Grenville, Essex, and Raleigh). *Crown 8vo.* 6s.

Spence (C. H.), M.A., Clifton College. HISTORY AND GEOGRAPHY EXAMINATION PAPERS. *Second Edition. Crown 8vo.* 2s. 6d.
[School Examination Series.

Spooner (W. A.), M.A., Warden of New College, Oxford. BISHOP BUTLER. With Portrait. *Crown 8vo.* 3s. 6d.
[Leaders of Religion.

Stanbridge (J. W.), B.D., late Canon of York, and sometime Fellow of St. John's College, Oxford. A BOOK OF DEVOTIONS. *Small Pott 8vo.* Cloth, 2s.; *leather,* 2s. 6d. net. [Library of Devotion.

'Stancliffe.' GOLF DO'S AND DONT'S. *Second Edition. Fcap. 8vo.* 1s.

Stedman (A. M. M.), M.A.
INITIA LATINA: Easy Lessons on Elementary Accidence. *Sixth Edition. Fcap. 8vo.* 1s.

FIRST LATIN LESSONS. *Eighth Edition. Crown 8vo.* 2s.

FIRST LATIN READER. With Notes adapted to the Shorter Latin Primer and Vocabulary. *Sixth Edition revised.* 18mo. 1s. 6d.

EASY SELECTIONS FROM CÆSAR. The Helvetian War. *Second Edition.* 18mo. 1s.

EASY SELECTIONS FROM LIVY. Part I. The Kings of Rome. 18mo. *Second Edition.* 1s. 6d.

EASY LATIN PASSAGES FOR UNSEEN TRANSLATION. *Ninth Edition. Fcap. 8vo.* 1s. 6d.

EXEMPLA LATINA. First Exercises in Latin Accidence. With Vocabulary. *Third Edition. Crown 8vo.* 1s.

EASY LATIN EXERCISES ON THE SYNTAX OF THE SHORTER AND REVISED LATIN PRIMER. With Vocabulary. *Ninth and Cheaper Edition, re-written. Crown 8vo.* 1s. 6d. KEY, 3s. net. *Original Edition.* 2s. 6d.

THE LATIN COMPOUND SENTENCE: Rules and Exercises. *Second Edition. Crown 8vo.* 1s. 6d. With Vocabulary. 2s.

NOTANDA QUAEDAM: Miscellaneous Latin Exercises on Common Rules and Idioms. *Fourth Edition. Fcap. 8vo.* 1s. 6d. With Vocabulary. 2s. Key, 2s. net.

LATIN VOCABULARIES FOR REPETITION: Arranged according to Subjects. *Eleventh Edition. Fcap. 8vo.* 1s. 6d.

A VOCABULARY OF LATIN IDIOMS. 18mo. *Second Edition.* 1s.

STEPS TO GREEK. *Second Edition, revised.* 18mo. 1s.

A SHORTER GREEK PRIMER. *Crown 8vo.* 1s. 6d.

EASY GREEK PASSAGES FOR UNSEEN TRANSLATION. *Third Edition, revised. Fcap. 8vo.* 1s. 6d.

GREEK VOCABULARIES FOR REPETITION. Arranged according to Subjects. *Third Edition. Fcap. 8vo.* 1s. 6d.

GREEK TESTAMENT SELECTIONS. For the use of Schools. With Introduction, Notes, and Vocabulary. *Third Edition. Fcap. 8vo.* 2s. 6d.

STEPS TO FRENCH. *Sixth Edition.* 18mo. 8d.

FIRST FRENCH LESSONS. *Sixth Edition, revised. Crown 8vo.* 1s.

EASY FRENCH PASSAGES FOR UNSEEN TRANSLATION. *Fifth Edition, revised. Fcap. 8vo.* 1s. 6d.

EASY FRENCH EXERCISES ON ELEMENTARY SYNTAX. With Vocabulary. *Fourth Edition. Crown 8vo.* 2s. 6d. KEY, 3s. net.

FRENCH VOCABULARIES FOR REPETITION: Arranged according to Subjects. *Eleventh Edition. Fcap. 8vo.* 1s.

FRENCH EXAMINATION PAPERS IN MISCELLANEOUS GRAMMAR AND IDIOMS. *Twelfth Edition. Crown 8vo.* 2s. 6d. [School Examination Series.

A KEY, issued to Tutors and Private Students only, to be had on application to the Publishers. *Fifth Edition. Crown 8vo.* 6s. net.

GENERAL KNOWLEDGE EXAMINA-TION PAPERS. *Fourth Edition. Crown 8vo.* 2s. 6d. [School Examination Series. KEY (*Third Edition*) issued as above. 7s. net.

GREEK EXAMINATION PAPERS IN MISCELLANEOUS GRAMMAR AND IDIOMS. *Seventh Edition. Crown 8vo.* 2s. 6d. [School Examination Series. KEY (*Third Edition*) issued as above. 6s. net.

LATIN EXAMINATION PAPERS IN MISCELLANEOUS GRAMMAR AND IDIOMS. *Twelfth Edition. Crown 8vo.* 2s. 6d. [School Examination Series. KEY (*Fourth Edition*) issued as above. 6s. net.

Steel (R. Elliott), M.A., F.C.S. THE WORLD OF SCIENCE. Including Chemistry, Heat, Light, Sound, Magnetism, Electricity, Botany, Zoology, Physiology, Astronomy, and Geology. 147 Illustrations. *Second Edition. Crown 8vo.* 2s. 6d.

PHYSICS EXAMINATION PAPERS. *Crown 8vo.* 2s. 6d. [School Examination Series.

Stephenson (C.), of the Technical College, Bradford, and Suddards (F.) of the York-shire College, Leeds. ORNAMENTAL DESIGN FOR WOVEN FABRICS. Illustrated. *Demy 8vo. Second Edition.* 7s. 6d.

Stephenson (J.), M.A. THE CHIEF TRUTHS OF THE CHRISTIAN FAITH. *Crown 8vo.* 3s. 6d.

Sterne (Laurence). A SENTIMENTAL JOURNEY. Edited by H. W. PAUL. *Small Pott 8vo. Cloth,* 1s. 6d. net; leather, 2s. 6d. net. [Little Library.

Sterry (W.), M.A. ANNALS OF ETON COLLEGE. With numerous Illustrations. *Demy 8vo.* 7s. 6d.

Steuart (Katherine). BY ALLAN WATER. *Second Edition. Crown 8vo.* 6s.

Stevenson (R. L.). THE LETTERS OF ROBERT LOUIS STEVENSON TO HIS FAMILY AND FRIENDS. Selected and Edited, with Notes and Intro-ductions, by SIDNEY COLVIN. *Sixth and Cheaper Edition. Crown 8vo.* 12s.

LIBRARY EDITION. *Demy 8vo.* 2 vols. 25s. net. A Colonial Edition is also published.

VAILIMA LETTERS. With an Etched Portrait by WILLIAM STRANG. *Third Edition. Crown 8vo. Buckram.* 6s. A Colonial Edition is also published.

THE LIFE OF R. L. STEVENSON. See G. Balfour.

Stoddart (Anna M.) ST. FRANCIS OF ASSISI. With 16 Illustrations. *Fcap. 8vo. Cloth,* 3s. 6d.; leather, 4s. net. [Little Biographies.

Stone (E. D.), M.A., late Assistant Master at Eton. SELECTIONS FROM THE ODYSSEY. *Fcap. 8vo.* 1s. 6d.

Stone (S. J.). POEMS AND HYMNS. With a Memoir by F. G. ELLERTON, M.A. With Portrait. *Crown 8vo.* 6s.

Straker (F.), Assoc. of the Institute of Bankers, and Lecturer to the London Chamber of Commerce. THE MONEY MARKET. *Crown 8vo.* 2s. 6d. net. [Books on Business. [Nearly Ready.

Streane (A. W.), D.D. ECCLESIASTES. With an Introduction and Notes. *Fcap. 8vo.* 1s. 6d. net. [Churchman's Bible.

Stroud (H.), D.Sc., M.A., Professor of Physics in the Durham College of Science, New-castle-on-Tyne. PRACTICAL PHYSICS. Fully Illustrated. *Crown 8vo.* 3s. 6d. [Textbooks of Technology.

Strutt (Joseph). THE SPORTS AND PASTIMES OF THE PEOPLE OF ENGLAND. Illustrated by many engrav-ings. Revised by J. Charles Cox, LL.D., F.S.A. *Quarto.* 21s. net.

Stuart (Capt. Donald). THE STRUGGLE FOR PERSIA. With a Map. *Crown 8vo.* 6s.

Suckling (Sir John). FRAGMENTA AUREA: a Collection of all the Incom-parable Peeces, written by. And published by a friend to perpetuate his memory. Printed by his own copies.

Printed for HUMPHREY MOSELEY, and are to be sold at his shop, at the sign of the Princes Arms in St. Paul's Churchyard, 1646. 6s. net. [Rariora. Nearly Ready.

Suddards (F.). See C. Stephenson.

Surtees (R. S.). HANDLEY CROSS. With 17 Coloured Plates and 100 Woodcuts in the Text by JOHN LEECH. *Fcap. 8vo.* 4s. 6d. net.

Also a limited edition on large Japanese paper. 30s. net. [Illustrated Pocket Library.

MR. SPONGE'S SPORTING TOUR. With 13 Coloured Plates and 90 Woodcuts in the Text by JOHN LEECH. *Fcap. 8vo.* 3s. 6d. net.

Also a limited edition on large Japanese paper. 30s. net. [Illustrated Pocket Library.

JORROCKS' JAUNTS AND JOLLITIES. With 15 Coloured Plates by H. ALKEN. *Fcap. 8vo.* 3s. 6d. net.

Also a limited edition on large Japanese paper. 30s. net. [Illustrated Pocket Library.

ASK MAMMA. With 13 Coloured Plates and 70 Woodcuts in the Text by JOHN LEECH. *Fcap. 8vo.* 3*s.* 6*d. net.*
Also a limited edition on large Japanese paper. 30*s. net.*
[Illustrated Pocket Library. NearlyReady.

Swift (Jonathan). THE JOURNAL TO STELLA. Edited by G. A. AITKEN. *Crown 8vo.* 6*s.*

Symes (J. E.), M.A. THE FRENCH REVOLUTION. *Crown 8vo.* 2*s.* 6*d.*
[University Extension Series.

Syrett (Netta). A SCHOOL YEAR. Illustrated. *Demy 16mo.* 2*s.* 6*d.*
[Little Blue Books.

Tacitus. AGRICOLA. With Introduction, Notes, Map, etc. By R. F. DAVIS, M.A., late Assistant Master at Weymouth College. *Crown 8vo.* 2*s.*
GERMANIA. By the same Editor. *Crown 8vo.* 2*s.*
AGRICOLA AND GERMANIA. Translated by R. B. TOWNSHEND, late Scholar of Trinity College, Cambridge. *Crown 8vo.* 2*s.* 6*d.* [Classical Translations.

Tauler (J.). THE INNER WAY. Being Thirty-six Sermons for Festivals by JOHN TAULER. Edited by A. W. HUTTON, M.A. *Small Pott 8vo. Cloth,* 2*s.; leather,* 2*s.* 6*d. net.* [Library of Devotion.

Taunton (E. L.). A HISTORY OF THE JESUITS IN ENGLAND. With Illustrations. *Demy 8vo.* 21*s. net.*

Taylor (A. E.). THE ELEMENTS OF METAPHYSICS. *Demy 8vo.* 10*s.* 6*d. net.*

Taylor (F. G.), M.A. COMMERCIAL ARITHMETIC. *Third Edition. Crown 8vo.* 1*s.* 6*d.* [Commercial Series.

Taylor (Miss J. A.). SIR WALTER RALEIGH. With 12 Illustrations. *Fcap. 8vo. Cloth,* 3*s.* 6*d.; leather,* 4*s. net.*
[Little Biographies.

Taylor (T. M.), M.A., Fellow of Gonville and Caius College, Cambridge. A CONSTITUTIONAL AND POLITICAL HISTORY OF ROME. *Crown 8vo.* 7*s.* 6*d.*

Tennyson (Alfred, Lord). THE EARLY POEMS OF. Edited, with Notes and an Introduction, by J. CHURTON COLLINS, M.A. *Crown 8vo.* 6*s.*
Also with 10 Illustrations in Photogravure by W. E. F. BRITTEN. *Demy 8vo.* 10*s.* 6*d.*
IN MEMORIAM, MAUD, AND THE PRINCESS. Edited by J. CHURTON COLLINS, M.A. *Crown 8vo.* 6*s.*
MAUD. Edited by ELIZABETH WORDSWORTH. *Small Pott 8vo. Cloth,* 1*s.* 6*d. net; leather,* 2*s.* 6*d. net.* [Little Library.
IN MEMORIAM. Edited by H. C. BEECHING, M.A. *Small Pott 8vo. Cloth,* 1*s.* 6*d. net; leather,* 2*s.* 6*d. net.* [Little Library.
THE EARLY POEMS OF. Edited by J. C. COLLINS, M.A. *Small Pott 8vo. Cloth,* 1*s.* 6*d. net; leather,* 2*s.* 6*d. net.* [Little Library.

THE PRINCESS. Edited by ELIZABETH WORDSWORTH. *Small Pott 8vo. Cloth,* 1*s.* 6*d. net; leather,* 2*s.* 6*d. net.* [Little Library.

Terry (C. S.). THE YOUNG PRETENDER. With 12 Illustrations. *Fcap. 8vo. Cloth,* 3*s.* 6*d.; leather,* 4*s. net.*
[Little Biographies.

Terton (Alice). LIGHTS AND SHADOWS IN A HOSPITAL. *Crown 8vo.* 3*s.* 6*d.*

Thackeray (W. M.). VANITY FAIR. Edited by STEPHEN GWYNN. *Three Volumes. Small Pott 8vo. Each volume, cloth,* 1*s.* 6*d. net; leather,* 2*s.* 6*d. net.*
[Little Library.
PENDENNIS. Edited by STEPHEN GWYNN. *Three Volumes. Small Pott 8vo. Each volume, cloth,* 1*s.* 6*d. net; leather,* 2*s.* 6*d. net.* [Little Library.
ESMOND. Edited by STEPHEN GWYNN. *Small Pott 8vo. Cloth,* 1*s.* 6*d. net; leather,* 2*s.* 6*d. net.* [Little Library.
CHRISTMAS BOOKS. Edited by STEPHEN GWYNN. *Small Pott 8vo. Cloth,* 1*s.* 6*d. net; leather,* 2*s.* 6*d. net.* [Little Library.
THE LOVING BALLAD OF LORD BATEMAN. With 11 Plates by GEORGE CRUIKSHANK. *Crown 16mo.* 1*s.* 6*d. net.*
From the edition published by C. Tilt, 1811.

Theobald (F. W.), M.A. INSECT LIFE. Illustrated. *Crown 8vo.* 2*s.* 6*d.*
[University Extension Series.

Thompson (A. H.). CAMBRIDGE AND ITS COLLEGES. Illustrated by E. H. NEW. *Small Pott 8vo. Cloth,* 3*s.; leather,* 3*s.* 6*d. net.* [Little Guides.

Tompkins (H. W.), F.R.H.S. HERTFORDSHIRE. Illustrated by E. H. NEW. *Small Pott 8vo. Cloth,* 3*s.; leather,* 3*s.* 6*d. net.* [Little Guides.

Toynbee (Paget), M.A., D.Litt. DANTE STUDIES AND RESEARCHES. *Demy 8vo.* 10*s.* 6*d. net.*
DANTE ALIGHIERI. With 12 Illustrations. *Second Edition. Fcap. 8vo. Cloth,* 3*s.* 6*d.; leather,* 4*s. net.*
[Little Biographies.

Trench (Herbert). DEIRDRE WED: and Other Poems. *Crown 8vo.* 5*s.*

Troutbeck (G. E.). WESTMINSTER ABBEY. Illustrated by F. D. BEDFORD. *Small Pott 8vo. Cloth,* 3*s.; leather,* 3*s.* 6*d. net.* [Little Guides.

Tuckwell (Gertrude). THE STATE AND ITS CHILDREN. *Crown 8vo.* 2*s.* 6*d.*
[Social Questions Series.

Twining (Louisa). WORKHOUSES AND PAUPERISM. *Crown 8vo.* 2*s.* 6*d.*
[Social Questions Series.

Tyler (E. A.), B.A., F.C.S. A JUNIOR CHEMISTRY. *Crown 8vo.* 2*s.* 6*d.*
[Junior School Books.

Tyrrell-Gill (Frances). TURNER. *Demy 16mo.* 2*s.* 6*d. net.*
[Little Books on Art. Nearly Ready.

Vaughan (Henry), THE POEMS OF. Edited by EDWARD HUTTON. *Small Pott 8vo. Cloth*, 1s. 6d. *net*; *leather*, 2s. 6d. *net*. [Little Library. [Nearly Ready.

Voegelin (A.), M.A. JUNIOR GERMAN EXAMINATION PAPERS. *Fcap. 8vo.* 1s. [Junior Examination Series.

Wade (G. W.), D.D. OLD TESTAMENT HISTORY. With Maps. *Second Edition. Crown 8vo.* 6s.

Walters (H. B.). GREEK ART. With many Illustrations. *Demy 16mo.* 2s. 6d. *net*. [Little Books on Art.

Walton (Izaac) and **Cotton (Charles)**. THE COMPLEAT ANGLER. With 14 Plates and 77 Woodcuts in the Text. *Fcap 8vo.* 3s. 6d. *net*. [Illustrated Pocket Library. This volume is reproduced from the beautiful edition of John Major of 1824-5. THE COMPLEAT ANGLER. Edited by J. BUCHAN. *Small Pott 8vo. Cloth*, 1s. 6d. *net*; *leather*, 2s. 6d. *net*. [Little Library.

Warmelo (D. S. Van). ON COMMANDO. With Portrait. *Crown 8vo.* 3s. 6d.

Waterhouse (Mrs. Alfred). A LITTLE BOOK OF LIFE AND DEATH. Selected. *Fourth Edition. Small Pott 8vo. Cloth*, 1s. 6d. *net*; *leather*, 2s. 6d. *net*. [Little Library.

Weatherhead (T. C.), M.A. EXAMINATION PAPERS IN HORACE. *Crown 8vo.* 2s. *net*. JUNIOR GREEK EXAMINATION PAPERS. *Fcap. 8vo.* 1s. [Junior Examination Series.

Webb (W. T.). A BOOK OF BAD CHILDREN. With 50 Illustrations by H. C. SANDY. *Demy 16mo.* 2s. 6d. [Little Blue Books.

Webber (F. C.). CARPENTRY AND JOINERY. With many Illustrations. *Third Edition. Crown 8vo.* 3s. 6d.

Wells (Sidney H.). PRACTICAL MECHANICS. With 75 Illustrations and Diagrams. *Second Edition. Crown 8vo.* 3s. 6d. [Textbooks of Technology.

Wells (J.), M.A., Fellow and Tutor of Wadham College. OXFORD AND OXFORD LIFE. By Members of the University. *Third Edition Crown 8vo.* 3s. 6d. A SHORT HISTORY OF ROME. *Fifth Edition*. With 3 Maps. *Cr. 8vo.* 3s. 6d. This book is intended for the Middle and Upper Forms of Public Schools and for Pass Students at the Universities. It contains copious Tables, etc. OXFORD AND ITS COLLEGES. Illustrated by E. H. New. *Fifth Edition. Pott 8vo. Cloth*, 3s.; *leather*, 3s. 6d. *net*. [Little Guides.

Wetmore (Helen C.). THE LAST OF THE GREAT SCOUTS ('Buffalo Bill'). With Illustrations. *Second Edition. Demy 8vo.* 6s.

Whibley (C.). See Henley and Whibley.

Whibley (L.), M.A., Fellow of Pembroke College, Cambridge. GREEK OLIGARCHIES: THEIR ORGANISATION AND CHARACTER. *Crown 8vo.* 6s.

Whitaker (G. H.), M.A. THE EPISTLE OF ST. PAUL THE APOSTLE TO THE EPHESIANS. With an Introduction and Notes. *Fcap. 8vo.* 1s. 6d. *net*. [Churchman's Bible.

White (Gilbert). THE NATURAL HISTORY OF SELBORNE. Edited by L. C. MIALL, F.R.S., assisted by W. WARDE FOWLER, M.A. *Crown 8vo.* 6s.

Whitfield (E. E.). PRECIS WRITING AND OFFICE CORRESPONDENCE. *Second Edition. Crown 8vo.* 2s. [Commercial Series. COMMERCIAL EDUCATION IN THEORY AND PRACTICE. *Crown 8vo.* 5s. [Commercial Series. An introduction to Methuen's Commercial Series treating the question of Commercial Education fully from both the point of view of the teacher and of the parent.

Whitley (Miss). See Lady Dilke.

Whyte (A. G.), B.Sc., Editor of *Electrical Investments*. THE ELECTRICAL INDUSTRY. *Crown 8vo.* 2s. 6d. *net*. [Books on Business. Nearly Ready.

Wilberforce (Wilfrid). VELASQUEZ. With many Illustrations. *Demy 16mo.* 2s. 6d. *net*. [Little Books on Art. Nearly Ready.

Wilkins (W. H.), B.A. THE ALIEN INVASION. *Crown 8vo.* 2s. 6d. [Social Questions Series.

Williamson (W.). THE BRITISH GARDENER. Illustrated. *Demy 8vo.* 10s. 6d.

Williamson (W.), B.A. JUNIOR ENGLISH EXAMINATION PAPERS. *Fcap. 8vo.* 1s. [Junior Examination Series. A JUNIOR ENGLISH GRAMMAR. With numerous passages for parsing and analysis, and a chapter on Essay Writing. *Crown 8vo.* 2s. [Junior School Books. A CLASS-BOOK OF DICTATION PASSAGES. *Eighth Edition. Crown 8vo.* 1s. 6d. [Junior School Books. EASY DICTATION AND SPELLING. *Second Edition. Fcap. 8vo.* 1s.

Wilmot-Buxton (E. M.). THE MAKERS OF EUROPE. *Crown 8vo. Second Edition.* 3s. 6d. A Text-book of European History for Middle Forms.

Wilson (Bishop). SACRA PRIVATA. Edited by A. E. BURN, B.D. *Small Pott 8vo. Cloth*, 2s.; *leather*, 2s. 6d. *net*. [Library of Devotion.

Willson (Beckles). LORD STRATHCONA: the Story of his Life. Illustrated. *Demy 8vo.* 7s. 6d. A Colonial Edition is also published.

Wilson (A. J.), Editor of the *Investor's Review*, City Editor of the *Daily Chronicle*. THE INSURANCE INDUSTRY. *Crown 8vo.* 2s. 6d. net. [Books on Business. Nearly Ready.

Wilson (H. A.). LAW IN BUSINESS. *Crown 8vo.* 2s. 6d. net. [Books on Business.

Wilton (Richard), M.A. LYRA PASTORALIS: Songs of Nature, Church, and Home. *Pott 8vo.* 2s. 6d.
A volume of devotional poems.

Winbolt (S. E.), M.A., Assistant Master in Christ's Hospital. EXERCISES IN LATIN ACCIDENCE. *Crown 8vo.* 1s.6d.
An elementary book adapted for Lower Forms to accompany the Shorter Latin Primer.
LATIN HEXAMETER VERSE: An Aid to Composition. *Crown 8vo.* 3s. 6d. KEY, 5s. net.

Windle (B. C. A.), D.Sc., F.R.S. SHAKESPEARE'S COUNTRY. Illustrated by E. H. NEW. *Second Edition. Small Pott 8vo. cloth,* 3s.; *leather,* 3s. 6d. net.
[Little Guides.
THE MALVERN COUNTRY. Illustrated by E. H. NEW. *Small Pott 8vo. Cloth,* 3s.; *leather,* 3s. 6d. net. [Little Guides.
REMAINS OF THE PREHISTORIC AGE IN ENGLAND. With numerous Illustrations and Plans. *Demy 8vo.* 7s. 6d. net. [Antiquary's Library. Nearly Ready.
CHESTER. Illustrated by E. H. New. *Crown 8vo.* 3s. 6d. net. [Ancient Cities.

Winterbotham (Canon), M.A.,B.Sc.,LL.B. THE KINGDOM OF HEAVEN HERE AND HEREAFTER. *Crown 8vo.* 3s. 6d.
[Churchman's Library.

Wood (J. A. E.). HOW TO MAKE A DRESS. Illustrated. *Second Edition. Cr. 8vo.* 1s. 6d. [Textbooks of Technology.

Wordsworth (Christopher), M.A., and **Littlehales (Henry).** OLD SERVICE BOOKS OF THE ENGLISH CHURCH. With Coloured and other Illustrations. *Demy 8vo.* 7s. 6d. net.
[Antiquary's Library.

Wordsworth (W.). SELECTIONS. Edited by NOWELL C. SMITH, M.A. *Small Pott 8vo. Cloth,* 1s. 6d. net; *leather,* 2s. 6d. net. [Little Library.

Wordsworth (W.) and Coleridge (S. T.). LYRICAL BALLADS. Edited by GEORGE SAMPSON. *Small Pott 8vo. Cloth,* 1s. 6d. net; *leather,* 2s. 6d. net. [Little Library.

Wright (Arthur), M.A., Fellow of Queen's College, Cambridge. SOME NEW TESTAMENT PROBLEMS. *Crown 8vo.* 6s. [Churchman's Library.

Wright (Sophie). GERMAN VOCABULARIES FOR REPETITION. *Fcap. 8vo.* 1s. 6d.

Wylde (A. B.). MODERN ABYSSINIA. With a Map and a Portrait. *Demy 8vo.* 15s. net.

Wyndham (G.), M.P. THE POEMS OF WILLIAM SHAKESPEARE. With an Introduction and Notes. *Demy 8vo. Buckram, gilt top.* 10s. 6d.

Wyon (R.) and Prance (G.). THE LAND OF THE BLACK MOUNTAIN. Being a description of Montenegro. With 40 Illustrations. *Crown 8vo.* 6s.
A Colonial Edition is also published.

Yeats (W. B.). AN ANTHOLOGY OF IRISH VERSE. *Revised and Enlarged Edition. Crown 8vo.* 3s. 6d.

Yendis (M.). THE GREAT RED FROG. A Story told in 40 Coloured Pictures. *Fcap. 8vo.* 1s. net.

Young (T. M.). THE AMERICAN COTTON INDUSTRY: A Study of Work and Workers. With an Introduction by ELIJAH HELM, Secretary to the Manchester Chamber of Commerce. *Crown 8vo. cloth,* 2s. 6d.; *paper boards,* 1s. 6d.

Antiquary's Library, The
General Editor, J. CHARLES COX, LL.D., F.S.A.

ENGLISH MONASTIC LIFE. By the Right Rev. Abbot Gasquet, O.S.B. Illustrated. *Demy 8vo.* 7s. 6d. net.

REMAINS OF THE PREHISTORIC AGE IN ENGLAND. By B. C. A. Windle, D.Sc., F.R.S. With numerous Illustrations and Plans. *Demy 8vo.* 7s. 6d. net.

OLD SERVICE BOOKS OF THE ENGLISH CHURCH. By Christopher Wordsworth, M.A., and Henry Littlehales. With Coloured and other Illustrations. *Demy 8vo.* 7s. 6d. net.

Business, Books on
Crown 8vo. 2s. 6d. net.

The first Twelve volumes are—

DOCKS AND PORTS. By Douglas Owen.
RAILWAYS. By E. R. McDermott.
THE STOCK EXCHANGE. By Chas. Duguid.
THE INSURANCE INDUSTRY. By A. J. Wilson.
THE ELECTRICAL INDUSTRY. By A. G. Whyte, B.Sc.
THE SHIPBUILDING INDUSTRY. By David Pollock, M.I.N.A.

THE MONEY MARKET. By F. Straker.
THE AGRICULTURAL INDUSTRY. By A. G. L. Rogers, M.A.
LAW IN BUSINESS. By H. A. Wilson.
THE BREWING INDUSTRY. By Julian L. Baker, F.I.C., F.C.S.
THE AUTOMOBILE INDUSTRY. By G. de H. Stone.
MINING AND MINING INVESTMENTS. By 'A. Moil.'

Byzantine Texts
Edited by J. B. BURY, M.A., Litt.D.

ZACHARIAH OF MITYLENE. Translated by F. J. Hamilton, D.D., and E. W. Brooks. *Demy 8vo.* 12s. 6d. net.

EVAGRIUS. Edited by Léon Parmentier and M. Bidez. *Demy 8vo.* 10s. 6d. net.

THE HISTORY OF PSELLUS. Edited by C. Sathas. *Demy 8vo.* 15s. net.
ECTHESIS CHRONICA. Edited by Professor Lambros. *Demy 8vo.* 7s. 6d. net.
THE CHRONICLE OF MOREA. Edited by John Schmitt. *Demy 8vo.* 15s. net.

Churchman's Bible, The
General Editor, J. H. BURN, B.D., F.R.S.E.

The volumes are practical and devotional, and the text of the Authorised Version is explained in sections, which correspond as far as possible with the Church Lectionary.

THE EPISTLE TO THE GALATIANS. Edited by A. W. Robinson, M.A. *Fcap. 8vo.* 1s. 6d. net.

ECCLESIASTES. Edited by A. W. Streane, D.D. *Fcap. 8vo.* 1s. 6d. net.

THE EPISTLE TO THE PHILIPPIANS. Edited by C. R. D. Biggs, D.D. *Fcap. 8vo.* 1s. 6d. net.

THE EPISTLE OF ST. JAMES. Edited by H. W Fulford, M.A. *Fcap. 8vo.* 1s. 6d. net.
ISAIAH. Edited by W. E. Barnes, D.D., Hulsean Professor of Divinity. *Two Volumes. Fcap. 8vo.* 2s. net each. With Map.
THE EPISTLE OF ST. PAUL THE APOSTLE TO THE EPHESIANS. Edited by G. H. Whitaker, M.A. *Fcap. 8vo.* 1s. 6d. net.

Churchman's Library, The
General Editor, J. H. BURN, B.D., F.R.S.E., Examining Chaplain to the Bishop of Aberdeen.

THE BEGINNINGS OF ENGLISH CHRISTIANITY. By W. E. Collins, M.A. With Map. *Crown 8vo.* 3s. 6d.
SOME NEW TESTAMENT PROBLEMS. By Arthur Wright, M.A. *Crown 8vo.* 6s.
THE KINGDOM OF HEAVEN HERE AND HEREAFTER. By Canon Winterbotham, M.A., B.Sc., LL.B. *Crown 8vo.* 3s. 6d.
THE WORKMANSHIP OF THE PRAYER BOOK: Its Literary and Liturgical Aspects. By J. Dowden, D.D. *Second Edition. Crown 8vo.* 3s. 6d.

EVOLUTION. By F. B. Jevons, M.A., Litt.D. *Crown 8vo.* 3s. 6d.
THE OLD TESTAMENT AND THE NEW SCHOLARSHIP. By J. W. Peters, D.D. *Crown 8vo.* 6s.
THE CHURCHMAN'S INTRODUCTION TO THE OLD TESTAMENT. Edited by A. M. Mackay, B.A. *Crown 8vo.* 3s. 6d.
THE CHURCH OF CHRIST. By E. T. Green, M.A. *Crown 8vo.* 6s.
COMPARATIVE THEOLOGY. By J. A. MacCulloch. *Crown 8vo.* 6s.

Classical Translations
Edited by H. F. Fox, M.A., Fellow and Tutor of Brasenose College, Oxford.
Crown 8vo.

ÆSCHYLUS—Agamemnon, Choephoroe, Eumenides. Translated by Lewis Campbell, LL.D. 5s.
CICERO—De Oratore I. Translated by E. N. P. Moor, M.A. 3s. 6d.
CICERO—Select Orations (Pro Milone, Pro Mureno, Philippic II., in Catilinam). Translated by H. E. D. Blakiston, M.A. 5s.
CICERO—De Natura Deorum. Translated by F. Brooks, M.A. 3s. 6d.
CICERO—De Officiis. Translated by G. B. Gardiner, M.A. 2s. 6d.
HORACE—The Odes and Epodes. Translated by A. Godley, M.A. 2s.

LUCIAN—Six Dialogues (Nigrinus, Icaro-Menippus, The Cock, The Ship, The Parasite, The Lover of Falsehood). Translated by S. T. Irwin, M.A. 3s. 6d.

SOPHOCLES—Electra and Ajax. Translated by E. D. A. Morshead, M.A. 2s. 6d.

TACITUS—Agricola and Germania. Translated by R. B. Townshend. 2s. 6d.

THE SATIRES OF JUVENAL. Translated by S. G. Owen. *Crown 8vo.* 2s. 6d.

Commercial Series, Methuen's
Edited by H. DE B. GIBBINS, Litt.D., M.A.
Crown 8vo.

COMMERCIAL EDUCATION IN THEORY AND PRACTICE. By E. E. Whitfield, M.A. 5s.
  An introduction to Methuen's Commercial Series treating the question of Commercial Education fully from both the point of view of the teacher and of the parent.

BRITISH COMMERCE AND COLONIES FROM ELIZABETH TO VICTORIA. By H. de B. Gibbins, Litt.D., M.A. *Third Edition.* 2s.
COMMERCIAL EXAMINATION PAPERS. By H. de B. Gibbins, Litt.D., M.A. 1s. 6d.

[Continued.

METHUEN'S COMMERCIAL SERIES—*continued.*

THE ECONOMICS OF COMMERCE. By H. de B. Gibbins, Litt.D., M.A. 1s. 6d.

A GERMAN COMMERCIAL READER. By S. E. Bally, With Vocabulary. 2s.

A COMMERCIAL GEOGRAPHY OF THE BRITISH EMPIRE. By L. W. Lyde, M.A. *Third Edition.* 2s.

A PRIMER OF BUSINESS. By S. Jackson, M.A. *Third Edition.* 1s. 6d.

COMMERCIAL ARITHMETIC. By F. G. Taylor, M.A. *Third Edition.* 1s. 6d.

FRENCH COMMERCIAL CORRESPONDENCE. By S. E. Bally. With Vocabulary. *Third Edition.* 2s.

GERMAN COMMERCIAL CORRESPONDENCE. By S. E. Bally. With Vocabulary. 2s. 6d.

A FRENCH COMMERCIAL READER. By S. E. Bally. With Vocabulary. *Second Edition.* 2s.

PRECIS WRITING AND OFFICE CORRESPONDENCE. By E. E. Whitfield, M.A. *Second Edition.* 2s.

A GUIDE TO PROFESSIONS AND BUSINESS. By H. Jones. 1s. 6d.

THE PRINCIPLES OF BOOK-KEEPING BY DOUBLE ENTRY. By J. E. B. M'Allen, M.A. 2s.

COMMERCIAL LAW. By W. Douglas Edwards. 2s.

Connoisseurs Library, The
Wide Royal 8vo. 25s. *net.*

Also a limited edition on Japanese vellum, with the photogravures on India paper. £7, 7s. *net.*

The first volumes will be—

MEZZOTINTS. By Cyril Davenport.
MINIATURES. By Dudley Heath.

PORCELAIN. By Edward Dillon.

Devotion, The Library of
With Introductions and (where necessary) Notes.
Small Pott 8vo, cloth, 2s. ; *leather,* 2s. 6d. *net.*

THE CONFESSIONS OF ST. AUGUSTINE. Edited by C. Bigg, D.D. *Third Edition.*

THE CHRISTIAN YEAR. Edited by Walter Lock, D.D. *Second Edition.*

THE IMITATION OF CHRIST. Edited by C. Bigg, D.D. *Second Edition.*

A BOOK OF DEVOTIONS. Edited by J. W. Stanbridge, B.D.

LYRA INNOCENTIUM. Edited by Walter Lock, D.D.

A SERIOUS CALL TO A DEVOUT AND HOLY LIFE. Edited by C. Bigg, D.D. *Second Edition.*

THE TEMPLE. Edited by E. C. S. Gibson, D.D.

A GUIDE TO ETERNITY. Edited by J. W. Stanbridge, B.D.

THE PSALMS OF DAVID. Edited by B. W. Randolph, D.D.

LYRA APOSTOLICA. Edited by Canon Scott Holland and Canon H. C. Beeching, M.A.

THE INNER WAY. Edited by A. W. Hutton, M.A.

THE THOUGHTS OF PASCAL. Edited by C. S. Jerram, M.A.

ON THE LOVE OF GOD. By St. Francis de Sales Edited by W. J. Knox-Little, M.A.

A MANUAL OF CONSOLATION FROM THE SAINTS AND FATHERS. Edited by J. H. Burn, B.D

THE SONG OF SONGS. Edited by B. Blaxland, M.A.

THE DEVOTIONS OF ST. ANSELM. Edited by C. C. J. Webb, M.A.

GRACE ABOUNDING. By John Bunyan. Edited by S. C. Freer, M.A.

BISHOP WILSON'S SACRA PRIVATA. Edited by A. E. Burn, B.D.

LYRA SACRA : A Book of Sacred Verse. Edited by H. C. Beeching, M.A., Canon of Westminster.

A DAY BOOK FROM THE SAINTS AND FATHERS. Edited by J. H. BURN, B.D.

HEAVENLY WISDOM. A Selection from the English Mystics. Edited by E. C. Gregory.

LIGHT, LIFE, AND LOVE. A Selection from the German Mystics. Edited by W. R. Inge, M.A.

Illustrated Pocket Library of Plain and Coloured Books, The
Fcap. 8vo. 3s. 6d. *net to* 4s. 6d. *net each volume.*

A series, in small form, of some of the famous illustrated books of fiction and general literature. These are faithfully reprinted from the first or best editions without introduction or notes.

COLOURED BOOKS

THE LIFE AND DEATH OF JOHN MYTTON, ESQ. By Nimrod. With 18 Coloured Plates by Henry Alken and T. J. Rawlins. *Third Edition.* 3s. 6d. *net.* Also a limited edition on large Japanese paper. 30s. *net.*

THE LIFE OF A SPORTSMAN. By Nimrod. With 35 Coloured Plates by Henry Alken. 4s. 6d. *net.* Also a limited edition on large Japanese paper. 30s. *net.*

HANDLEY CROSS, By R. S. Surtees. With 17 Coloured Plates and 100 Woodcuts in the Text by John Leech. 4s. 6d. *net.* Also a limited edition on large Japanese paper. 30s. *net.*

MR. SPONGE'S SPORTING TOUR. By R. S. Surtees. With 13 Coloured Plates and 90 Woodcuts in the Text by John Leech. 3s. 6d. *net.* Also a limited edition on large Japanese paper. 30s. *net.*

JORROCKS' JAUNTS AND JOLLITIES. By R. S. Surtees. With 15 Coloured Plates by H. Alken. 3s. 6d. *net.* Also a limited edition on large Japanese paper. 30s. *net.* This volume is reprinted from the extremely rare and costly edition of 1843, which contains Alken's very fine illustrations instead of the usual ones by Phiz.

Continued.

THE ILLUSTRATED POCKET LIBRARY—continued.

ASK MAMMA. By R. S. Surtees. With 13 Coloured Plates and 70 Woodcuts in the Text by John Leech. 3s. 6d. net.
Also a limited edition on large Japanese paper. 30s. net.

THE ANALYSIS OF THE HUNTING FIELD. By R. S. Surtees. With 7 Coloured Plates by Henry Alken, and 43 Illustrations on Wood. 3s. 6d. net.

THE TOUR OF DR. SYNTAX IN SEARCH OF THE PICTURESQUE. By William Combe. With 30 Coloured Plates by T. Rowlandson. 3s. 6d. net.
Also a limited edition on large Japanese paper. 30s. net.

THE TOUR OF DOCTOR SYNTAX IN SEARCH OF CONSOLATION. By William Combe. With 24 Coloured Plates by T. Rowlandson. 3s. 6d. net.
Also a limited edition on large Japanese paper. 30s. net.

THE THIRD TOUR OF DOCTOR SYNTAX IN SEARCH OF A WIFE. By William Combe. With 24 Coloured Plates by T. Rowlandson. 3s. 6d. net.
Also a limited edition on large Japanese paper. 30s. net.

THE HISTORY OF JOHNNY QUAE GENUS: the Little Foundling of the late Dr. Syntax. By the Author of 'The Three Tours.' With 24 Coloured Plates by Rowlandson. 3s. 6d. net. 100 copies on large Japanese paper. 21s. net.
Also a limited edition on large Japanese paper. 30s. net.

THE ENGLISH DANCE OF DEATH, from the Designs of T. Rowlandson, with Metrical Illustrations by the Author of 'Doctor Syntax.' Two Volumes. 9s. net.
This book contains 76 Coloured Plates.
Also a limited edition on large Japanese paper. 30s. net.

THE DANCE OF LIFE: A Poem. By the Author of 'Doctor Syntax.' Illustrated with 26 Coloured Engravings by T. Rowlandson. 3s. 6d. net.
Also a limited edition on large Japanese paper. 30s. net.

LIFE IN LONDON: or, the Day and Night Scenes of Jerry Hawthorn, Esq., and his Elegant Friend, Corinthian Tom. By Pierce Egan. With 36 Coloured Plates by I. R. and G. Cruikshank. With numerous Designs on Wood. 3s. 6d. net.
Also a limited edition on large Japanese paper. 30s. net.

REAL LIFE IN LONDON: or, the Rambles and Adventures of Bob Tallyho, Esq., and his Cousin, The Hon. Tom Dashall. By an Amateur (Pierce Egan). With 31 Coloured Plates by Alken and Rowlandson, etc. Two Volumes. 9s. net.

THE LIFE OF AN ACTOR. By Pierce Egan. With 27 Coloured Plates by Theodore Lane, and several Designs on Wood. 4s. 6d. net.

THE VICAR OF WAKEFIELD. By Oliver Goldsmith. With 24 Coloured Plates by T. Rowlandson. 3s. 6d. net.
Also a limited edition on large Japanese paper. 30s. net.
A reproduction of a very rare book.

THE MILITARY ADVENTURES OF JOHNNY NEWCOME. By an Officer. With 15 Coloured Plates by T. Rowlandson. 3s. 6d. net.

THE NATIONAL SPORTS OF GREAT BRITAIN. With Descriptions and 51 Coloured Plates by Henry Alken. 4s. 6d. net.
Also a limited edition on large Japanese paper. 30s. net.
This book is completely different from the large folio edition of 'National Sports' by the same artist, and none of the plates are similar.

PLAIN BOOKS

THE GRAVE: A Poem. By Robert Blair. Illustrated by 12 Etchings executed by Louis Schiavonetti from the Original Inventions of William Blake. With an Engraved Title Page and a Portrait of Blake by T. Phillips, R.A. 3s. 6d. net.
The Illustrations are reproduced in photogravure. Also a limited edition on large Japanese paper, with India proofs and a duplicate set of the plates. 15s. net.

ILLUSTRATIONS OF THE BOOK OF JOB. Invented and engraved by William Blake. 3s. 6d. net.
These famous Illustrations—21 in number—are reproduced in photogravure. Also a limited edition on large Japanese paper, with India proofs and a duplicate set of the plates. 15s. net.

ÆSOP'S FABLES. With 380 Woodcuts by Thomas Bewick. 3s. 6d. net.

WINDSOR CASTLE. By W. Harrison Ainsworth. With 22 Plates and 87 Woodcuts in the Text by George Cruikshank. 3s. 6d. net.

THE TOWER OF LONDON. By W. Harrison Ainsworth. With 40 Plates and 58 Woodcuts in the Text by George Cruikshank. 3s. 6d. net.

FRANK FAIRLEGH. By F. E. Smedley. With 30 Plates by George Cruikshank. 3s. 6d. net.

HANDY ANDY. By Samuel Lover. With 24 Illustrations by the Author. 3s. 6d. net.

THE COMPLEAT ANGLER. By Izaak Walton and Charles Cotton. With 14 Plates and 77 Woodcuts in the Text. 3s. 6d. net.
This volume is reproduced from the beautiful edition of John Major of 1824.

THE PICKWICK PAPERS. By Charles Dickens. With the 43 Illustrations by Seymour and Phiz, the two Buss Plates, and the 32 Contemporary Onwhyn Plates. 3s. 6d. net.

Junior Examination Series
Edited by A. M. M. STEDMAN, M.A.   Fcap. 8vo.   1s.

JUNIOR FRENCH EXAMINATION PAPERS. By F. Jacob, B.A.

JUNIOR LATIN EXAMINATION PAPERS. Second Edition. By C. G. Botting, M.A.

JUNIOR ENGLISH EXAMINATION PAPERS. By W. Williamson, B.A.

JUNIOR ARITHMETIC EXAMINATION PAPERS. By W. S. Beard. Second Edition.

JUNIOR ALGEBRA EXAMINATION PAPERS. By W. S. Finn, M.A.

JUNIOR GREEK EXAMINATION PAPERS. By T. C. Weatherhead, M.A.

JUNIOR GENERAL INFORMATION EXAMINATION PAPERS. By W. S. Beard.

JUNIOR GEOGRAPHY EXAMINATION PAPERS. By W. G. Baker, M.A.

JUNIOR GERMAN EXAMINATION PAPERS. By A. Voegelin, M.A.

Junior School-Books, Methuen's
Edited by O. D. INSKIP, LL.D., and W. WILLIAMSON, B.A.

A CLASS-BOOK OF DICTATION PASSAGES. By W. Williamson, B.A. Eighth Edition. Crown 8vo. 1s. 6d.

THE GOSPEL ACCORDING TO ST. MATTHEW. Edited by E. Wilton South, M.A. Crown 8vo. 1s. 6d.

Continued.

METHUEN'S JUNIOR SCHOOL-BOOKS—*continued.*

THE GOSPEL ACCORDING TO ST. MARK. Edited by A. E. Rubie, M.A., Headmaster of College, Eltham. With Three Maps. *Crown 8vo.* 1s. 6d.

A JUNIOR ENGLISH GRAMMAR. By W. Williamson, B.A. With numerous passages for parsing and analysis, and a chapter on Essay Writing. *Crown 8vo.* 2s.

A JUNIOR CHEMISTRY. By E. A. Tyler, B.A., F.C.S., Science Master at Swansea Grammar School. With 73 Illustrations. *Crown 8vo.* 2s. 6d.

THE ACTS OF THE APOSTLES. Edited by A. E. Rubie, M.A., Headmaster of College, Eltham. *Crown 8vo.* 2s.

A JUNIOR FRENCH GRAMMAR. By L. A. Sornet and M. J. Acatos, Modern Language Masters at King Edward's School, Birmingham. *Cr. 8vo.* 2s.

ELEMENTARY EXPERIMENTAL SCIENCE. PHYSICS by W. T. Clough, A.R.C.S. CHEMISTRY by A. E. Dunstan, B.Sc. With numerous Diagrams. *Crown 8vo.* 2s.

A JUNIOR GEOMETRY. By Noel S. Lydon. With numerous Diagrams. *Crown 8vo.* 2s.

Leaders of Religion

Edited by H. C. BEECHING, M.A. *With Portraits. Crown 8vo.* 3s. 6d.

A series of short biographies of the most prominent leaders of religious life and thought of all ages and countries.

CARDINAL NEWMAN. By R. H. Hutton.
JOHN WESLEY. By J. H. Overton, M.A.
BISHOP WILBERFORCE. By G. W. Daniell, M.A.
CARDINAL MANNING. By A. W. Hutton, M.A.
CHARLES SIMEON. By H. C. G. Moule, D.D.
JOHN KEBLE. By Walter Lock, D.D.
THOMAS CHALMERS. By Mrs. Oliphant.
LANCELOT ANDREWES. By R. L. Ottley, M.A.
AUGUSTINE OF CANTERBURY. By E. L. Cutts, D.D.
WILLIAM LAUD. By W. H. Hutton, M.A.

JOHN KNOX. By F. MacCunn.
JOHN HOWE. By R. F. Horton, D.D.
BISHOP KEN. By F. A. Clarke, M.A.
GEORGE FOX, THE QUAKER. By T. Hodgkin, D.C.L.
JOHN DONNE. By Augustus Jessopp, D.D.
THOMAS CRANMER. By A. J. Mason.
BISHOP LATIMER. By R. M. Carlyle and A. J. Carlyle, M.A.
BISHOP BUTLER. By W. A. Spooner, M.A.

Little Biographies

Fcap. 8vo. Each volume, cloth, 3s. 6d. ; leather, 4s. net.

DANTE ALIGHIERI. By Paget Toynbee, M.A., D.Litt. With 12 Illustrations. *Second Edition.*
SAVONAROLA. By E. L. S. Horsburgh, M.A. With 12 Illustrations. *Second Edition.*
JOHN HOWARD. By E. C. S. Gibson, D.D., Vicar of Leeds. With 12 Illustrations.
TENNYSON. By A. C. Benson, M.A. With 9 Illustrations.
WALTER RALEIGH. By J. A. Taylor. With 12 Illustrations.
ERASMUS. By E. F. H. Capey. With 12 Illustrations.

THE YOUNG PRETENDER. By C. S. Terry. With 12 Illustrations.
ROBERT BURNS. By T. F. Henderson. With 12 Illustrations.
CHATHAM. By A. S. M'Dowall. With 12 Illustrations.
ST. FRANCIS OF ASSISI. By Anna M. Stoddart. With 16 Illustrations.
CANNING. By W. A. Phillips. With 12 Illustrations.
BEACONSFIELD. By Walter Sichel. With 12 Illustrations.
GOETHE. By H. G. Atkins. With 12 Illustrations.

Little Blue Books, The

General Editor, E. V. LUCAS.

Illustrated. Demy 16mo. 2s. 6d.

1. THE CASTAWAYS OF MEADOWBANK. By T. Cobb.
2. THE BEECHNUT BOOK. By Jacob Abbott. Edited by E. V. Lucas.
3. THE AIR GUN. By T. Hilbert.
4. A SCHOOL YEAR. By Netta Syrett.
5. THE PEELES AT THE CAPITAL. By Roger Ashton.
6. THE TREASURE OF PRINCEGATE PRIORY. By T. Cobb.
7. MRS. BARBERRY'S GENERAL SHOP. By Roger Ashton.
8. A BOOK OF BAD CHILDREN. By W. T. Webb.
9. THE LOST BALL. By Thomas Cobb.

Little Books on Art

Demy 16mo. 2s. 6d. net.

GREEK ART. H. B. Walters.
BOOKPLATES. E. Almack.
MINIATURES. Alice Corkran.
REYNOLDS. J. Sime.
ROMNEY. George Paston.
WATTS. Miss R. E. D. Sketchley.

LEIGHTON. Alice Corkran.
VELASQUEZ. Wilfrid Wilberforce and A. R. Gilbert.
GREUZE AND BOUCHER. Eliza F. Pollard.
VANDYCK. M. G. Smallwood.
TURNER. F. Tyrell-Gill.
DURER. Jessie Allen.

Little Galleries, The

Demy 16mo.   2s. 6d. net.

A LITTLE GALLERY OF REYNOLDS.
A LITTLE GALLERY OF ROMNEY.

A LITTLE GALLERY OF HOPPNER.
A LITTLE GALLERY OF MILLAIS.

Little Guides, The

Small Pott 8vo, cloth, 3s.; leather, 3s. 6d. net.

OXFORD AND ITS COLLEGES. By J. Wells, M.A. Illustrated by E. H. New. *Fourth Edition.*
CAMBRIDGE AND ITS COLLEGES. By A. Hamilton Thompson. Illustrated by E. H. New.
THE MALVERN COUNTRY. By B. C. A. Windle, D.Sc., F.R.S. Illustrated by E. H. New.
SHAKESPEARE'S COUNTRY. By B. C. A. Windle, D.Sc., F.R.S. Illustrated by E. H. New. *Second Edition.*
SUSSEX. By F. G. Brabant, M.A. Illustrated by E. H. New.
WESTMINSTER ABBEY. By G. E. Troutbeck. Illustrated by F. D. Bedford.
NORFOLK. By W. A. Dutt. Illustrated by B. C. Boulter.
CORNWALL. By A. L. Salmon. Illustrated by B. C. Boulter.
BRITTANY. By S. Baring-Gould. Illustrated by J. Wylie.

THE ENGLISH LAKES. By F. G. Brabant, M.A. Illustrated by E. H. New. 4s.; leather, 4s. 6d. net.
KENT. By G. Clinch. Illustrated by F. D. Bedford.
HERTFORDSHIRE. By H. W. Tompkins, F.R.H.S. Illustrated by E. H. New.
ROME. By C. G. Ellaby. Illustrated by B. C. Boulter.
THE ISLE OF WIGHT. By G. Clinch. Illustrated by F. D. Bedford.
SURREY. By F. A. H. Lambert. Illustrated by E. H. New.
BUCKINGHAMSHIRE. By E. S. Roscoe. Illustrated by F. D. Bedford.
SUFFOLK. By W. A. Dutt. Illustrated by J. Wylie.
DERBYSHIRE. By J. Charles Cox, LL.D., F.S.A. Illustrated by J. C. Wall.
THE NORTH RIDING OF YORKSHIRE. By J. E. Morris. Illustrated by R. J. S. Bertram.

Little Library, The

With Introductions, Notes, and Photogravure Frontispieces.

Small Pott 8vo.   Each Volume, cloth, 1s. 6d. net ; leather, 2s. 6d. net.

VANITY FAIR. By W. M. Thackeray. Edited by S. Gwynn. *Three Volumes.*
PENDENNIS. By W. M. Thackeray. Edited by S. Gwynn. *Three Volumes.*
ESMOND. By W. M. Thackeray. Edited by S. Gwynn.
CHRISTMAS BOOKS. By W. M. Thackeray. Edited by S. Gwynn.
CHRISTMAS BOOKS. By Charles Dickens. Edited by S. Gwynn. *Two Volumes.*
SELECTIONS FROM GEORGE CRABBE. Edited by A. C. Deane.
JOHN HALIFAX, GENTLEMAN. By Mrs. Craik. Edited by Annie Matheson. *Two Volumes.*
PRIDE AND PREJUDICE. By Jane Austen. Edited by E. V. Lucas. *Two Volumes.*
NORTHANGER ABBEY. By Jane Austen. Edited by E. V. Lucas.
THE PRINCESS. By Alfred, Lord Tennyson. Edited by Elizabeth Wordsworth.
MAUD. By Alfred, Lord Tennyson. Edited by Elizabeth Wordsworth.
IN MEMORIAM. By Alfred, Lord Tennyson. Edited by H. C. Beeching, M.A.
THE EARLY POEMS OF ALFRED, LORD TENNYSON. Edited by J. C. Collins, M.A.
A LITTLE BOOK OF ENGLISH LYRICS. With Notes.
THE INFERNO OF DANTE. Translated by H. F. Cary. Edited by Paget Toynbee, M.A., D.Litt.
THE PURGATORIO OF DANTE. Translated by H. F. Cary. Edited by Paget Toynbee, M.A., D.Litt.
THE PARADISO OF DANTE. Translated by H. F. Cary. Edited by Paget Toynbee, M.A., D.Litt.
A LITTLE BOOK OF SCOTTISH VERSE. Edited by T. F. Henderson.
A LITTLE BOOK OF LIGHT VERSE. Edited by A. C. Deane.
A LITTLE BOOK OF ENGLISH SONNETS. Edited by J. B. B. Nichols.

POEMS. By John Keats. With an Introduction by L. Binyon, and Notes by J. Masefield. A complete Edition.
THE MINOR POEMS OF JOHN MILTON. Edited by H. C. Beeching, M.A.
THE POEMS OF HENRY VAUGHAN. Edited by Edward Hutton.
SELECTIONS FROM WORDSWORTH. Edited by Nowell C. Smith.
SELECTIONS FROM THE EARLY POEMS OF ROBERT BROWNING. Edited by W. Hall Griffin, M.A.
THE ENGLISH POEMS OF RICHARD CRASHAW. Edited by Edward Hutton.
SELECTIONS FROM WILLIAM BLAKE. Edited by M. Perugini.
SELECTIONS FROM THE POEMS OF GEORGE DARLEY. Edited by R. A. Streatfeild.
LYRICAL BALLADS. By W. Wordsworth and S. T. Coleridge. Edited by George Sampson.
SELECTIONS FROM LONGFELLOW. Edited by Lilian M. Faithfull.
SELECTIONS FROM THE ANTI-JACOBIN; with George Canning's additional Poems. Edited by Lloyd Sanders.
THE POEMS OF ANDREW MARVELL. Edited by Edward Wright.
A LITTLE BOOK OF LIFE AND DEATH. Edited by Mrs. Alfred Waterhouse. *Fourth Edition.*
A LITTLE BOOK OF ENGLISH PROSE. Edited by Mrs. P. A. Barnett.
EOTHEN. By A. W. Kinglake. With an Introduction and Notes.
CRANFORD. By Mrs. Gaskell. Edited by E. V. Lucas.
LAVENGRO. By George Borrow. Edited by F. Hindes Groome. *Two Volumes.*
THE ROMANY RYE. By George Borrow. Edited John Sampson.
THE HISTORY OF THE CALIPH VATHEK. By William Beckford. Edited by E. Denison Ross.

[Continued.

THE LITTLE LIBRARY—*continued*.

THE COMPLEAT ANGLER. By Izaak Walton. Edited by J. Buchan.

MARRIAGE. By Susan Ferrier. Edited by Miss Goodrich-Freer and Lord Iddesleigh. *Two Volumes.*

THE INHERITANCE. By Susan Ferrier. Edited by Miss Goodrich-Freer and Lord Iddesleigh. *Two Volumes.*

ELIA, AND THE LAST ESSAYS OF ELIA. By Charles Lamb. Edited by E. V. Lucas.

THE ESSAYS OF ABRAHAM COWLEY. Edited by H. C. Minchin.

THE ESSAYS OF FRANCIS BACON. Edited by Edward Wright.

THE MAXIMS OF LA ROCHEFOUCAULD. Translated by Dean Stanhope. Edited by G. H. Powell.

A SENTIMENTAL JOURNEY. By Laurence Sterne. Edited by H. W. Paul.

MANSIE WAUCH. By D. M. Moir. Edited by T. F. Henderson.

THE INGOLDSBY LEGENDS. By R. H. Barham. Edited by J. B. Atlay. *Two Volumes.*

THE SCARLET LETTER. By Nathaniel Hawthorne. Edited by P. Dearmer.

REJECTED ADDRESSES. By Horace and James Smith. Edited by A. D. Godley, M.A.

LONDON LYRICS. By F. Locker. Edited by A. D. Godley, M.A. A reprint of the First Edition.

Miniature Library, Methuen's

EUPHRANOR: a Dialogue on Youth. By Edward FitzGerald. From the edition published by W. Pickering in 1851. *Leather, 2s. net.*

POLONIUS: or Wise Saws and Modern Instances. By Edward FitzGerald. From the edition published by W. Pickering in 1852. *Leather, 2s. net.*

THE RUBAIYAT OF OMAR KHAYYAM. By Edward FitzGerald. From the 1st edition of 1859. *Leather, 1s. net.*

THE LIFE OF EDWARD, LORD HERBERT OF CHERBURY. Written by himself. From the edition printed at Strawberry Hill in the year 1764. *Leather, 2s. net.*

THE VISIONS OF DOM FRANCISCO DE QUEVEDO VILLEGAS, Knight of the Order of St. James.

Made English by R. L. From the edition printed for H. Herringman, 1668. *Leather, 2s. net.*

POEMS. By Dora Greenwell. From the edition of 1848. *Leather, 2s. net.*

A book called in Latin ENCHIRIDION MILITIS CHRISTIANI, and in English the manual of the Christian Knight, replenished with most wholesome precepts, made by the famous clerk Erasmus of Roterdame, to the which is added a new and marvellous profitable preface. From the edition printed by Wynken de Worde for John Byddell, 1533. *Leather 2s. net.*

DE CONTEMPTU MUNDI. By Erasmus. From the edition printed by Thomas Berthelet, 1533. *Leather, 2s. net.*

Rariora

ADONAIS; an Elegy on the death of John Keats, Author of Endymion, etc. Pisa. From the types of Didot, 1821. *2s. net.*

FRAGMENTA AUREA: a Collection of all the Incomparable Peeces, written by Sir John Suckling. And published by a friend to perpetuate his memory. Printed by his own copies. Printed for Humphrey Moseley, and are to be sold at his shop, at the sign of the Princes Arms in St. Pauls Churchyard, 1646. *6s. net.*

POEMS OF MR. JOHN MILTON, BOTH ENGLISH AND LATIN Compos'd at several times. Printed by his true Copies. The Songs were set in Musick by Mr. Henry Lawes, Gentleman of the King's Chappel, and one of His Majesty's Private Musick. Printed and Publish'd according to Order. Printed by Ruth Raworth for Humphrey Moseley, and are to be sold at the signe of the Princes Arms in Pauls Churchyard, 1645. *3s. 6d. net.*

School Examination Series

Edited by A. M. M. STEDMAN, M.A. *Crown 8vo.* *2s. 6d.*

FRENCH EXAMINATION PAPERS. By A. M. M. Stedman, M.A. *Twelfth Edition.*

A KEY, issued to Tutors and Private Students only, to be had on application to the Publishers. *Fifth Edition. Crown 8vo. 6s. net.*

LATIN EXAMINATION PAPERS. By A. M. M. Stedman, M.A. *Twelfth Edition.*

KEY (*Fourth Edition*) issued as above. *6s. net.*

GREEK EXAMINATION PAPERS. By A. M. M. Stedman, M.A. *Seventh Edition.*

KEY (*Second Edition*) issued as above. *6s. net.*

GERMAN EXAMINATION PAPERS. By R. J. Morich. *Fifth Edition.*

KEY (*Second Edition*) issued as above. *6s. net.*

HISTORY AND GEOGRAPHY EXAMINATION PAPERS. By C. H. Spence, M.A., Clifton College. *Second Edition.*

PHYSICS EXAMINATION PAPERS. By R. E. Steel, M.A., F.C.S.

GENERAL KNOWLEDGE EXAMINATION PAPERS. By A. M. M. Stedman, M.A. *Fourth Edition.*

KEY (*Third Edition*) issued as above. *7s. net.*

EXAMINATION PAPERS IN ENGLISH HISTORY. By J. Tait Plowden-Wardlaw, B.A.

Social Questions of To-day

Edited by H. DE B. GIBBINS, Litt.D., M.A.

Crown 8vo. *2s. 6d.*

TRADE UNIONISM—NEW AND OLD. By G. Howell. *Third Edition.*

THE CO-OPERATIVE MOVEMENT TO-DAY. By G. J. Holyoake. *Second Edition.*

PROBLEMS OF POVERTY. By J. A. Hobson, M.A. *Fourth Edition.*

THE COMMERCE OF NATIONS. By C. F. Bastable, M.A. *Third Edition.*

THE ALIEN INVASION. By W. H. Wilkins, B.A.

THE RURAL EXODUS. By P. Anderson Graham.

LAND NATIONALIZATION. By Harold Cox, B.A.

A SHORTER WORKING DAY. By H. de B. Gibbins and R. A. Hadfield.

BACK TO THE LAND: An Inquiry into Rural Depopulation. By H. E. Moore.

Continued.

SOCIAL QUESTIONS OF TO-DAY—*continued.*

TRUSTS, POOLS, AND CORNERS. By J. Stephen Jeans.

THE FACTORY SYSTEM. By R. W. Cooke-Taylor.

THE STATE AND ITS CHILDREN. By Gertrude Tuckwell.

WOMEN'S WORK. By Lady Dilke, Miss Bulley, and Miss Whitley.

SOCIALISM AND MODERN THOUGHT. By M. Kauffmann.

THE HOUSING OF THE WORKING CLASSES. By E. Bowmaker.

THE PROBLEM OF THE UNEMPLOYED. By J. A. Hobson, M.A.

LIFE IN WEST LONDON. By Arthur Sherwell, M.A. *Third Edition.*

RAILWAY NATIONALIZATION. By Clement Edwards.

WORKHOUSES AND PAUPERISM. By Louisa Twining.

UNIVERSITY AND SOCIAL SETTLEMENTS. By W. Reason, M.A.

Technology, Textbooks of
Edited by PROFESSOR J. WERTHEIMER, F.I.C.
Fully Illustrated.

HOW TO MAKE A DRESS. By J. A. E. Wood. *Second Edition. Crown 8vo. 1s. 6d.*

CARPENTRY AND JOINERY. By F. C. Webber. *Third Edition. Crown 8vo. 3s. 6d.*

PRACTICAL MECHANICS. By Sidney H. Wells. *Second Edition. Crown 8vo. 3s. 6d.*

PRACTICAL PHYSICS. By H. Stroud, D.Sc., M.A. *Crown 8vo. 3s. 6d.*

MILLINERY, THEORETICAL AND PRACTICAL. By Clare Hill. *Crown 8vo. 2s.*

PRACTICAL CHEMISTRY. By W. French, M.A. *Crown 8vo. Part I. Second Edition. 1s. 6d.* Part II.

TECHNICAL ARITHMETIC AND GEOMETRY. By C. T. Millis, M.I.M.E. With Diagrams. *Crown 8vo. 3s. 6d.*

Theology, Handbooks of

THE XXXIX. ARTICLES OF THE CHURCH OF ENGLAND. Edited by E. C. S. Gibson, D.D. *Third and Cheaper Edition in One Volume. Demy 8vo. 12s. 6d.*

AN INTRODUCTION TO THE HISTORY OF RELIGION. By F. B. Jevons, M.A., Litt.D. *Second Edition. Demy 8vo. 10s. 6d.*

THE DOCTRINE OF THE INCARNATION. By R. L. Ottley, M.A. *Second and Cheaper Edition. Demy 8vo. 12s. 6d.*

AN INTRODUCTION TO THE HISTORY OF THE CREEDS. By A. E. Burn, B.D. *Demy 8vo. 10s. 6d.*

THE PHILOSOPHY OF RELIGION IN ENGLAND AND AMERICA. By Alfred Caldecott, D.D. *Demy 8vo. 10s. 6d.*

A HISTORY OF EARLY CHRISTIAN DOCTRINE. By J. F. Bethune-Baker, M.A., Fellow of Pembroke College, Cambridge. *Demy 8vo. 10s. 6d.*

University Extension Series
Edited by J. E. SYMES, M.A.,
Principal of University College, Nottingham.
Crown 8vo. Price (with some exceptions) 2s. 6d.

A series of books on historical, literary, and scientific subjects, suitable for extension students and home-reading circles. Each volume is complete in itself, and the subjects are treated by competent writers in a broad and philosophic spirit.

THE INDUSTRIAL HISTORY OF ENGLAND. By H. de B. Gibbins, Litt.D., M.A. *Tenth Edition.* Revised. With Maps and Plans. *3s.*

A HISTORY OF ENGLISH POLITICAL ECONOMY. By L. L. Price, M.A. *Third Edition.*

VICTORIAN POETS. By A. Sharp.

THE FRENCH REVOLUTION. By J. E. Symes, M.A.

PSYCHOLOGY. By F. S. Granger, M.A. *Second Edition.*

THE EVOLUTION OF PLANT LIFE: Lower Forms. By G. Massee. Illustrated.

AIR AND WATER. By V. B. Lewes, M.A. Illustrated.

THE CHEMISTRY OF LIFE AND HEALTH. By C. W. Kimmins, M.A. Illustrated.

THE MECHANICS OF DAILY LIFE. By V. P. Sells, M.A. Illustrated.

ENGLISH SOCIAL REFORMERS. By H. de B. Gibbins, Litt.D., M.A. *Second Edition.*

ENGLISH TRADE AND FINANCE IN THE SEVENTEENTH CENTURY. By W. A. S. Hewins, B.A.

THE CHEMISTRY OF FIRE. By M. M. Pattison Muir, M.A. Illustrated.

A TEXT-BOOK OF AGRICULTURAL BOTANY. By M. C. Potter, M.A., F.L.S. Illustrated. *Second Edition. 4s. 6d.*

THE VAULT OF HEAVEN. A Popular Introduction to Astronomy. By R. A. Gregory. With numerous Illustrations.

METEOROLOGY. By H. N. Dickson, F.R.S.E., F.R. Met. Soc. Illustrated.

A MANUAL OF ELECTRICAL SCIENCE. By George J. Burch, M.A., F.R.S. Illustrated. *3s.*

THE EARTH. An Introduction to Physiography. By Evan Small, M.A. Illustrated.

INSECT LIFE. By F. W. Theobald, M.A. Illustrated.

ENGLISH POETRY FROM BLAKE TO BROWNING. By W. M. Dixon, M.A. *Second Edition.*

ENGLISH LOCAL GOVERNMENT. By E. Jenks, M.A.

THE GREEK VIEW OF LIFE. By G. L. Dickinson. *Third Edition.*

Westminster, Commentaries The
General Editor, WALTER LOCK, D.D., Warden of Keble College,
Dean Ireland's Professor of Exegesis in the University of Oxford.

THE BOOK OF GENESIS. Edited with Introduction and Notes by S. R. Driver, D.D., Canon of Christ Church, and Regius Professor of Hebrew at Oxford. *Demy 8vo. 10s. 6d.*

THE BOOK OF JOB. Edited by E. C. S. Gibson, D.D. *Demy 8vo. 6s.*

THE ACTS OF THE APOSTLES. Edited by R. B. Rackham, M.A. *Demy 8vo. 12s. 6d.*

THE FIRST EPISTLE OF PAUL THE APOSTLE TO THE CORINTHIANS. Edited by H. L. Goudge, M.A. *Demy 8vo. 6s.*

PART II.—FICTION

Marie Corelli's Novels.
Crown 8vo.   6s. each.

A ROMANCE OF TWO WORLDS. *Twenty-Fourth Edition.*

VENDETTA. *Nineteenth Edition.*

THELMA. *Twenty-Ninth Edition.*

ARDATH: THE STORY OF A DEAD SELF. *Fourteenth Edition.*

THE SOUL OF LILITH. *Twelfth Edit.*

WORMWOOD. *Thirteenth Edition.*

BARABBAS: A DREAM OF THE WORLD'S TRAGEDY. *Thirty-Ninth Edition.*

'The tender reverence of the treatment and the imaginative beauty of the writing have reconciled us to the daring of the conception. This "Dream of the World's Tragedy" is a lofty and not inadequate paraphrase of the supreme climax of the inspired narrative.'—*Dublin Review.*

THE SORROWS OF SATAN. *Forty-Sixth Edition.*

'A very powerful piece of work. . . . The conception is magnificent, and is likely to win an abiding place within the memory of man. . . . The author has immense command of language, and a limitless audacity. . . . This interesting and remarkable romance will live long after much of the ephemeral literature of the day is forgotten. . . . A literary phenomenon . . . novel, and even sublime.—W. T. STEAD in the *Review of Reviews.*

THE MASTER CHRISTIAN.

[*165th Thousand.*

'It cannot be denied that "The Master Christian" is a powerful book ; that it is one likely to raise uncomfortable questions in all but the most self-satisfied readers, and that it strikes at the root of the failure of the Churches—the decay of faith—in a manner which shows the inevitable disaster heaping up . . . The good Cardinal Bonpré is a beautiful figure, fit to stand beside the good Bishop in "Les Misérables." It is a book with a serious purpose expressed with absolute unconventionality and passion . . . And this is to say it is a book worth reading.'—*Examiner.*

TEMPORAL POWER: A STUDY IN SUPREMACY.   [*150th Thousand.*

'It is impossible to read such a work as "Temporal Power" without becoming convinced that the story is intended to convey certain criticisms on the ways of the world and certain suggestions for the betterment of humanity. . . . The chief characteristics of the book are an attack on conventional prejudices and manners and on certain practices attributed to the Roman Church and the propounding of theories for the improvement of the social and political systems. . . . If the chief intention of the book was to hold the mirror up to shams, injustice, dishonesty, cruelty, and neglect of conscience, nothing but praise can be given to that intention.'—*Morning Post.*

Anthony Hope's Novels.
Crown 8vo.   6s. each.

THE GOD IN THE CAR. *Ninth Edition.*

'A very remarkable book, deserving of critical analysis impossible within our limit ; brilliant, but not superficial ; well considered, but not elaborated ; constructed with the proverbial art that conceals, but yet allows itself to be enjoyed by readers to whom fine literary method is a keen pleasure.'—*The World.*

A CHANGE OF AIR. *Sixth Edition.*

'A graceful, vivacious comedy, true to human nature. The characters are traced with a masterly hand.'—*Times.*

A MAN OF MARK. *Fifth Edition.*

'Of all Mr. Hope's books, "A Man of Mark" is the one which best compares with "The Prisoner of Zenda."'—*National Observer.*

THE CHRONICLES OF COUNT ANTONIO. *Fifth Edition.*

'It is a perfectly enchanting story of love and chivalry, and pure romance. The Count is the most constant, desperate, and

modest and tender of lovers, a peerless gentleman, an intrepid fighter, a faithful friend, and a magnanimous foe.'—*Guardian.*

PHROSO. Illustrated by H. R. MILLAR. *Sixth Edition.*

'The tale is thoroughly fresh, quick with vitality, stirring the blood.'—*St. James's Gazette.*

SIMON DALE. Illustrated. *Sixth Edition.*

'There is searching analysis of human nature, with a most ingeniously constructed plot. Mr. Hope has drawn the contrasts of his women with marvellous subtlety and delicacy.'—*Times.*

THE KING'S MIRROR. *Fourth Edition.*

'In elegance, delicacy, and tact it ranks with the best of his novels, while in the wide range of its portraiture and the subtilty of its analysis it surpasses all his earlier ventures.'—*Spectator.*

QUISANTE. *Fourth Edition.*

'The book is notable for a very high literary quality, and an impress of power and mastery on every page.'—*Daily Chronicle.*

W. W. Jacobs' Novels

Crown 8vo. 3s. 6d. each.

MANY CARGOES. *Twenty-Seventh Edition.*
SEA URCHINS. *Tenth Edition.*
A MASTER OF CRAFT. Illustrated.
Sixth Edition.
    'Can be unreservedly recommended to
all who have not lost their appetite for
wholesome laughter.'—*Spectator.*
    'The best humorous book published for
many a day.'—*Black and White.*

LIGHT FREIGHTS. Illustrated. *Fourth
Edition.*
    'His wit and humour are perfectly irresis-
tible. Mr. Jacobs writes of skippers, and
mates, and seamen, and his crew are the
jolliest lot that ever sailed.'—*Daily News.*
    'Laughter in every page.'—*Daily Mail.*

Lucas Malet's Novels

Crown 8vo. 6s. each.

COLONEL ENDERBY'S WIFE. *Third
Edition.*
A COUNSEL OF PERFECTION. *New
Edition.*
LITTLE PETER. *Second Edition.* 3s. 6d.
THE WAGES OF SIN. *Fourteenth Edition.*
THE CARISSIMA. *Fourth Edition.*
THE GATELESS BARRIER. *Fourth
Edition.*
    'In "The Gateless Barrier" it is at once
evident that, whilst Lucas Malet has pre-
served her birthright of originality, the
artistry, the actual writing, is above even
the high level of the books that were born
before.'—*Westminster Gazette.*

THE HISTORY OF SIR RICHARD
CALMADY. *Seventh Edition.* A Limited
Edition in Two Volumes. *Crown 8vo.* 12s.
    'A picture finely and amply conceived.
In the strength and insight in which the
story has been conceived, in the wealth of
fancy and reflection bestowed upon its
execution, and in the moving sincerity of its
pathos throughout, "Sir Richard Calmady"
must rank as the great novel of a great
writer.'—*Literature.*
    'The ripest fruit of Lucas Malet's genius.
A picture of maternal love by turns tender
and terrible.'—*Spectator.*
    'A remarkably fine book, with a noble
motive and a sound conclusion.'—*Pilot.*

Gilbert Parker's Novels

Crown 8vo. 6s. each.

PIERRE AND HIS PEOPLE. *Fifth Edi-
tion.*
    'Stories happily conceived and finely ex-
ecuted. There is strength and genius in
Mr. Parker's style.'—*Daily Telegraph.*
MRS. FALCHION. *Fourth Edition.*
    'A splendid study of character.'—
                     '*Athenæum.*
THE TRANSLATION OF A SAVAGE.
Second Edition.
THE TRAIL OF THE SWORD. Illus-
trated. *Eighth Edition.*
    'A rousing and dramatic tale. A book
like this is a joy inexpressible.'—
                    Daily Chronicle.
WHEN VALMOND CAME TO PONTIAC:
The Story of a Lost Napoleon. *Fifth
Edition.*
    'Here we find romance—real, breathing,
living romance. The character of Valmond
is drawn unerringly.'—*Pall Mall Gazette.*

AN ADVENTURER OF THE NORTH:
The Last Adventures of 'Pretty Pierre.'
Third Edition.
    'The present book is full of fine and mov-
ing stories of the great North.'—*Glasgow
Herald.*
THE SEATS OF THE MIGHTY. Illus-
trated. *Thirteenth Edition.*
    'Mr. Parker has produced a really fine
historical novel.'—*Athenæum.*
    'A great book.'—*Black and White.*
THE BATTLE OF THE STRONG: a
Romance of Two Kingdoms. Illustrated.
Fourth Edition.
    'Nothing more vigorous or more human
has come from Mr. Gilbert Parker than this
novel.'—*Literature.*
THE POMP OF THE LAVILETTES.
Second Edition. 3s. 6d.
    'Unforced pathos, and a deeper know-
ledge of human nature than he has displayed
before.'—*Pall Mall Gazette.*

Arthur Morrison's Novels
Crown 8vo. 6s. each.

TALES OF MEAN STREETS. *Sixth Edition.*

'A great book. The author's method is amazingly effective, and produces a thrilling sense of reality. The writer lays upon us a master hand. The book is simply appalling and irresistible in its interest. It is humorous also; without humour it would not make the mark it is certain to make.'—*World.*

A CHILD OF THE JAGO. *Fourth Edition.*

'The book is a masterpiece.'—*Pall Mall Gazette.*

TO LONDON TOWN. *Second Edition.*

'This is the new Mr. Arthur Morrison, gracious and tender, sympathetic and human.'—*Daily Telegraph.*

CUNNING MURRELL.

'Admirable. . . . Delightful humorous relief . . . a most artistic and satisfactory achievement.'—*Spectator.*

THE HOLE IN THE WALL. *Third Edition.*

'A masterpiece of artistic realism. It has a finality of touch that only a master may command.'—*Daily Chronicle.*

'An absolute masterpiece, which any novelist might be proud to claim.'—*Graphic.*

'"The Hole in the Wall" is a masterly piece of work. His characters are drawn with amazing skill. Extraordinary power.'—*Daily Telegraph.*

Eden Phillpotts' Novels
Crown 8vo. 6s. each.

LYING PROPHETS.

CHILDREN OF THE MIST. *Fifth Edition.*

THE HUMAN BOY. With a Frontispiece. *Fourth Edition.*

'Mr. Phillpotts knows exactly what school-boys do, and can lay bare their inmost thoughts; likewise he shows an all-pervading sense of humour.'—*Academy.*

SONS OF THE MORNING. *Second Edition.*

'A book of strange power and fascination.'—*Morning Post.*

THE STRIKING HOURS. *Second Edition.*

'Tragedy and comedy, pathos and humour, are blended to a nicety in this volume.'—*World.*

'The whole book is redolent of a fresher and ampler air than breathes in the circumscribed life of great towns.'—*Spectator.*

FANCY FREE. Illustrated. *Second Edition.*

'Of variety and racy humour there is plenty.'—*Daily Graphic.*

THE RIVER. *Third Edition.*

'"The River" places Mr. Phillpotts in the front rank of living novelists.'—*Punch.*

'Since "Lorna Doone" we have had nothing so picturesque as this new romance.' *Birmingham Gazette.*

'Mr. Phillpotts's new book is a masterpiece which brings him indisputably into the front rank of English novelists.'—*Pall Mall Gazette.*

'This great romance of the River Dart. The finest book Mr. Eden Phillpotts has written.'—*Morning Post.*

THE AMERICAN PRISONER. *Second Edition.*

S. Baring-Gould's Novels
Crown 8vo. 6s. each.

ARMINELL. *Fifth Edition.*

URITH. *Fifth Edition.*

IN THE ROAR OF THE SEA. *Seventh Edition.*

MRS. CURGENVEN OF CURGENVEN. *Fourth Edition.*

CHEAP JACK ZITA. *Fourth Edition.*

THE QUEEN OF LOVE. *Fifth Edition.*

MARGERY OF QUETHER. *Third Edition.*

JACQUETTA. *Third Edition.*

KITTY ALONE. *Fifth Edition.*

NOÉMI. Illustrated. *Fourth Edition.*

THE BROOM-SQUIRE. Illustrated. *Fourth Edition.*

THE PENNYCOMEQUICKS. *Third Edition.*

DARTMOOR IDYLLS.

GUAVAS THE TINNER. Illustrated. *Second Edition.*

BLADYS. Illustrated. *Second Edition.*

DOMITIA. Illustrated. *Second Edition.*

PABO THE PRIEST.

WINIFRED. Illustrated. *Second Edition.*

THE FROBISHERS.

ROYAL GEORGIE. Illustrated

MISS QUILLET. Illustrated.

LITTLE TU'PENNY. *A New Edition.* 6d.

CHRIS OF ALL SORTS.

Robert Barr's Novels

Crown 8vo. 6s. each.

IN THE MIDST OF ALARMS. *Third Edition.*

'A book which has abundantly satisfied us by its capital humour.'—*Daily Chronicle.*

THE MUTABLE MANY. *Second Edition.*

'There is much insight in it, and much excellent humour.'—*Daily Chronicle.*

THE COUNTESS TEKLA. *Third Edition.*

'Of these mediæval romances, which are now gaining ground "The Countess Tekla" is the very best we have seen.'—*Pall Mall Gazette.*

THE STRONG ARM. Illustrated. *Second Edition.*

THE VICTORS.

'Mr. Barr has a rich sense of humour.'—*Onlooker.*

'A very convincing study of American life in its business and political aspects.'—*Pilot.*

'Good writing, illuminating sketches of character, and constant variety of scene and incident.'—*Times.*

THE LADY ELECTRA. [*Nearly Ready.*

Abbot (J. H. M.) Author of 'Tommy Cornstalk.' PLAIN AND VELDT. *Crown 8vo. 6s.*

Albanesi (E. Maria). SUSANNAH AND ONE OTHER. *Third Edition. Crown 8vo. 6s.*

Anstey (F.), Author of 'Vice Versâ. A BAYARD FROM BENGAL. Illustrated by BERNARD PARTRIDGE. *Third Edition. Crown 8vo. 3s. 6d.*

Bacheller (Irving), Author of 'Eben Holden.' DARREL OF THE BLESSED ISLES. *Third Edition. Crown 8vo. 6s.*

Bagot (Richard). A ROMAN MYSTERY. *Third Edition. Crown 8vo. 6s.*

Balfour (Andrew). BY STROKE OF SWORD. Illustrated. *Fourth Edition. Crown 8vo. 6s.*

VENGEANCE IS MINE. Illustrated. *Crown 8vo. 6s.*

See also Fleur de Lis Novels.

Balfour (M. C.). THE FALL OF THE SPARROW. *Crown 8vo. 6s.*

Baring-Gould (S.). See page 33.

Barlow (Jane). THE LAND OF THE SHAMROCK. *Crown 8vo. 6s.*

FROM THE EAST UNTO THE WEST. *Crown 8vo. 6s.*

THE FOUNDING OF FORTUNES. *Crown 8vo.*

See also Fleur de Lis Novels.

Barr (Robert). See page 34.

Barry (J. A.). IN THE GREAT DEEP. *Crown 8vo. 6s.*

Bartram (George), Author of 'The People of Clopton.' THE THIRTEEN EVENINGS. *Crown 8vo. 6s.*

Begbie (Harold). THE ADVENTURES OF SIR JOHN SPARROW. *Crown 8vo. 6s.*

Benson (E. F.). DODO: A Detail of the Day. *Crown 8vo. 6s.*

THE CAPSINA. *Crown 8vo. 6s.*

See also Fleur de Lis Novels.

Benson (Margaret). SUBJECT TO VANITY. *Crown 8vo. 3s. 6d.*

Besant (Sir Walter). A FIVE YEARS' TRYST, and Other Stories. *Crown 8vo. 6s.*

Bowles (G. Stewart). A STRETCH OFF THE LAND. *Crown 8vo. 6s.*

Brooke (Emma). THE POET'S CHILD. *Crown 8vo. 6s.*

Bullock (Shan. F.). THE SQUIREEN. *Crown 8vo. 6s.*

THE RED LEAGUERS. *Crown 8vo. 6s.*

Burton (J. Bloundelle). THE YEAR ONE: A Page of the French Revolution. Illustrated. *Crown 8vo. 6s.*

DENOUNCED. *Crown 8vo. 6s.*

THE CLASH OF ARMS. *Crown 8vo. 6s.*

ACROSS THE SALT SEAS. *Cr. 8vo. 6s.*

SERVANTS OF SIN. *Crown 8vo. 6s.*

THE FATE OF VALSEC. *Cr. 8vo. 6s.*

A BRANDED NAME. *Crown 8vo. 6s.*

See also Fleur de Lis Novels.

Cambridge (Ada). THE DEVASTATORS. *Crown 8vo. 6s.*

PATH AND GOAL. *Crown 8vo. 6s.*

Capes (Bernard), Author of 'The Lake of Wine.' PLOTS. *Crown 8vo. 6s.*

Chesney (Weatherby). JOHN TOPP, PIRATE. *Second Edition. Crown 8vo. 6s.*

THE FOUNDERED GALLEON. *Crown 8vo. 6s.*

THE BRANDED PRINCE. *Cr. 8vo. 6s.*

THE BAPTIST RING. *Crown 8vo. 6s.*

THE TRAGEDY OF THE GREAT EMERALD. *Crown 8vo. 6s.* [*Nearly Ready.*

Clifford (Mrs. W. K.). A WOMAN ALONE. *Crown 8vo. 3s. 6d.*

See also Fleur de Lis Novels.

Clifford (Hugh). A FREE LANCE OF TO-DAY. *Crown 8vo. 6s.*

Cobb (Thomas). A CHANGE OF FACE. *Crown 8vo. 6s.*

Cobban (J. Maclaren). THE KING OF ANDAMAN: A Saviour of Society. *Crown 8vo. 6s.*

WILT THOU HAVE THIS WOMAN? *Crown 8vo. 6s.*

THE ANGEL OF THE COVENANT. *Crown 8vo. 6s.*

Cooper (E. H.), Author of 'Mr. Blake of Newmarket.' A FOOL'S YEAR. *Crown 8vo. 6s.*

Corbett (Julian). A BUSINESS IN GREAT WATERS. *Crown 8vo. 6s.*

Corelli (Marie). See page 31.

Cornford (L. Cope). CAPTAIN JACOBUS: A Romance of the Road. *Cr. 8vo. 6s.*
See also Fleur de Lis Novels.

Crane (Stephen). WOUNDS IN THE RAIN. *Crown 8vo. 6s.*

Crockett (S. R.), Author of 'The Raiders,' etc. LOCHINVAR. Illustrated. *Second Edition. Crown 8vo. 6s.*
THE STANDARD BEARER. *Cr. 8vo. 6s.*

Croker (B. M.). ANGEL. *Third Edition. Crown 8vo. 6s.*
PEGGY OF THE BARTONS. *Cr. 8vo. 6s.*
A STATE SECRET. *Crown 8vo. 3s. 6d.*
JOHANNA. *Second Edition. Cr. 8vo. 6s.*

Dawlish (Hope). A SECRETARY OF LEGATION. *Crown 8vo. 6s.*

Denny (C. E.). THE ROMANCE OF UPFOLD MANOR. *Crown 8vo. 6s.*

Dickinson (Evelyn). A VICAR'S WIFE. *Crown 8vo. 6s.*
THE SIN OF ANGELS. *Crown 8vo. 3s. 6d.*

Dickson (Harris). THE BLACK WOLF'S BREED. Illustrated. *Second Edition. Crown 8vo. 6s.*

Doyle (A. Conan), Author of 'Sherlock Holmes,' 'The White Company,' etc. ROUND THE RED LAMP. *Ninth Edition. Crown 8vo. 6s.*

Duncan (Sara Jeannette) (Mrs. Everard Cotes), Author of 'A Voyage of Consolation.' THOSE DELIGHTFUL AMERICANS. Illustrated. *Third Edition. Crown 8vo. 6s.*
THE PATH OF A STAR. Illustrated. *Second Edition. Crown 8vo. 6s.*
THE POOL IN THE DESERT. *Crown 8vo. 6s.*
See also Fleur de Lis Novels.

Embree (C. F.). A HEART OF FLAME. *Crown 8vo. 6s.*

Fenn (G. Manville). AN ELECTRIC SPARK. *Crown 8vo. 6s.*
ELI'S CHILDREN. *Crown 8vo. 2s. 6d.*
A DOUBLE KNOT. *Crown 8vo. 2s. 6d.*
See also Fleur de Lis Novels.

Findlater (J. H.). THE GREEN GRAVES OF BALGOWRIE. *Fourth Edition. Crown 8vo. 6s.*
A DAUGHTER OF STRIFE. *Cr. 8vo. 6s.*
See also Fleur de Lis Novels.

Findlater (Mary). OVER THE HILLS. *Second Edition. Crown 8vo. 6s.*
BETTY MUSGRAVE. *Second Edition. Crown 8vo. 6s.*
A NARROW WAY. *Third Edition. Crown 8vo. 6s.*
THE ROSE OF JOY. *Second Edition. Crown 8vo. 6s.*

Fitzstephen (Gerald). MORE KIN THAN KIND. *Crown 8vo. 6s.*

Fletcher (J. S.). THE BUILDERS. *Crown 8vo. 6s.*
LUCIAN THE DREAMER. *Crown 8vo. 6s.*
DAVID MARCH. *Crown 8vo. 6s.*
See also Fleur de Lis Novels.

Forrest (R. E.). THE SWORD OF AZRAEL, a Chronicle of the Great Mutiny. *Crown 8vo. 6s.*

Francis (M. E.). MISS ERIN. *Second Edition. Crown 8vo. 6s.*

Gallon (Tom), Author of 'Kiddy.' RICKERBY'S FOLLY. *Crown 8vo. 6s.*

Gaunt (Mary). DEADMAN'S. *Crown 8vo. 6s.*
THE MOVING FINGER. *Crown 8vo. 3s. 6d.*
See also Fleur de Lis Novels.

Gerard (Dorothea), Author of 'Lady Baby.' THE MILLION. *Crown 8vo. 6s.*
THE CONQUEST OF LONDON. *Second Edition. Crown 8vo. 6s.*
THE SUPREME CRIME. *Cr. 8vo. 6s.*
HOLY MATRIMONY. *Second Edition. Crown 8vo. 6s.*
THINGS THAT HAVE HAPPENED. *Crown 8vo. 6s.*
MADE OF MONEY. *Crown 8vo. 6s.* [Nearly Ready.

Gilchrist (R. Murray). WILLOWBRAKE. *Crown 8vo. 6s.*

Gissing (Algernon). THE KEYS OF THE HOUSE. *Crown 8vo. 6s.*

Gissing (George), Author of 'Demos,' 'In the Year of Jubilee,' etc. THE TOWN TRAVELLER. *Second Edition. Crown 8vo. 6s.*
THE CROWN OF LIFE. *Crown 8vo. 6s.*

Glanville (Ernest). THE KLOOF BRIDE. *Crown 8vo. 3s. 6d.*
THE LOST REGIMENT. *Crown 8vo. 3s. 6d.*
THE DESPATCH RIDER. *Crown 8vo. 3s. 6d.*
THE INCA'S TREASURE. Illustrated. *Crown 8vo. 3s. 6d.*

Gleig (Charles). BUNTER'S CRUISE. Illustrated. *Crown 8vo. 3s. 6d.*

Gordon (Julien). MRS. CLYDE. *Crown 8vo. 6s.*
WORLD'S PEOPLE. *Crown 8vo. 6s.*

Gordon (S.). A HANDFUL OF EXOTICS. *Crown 8vo. 3s. 6d.*

Goss (C. F.). THE REDEMPTION OF DAVID CORSON. *Third Edition. Crown 8vo. 6s.*

Gray (E. M'Queen). ELSA. *Crown 8vo. 6s.*
MY STEWARDSHIP. *Crown 8vo. 2s. 6d.*

Hales (A. G.). JAIR THE APOSTATE. Illustrated. *Crown 8vo. 6s.*

Hamilton (Lord Ernest). MARY HAMILTON. *Third Edition. Crown 8vo. 6s.*

Harrison (Mrs. Burton). A PRINCESS OF THE HILLS. Illustrated. *Crown 8vo.* 6s.

Herbertson (Agnes G.). PATIENCE DEAN. *Crown 8vo.* 6s. [Nearly Ready.

Hichens (Robert). Author of 'Flames,' etc. THE PROPHET OF BERKELEY SQUARE. *Second Ed. Crown 8vo.* 6s.
TONGUES OF CONSCIENCE. *Second Edition. Crown 8vo.* 6s.
FELIX. *Fourth Edition. Crown 8vo.* 6s.
THE WOMAN WITH THE FAN. *Crown 8vo.* 6s. [Nearly Ready.
See also Fleur de Lis Novels.

Hobbes (John Oliver). Author of 'Robert Orange.' THE SERIOUS WOOING. *Crown 8vo.* 6s.

Hooper (I.). THE SINGER OF MARLY. *Crown 8vo.* 6s.

Hope (Anthony). See page 31. [Nearly Ready.

Hough (Emerson). THE MISSISSIPPI BUBBLE. Illustrated. *Crown 8vo.* 6s.

Housman (Clemence). SCENES FROM THE LIFE OF AGLOVALE. Illustrated. *Crown 8vo.* 3s. 6d.

Hunt (Violet). THE HUMAN INTEREST. *Crown 8vo.* 6s.

Hyne (C. J. Cutcliffe). Author of 'Captain Kettle.' PRINCE RUPERT THE BUCCANEER. With 8 Illustrations. *Second Edition. Crown 8vo.* 6s.
MR. HORROCKS, PURSER. *Third Edition. Crown 8vo.* 6s.

Jacobs (W. W.). See page 32.

James (Henry). Author of 'What Maisie Knew.' THE SACRED FOUNT. *Crown 8vo.* 6s.
THE SOFT SIDE. *Second Edition. Crown 8vo.* 6s.
THE BETTER SORT. *Crown 8vo.* 6s.
THE AMBASSADORS. *Second Edition. Crown 8vo.* 6s.

Janson (Gustaf). ABRAHAM'S SACRIFICE. *Crown 8vo.* 6s.

Keary (C. F.). THE JOURNALIST. *Crown 8vo.* 6s.

Kelly (Florence Finch). WITH HOOPS OF STEEL. *Crown 8vo.* 6s.

Larkin (L.). LARKS AND LEVITIES. *Small Quarto.* 1s.

Lawless (Hon. Emily). TRAITS AND CONFIDENCES. *Crown 8vo.* 6s.
WITH ESSEX IN IRELAND. *New Edition. Crown 8vo.* 6s.
See also Fleur de Lis Novels.

Lawson (Harry). Author of 'When the Billy Boils.' CHILDREN OF THE BUSH. *Crown 8vo.* 6s.

Linden (Annie). A WOMAN OF SENTIMENT. *Crown 8vo.* 6s. [Nearly Ready.

Linton (E. Lynn.) THE TRUE HISTORY OF JOSHUA DAVIDSON, Christian and Communist. *Twelfth Edition. Medium 8vo.* 6d.

Lorimer (Norma). MIRRY ANN. *Crown 8vo.* 6s.
JOSIAH'S WIFE. *Crown 8vo.* 6s.

Lowis (Cecil). THE MACHINATIONS OF THE MYO-OK. *Crown 8vo.* 6s.

Lush (Charles K.). THE AUTOCRATS. *Crown 8vo.* 6s.

Lyall (Edna). DERRICK VAUGHAN, NOVELIST. *42nd thousand. Crown 8vo.* 3s. 6d.

Macdonell (A.). THE STORY OF TERESA. *Crown 8vo.* 6s.

Macgrath (Harold). THE PUPPET CROWN. Illustrated. *Crown 8vo.* 6s.

Mackie (Pauline Bradford). THE VOICE IN THE DESERT. *Crown 8vo.* 6s. [Nearly Ready.

Macnaughtan (S.). THE FORTUNE OF CHRISTINA MACNAB. *Third Edition. Crown 8vo.* 6s.

Makgill (G.). OUTSIDE AND OVERSEAS. *Crown 8vo.* 6s.

Malet (Lucas). See page 32.

Mann (Mrs. M. E.). OLIVIA'S SUMMER. *Second Edition. Crown 8vo.* 6s.
A LOST ESTATE. *A New Edition. Crown 8vo.* 6s.
THE PARISH OF HILBY. *A New Edition. Crown 8vo.* 6s.
GRAN'MA'S JANE. *Crown 8vo.* 6s.
MRS. PETER HOWARD. *Cr. 8vo.* 6s.
A WINTER'S TALE. *Crown 8vo.* 6s. [Nearly Ready.

Marsh (Richard). BOTH SIDES OF THE VEIL. *Second Edition. Crown 8vo.* 6s.
THE SEEN AND THE UNSEEN. *Crown 8vo.* 6s.
MARVELS AND MYSTERIES. *Crown 8vo.* 6s.
THE TWICKENHAM PEERAGE. *Second Edition. Crown 8vo.* 6s.
A METAMORPHOSIS. *Crown 8vo.* 6s.
GARNERED. *Crown 8vo.* 6s.

Mason (A. E. W.). Author of 'The Courtship of Morrice Buckler,' 'Miranda of the Balcony,' etc. CLEMENTINA. Illustrated. *Crown 8vo. Second Edition.* 6s.

Mathers (Helen). Author of 'Comin' thro' the Rye.' HONEY. *Fourth Edition. Crown 8vo.* 6s.
GRIFF OF GRIFFITHSCOURT. *Crown 8vo.* 6s.

Mayall (J. W.). THE CYNIC AND THE SYREN. *Crown 8vo.* 6s.

Meade (L. T.). DRIFT. *Crown 8vo.* 6s.
RESURGAM. *Crown 8vo.* 6s.

Miss Molly. (The Author of). THE GREAT RECONCILER. *Crown 8vo.* 6s.

Mitford (Bertram). THE SIGN OF THE SPIDER. Illustrated. *Sixth Edition. Crown 8vo.* 3s. 6d.
A NEW NOVEL. *Crown 8vo.* 6s. [Nearly Ready.

Monkhouse (Allan). LOVE IN A LIFE. *Crown 8vo.* 6s.

Montresor (F. F.), Author of 'Into the Highways and Hedges.' THE ALIEN. *Third Edition. Crown 8vo.* 6s.

Moore (Arthur). THE KNIGHT PUNCTILIOUS. *Crown 8vo.* 6s.

Morrison (Arthur). See page 33.

Nesbit (E.) (Mrs. E. Bland). THE RED HOUSE. Illustrated. *Crown 8vo.* 6s.
THE LITERARY SENSE. *Cr. 8vo.* 6s.

Norris (W. E.). THE CREDIT OF THE COUNTY. Illustrated. *Second Edition. Crown 8vo.* 6s.
THE EMBARRASSING ORPHAN. *Crown 8vo.* 6s.
HIS GRACE. *Third Edition. Cr. 8vo.* 6s.
THE DESPOTIC LADY. *Crown 8vo.* 6s.
CLARISSA FURIOSA. *Crown 8vo.* 6s.
GILES INGILBY. *Illustrated. Second Edition. Crown 8vo.* 6s.
AN OCTAVE. *Second Edition. Crown 8vo.* 6s.
A DEPLORABLE AFFAIR. *Crown 8vo.* 3s. 6d.
JACK'S FATHER. *Crown 8vo.* 2s. 6d.
LORD LEONARD THE LUCKLESS. *Crown 8vo.* 6s.
See also Fleur de Lis Novels.

Oliphant (Mrs.). THE TWO MARYS. *Crown 8vo.* 6s.
THE LADY'S WALK. *Crown 8vo.* 6s.
THE PRODIGALS. *Crown 8vo.* 3s. 6d.
See also Fleur de Lis Novels.

Ollivant (Alfred). OWD BOB, THE GREY DOG OF KENMUIR. *Sixth Edition. Crown 8vo.* 6s.

Oppenheim (E. Phillips). MASTER OF MEN. *Second Edition. Crown 8vo.* 6s.

Oxenham (John), Author of 'Barbe of Grand Bayou.' A WEAVER OF WEBS. *Crown 8vo.* 6s.

Pain (Barry). THREE FANTASIES. *Crown 8vo.* 1s. [Nearly Ready.

Parker (Gilbert). See page 32.

Patton James (Blythe). BIJLI, THE DANCER. *Crown 8vo.* 6s.

Pemberton (Max). THE FOOTSTEPS OF A THRONE. Illustrated. *Second Edition. Crown 8vo.* 6s.
I CROWN THEE KING. With Illustrations by Frank Dadd and A. Forrestier. *Crown 8vo.* 6s.

Penny (Mrs. F. E.). A FOREST OFFICER. *Crown 8vo.* 6s.
A MIXED MARRIAGE. *Crown 8vo.* 6s.

Phillpotts (Eden). See page 33.

Pickthall (Marmaduke). SAID THE FISHERMAN. *Third Edition. Crown 8vo.* 6s.

Prowse (R. Orton). THE POISON OF ASPS. *Crown 8vo.* 3s. 6d.

Pryce (Richard). TIME AND THE WOMAN. *Crown 8vo.* 6s.
THE QUIET MRS. FLEMING. *Crown 8vo.* 3s. 6d.

'Q,' Author of 'Dead Man's Rock.' THE WHITE WOLF. *Second Edition. Crown 8vo.* 6s.

Queux (W. le). THE HUNCHBACK OF WESTMINSTER. *Crown 8vo.* 6s. [Nearly Ready.

Randal (J.). AUNT BETHIA'S BUTTON. *Crown 8vo.* 6s.

Raymond (Walter), Author of 'Love and Quiet Life.' FORTUNE'S DARLING. *Crown 8vo.* 6s.

Rhys (Grace). THE WOOING OF SHEILA. *Second Edition. Crown 8vo.* 6s.
THE PRINCE OF LISNOVER. *Crown 8vo.* 6s. [Nearly Ready.

Rhys (Grace) and Another. THE DIVERTED VILLAGE. With Illustrations by DOROTHY GWYN JEFFRIES. *Crown 8vo.* 6s.

Rickert (Edith). OUT OF THE CYPRESS SWAMP. *Crown 8vo.* 6s.

Ridge (W. Pett). LOST PROPERTY. *Second Edition. Crown 8vo.* 6s.
SECRETARY TO BAYNE, M.P. *Crown 8vo.* 6s.
ERB. *Second Edition. Crown 8vo.* 6s.
A SON OF THE STATE. *Crown 8vo.* 3s. 6d.
A BREAKER OF LAWS. *Cr. 8vo.* 3s. 6d.

Ritchie (Mrs. David G.). THE TRUTHFUL LIAR. *Crown 8vo.* 6s.

Roberts (C. G. D.). THE HEART OF THE ANCIENT WOOD. *Crown 8vo.* 3s. 6d.

Roberton (Mrs. M. H.). A GALLANT QUAKER. Illustrated. *Crown 8vo.* 6s.

Russell (W. Clark). MY DANISH SWEETHEART. Illustrated. *Fourth Edition. Crown 8vo.* 6s.
ABANDONED. *Second Edition. Crown 8vo.* 6s.

Satchell (W.). THE LAND OF THE LOST. *Crown 8vo.* 6s.

Saunders (Marshall). ROSE A CHARLITTE. *Crown 8vo.* 6s.

Scully (W. C.). THE WHITE HECATOMB. *Crown 8vo.* 6s.
BETWEEN SUN AND SAND. *Crown 8vo.* 6s.
A VENDETTA OF THE DESERT. *Crown 8vo.* 3s. 6d.

Sergeant (Adeline), Author of 'The Story of a Penitent Soul.' A GREAT LADY. *Crown 8vo.* 6s.
THE MASTER OF BEECHWOOD. *Crown 8vo.* 6s.
BARBARA'S MONEY. *Second Edition. Crown 8vo.* 6s.
ANTHEA'S WAY. *Crown 8vo.* 6s.
THE YELLOW DIAMOND. *Crown 8vo.* 6s.
UNDER SUSPICION. *Crown 8vo.* 6s. [Nearly Ready.
THE LOVE THAT OVERCAME. *Crown 8vo.* 6s.
THE ENTHUSIAST. *Crown 8vo.* 6s.

Shannon (W. F.). THE MESS DECK. Crown 8vo. 3s. 6d.
JIM TWELVES. Second Edition. Crown 8vo. 3s. 6d.

Shipton (Helen). THE STRONG GOD CIRCUMSTANCE. Crown 8vo. 6s.

Sonnichsen (Albert). DEEP SEA VAGABONDS. Crown 8vo. 6s.
[Nearly Ready.

Stephens (R. N.). A GENTLEMAN PLAYER. Crown 8vo. 6s.
See also Fleur de Lis Novels.

Strain (E. H.). ELMSLIE'S DRAG-NET. Crown 8vo. 6s.

Stuart (Esmé). A WOMAN OF FORTY. Crown 8vo. 3s. 6d.
CHRISTALLA. Crown 8vo. 6s.

Sutherland (Duchess of). ONE HOUR AND THE NEXT. Third Edition. Crown 8vo. 6s.

Swan (Annie). LOVE GROWN COLD. Second Edition. Crown 8vo. 5s.

Swift (Benjamin). SIREN CITY. Crown 8vo. 6s.
SORDON. Crown 8vo. 6s.

Tanqueray (Mrs. B. M.). THE ROYAL QUAKER. Crown 8vo. 6s.

Townshend (R. B.). LONE PINE: A Romance of Mexican Life. Crown 8vo. 6s.

Trafford-Taunton (Mrs. E. W.). SILENT DOMINION. Crown 8vo. 6s.

Wainaman (Paul). A HEROINE FROM FINLAND. Crown 8vo. 6s.
BY A FINNISH LAKE. Crown 8vo. 6s.

A SONG OF THE FOREST. Crown 8vo. 6s.

Waite (Victor). CROSS TRAILS. Crown 8vo. 6s.

Watson (H. B. Marriott). THE SKIRTS OF HAPPY CHANCE. Illustrated. Second Edition. Crown 8vo. 6s.
ALARUMS AND EXCURSIONS. Cr. 8vo. 6s.

Weyman (Stanley), Author of 'A Gentleman of France.' UNDER THE RED ROBE. With Illustrations by R. C. WOODVILLE. Eighteenth Edition. Crown 8vo. 6s.

White (Stewart E.), Author of 'The Blazed Trail.' CONJUROR'S HOUSE. A Romance of the Free Trail. Second Edition. Crown 8vo. 6s.

Williamson (Mrs. C. N.), Author of 'The Barnstormers.' PAPA. Second Edition. Crown 8vo. 6s.
THE ADVENTURE OF PRINCESS SLYVIA. Crown 8vo. 3s. 6d.
THE WOMAN WHO DARED. Crown 8vo. 6s.
THE SEA COULD TELL. Cr. 8vo. 6s.
[Nearly Ready.

Williamson (C. N. and A. M.). THE LIGHTNING CONDUCTOR: Being the Romance of a Motor Car. Illustrated. Fourth Edition. Crown 8vo. 6s.

X.L. AUT DIABOLUS AUT NIHIL. Crown 8vo. 3s. 6d.

Zack, Author of 'Life is Life.' TALES OF DUNSTABLE WEIR. Crown 8vo. 6s.

Boys and Girls, Books for
Crown 8vo. 3s. 6d.

THE ICELANDER'S SWORD. By S. Baring-Gould.
TWO LITTLE CHILDREN AND CHING. By Edith E. Cuthell.
TODDLEBEN'S HERO. By M. M. Blake.
ONLY A GUARD-ROOM DOG. By Edith E. Cuthell.
THE DOCTOR OF THE JULIET. By Harry Collingwood.
MASTER ROCKAFELLAR'S VOYAGE. By W. Clark Russell.

SYD BELTON: Or, the Boy who would not go to Sea. By G. Manville Fenn.
THE RED GRANGE. By Mrs. Molesworth.
THE SECRET OF MADAME DE MONLUC. By the Author of 'Mdle. Mori.'
DUMPS. By Mrs. Parr.
A GIRL OF THE PEOPLE. By L. T. Meade.
HEPSY GIPSY. By L. T. Meade. 2s. 6d.
THE HONOURABLE MISS. By L. T. Meade.

Dumas, The Novels of Alexandre
Price 6d. Double Volume, 1s.

THE THREE MUSKETEERS. With a long Introduction by Andrew Lang. Double volume.
THE PRINCE OF THIEVES. Second Edition.
ROBIN HOOD. A Sequel to the above.
THE CORSICAN BROTHERS.
GEORGES.
CROP-EARED JACQUOT.
TWENTY YEARS AFTER. Double volume.
AMAURY.
THE CASTLE OF EPPSTEIN.
THE SNOWBALL.
CECILE; OR, THE WEDDING GOWN.
ACTE.
THE BLACK TULIP.
THE VISCOMTE DE BRAGELONNE. [Nearly Ready.
THE CONVICT'S SON.
THE WOLF-LEADER. [Nearly Ready.

NANON; OR, THE WOMEN'S WAR. [Nearly Ready.
PAULINE; MURAT; AND PASCAL BRUNO. [Nearly Ready.
THE ADVENTURES OF CAPTAIN PAMPHILE. [Nearly Ready.
FERNANDE.
GABRIEL LAMBERT. [Nearly Ready.
THE REMINISCENCES OF ANTONY
CATHERINE BLUM.
THE CHEVALIER D'HARMENTAL.
CONSCIENCE.

ILLUSTRATED EDITION. Demy 8vo. 2s. 6d.
THE THREE MUSKETEERS. Illustrated in Colour by Frank Adams.
THE PRINCE OF THIEVES. Illustrated in Colour by Frank Adams.

Continued.

DUMAS—*continued*.

ROBIN HOOD THE OUTLAW. Illustrated in Colour by Frank Adams.
THE CORSICAN BROTHERS. Illustrated in Colour by A. M. M'Lellan.
FERNANDE. Illustrated in Colour by Munro Orr.
THE BLACK TULIP. Illustrated in Colour by A. Orr.
ACTÉ. Illustrated in Colour by Gordon Browne.
GEORGES. Illustrated in Colour by Munro Orr.
THE CASTLE OF EPPSTEIN. Illustrated in Colour by A. Orr.

TWENTY YEARS AFTER. Illustrated in Colour by Frank Adams.
THE SNOW BALL AND SULTANETTA. Illustrated in Colour by Frank Adams.
THE VICOMTE DE BRAGELONNE. Illustrated in Colour by Frank Adams.
AMAURY. Illustrated in Colour by Gordon Browne.
CROP-EARED JACQUOT. Illustrated in Colour by Gordon Browne.

Fleur de Lis, Novels The

Crown 8vo. 3s. 6d.

MESSRS. METHUEN are now publishing a cheaper issue of some of their popular Novels in a new and most charming style of binding.

Andrew Balfour.
TO ARMS!

Jane Barlow.
A CREEL OF IRISH STORIES.

E. F. Benson.
THE VINTAGE.

J. Bloundelle-Burton.
IN THE DAY OF ADVERSITY.

Mrs. Caffyn (Iota).
ANNE MAULEVERER.

Mrs. W. K. Clifford.
A FLASH OF SUMMER.

L. Cope Cornford.
SONS OF ADVERSITY.

A. J. Dawson.
DANIEL WHYTE.

Menie Muriel Dowie.
THE CROOK OF THE BOUGH.

Mrs. Dudeney.
THE THIRD FLOOR.

Sara Jeannette Duncan.
A VOYAGE OF CONSOLATION.

G. Manville Fenn.
THE STAR GAZERS.

Jane H. Findlater.
RACHEL.

Jane H. and Mary Findlater.
TALES THAT ARE TOLD.

J. S. Fletcher.
THE PATHS OF THE PRUDENT.

Mary Gaunt.
KIRKHAM'S FIND.

Robert Hichens.
BYEWAYS.

Emily Lawless.
HURRISH.
MAELCHO.

W. E. Norris.
MATTHEW AUSTIN.

Mrs. Oliphant.
SIR ROBERT'S FORTUNE.

Mary A. Owen.
THE DAUGHTER OF ALOUETTE.

Mary L. Pendered.
AN ENGLISHMAN.

Morley Roberts.
THE PLUNDERERS.

R. N. Stephens.
AN ENEMY TO THE KING.

Mrs. Walford.
SUCCESSORS TO THE TITLE.

Percy White.
A PASSIONATE PILGRIM.

Novelist, The

MESSRS. METHUEN are issuing under the above general title a Monthly Series of Novels by popular authors at the price of Sixpence. Each number is as long as the average Six Shilling Novel. The first numbers of 'THE NOVELIST' are as follows:—

I. DEAD MEN TELL NO TALES. By E. W. Hornung.
II. JENNIE BAXTER, JOURNALIST. By Robert Barr.
III. THE INCA'S TREASURE. By Ernest Glanville.
IV. A SON OF THE STATE. By W. Pett Ridge.
V. FURZE BLOOM. By S. Baring-Gould.
VI. BUNTER'S CRUISE. By C. Gleig.
VII. THE GAY DECEIVERS. By Arthur Moore.
VIII. PRISONERS OF WAR. By A. Boyson Weekes.
IX. A FLASH OF SUMMER. By Mrs. W. K. Clifford.
X. VELDT AND LAAGER: Tales of the Transvaal. By E. S. Valentine.
XI. THE NIGGER KNIGHTS. By F. Norreys Connel.
XII. A MARRIAGE AT SEA. By W. Clark Russell.
XIII. THE POMP OF THE LAVILETTES. By Gilbert Parker.
XIV. A MAN OF MARK. By Anthony Hope.
XV. THE CARISSIMA. By Lucas Malet.
XVI. THE LADY'S WALK. By Mrs. Oliphant.
XVII. DERRICK VAUGHAN. By Edna Lyall.
XVIII. IN THE MIDST OF ALARMS. By Robert Barr.
XIX. HIS GRACE. By W. E. Norris.
XX. DODO. By E. F. Benson.
XXI. CHEAP JACK ZITA. By S. Baring-Gould.
XXII. WHEN VALMOND CAME TO PONTIAC. By Gilbert Parker.
XXIII. THE HUMAN BOY. By Eden Phillpotts.
XXIV. THE CHRONICLES OF COUNT ANTONIO. By Anthony Hope.
XXV. BY STROKE OF SWORD. By Andrew Balfour.
XXVI. KITTY ALONE. By S. Baring-Gould.
XXVII. GILES INGILBY. By W. E. Norris.
XXVIII. URITH. By S. Baring-Gould.
XXIX. THE TOWN TRAVELLER. By George Gissing.

Continued.

THE NOVELIST—*continued.*

XXX. MR. SMITH. By Mrs. Walford.
XXXI. A CHANGE OF AIR. By Anthony Hope.
XXXII. THE KLOOF BRIDE. By Ernest Glanville.
XXXIII. ANGEL. By B. M. Croker.
XXXIV. A COUNSEL OF PERFECTION. By Lucas Malet.
XXXV. THE BABY'S GRANDMOTHER. By Mrs. Walford.
XXXVI. THE COUNTESS TEKLA. By Robert Barr.
XXXVII. DRIFT. By L. T. Meade.
XXXVIII. THE MASTER OF BEECHWOOD. By Adeline Sergeant.
XXXIX. CLEMENTINA. By A. E. W. Mason.
XL. THE ALIEN. By F. F. Montresor.
XLI. THE BROOM SQUIRE. By S. Baring-Gould.
XLII. HONEY. By Helen Mathers.
XLIII. THE FOOTSTEPS OF A THRONE. By Max Pemberton.
XLIV. ROUND THE RED LAMP. By A. Conan Doyle.

XLV. LOST PROPERTY. By W. Pett Ridge.
XLVI. THE TWICKENHAM PEERAGE. By Richard Marsh.
XLVII. HOLY MATRIMONY. By Dorothea Gerard.
XLVIII. THE SIGN OF THE SPIDER. By Bertram Mitford.
XLIX. THE RED HOUSE. By E. Nesbit.
L. THE CREDIT OF THE COUNTY. By W. E. Norris.
LI. A ROMAN MYSTERY. By Richard Bagot. [Nearly Ready.
LII. A MOMENT'S ERROR. By A. W. Marchant. [Nearly Ready.
LIII. THE HOLE IN THE WALL. By A. Morrison. [Nearly Ready.
LIV. PHROSO. By Anthony Hope. [Nearly Ready.
LV. I CROWN THEE KING. By Max Pemberton. [Nearly Ready.

Sixpenny Library

THE MATABELE CAMPAIGN. By Major-General Baden-Powell.
THE DOWNFALL OF PREMPEH. By Major-General Baden-Powell.
MY DANISH SWEETHEART. By W. Clark Russell.
IN THE ROAR OF THE SEA. By S. Baring-Gould.
PEGGY OF THE BARTONS. By B. M. Croker.
THE GREEN GRAVES OF BALGOWRIE. By Jane H. Findlater.
THE STOLEN BACILLUS. By H. G. Wells.
MATTHEW AUSTIN. By W. E. Norris.
THE CONQUEST OF LONDON. By Dorothea Gerard.
A VOYAGE OF CONSOLATION. By Sara J. Duncan.
THE MUTABLE MANY. By Robert Barr.
BEN HUR. By General Lew Wallace.
SIR ROBERT'S FORTUNE. By Mrs. Oliphant.
THE FAIR GOD. By General Lew Wallace.
CLARISSA FURIOSA. By W. E. Norris.
CRANFORD. By Mrs. Gaskell.
NOEMI. By S. Baring-Gould.
THE THRONE OF DAVID. By J. H. Ingraham.
ACROSS THE SALT SEAS. By J. Bloundelle Burton.
THE MILL ON THE FLOSS. By George Eliot.
PETER SIMPLE. By Captain Marryat.
MARY BARTON. By Mrs. Gaskell.

PRIDE AND PREJUDICE. By Jane Austen.
NORTH AND SOUTH. By Mrs. Gaskell.
JACOB FAITHFUL. By Captain Marryat.
SHIRLEY. By Charlotte Brontë.
FAIRY TALES RE-TOLD. By S. Baring Gould.
THE TRUE HISTORY OF JOSHUA DAVIDSON. By Mrs. Lynn Linton.
A STATE SECRET. By B. M Croker.
SAM'S SWEETHEART. By Helen Mathers.
HANDLEY CROSS. By R. S. Surtees.
ANNE MAULEVERER. By Mrs. Caffyn.
THE ADVENTURERS. By H. B. Marriott Watson.
DANTE'S DIVINE COMEDY. Translated by H. F. Cary.
THE CEDAR STAR. By M. E. Mann.
MASTER OF MEN. By E. P. Oppenheim.
THE TRAIL OF THE SWORD. By Gilbert Parker.
THOSE DELIGHTFUL AMERICANS. By Mrs. Cotes.
MR. SPONGE'S SPORTING TOUR. By R. S. Surtees.
ASK MAMMA. By R. S. Surtees.
GRIMM'S FAIRY STORIES. Illustrated by George Cruikshank.
GEORGE AND THE GENERAL. By W. Pett Ridge. [Nearly Ready.
THE JOSS. By Richard Marsh. [Nearly Ready.
MISER HOADLEY' SECRET. By A. W. Marchmont. [Nearly Ready.

Methuen's Colonial Library

FICTION—continued

Oliphant, Mrs.
SIR ROBERT'S FORTUNE.
THE TWO MARYS.
THE LADY'S WALK.

Ollivant, Alfred
OWD BOB, THE GREY DOG OF KENMUIR.

Oppenheim, E. Phillips
MASTER OF MEN.

Oxenham, John
A MODERN MASQUER.

Parker, Sir Gilbert
THE TRAIL OF THE SWORD. Illustrated.
WHEN VALMOND CAME TO PONTIAC.
AN ADVENTURER OF THE NORTH.
PIERRE AND HIS PEOPLE.
MRS. FALCHION.
THE SEATS OF THE MIGHTY. Illustrated.
THE POMP OF THE LAVILETTES.
THE BATTLE OF THE STRONG. Illustrated.
THE TRANSLATION OF A SAVAGE.

Pemberton, Max
THE FOOTSTEPS OF A THRONE.
I CROWN THEE KING. Illustrated.

Pendered, Mary L.
AN ENGLISHMAN.

Penny, Mrs. Frank
A FOREST OFFICER.
A MIXED MARRIAGE.

Pett Ridge, W.
SECRETARY TO BAYNE, M.P.
A SON OF THE STATE.
LOST PROPERTY.
'ERB.
A BREAKER OF LAWS

Phillpotts, Eden
SONS OF THE MORNING.
CHILDREN OF THE MIST.
LYING PROPHETS.
THE STRIKING HOURS.
FANCY FREE. Illustrated.
THE RIVER.
THE HUMAN BOY.
THE AMERICAN PRISONER.

Pickthall, Marmaduke
SAID THE FISHERMAN.

'Q'
THE WHITE WOLF, and other Fireside Tales.

Randal, J.
AUNT BETHIA'S BUTTON.

Raymond, Walter
FORTUNE'S DARLING.

Rhys, Grace
THE WOOING OF SHEILA.
THE DIVERTED VILLAGE.
THE PRINCE OF LISNOVER.

Rickert, Edith
OUT OF THE CYPRESS SWAMP.

Roberts, Morley
THE PLUNDERERS.

Rousseau, Victor
DERWENT'S HORSE.

Russell, W. Clark
MY DANISH SWEETHEART. Illustrated.
ABANDONED.

Satchell, Wm.
THE LAND OF THE LOST.

Scully, W. C.
THE WHITE HECATOMB.
A VENDETTA OF THE DESERT.

Sergeant, Adeline
A GREAT LADY.
THE MASTER OF BEECHWOOD.
ANTHEA'S WAY.
BARBARA'S MONEY.
THE LOVE THAT OVERCAME.
THE ENTHUSIAST.
THE YELLOW DIAMOND.
UNDER SUSPICION.

Shannon, Edgar
THE MESS DECK.

Shannon, W. F.
JIM TWELVES.

Sonnischen, Albert
DEEP SEA VAGABONDS.

Stephens, R. N.
A GENTLEMAN PLAYER.
AN ENEMY TO THE KING.

Swan, Annie
LOVE GROWN COLD

Swift, Benjamin
SIREN CITY.
SORDON.

Tanqueray, B. M.
THE ROYAL QUAKER.

Trafford-Taunton, Winefride
SILENT DOMINION.

Waineman, Paul
A HEROINE FROM FINLAND.
BY A FINNISH LAKE.

Walford, L. B.
SUCCESSORS TO THE TITLE.

Watson, H. B. Marriott
THE SKIRTS OF HAPPY CHANCE.
ALARMS AND EXCURSIONS.

Wells, H. G.
THE STOLEN BACILLUS.
THE PLATTNER STORY.
THE SEA LADY.
TALES OF SPACE AND TIME.
WHEN THE SLEEPER WAKES.
LOVE AND MR. LEWISHAM.
THE INVISIBLE MAN.

Weyman, Stanley J.
UNDER THE RED ROBE. Illustrated.

White, Percy
A PASSIONATE PILGRIM.

White, Stewart E.
CONJUROR'S HOUSE. Illustrated.

Williamson, Mrs. C. N.
THE ADVENTURE OF PRINCESS SYLVIA.
PAPA.
THE WOMAN WHO DARED.
THE SEA COULD TELL.

Williamson, C. N. and A. M.
THE LIGHTNING CONDUCTOR.

Zack
TALES OF DUNSTABLE WEIR.

Methuen's Colonial Library

GENERAL LITERATURE

Crown 8vo

CPSIA information can be obtained at www.ICGtesting.com
Printed in the USA
LVOW02s0024050913

351066LV00005B/147/P